P9-ECO-311

NOBODY CALLED ME CHARLIE

NOBODY CALLED ME CHARLIE

The Story of a Radical White Journalist Writing
for a Black Newspaper in the Civil Rights Era

by CHARLES PRESTON

MONTHLY REVIEW PRESS
New York

Copyright © 2010 by Gregor Preston

All rights reserved

Library of Congress Cataloging-in-Publication Data

Preston, Charles, 1911-1982.

  Nobody called me Charlie: the story of a radical white journalist writing
for a Black newspaper in the Civil Rights era / by Charles Preston.

    p. cm.

  ISBN 978-1-58367-202-0 (cloth)

  1. Preston, Charles, 1911-1982—Fiction. 2. Reporters and reporting—United
States—Fiction. 3. Communists--Fiction. 4. African American newspapers—
Fiction. 5. Race relations—United States—Fiction. 6. Civil rights movements—
Press coverage—United States—Fiction. I. Title.

  PS3566.R3975N63 2010

  813'.54—dc22

                          2009045084

Monthly Review Press

146 West 29th Street, Suite 6W

New York, NY 10001

www.monthlyreview.org

5 4 3 2 1

Contents

Editor's Note

This book came to us by way of the author's son Gregor, who wrote the moving introduction. It was written more than thirty-five years ago. This is both a blessing and a curse. It is a blessing because it gives readers an unfiltered account of a time in the history of the United States with which most of us are unfamiliar. While we live in a society that is still racially stratified, we no longer inhabit the completely segregated world that existed in this country for nearly two hundred years. The Civil War might have ended slavery, but from the end of Reconstruction in 1877 until the full flowering of the civil rights movement, there existed the "Jim Crow" system, in which black people were denied even the most basic rights.

Despite their harsh exploitation and brutalized lives, the former slaves and their progeny built a vibrant black culture. There were black professionals, black businesses of every kind, black athletic teams, black clubs, black colleges, black fraternal organizations, and, at the heart of this story, black newspapers. The black press played a critical role in black communities. It was a source of vital information to its overwhelmingly black readers; it provided a kind of social glue for the places it served; and it acted as a major protagonist in the struggle for black liberation. It kept the flame of black freedom alive in the worst of times and fanned freedom's fires when the times were more auspicious. And it showed more clearly than any other institution that there were two Americas, which saw the world in fundamentally different ways. For example, the case of the murdered teenager Emmett Till was seen in an entirely different light by the leading black newspapers than it was by the influential mainstream journals, much less the racist press of most of the South. James L. Hicks, bureau chief for the National Negro Press Association, did some remarkable investigative journalism into the case, at considerable risk to his life, while the mainstream papers were pretty much Johnny Come Latelies, following the lead of the black journalists. The daily racism that was taken for granted by white America was presented in the black newspapers as the affront to human dignity that it should have been to any thinking person.

Black America was a mystery to most whites, but not all. There have always been white persons who were interested in various aspects of the black experience, and there were a few who championed their fight for equality. White concern for the black cause, or as it was called, The Question, grew considerably during the Great Depression, a product in part of the prominence of radicals in the burgeoning labor movement. The Congress of Industrial Organizations (CIO) would never have succeeded in organizing the mass production industries without the leadership of socialists and especially of members of the Communist Party. The Communists were committed to the principle of racial equality, and they strove mightily to put this principle into practice in their daily organizing activities.

Charles Preston became a Party member during the 1930s, and he fully embraced its racial egalitarianism. When personal circumstances forced him and his wife to return to Indiana from New York City, he put his commitment to the full integration of black people into every aspect of life in the United States into practice by going to work for a black newspaper, the *Indianapolis Recorder*, the third oldest black newspaper in the country. His time at the paper and his life as a white person in a thoroughly black milieu, not just at work but in his daily life, are the subjects of this memoir. It is an account readers are not likely to find anywhere else, and it is, in this sense, a unique historical document.

But if *Nobody Called Me Charlie* provides a perspective not often encountered, the fact that it was written when it was is also something of a curse. The language used and some of the views expressed might irritate modern sensibilities. First of all, the word "Charlie" in the title refers to a derogatory word black people used for whites. It is no longer used this way, at least not in ordinary conversation. We thought of other titles for the book to avoid using a word modern readers wouldn't recognize. But in the end, we decided to stick to the original, since this is what Preston himself used. Second, the author uses the word "Negro" throughout the book, something he probably would not have done had he written the book today. And finally, Preston is also a product of his times, and, despite his radical sensibilities, he is not immune to some of what are, today, at least questionable points of view. The most striking examples almost always involve gender relationships. The author's world is very much a man's world, and he occasionally says things that to a modern ear are sexist. Readers should keep in mind that while the Communist Party preached gender equality, it did not always practice it. Neither did Charles Preston, although he frequently did do political work with women, and in this, he did indeed participate as an equal and often took the lead from women.

These caveats aside, *Nobody Called Me Charlie* is a remarkable story, one that Monthly Review Press is proud to publish.

—Michael D. Yates

Introduction

My father, Charles Smith Preston, was born in the small town of Monticello, Indiana, on June 1, 1911, and grew up in the larger town of Anderson (pop. 38,000 in 1930). His father, a newspaperman, died at a young age in 1919. His mother, a high school teacher, raised him and his younger brother, Dick, who became a journalist for the Scripps chain.

Chuck, as many of his friends knew him, went to DePauw College in Greencastle, Indiana, starting in the foreboding year of 1929. There were few jobs for an English major when he graduated four years later in 1933.

Sometime after graduation, he met my mother, Lucy Ashjian, at a John Reed Club social function. The club, named after the famous revolutionary journalist, was sponsored by the Communist Party (CP). Both of my parents joined the Communist Party sometime in the 1930s, as did upwards of 100,000 others during this period. I don't recall them describing any specific incidents that led them to communism. Both were intellectuals who read widely in the radical material available at the time. Marx and Engels seemed to them to have the answers to the terrible crises brought on by the capitalist system.

They were rank-and-file Party members until the heyday of McCarthyism in the early 1950s. My father described a meeting with a CP functionary during that time in which CP members were given dispensation to resign their membership. My parents accepted the idea as the wisest course of action. Both remained communists in spirit for the rest of their lives and activists on the left, especially in the anti-Vietnam War movement.

Both my mother and father were enamored of life in New York City where they were married in 1937. Mother studied photography and was a member of the Photo League. Her photos are held in collections at The Metropolitan Museum of Art, The Philadelphia Museum of Art, George Eastman House, Princeton Museum of Art, Columbus (Ohio) Museum of Art, and The Jewish Museum. The remaining photographs and all materials relating to her photography career are deposited in the Center for Creative Photography at the University of Arizona.

During the 1930s, Chuck worked at *Junior Scholastic* and was an editor of *The Fight Against War and Fascism*. He published short stories and verse in *Story*, *Partisan Review*, and *The New Masses*. He wrote a long unpublished novel, *Richard Perhaps* or *Passion and Action*, about a young fellow who travels from Indiana to New York City and gets involved in the left-wing movement. Most of his writing was unpublished, but he never stopped writing. He wrote many poems and three plays, one of which, *T'e Tragedy of King Richard T'e T'ird*, was subtitled "With Apologies to William Shakespeare and Barbara Garson" and was a satire, *MacBird*-like, of the Nixon-McGovern presidential race. He advertised and distributed this one himself.

My father was not without his demons. When I was struggling with some of my own, in 1969, he told me that he considered himself a "psychoneurotic." Shortly after I was born in February 1943, he had what he considered a nervous breakdown and he was hospitalized. Unable to take care of me and also earn a living, my mother took me and moved us to her parents' home in Indianapolis in December 1943. After recuperation with the help of a relative, father rejoined the family and not long after, they bought a modest home not far from my mother's parents, who loaned them the money for the mortgage. My mother got a decent secretarial job with the International

Typographical Union. The local Negro weekly newspaper, *The Indianapolis Recorder*, was publishing a special huge "Victory" edition celebrating the Allies' victory and the Negroes'—as they were then known—role in the nation's history and its hopes for "a new world a-comin'." They needed people to do research and write short articles. It was just the thing that appealed to a fellow still feeling a little shaky and who believed in the solidarity of black and white.

This is where *Nobody Called Me Charlie* begins. Chuck wrote it beginning in 1969 and he revised it up through 1973. In a letter to publishers in June 1973, he wrote: "This is a query in search of a publisher. . . . I take this recourse after the book has been handled by two reputable literary agents in turn, because I despair of their methods reaching a satisfactory sampling of publishers in any reasonable time." And he described it thus: It "is a memoir, with names and place-names changed, of the eighteen years during which I, a white man, worked as a regular employee on the staff of a Black weekly newspaper. At the same time I was an activist in the NAACP and countless other movements for Negro freedom and advancement. The book is in no sense sociology, but an autobiographical novel or 'narrative with a human face.' My principal interest has been to examine the Black society and every aspect of black-white relationships as they came to me in the concreteness of experience. I have tried to portray various Black personalities whom I knew, reacting to their continually desperate situation with ingenuity, paranoia, humor, alcoholism, incredible courage, and abiding fear. In all, I found an 'extended family' filled with life and mutual support despite the grave wounds inflicted on it by racism and poverty."

Finally, he wrote: "I have also been concerned to draw the white people as I saw them from the other side of the line: their crude and frightful, or subtle and sickening, manifestations of prejudice (including my own); the antics of various exploiters and opportunists. And by no means least, I have taken particular pains to tell the stories of those white individuals who found one way or another to assert their fellowship with the Blacks."

For obvious reasons, he had to change the names of people and places. It would make a more informative book today if we had the real names in front of us, but it does not detract in any meaningful way from the power of the narrative. For, it is what he describes that holds our interest, not who he describes. However, there are two famous personalities Chuck mentions in the book whom I would like to identify. One is the All-American basketball player, Oscar Robertson, who is called "Oscar Bentley" in the book. The author, along with the rest of Indianapolis, had the good fortune to watch Oscar grow into one of the all-time great basketball players, bringing two state championships to his high school, Crispus Attucks, on his way to collegiate and professional stardom. The other is the Reverend Jim Jones, of Jonestown, Guyana, infamy, who led hundreds of his followers to their deaths by "drinking the Kool-Aid" in their jungle encampment.

The Rev. Jones and my father met and became friends in the 1950s; they kept in touch over the years and Jones was skilled at pushing my dad's buttons—and mine, to a certain degree. When I visited Jones and his church in late 1969 in Ukiah, California, I was surprised—and pleased, as well—to hear the group launch into a chorus of "the Internationale." My father received similar treatment when Jones came through Philadelphia. So it was very difficult for my father to believe that Jones had become a madman, despite the phony "faith-healings" he had observed so many years ago in Indianapolis.

My father was especially affected by the Jonestown tragedy of 1978. Although none of the books later written about Jones ever uncovered the relationship between them, Chuck was assuredly the first white friend Jones had outside church circles. Jones urged him to come to Jonestown, and were it not for my dad's ill health and most importantly my mother's refusal to go, it is likely that they, too, would have perished at Jonestown.

Although I never got to know my father's coworkers at the *Recorder* while I was growing up (I went to the office only once and it was as dirty and messy as he describes), I did identify with black people, especially when rooting for Negroes in sporting events. The family employed a black domestic who enabled both parents to work and me to be looked after in the early years. Especially when very young, there is some evidence that I considered Mildred to be another mother. From the first to sixth grade, I lived in an integrated neighborhood and thus went to an integrated school. Until the age of thirteen, when the Prestons moved a few blocks north, to an all-white school district, most of my friends were black. From then until I went to college, I was a pretty unhappy camper. My parents explained the move by the need for another room for my maternal grandmother. An unspoken reason may have been their desire that I attend a more academic junior high.

On the other hand, I felt like the prince of the city when, for a couple of years, I went with my dad to sit in the press box to watch all the Triple A Indianapolis Indians home baseball games. We even got to order free food and drinks during the fifth inning. I thought that was integration at its best and as it should be!

As for politics, communism was so far beyond the pale of Hoosier experience that it never came up in my circles. It is possible that in 1950 or 1951, on one of the annual vacations that our family took to Canada, we visited the Soviet Embassy in Ottawa. I was so impressed that I thought we were going to visit the Queen. That may have been the time that Chuck asked for an audience with a Soviet functionary about the possibility of emigrating to the Soviet Union—that's how bad things looked under the Red Scare juggernaut then sweeping the United States. He estimates that there might have been possibly forty Communists in Indianapolis at the time of the Progressive Party campaign in 1948, no more than eight to ten of them black. I cannot think of more than three or four whom I may have met. All this meant that there were no "red diaper" babies to become friends with in Indianapolis. I remember only one family who might have qualified, but our get-togethers never became anything more political. For my college freshman English class in 1961, I did write my first essay, entitled "Why I Am a Socialist." So there is no doubt that something stuck in my mind from my parents' tutelage as well as surprising the hell out of my teacher—who asked me, favorably, I thought, where I got my ideas from!

After he finally left *The Recorder*, Chuck got a position as public relations director for the Job Corps in 1965 at Camp Breckinridge in Morganfield, Kentucky. He was fired from that position when he didn't "manage" the press releases following a "riot" at the camp as the executives would have liked. He tried but failed to get his job back despite a strong editorial in the *Louisville Courier-Journal*. He thought it was because his name was on a list in Washington.

His last regular job was with the York, Pennsylvania, *Gazette & Daily*, a newspaper owned by a homegrown radical. During this time he made many good friends in the local antiwar and anti-nuclear movement (Three Mile Island was only a few miles from his home) and became the first editor of Maggie Kuhn's *Grey Panther Newsletter*. In 1980, my parents moved to Davis, California, and we were together again, as I worked as a librarian at the University of California, Davis. Chuck again made many friends in the short time he was with us before his death at age seventy-one in 1983 of heart failure. He even managed to join yet another Unitarian church.

I only wish there really was a hereafter. My father would be so thrilled to see *Nobody Called Me Charlie* finally in print. And I believe he would think it very timely, what with a black president and people having "beer summits" on the subject of race. We still have a lot to learn, but we're getting there, and thanks to Monthly Review Press, Chuck Preston can add his bit. I happen to think it's a unique viewpoint. I hope you enjoy it.

—Gregor A. Preston, August 2009
Davis, California

NOBODY CALLED ME CHARLIE

PART ONE

It is a more difficult matter to get rid of the communal guilt. One lives in a colour-bar world, and one cannot behave in all respects as though one did not. But one must begin by challenging the customs; there can be no relief from melancholy until we do.

—ALAN PATON

For I was hungry, and ye gave me meat.

—THE GOSPEL ACCORDING TO ST. MATTHEW

1. A White Man among Them

The fact that I was a white man working among them was for a long time seldom alluded to by my fellow workers of *The Clarion*. Since my presence was an example of racial equality and integration—ideals which they all held in their hearts like an obsession—their attitude was that it should be taken absolutely in stride. This made a very pleasant and agreeable working atmosphere for me. I was annoyed only when I realized that to a considerable extent this point of honor was undergirded by a feeling that I should be treated with deference for the very reason that I was white, and that well-behaved Negroes should show respect for white people. I tried to get across my objections to it, but with little success. I think no one had yet figured out how to treat me.

I use the word "Negroes" because it was then, in the closing years of the Second World War, the expression finally replacing "colored people."

Among themselves, however, Negroes still said "colored" or much more generally, "nigger." Frequently one of them, after saying "nigger," would turn to me and beg my pardon. "Spade" and "spook" were used by the more lively talkers, along with "ofay" and "paddy" for a white. (I speculated that the curious "ofay" originated as Pig Latin for "foe.")

Euphemisms such as "tan" were popular in sports writing and sometimes elsewhere, as in "tan GIs." "Tan" was a beautifully short word for headlines. "Sepia" also was used in journalism.

"Black," now the obligatory term, at that time was nearly always disparaging, as in, "You black bastard, get your black ass out of here." There was a lot of playing the dozens on the theme of one another's degree of blackness, or more properly the blackness of someone's mother.

The subject of my color was at last brought down out of the clouds through an incident resulting from the explosive pressures of the weekly Thursday night poker game, which was always straight five-card stud.

The hand had come down to a battle between Mike and me. Mike was a short and ancient man, dressed in poorly fitting secondhand clothes, who eked out a living as a numbers runner. He was considered a member of the newspaper fraternity because he played some part many years before with *The Clarion*'s predecessor, *The Freeman*. I think he might have sold copies on the street. He was bald, and he was jet black.

I held a pair of aces showing and another ace down. Mike had two kings showing and a third in the hole. After the others had dropped out, we kept raising and back-raising each other. Blue chips were a quarter, and eventually a nice pile of them was amassed on the table.

"Blue up," I would say, as I sat there with my mortal.

"See you and a bluedy up on you," said Mike, squeezing his "three kings of Orient."

"And a bluedy up on you," I retorted.

Finally, Mike reached the point where his self-confidence was shaken. He sat there for a long time, bending his cards in his hand so he could glimpse that king in the hole, peering across at my double aces.

Suddenly he shouted, "That black motherfucker's got an ace!" and threw in his cards.

The others roared with laughter and Lehman Scott, the old pro who presided over the game, wiped his eyes and said, "Preston's made it at last! Mike has done put him in the club!"

From that moment on, it seemed to me, things were easier regarding my color. I was openly acknowledged as being white; discussions were held with me about it; and I even began to take some kidding on the score. If I was still occasionally spoken to obsequiously, it was frankly satirical and with a memory of Mike Gale's *mot*.

I thought it was about time. I had been there for seven years.

I suppose that because of the earlier avoidance of communication on the subject, I had not realized how great an object of curiosity I was. When my fellow workers felt the necessity to account for my presence, they did so by some motive other than the obvious one. They seemed to be embarrassed for me because I had fallen out of white society into their own.

"He's getting material for a book," George Brown, somewhat spifflicated, once ventured with his leer.

Bill Whitcomb had another explanation. He would spin a great yarn that depicted me as "the scion of Quaker forebears" who had been working for Negro liberation since the Underground Railroad days.

They were all wrong. My Quaker ancestry ended when my great-grandfather joined the Methodist Church. The only person I ever heard of him rescuing was a Lincoln-hating congressman who was threatened by Unionists with a lynching on his way home from a Copperhead convention. My grandfather used to say that he first saw my grandmother when she was riding in a parade on a float bearing the sign, "God Save Us from Nigger Husbands." In fact, I never knew of my family's Quaker past until several years after I started working at *The Clarion*. But Bill Whitcomb seized on the "Quaker" story and elaborated it like a Negro mother making a neck-bone stew.

Nor had I any serious intention in those days of writing a book. Occasionally I took notes of some colorful turns of speech, but all together they never filled four pages of a notebook, and years went by without an entry.

The truth was that I needed a job that wouldn't make too heavy demands. I was recovering from an illness that had obliged me to come home from New York. My field was editorial work, but I didn't wish to become associated with the city's daily newspapers, two of them notoriously reactionary, and the third, which had once been liberal, at that time trying too hard to "me-too" the others.

As for the race question, I was amongst the first generation of white people who joined in the integration movement of the postwar decades. I had been educated by the Communist Party, of which I had been a member since shortly after I came out of college into the depths of the Great Depression. It was the Party that taught me to identify fully with the cause of the Negro.

I was an "underground" member in that I didn't make my affiliation public knowledge. My employer at *The Clarion* never inquired into my politics, though he several times resisted outside pressure to do so. It was a matter of principle with him, and also, he didn't think I was a Communist. The more the police and the "respectable" people, Negro and white, told him he was harboring a Red, the less inclined he was to believe it.

At the same time, of course, I was still a white man from the Midwest. Anyone who has lived as such a person for his first twenty-five years won't need to be told what racism is, for he will taste it on his own tongue. Even when he is trying to help the black man, he must recognize the motive of noblesse oblige, with its measure of racial vanity.

But if there was one lesson I learned from Cassius M. Talbott and the staff of his weekly paper, it was not to be fussy about motives. "The Devil may have brought you, but the Lord sent you. Praise the Lord, I'll make use of you."

It was Penelope Parker, a radical friend from the John Reed Club days, who told Susan and me about *The Clarion* and its "Victory Edition." This was planned as a special project of 192 eight-column newspaper pages—the largest Negro newspaper ever published—celebrating the Allies' triumph in the war and also recounting the Negro's history throughout the ages and projecting his "Fair Hopes. . . . For a New World a-Comin'." This was Bill Whitcomb's phrase. He was editor of the edition and it was to be blazoned across the top of page one. The work was being done in a separate office from *The Clarion*'s, a dank basement across the street from the newspaper's regular offices.

Penny was a statuesque redhead whom Susan had known since grade school. She had gone to Ward Belmont, and she lived with flair—working for a Negro newspaper was just the sort of thing she would do. She introduced me to Whitcomb; we were at once drawn to each other as kindred spirits, and he said help was needed and urged me to make an application.

I went to see Mr. Talbott, as I was always to call him, and was hired for part-time work on the special edition. Little did either of us dream that I was signing up for the better part of a lifetime.

2. The Special Edition

Our editor, Mr. Talbott, had grey eyes that he said came from a white grandmother in the family's old hometown, a place that dated from French control of the territory. He and I used to engage in mock arguments on the subject, with me saying, "You must mean your grandfather," and him replying, "No, my grandmother!" There was an albino strain in his family, most strikingly exemplified in his younger sister, Mrs. Luvenia Weyhouse, who was office manager of *The Clarion*.

The staff of *The Clarion*, not counting white people such as Penny and myself and "Senator" Anderson, a little old ex-convict who sold advertising for a while, ranged in color from Lehman Scott, the advertising manager, who could have been taken for a swarthy white person, to such an ebony-skinned person as John Elliott.

Lehman told me he was from Darke County, Ohio. He said the town was unusual, in that there were numerous families with white branches and black branches, who, instead of avoiding each other went so far as to hold reunions together. I can't vouch for that—I suspected that light-skinned persons like Lehman exaggerated such stories—but I once got the surprise of my life when I covered a meeting of the Negro Masons in Weaver, Indiana, a ghost-town community descended from a very early Negro settlement. Several blue-eyed, red-necked, prosperous-appearing farmers drove up in big cars and began talking in the nasal Hoosier twang. They were, however, "Negroes."

In between, on our staff one found the complexions of Smitty
Smith, café au lait; George Brown, who might have had Puerto Rican
blood; and Walt Evers, a wandering Mexican, if one ever wandered.
But they were all Negroes, because that's how they were treated. By
the same token, they were all colored people or niggers, and I assume
they are now all blacks.

The subject of color was continuously a matter of detailed discussion, as was the topic of "good hair," meaning straight like a white person's. Most of my coworkers would imply quotation marks about
"good" with a little laugh, but others used it as a simple adjective.

But while I triumphantly demonstrated that it was impossible to
define "Negro" in biological terms, I was burningly aware that Negroes
existed as members of an oppressed social group, and it was my aim to
destroy the arbitrary groundwork for such oppression. Since there was
"no difference," I reasoned, there should be no disparity in citizenship.
In an editorial I wrote for the Victory Edition, I addressed the constituency as "Americans of Negro origin." In my endeavor to wipe out all
distinction, I even asserted, "there have been many nations of black masters and white slaves." Perhaps I had in mind cases of Europeans being
captured and enslaved by the Moors and Berbers. It seemed to me that,
theoretically, there could just as well have been nations of black masters
and white slaves, for there were black masters and black slaves, and
white masters and white slaves. But I'm afraid my history was lacking.

This piece was accompanied by my picture, which showed that I
was presumably white. Every member of the staff had his picture published. Mr. Talbott, his mother, Smitty Smith (who was then city editor), and Mr. Talbott's older sister, Mrs. Peggy Talbott Lewis, had
double-column pictures, as, of course, did Bill Whitcomb as editor of
the edition. So did Frederick Douglass, Booker T. Washington, and
other historical figures. So did Neanderthal Man and Paleanthropus,
who were thus tacitly claimed as early Negroes.

Mr. Talbott's deceased father, George W. Talbott Sr., founder of
The Clarion, had a four-column cut, as did Abraham Lincoln.

Page one of the edition bore the banner "UNITED NATIONS
PLEDGE NEW WORLD," and beneath it were four photos:

Roosevelt, Truman, Churchill, and Stalin. Mr. Talbott, who stuck to the business side of the publication and rarely intruded into our sanctum, argued that Haile Selassie should be included in the group. But Bill Whitcomb, with my support, rebuffed this intervention into his province, and stood by his duty to protect the work from what we thought was Mr. Talbott's crass desire to sell newspapers. "Ya can't put him in with these men just because he's a nigger," he thundered. "These are the biggest men in the world!"

Keeping his opinion, Mr. Talbott lapsed into silence. This continued for several years, when he exercised his power of command hardly at all. There was an atmosphere in which freedom of the press seemed to mean freedom of the writer rather than freedom of the owner. Even later on, when he began throwing his weight around more like a publisher, his rule was far from dictatorial, and he lost his battles as often as he won them. I wished all the newspapermen on the tyranny-structured white newspapers of America could have had a taste of working at *The Clarion*.

On the question of Haile Selassie, Mr. Talbott, of course, was right. The newspaper's significance was not well represented by the pictures of three white men and a Caucasian Red. When this became obvious after publication, the difficulty was circumvented by wrapping Section II on the outside instead of Section I. Section II dealt with "The Armed Forces," and displayed a full-page drawing of a tan GI in battle garb with a smoking automatic in his hand. That was more like it.

Besides getting our pictures in the Victory Edition, all the workers were granted titles. Penny was Women's Editor, while Kitty Curtis, a Negro woman, was Society Editor. I was Copy Editor. In later years, when I would speak at meetings in Negro churches, the minister often would introduce me as "the Editor of *The Clarion*." He knew, as presumably did all the members of the congregation, that the editor and publisher of *The Clarion* was Cassius M. Talbott. I might have suspected it was because I was white, and even a satirical motive, if I hadn't seen that black people were also the recipients of this courteous upgrading. It was the gift of dignity, which people without it can still confer on each other. Its widespread dispensing was part of what I understand as "soul."

The special edition boasted a large number of "editors," most of whom prepared their articles and brought or mailed them in, but only four of us were on-the-job workers. Bill Whitcomb—William Jefferson Whitcomb from Hopkinsville, Kentucky—was a tall, handsome man with a neat mustache and a serious demeanor, a man of great sensitivity who larded his talk with rich folk expressions. I often felt that one could have written a classic simply by following him around with a tape recorder. But when he sat down to write, he thought it incumbent to put all that aside and employ long, Latin-derived words and contrived sentence structures to the degree that sometimes you actually could not tell what he was trying to say. I surmised this attitude went back to his school days in Hopkinsville; it seemed to me a bitter commentary on the Negro's condition in America: the mind of a Bobby Burns, lynched in childhood. I didn't feel it was possible to speak to him about it.

There was Penny, flouncing around our basement hangout in her bizarre and gay-colored clothes, and there was Robert Morgan, who was the Fine Arts Editor. Robert, who was then in his early twenties, was undoubtedly a genius or near it, not only in the field of music, but in general intellectual competence. He had already written a serious musical work, "Prelude to a Symphony at Sundown." He wrote and edited newspaper articles rapidly and with great ease, always turning out perfect copy.

Robert was a homosexual. As I got to know him, I learned he was from a broken home and had been brought up by his grandmother. There had been no money for college; he had given himself a higher education by reading. I couldn't imagine why he should not have received a scholarship and financial aid from some institution. If it was any consolation, of all the persons I have known, no one was better equipped to get along without a college education than Robert Morgan. At the same time, he was entirely without ambition to rise out of his environment and to do something with either his musical talent or other abilities. Or almost entirely, as we later saw.

So the four of us worked through the spring months and into the early summer of 1945, in the basement of the decrepit building tucked away on the shore of the broad avenue that, like a mighty river, bore its fish of many hues on the myriad errands of their existence. There was none of the wound-up tautness that marks the operations of daily and even weekly white newspapers. We had frequent visitors, and even when we did not, we often got into discussions that lasted for hours. The publication deadline had to be posted several times.

We were working for beggars' wages, but the wonder was that Mr. Talbott was able to come up even with these week after week. The edition carried little advertising and there were no foundations in those days. I assumed that the bite had been put on some politicians for money. In fact, I heard later of a U.S. senator who was quite nettled because I, not knowing he was a donor, had landed hard on him in an article. Aside from this case, I never learned the sources of *The Clarion*'s financing.

The edition was sold for a dollar, and as a virtual encyclopedia of Negro life, it was well worth it. Unfortunately, there was no money for promotion, and the organization of a wider circulation proved too difficult a task. Years later, I was told that thousands of copies were gathering dust in a warehouse.

When our work was complete, Penny got a job in the union office where Susan was employed. I took the course of least resistance and moved across the street to *The Clarion*.

3. Mr. Talbott's Newspaper

The first thing that struck me about *The Clarion*'s offices and composing room was that they were filthy. They were in a ramshackle frame building that may have been a century old, a firetrap, and indeed it was well-nigh destroyed by a three-alarm fire one night. Whether there was insufficient insurance (or none), or whether the insurance money was used for something else, the walls remained smoke-blackened for a long time. Some of them were never repainted, as far as I know.

In winter, the office was heated by an oil stove, and the composing room by a coal stove. A newsroom, which was built from cement blocks by Harry Martin, one of the linotypists, relied on an ancient gas heater. The oil stove was always getting out of kilter, and the pipe of the coal stove frequently became clogged. When these things happened, the place quickly filled with smoke. The offending stove or stoves then would have to be taken out of operation, even in zero-degree weather. We shivered through many a frigid winter day, wearing our overcoats and scarves. My own desk was against the wall without insulation, so I brought in a large electric heater and placed it so that it bore directly on my feet and legs. Even so, I was thoroughly chilled most of the time.

Coal for the printers' stove was kept in the unlit basement, with its horizontal door that was part of the composing room floor. It goes without saying that rats lived down there. Every now and then a big one would escape into the offices. The women would scream and climb on chairs and tables, and all work halted while Harold Price, the composing room foreman, stalked the intruder. Usually the rat got away, and after a certain length of time our work would resume.

Most of the men weren't much concerned about the live rats, but from time to time, when it became obvious that one of them had died somewhere about the premises, there was nothing to do but endure the odor for a few days.

There was only one bathroom in the facility, and it too was in a dilapidated and grimy condition. Both the faucets gave cold water, and the washbowl was usually encrusted with printer's ink. That hardly mattered, because there was no plug to hold water anyway. The door to the little room was locked on the inside by a hook arrangement, on the outside by a small wooden bar. Occasionally an occupant would have to cry for help after a passerby thoughtlessly or in sport turned the bar.

The windows were usually unwashed, and showed it. The lot in back where we parked our cars was either blowing with dust or thick with mud. Above *The Clarion*'s newsroom, and reached by a stairway from the street, were more musty rooms, one of which was the office of the theatrical editor, St. John Ashley (who signed his column "The Saint"). Robert Morgan inhabited another of these rooms for a period. Since he preferred to keep irregular hours, in the afternoons we often heard classical records drifting down endlessly. Once, when passing by yet another of the rooms, I glanced inside and saw a totally nude black woman stretched out on a bed. I can't explain her, because I didn't inquire further.

I accepted all this poverty, in which *The Clarion* was compelled to operate, as due to the white people's prejudice. For example, the downtown department store—even with its thousands of black customers—would not advertise in the paper. Mr. Talbott said the secretary of the Chamber of Commerce, a man from the Deep South, had been organizing a merchants' boycott of *The Clarion* for years because of its militant stands. Considering these things, the dirt and smells were like the stigmata of martyrdom.

Later on, after young George Lewis became business manager, plans were announced for a new, modern building for *The Clarion*. An architect's conception of the projected new quarters was published on the front page. The rendering was even displayed in the window for several months, until it too became flyspecked. But the plans did not materialize, and after a couple of years they were no longer mentioned.

Mr. Talbott then, for a time, had a project to move to an old but more spacious brick building on the bank of the unused canal that made its way through the district. I think he had some financial interest in this edifice, which served as a hotel and whorehouse until the death of its proprietor. I for one didn't relish looking out on the murky, sinister (bodies were always being fished out of them) waters of the canal, and was just as happy that we stayed where we were.

Despite its physical backwardness, every Thursday night *The Clarion*'s humble plant issued forth a sixteen-page, full-sized, vigorous and interesting newspaper, and every Friday the more than a score of staff workers received their pay envelopes. In all my years, Mr. Talbott never missed a payroll.

The printer's bill was something else. *The Clarion* men set the type and made up the forms, which then were taken to the Hoadley

Printing Company—a large, white establishment—for printing. I
used to hear of tremendous amounts owed to Hoadley's, and yet the
firm seemed cordial and eager to continue business with us. I speculated that *The Clarion*'s account had been allowed to lurch and slip
behind at some period of hard times; it couldn't erase this deficit but
probably was meeting its current payments. Of course, a newspaper
can't be allowed to miss even one issue or it is out of existence—
deficit and all.

It struck me as a good example of the business axiom that if you
can get yourself deeply enough in debt, your creditors will be obliged
to support you.

Mr. Talbott once observed that we made work for his printers
every week. Otherwise, he'd have to pay them for standing around or
they'd get away from him. Beyond this, he was close-mouthed about
Hoadley's, just as he was about the bank and his other business
affairs. Whatever it was, it was a relationship that held firm through
the decades. Years later, near the end of my stay at *The Clarion*, something happened that might have had some bearing on the question.
Young John Hoadley, the heir to the printing firm, just out of
Harvard, suddenly launched on a course of philanthropic Christian
social work. For one year, at his own expense, he operated a home in
Boston where penniless alcoholics could stay and attempt to overcome their affliction, guided by the influence of Christian love. When
he returned to our city, he immediately took up his duties with the
firm and also plunged into the great racial and poverty conflicts that
were then arising in society. It struck an odd note: a representative of
a prominent business family, a Republican, intervening vigorously on
behalf of the black and the poor, in the name of Christianity! One
hardly knew what to think.

Did he do it out of sympathy or a guilty conscience? Was it the
strain of youthful rebellion that was beginning to show up everywhere,
or conversely something he had inherited from his father? While the
particulars were blurred, it seemed to me that the symbiosis of
Hoadley's and *The Clarion* was somehow behind it. I reflected that
John Hoadley had known of *The Clarion* since he was a boy, had

heard his father discuss it, undoubtedly had read it, and perhaps had worked on its production in the printing plant.

The wonder didn't last forever. I left town about then, and when in a few years I returned for a visit, I learned that John Hoadley had veered to a rightist position. Nevertheless, Mr. Talbott often asserted, and I had occasion to confirm by my observations, that despite all the brutality and hatred, there at the same time existed bonds between white and Negro Americans as deep as their very lives. And he was not by any means referring only to liberal thinkers. One day he stood talking in a friendly way at the counter with a well-dressed white man. When the visitor had gone, Mr. Talbott waited pensively a minute and then said to me:

"Did you see that man? Do you know who he is? He was the mayor of M— twenty years ago, when the Negroes were lynched.

"He knew it was going to be done. He wasn't for it, but he was afraid to stop it. So he took a private plane and flew down here, in order to be away when it happened. And of course the mob broke into the jail and hung them in the courthouse square.

"I met him when Smitty and I drove up to cover the story. And ever since then, all this time, he stops by every couple of months. He ain't especially helpful, though he's done a few things. But he's always got to come by."

Another time, I was standing in the front office when a poorly dressed white youth came in to panhandle the price of a meal. Mr. Talbott gave him a quarter. I must have looked surprised, for Mr. Talbott smiled and said, "That happens all the time. When the white man is down and needs a handout, he comes to the nigger neighborhood. Just watch and you'll see."

In fact, I did see numerous cases throughout the years of whites coming to the Avenue for money, votes, love, and human fellowship. It was then a little early in the game for me to realize that I had done so myself.

It worked the other way around too, Mr. Talbott observed. He ridiculed the commonly voiced statement that Negroes hated white people. "The white man is the Negro's god," he said flatly.

The workers didn't take so charitable a view as I did on Mr. Talbott's responsibility for *The Clarion*'s shabbiness. They vociferously and endlessly blamed it on his backward character. Shaking their heads, they spoke of the modern plants that they said other Negro newspapers possessed. "No excuse for it," they declared. "It's just his way." Bill Whitcomb used to complain of Mr. Talbott's habit of leaving a burning cigarette, its end wet with spittle, on the edge of your desk after he had come to speak with you. On the other hand, Mr. Talbott openly rebuked Bill for his nervous trait of taking a mouthful of water and then spitting it into, or near, the water cooler.

"Why, Gawd damn it, man, I wouldn't do a thing like that!" Bill replied furiously.

Quietly but firmly Mr. Talbott said, "You just did, Bill, you know you did. You do it all the time."

At such times, Bill's nerves ran away with him. He would either launch into a yelling spree or step out to the bar next door for a drink of gin.

Mr. Talbott, like a good businessman, kept the front sidewalk swept in summer and cleared of snow in the winter. And he kept the front window clean. He unassumingly did such tasks on his own, which lowered his prestige among the workers to the vanishing point. Moreover, he was a ragged dresser. It sometimes happened that a stranger, entering on a business call, for that reason would address himself to any man on the premises other than the boss. He could not believe that that short fellow wearing old, oddly-matched coat and trousers, a frayed shirt with no tie—perhaps in need of a shave and with a smudge of printer's ink on his forehead—could be the proprietor. These incidents caused no end of stifled merriment among the paper's employees.

He kept a very untidy desk, a trait which any newspaperman who has been around can testify is not confined to Negro editors. Mr. Talbott's was covered several inches deep with opened and unopened letters, magazines, newspapers, and other bric-a-brac. To work at it—when he didn't simply move to another desk—he would clear a space by pushing the debris to the sides, as if with a bulldozer. But then he didn't do much desk work; he wasn't a writer at all. He would tear stories out of other papers, scribble on them "eddy" (editorial) or "short" or "three inches" and hand them to Whitcomb or me for rewriting. Usually he forgot to date them, which infuriated us. Now and then, they were items that had already appeared in *The Clarion*, which gave us a high sense of tongue-clucking superiority.

Mr. Talbott's telephone manners were impeccable—courteous, very clear enunciation, replete with *sirs* or *madams*—but he had one habit that nettled Bill and me, which was to say in conversation:

"This is Cassius Talbott, down at *The Clarion* . . ."

Why "down"? The office was in no sense at the bottom of a hill, or downtown from the white businessmen with whom he was usually talking, or south so as to be on the lower part of a map of the city. If anything, we were "up" or "out" from the business district. But he almost invariably said it, and he had gotten Lehman Scott and George Weyhouse, the paper's advertising men, saying it too.

Shabby, raggedy, "down"—was there somewhere within him, as the workers said, a child who loved filth and disorder? I was told he had been wild in his youth. At the same time, paradoxically, I found him self-representing, adamant against the white ruler of his world, and not for sale to them in the important things. I used to read the other Negro newspapers that the men said had modern plants and well-dressed editors with big cars. It seemed to me that when "push came to shove," most of them were not quite so hard-hitting as *The Clarion*, which a daily writer once dubbed "the militant voice of Illinois Avenue." I believed that Mr. Talbott, in the silence of the night, had considered the cost of a new building and concluded it was his independence. And that was too high a price.

Once the decision was made that you weren't going to be a well-decked-out cipher, there were about two alternatives in our city at the time. You could have got a mile high and carried yourself as the new, unfamiliar, cold, and incomprehensible Negro insisting on his dignity, in which case the white folks (except for the handful of "good white people") would have turned their faces away, and most of the black folks would have also. Or, you could be the old-fashioned poor harmless darky, begging for help, and then on Thursday you could turn around and clobber a couple of segregationists good. The black people would admire these tactics, and strangely enough so would a lot of white people who hadn't been clobbered.

We had in our town an old, black, filthy, stinking, ragged woman named Minnie the Moocher. She had the foulest vocabulary of any human being I have ever heard. She would stand on the sidewalk in front of the Union Club and other haunts of the high and the mighty, and as they went in and out she would curse them to a fare-thee-well. (Although "curse" is much too mild a word.) If a policeman should approach, she would round on him and call him names he hadn't known existed. Minnie was never arrested; she was an institution.

The Clarion was an institution; it had survived half a century when I arrived. Later on, it became the third-oldest Negro newspaper in the United States, as two of three others folded. Every Monday, Lehman Scott would collect any traffic tickets we staff members had received and take them to police headquarters to be fixed. And every Thursday, if they deserved it, *The Clarion* would give the police hell. Of course, the inspector who fixed the tickets was one of the cops who beat on the heads of Negroes. Still and all, it was a *modus vivendi*. The Police Department and *The Clarion* could not put each other out of business, and in fact did not desire to do so, however often they might be in the position of adversaries. They were settled down like an old married couple.

This was not a matter of race, creed, or color, but of power. Even I benefited by it at least once. A young white officer flagged me for speeding. While he was writing the ticket, I was looking through my wallet for my driver's license, and as it happened, came first on my *Clarion* press card.

"How long have you worked at *The Clarion*?" he asked, suspicious of my color.

When I replied he said, "Well, Mr. Preston, you really ought to watch it on the city streets," and he tore up the ticket and departed.

The Clarion's parking lot was a sight during the weeks after the annual deadline for new auto licenses. As many as three or four cars would have homemade cardboard plates stuck in their back windows, bearing the line "plate lost" or "plate stolen." What had really happened was that the owners had failed to ante up the fees for their new plates. The cops must have known it as well as we did. Our city's policemen, except for individual "bad actors," didn't want to "get down wrong with *The Clarion.*" Who of them could ever say from what direction trouble, or even support, might come?

This isn't to say that our law officers were less brutal toward Negroes than those of any other American city. But they respected the power of the press *The Clarion* had achieved. I remember one morning, shortly after my arrival, when a hard-bitten white gold-badge man questioned me as to what I, as a white man, was doing on the Avenue. Bill Whitcomb came to my rescue—very politely, calling the officer "sir"—and that was the end of it. It was precisely this combination of apparent deference with the unspoken threat of what might come out in next Thursday's edition that kept the authorities and the white people off balance and enabled *The Clarion* to survive. It was heeding the admonition of St. Paul to be as "cunning as serpents, and harmless as doves."

The Clarion's news policy, which many whites and some Negroes regarded as bizarre, actually was in my opinion a very intelligent expansion on this text. In the first place there were bloody murders (of Negroes by Negroes), which we played sensationally on page one with screaming headlines. These not only reassured the big white folks that all was normal in Darktown, but they were what sold the paper on the streets. There was no doubt whatsoever that a juicy killing was good for a couple of thousand extra sales.

The efforts of well-meaning persons to reduce the display of violence by the press found no supporters at *The Clarion*. It was not only the staff's bread and butter; it was the life or death of the only real Negro newspaper in the state. And so on Thursday night, when the printers were making up the forms on the stone, the circulation manager would come by and take a look at the front-page headlines as they lay backward in type. The paper customarily carried two or three streamers, and if one of them was on the order of "Eastside Man

Fatally Knifed by Mate," he would beam. But if it was something like
"Truman Supports Housing Bill," he would say, "Oh lord," and his
face would fall a foot. Sometimes he would protest and scurry around
in search of some "like" story that could be elevated into headline status. But by that time, the work was usually well behind schedule,
Hoadley's pair of stout white men were waiting to hoist the forms into
their truck, and Mr. Talbott would hardly ever authorize a change.

Clear in my memory is the front page I held to be the "best," from
this point of view, during my years at *The Clarion*. The top story was
the slaying of one homosexual by another who suspected his mate of
paying attention to a woman. Smitty Smith had even managed to get
hold of a photograph of the victim dressed in woman's garb. That was
one hell of a story! And for the icing there was another, which was
headlined "GIRL NIPS IN SCHOOL FROM MAN'S BOTTLE."
As I remember, Mr. Talbott called Hoadley's and ordered the press
run increased by twenty-five hundred.

There was a certain amount of backlash from middle-class readers
to these stories, mainly women, who deplored the "image of the
Negro" *The Clarion* was presenting. There were times when one realized that tongues were wagging over their bridge tables. Now and then
we received a scolding letter to the editor. These were published, as
were all letters, but the staff viewed them coldly. Sometimes the circulation manager checked on the critics, and found they were not even
subscribers! One woman phone-caller said, "Of course, I don't read
your newspaper myself, but . . ."

Placed side by side with this steady menu of violence was the
theme of civil rights, or more precisely, the exposure of civil wrongs.
That included everything from the refusal of a local stand to sell a
hamburger to a black person to the murder of fourteen-year-old
Emmett Till in Mississippi. It was the great crusade of protest on
which such eminent newspapers as the *Pittsburgh Courier* and the
Chicago Defender had been built. There was no lack of material. The
seventy-five thousand Negroes of our city—later almost double that
number—and as many more elsewhere in the state were continually
being subjected to segregation and discrimination in every area of life,

from economic exploitation to police brutality. In this postwar period
when greater expectations were loose in the world, they were fighting
back on a wider scale than before.

As anyone who has worked for a crusading newspaper knows, stories of these injustices and struggles flew into *The Clarion*'s office
from every quarter. Many who might not even buy the paper in fair
weather beat a path to its door when a storm struck them. In every
town, *The Clarion* had its contact, a stalwart of the National
Association for the Advancement of Colored People, the National
Urban League, the YMCA, a minister, or race-minded private citizen.
Many times, it scooped the dailies, as either the victim or a relative or
some representative of the famous "black dispatch" (not an organization but a figurative term for the spread of news by word-of-mouth
amongst Negroes, as in an underground) would call with the first tip
of the story. Occasionally, *The Clarion* would receive some pencil-
scrawled account in the mail, perhaps on a sheet from a lined school
tablet—some of these from men in prison. Or maybe a sad-faced group
of people, a family with a young man wearing a bandage around his
head or with his arm in a sling, would come into the office.

The informants were by no means all Negroes. Frequently the tips
came from liberal whites, lawyers with clients in the black community,
or white people with axes to grind.

Much news was made by organizations, particularly the NAACP,
which had vigorous local and state branches. Paradoxically, I became
the only member of *The Clarion*'s staff who was active in that body
(except Robert Morgan for a short time). And I wasn't an "impartial
observer." Often, I would introduce a motion, speak on behalf of it,
take part in the resulting action, and then report the whole thing in
The Clarion. I didn't see any contradiction in this: there is a difference
between respecting the truth and pretending to be neutral. In my stories, which were usually bylined, I made every effort to present both
sides of intra-NAACP fights (of which there were many), accurately
and fairly. I ran into a good deal of static from members who thought
I shouldn't wash the dirty linen in public. As a *Clarion* man, I firmly
believed just the opposite—the public is always interested in contro-

versy and an organization presented as being without controversy will die on the vine.

Grist for the mill of *The Clarion* was also supplied by many other organizations. There were long-established bodies, such as the civil liberties department of the Elks, and emerging ones such as Frontiers, Inc. (for businessmen and other professionals), and the Fair Play Officials' Association (for sports referees). There were interchurch groups, integrated neighborhood groups—one couldn't begin to list all the Community Civil Leagues, Human Relations Councils, Yankee Doodle Federations, and Ad Hoc Committees that were waging the good fight with maximum possible exposure by the press and television.

Some of them may have resembled the David vs. Goliath Society, of which *The Clarion*'s good friend and my personal attorney, Davis R. Peckham, was president. After several unsuccessful attempts to attend its meetings, I came to the conclusion that it had no membership whatsoever. But it played its part, issuing blistering press releases on civil issues and sponsoring television statements by Attorney Peckham that challenged the powerful on behalf of God's black people, especially those on the east side of town, where generally the Negroes were more recently from the South and poorer than those on the west side.

Why didn't these aggrieved hordes take their troubles to the vastly more influential daily newspapers, which, incidentally, they bought in greater numbers than *The Clarion*? Some did, and they weren't always turned away with empty hands, but most came instinctively to the decrepit office on Illinois Avenue. For whatever outrage they had to speak of, there was not a man or woman at *The Clarion* who hadn't suffered something like it. Mr. Talbott himself once recounted to me what he said was one of the most harrowing experiences of his life, in connection with his sons and a discriminating amusement park.

"It was when George was about seven and Cashy was about five," he recalled. "I used to drive miles out of the way so as not to take them past Lakeside Park. They didn't know it existed and never would if I could help it.

"And then one day—it was a Sunday—for some reason, I was in a hurry and thinkin' about somethin' else, and all of a sudden there we were. And they began yellin', 'Daddy, look, Daddy, I want to go there, Daddy! Daddy, there's ponies, I want to ride a pony!'"

"My God, what could I do!" he cried. "What could I tell them!"

It goes without saying that the campaign to compel Lakeside Amusement Part to admit Negroes received stronger support from *The Clarion* than from the dailies, no matter how sympathetic their editors might profess to be toward integration.

4. Putting on the Dog

When I first came to *The Clarion*, my cause was civil rights, and I could swallow the bloody murder—perhaps I fancied myself tougher than the average liberal. But I was repelled by another stock-in-trade of the paper, which might be described as ministering to the wounded egos of the dark victims of white society.

This was not so much a matter of celebrating the genuine accomplishments of Negroes as of ladling out flattery to individuals. Bill Whitcomb called it "putting on the dog." It was the sort of thing one had seen in small-town newspapers of an earlier time, and was exhibited at its grossest in the column of correspondence from points south. Here—just as the minister had called me "editor"—every teacher became "professor," every jackleg preacher was a "doctor." Instead of driving, people "motored" to a town twenty miles away. "Delicious luncheons" were served and "many lovely gifts" (or sometimes "many useful gifts") were received at bridal showers or anniversaries. Everyone was a "prominent" something-or-other, if only a "prominent fraternal leader," which might mean he was a member of the Improved Benevolent Protective Order of Elks of the World (IBPOE of W). (If you didn't know, the "of W" signifies a black rather than a white Elk, just as Prince Hall Affiliation denotes a black Mason. On the college campuses a black Kappa will be a man and a white Kappa a coed.)

On various occasions, such as moving to town, getting a new job, assuming the pastorate of a church, or even being scheduled to make a talk, people would call on *The Clarion* to publish their pictures, together with an account of their qualifications. They paid for the engravings and the photos themselves if *Clarion* photographers took them. Sometimes, if they looked good for it, they paid for the space. And what qualifications! The great list of schools attended, degrees, awards, church and fraternal and civic committee memberships and the like might run on and on for ten to twenty solid inches of type. On the face of it, it was inconceivable that anyone would read all this except the subject and members of his or her immediate circle. And when one met the person involved, he would often turn out to be quite an ordinary-seeming individual.

My cold white mind at first had difficulty digesting this. Bill Whitcomb also kept up a running fire of sarcasm about it as not being the "modern way" of doing things, though I came to realize he was chiefly expressing his jealousy of other "puffed-up" Negroes. Mr. Talbott, as always, had a more down-to-earth attitude, seeking to give the people what they wanted and needed.

It was only after working among Negroes for a good many years, after visiting many Negro homes in their humble poverty, after going to the towns where the ghettoes huddled in the deadly backwash of forgotten time—it was only after doing all these things that I reached a place where I felt, not the boastfulness of the autobiographies, but the pity of them. If only God Almighty could be shown what an able sort of person He was allowing to fall into a bottomless pit, surely He would reach down His hand of rescue!

Robert Morgan presided over the society pages of *The Clarion*—the only male society editor I ever heard of at the time—and he dispensed the nostrums of "social standing" with the skill of a chemist. Society writing was just then starting to be deemphasized by the white newspaper, or so I was told, but it was in full flood in the Negro press. And, contrary to what I expected from an oppressed and generally impoverished people, I found that Negro society affairs—not that I went to any, but that was another matter—were as lavish and resplendent as those of the whites. I thought the fact that the American Negro was originally a Southerner had something to do with it, as it did with so many other things, and also his historically close relation—in the capacities of slave and then domestic servant—with the upper reaches of white "society." We Communists were often mystified by the failure of Negroes to flock to our working-class banner, but after some observation, I decided it was a result of the black people's intimacy (albeit on unjust terms) with wealthy whites. What did the Negro want with the *poor* white man?

There was one respect, I was happy to see, in which the good healthy democracy of *The Clarion* shone through the society flimflam. In reading the Negro newspapers from more metropolitan areas, one couldn't help noticing that social status was based largely on skin color; the lighter a person was the more "well placed" they tended to be. I won't say Robert was immune to this, because it was an ever-present law of this side of Negro life, but his intelligence rebelled against it, and to a certain extent he played up Mrs. Darkskin as well as Mrs. Fairskin. From the economic standpoint, too, it may have been that our community was more democratic because we lacked the really wealthy circles that I heard existed in such places as Washington, D.C., and Atlanta. We had a reputedly wealthy man, Hatteras Thompson, but for other reasons he wasn't ordinarily regarded as "society."

And so, black women who weren't "society," or the wives of professional men, nor teachers or even social workers made it into Robert's pages.

Then, however, there was the case of Mrs. Dorothy Hill Boatner, a beautiful and elegant woman who had a special relationship with *The Clarion*. The wife of a well-to-do lawyer, Mrs. Boatner headed the group who conducted the newspaper's annual Christmas charity drive for the poor. She rarely visited the office, but when she did, slender and olive-skinned with an air of New Orleans about her, wearing soft furs and trailing a bewitching scent, it was as if a queen was among us.

The thing about Mrs. Boatner was that her picture graced *The Clarion*'s pages not two or three times a year, but dozens of times every year, sometimes week after week. Every time it was a double-column of space and a glamorous portrait taken by some commercial photographer. Robert would have his pages filled and made up when the word would come from Mrs. Weyhouse to make space for a picture of Mrs. Boatner. "What, again? It was in last week and also three weeks ago." "But this is a new one—it's a must. Come on, Robert, you know it has to go." Or, "Richard [her son, with whom she seemed to identify herself more closely than her husband] is in this one with her."

Robert, grumbling, would make a hole in his page.

In the files where used engravings were kept, there was a large envelope filled with those of Mrs. Boatner. If God clipped *The Clarion*, He will recognize her, with her large, sad eyes on Judgment Day.

Mrs. Boatner furnished her own photographs, but I doubt that she paid for the engraving, because she was "*Clarion*." Most often, a *Clarion* photographer would go and take the picture, in which case he picked up a ten-dollar bill. Walt Evers was the paper's photographer before he became circulation manager; then Dick Nelson, who worked on a freelance basis while he held a factory job; and pretty soon, Mr. Talbott's sons came along. Because these jobs were cash in hand, men vied for the assignments. Nelson complained to me endlessly that Mr. Talbott favored his son George.

As for the church page, every line of type in stories, as well as advertisements, was cash on the barrelhead. In return, the ministers wrote their own articles, and said whatever they pleased. That the preachers should pay was held to be only fair. They were seeking the patronage of the public, and they took in money regularly in the Sunday collections (and sometimes up to three or four collections, for various purposes, on the same Sunday). They were looked on as entrepreneurs. Which is not to say that the Talbott family, which belonged to the African Methodist Episcopal Church, was cynical about religion. They were only being practical.

The theatrical pages were also solidly commercial ads, except for the Saint's column, "The Avenoo," and an occasional musicians' column by Don West, an alcoholic member of those circles. I suspected that some of the items in those columns also entailed considerations, probably going directly to the columnists, though I never saw any money change hands. The Saint, a large and saturnine man, rarely came down from his pigeon's roost, and to tell the truth, he and I did not get along too well. He was an extremely Negro Negro, and did not put much stock in the carryings-on of mere integrationists. He seemed full of the dark distrust that in the 1920s had characterized Marcus Garvey's followers, and was to emerge again with the Muslims.

In short, the Saint and I were as far apart as black and white. It took me a long time to admit that his column was as good as it was. Of course, I couldn't begin to write as he did, in vivid street language, and I suppose he made me feel like a white liberal who had been expelled from the SNCC. Not that we ever had words—neither of us was the type, and he less than I—although we came close to it once.

The Saint made a mistake in his column, I forget about what, and he corrected it in the next week and wrote, "Due to an error in proofreading." I was doing the proofreading at that time, and I refused to pass the explanation.

"Well, I know that," he said. "It's just the easiest way to get rid of it—you know, without hurting anybody's feelings."

But something had got into me, and I wasn't in a mood for common sense. I declared that people knew who the proofreader at *The Clarion* was, and it would hurt my standing in the profession and other rubbish. The Saint kept saying, "Well, yeah," and "Well, but you know," but I didn't let him wriggle off. Being the proofreader, I had the final word. I made it, "Due to an error in last week's column."

This brush with the Saint, seen in retrospect after I began to be aware that there was still a "white man" within me, reminded me of an incident on King Avenue—the west side's killer traffic street—that took place as I was driving home one day. I was approaching the intersection with 18th Street, where King jogged to the left around the gas works. Here came a Negro in a ramshackle car, with a woman and maybe a child or two, passing me near the intersection. To be safe, I should have slowed and let him go by, because there were cars coming toward us, and there might be others around the jog. But I had another alternative, to stand on my right and make him brake behind me.

It all happened in a flash, so that I didn't have time to consider. I accelerated, and, as in a discovered check in chess, he was caught in the intersection with nowhere to go and the traffic coming on. He turned his head and I can still remember his bearded dark face as he yelled, "Oh, no you don't!" I forget how it ended—whether he put on a burst of speed and cut ahead or, more likely, fell behind. But I reflected that he had thought I was a white race-hater who had deliberately tried to murder him and his family.

The sports page, to which I eventually gravitated, was mostly not for sale. It hardly ever levied a toll—or brought in a dime, if you look at it that way—for pictures or space. For one thing, most of the sports events covered were either amateur (such as high school games) or national, and there was no way of putting the bite on their sponsors. Then, when I became sports editor, I insisted on operating according to the Puritan ethic, which was great for idealism but not so much for survival. I high-mindedly resisted any considerations of filthy lucre, not only for myself but for the paper. Looking back, I am not so proud as I once was of this attitude. I can see that I was holding myself "above" the other editors, as if I were not going to stoop to "Negro dishonesty." Actually, the course they followed of bringing in revenue while at the same time getting across the truth to readers was much more complicated and difficult than I had made it out to be. But I was as I was, and couldn't change all that fast. Had I not been a good deal of a fanatic on such things, of course, I wouldn't have been there. I sometimes saw a look of bafflement in Mr. Talbott's eyes when he found me disdaining some opportunity to bring in a few dollars. Usually he said nothing, being prevented, I think, by consideration that if he wanted to have me on the staff, he must respect my quirks. There were times when I had a feeling that he was quietly going behind my back to the Braves' professional baseball club, for instance, or the Harlem Globetrotters' management, and negotiating a financial arrangement unbeknownst to me. If so, it was a reasonable solution, for it left me with my illusion of being clean-handed while compelling the well-to-do beneficiaries of my writings to help support *The Clarion.*

As the years went by, and I came to understand Mr. Talbott's motivations better—he wasn't personally getting rich, after all—I'm happy to report that I shook down into a more human state of mind on this subject, so that I was no longer ashamed to exact a charge for *The Clarion* in certain situations.

The Clarion's editorial page was also free of commercialism, unless once in a blue moon someone might buy a "puff" editorial. The star of the page was Abraham L. Jackson, whose column, "Crying in the Wilderness," was an acid commentary on our segregated society. I used to say it was the most interesting column in the United States, black, white, or indigo. I think we don't have people like Jackson in white America. He was a teacher at Dunbar High School (which was all Negro), yet the most outspoken critic of segregated schools; he was a prominent lay worker in the Disciples of Christ Church, but was fond of writing that "the most segregated hour in American life is eleven o'clock on Sunday morning." He was also active in not only the NAACP and the Teachers' Union, but in the Masons, the Kappas or Alphas, organized duplicate bridge and, with his wife, was the social whirl. In his column he frequently came down hard on the "black bourgeoisie," and I sometimes thought he was being self-critical. The corollary, in an earlier time, would have been Mencken being president of the Rotary Club.

Whitcomb, Morgan, and I wrote the editorials. They didn't often reflect the paper's "politics," which was, strange as it seemed to me, Republican. As every Election Day drew near, *The Clarion* would solemnly publish its slate, consisting of all or most of the Republican candidates, with occasionally the odd Democrat for some minor office. And as every election took place, its readers would vote up to eighty-five percent Democratic.

When the election was over *The Clarion* immediately dropped the subject and returned to its civil themes—which, of course, brought it into conflict with most of the Republicans. And the readers, holding no grudge, went on buying the paper as before.

At first, I was inclined to take a cynical view of all this. I had lived through the Depression and the New Deal, and I couldn't see how any poor man in his right mind would be Republican. But since the big money was with the Grand Old Party—the senator whose foot I had stepped on, for example, was a millionaire industrialist—I could easily see how a poor man might pretend to be Republican.

It was said by waiters, janitors, and other strategically placed persons that *The Clarion* was read in the Union Club, the Chamber of Commerce, and similar haunts of the wealthy. It stood to reason that it was read with special attention when it endorsed candidates. And one could picture the money-men reading and noting with gratification, "Well, Cassius is safe. Right down the line for the ticket."

Something happened one day that led me to think it was also read when certain shibboleth names were printed. In those years, Paul Robeson was often in the news, raising his mighty voice as a singer and speaker against the reactionaries. He was a Negro white people had heard of, and so he had been made a particular target of red-baiters. (I don't know whether or not he was a Communist, but he refused to be anti-Communist, which set the right-wingers to having nightmares of a slave uprising.)

I wrote several editorials holding up Robeson's hand, until Mr. Talbott came to me and, with some embarrassment, said, "Listen, don't use Robeson's name anymore. Neither favorably nor unfavorably. Just don't put his name in the paper."

I felt certain that Mr. Talbott was not opposed to Robeson, and, in fact, admired him greatly, but for once he was acting out of fear. I concluded that "somebody downtown" must be having fits at the appearance of the powerful combination of letters "P-A-U-L R-O-B-E-S-O-N" in *The Clarion*'s pages.

I was mistaken about Mr. Talbott and the Republicans, however. He really meant it. His revered father had been a supporter of the party of Lincoln, and he wasn't about to turn to false gods.

He could give you an argument over it, too. Since he was a businessman, the mere name of FDR held no magic for him, as it did for most Negroes. And when he looked around at the state and local white politicians, many of whom he was acquainted with, while I was not, he defied you to say that the Democrats were any more liberal on the race question than the Republicans. "They're all Kluckers!" he snorted. "Some of 'em got on Roosevelt's coattails for votes, and the rest are just plain Kluckers. What does it mean to the black man? Nothin'!"

I had to admit that, seen up close, the local Democrats offered little inspiration. And, on the other hand, the county Republican boss, while deemed a "crooked politician," had the reputation of being personally fair to Negroes in the dispensing of small patronage jobs.

Mr. Talbott and I came as close to hard words as we ever would when I once observed that the Republicans, after all, were the party of money.

"Shit!" he countered. "Roosevelt took all of the money in the country and used it to keep himself in the White House. The Democrats have three times the money of the Republicans. They've got the whole God-damned budget!"

This sounded so like an ordinary white Republican of our state that I realized Mr. Talbott was sincere. I used to watch him from time to time to see whether he still believed in Republicanism. I always concluded that he did, though he would make an exception when a truly liberal Democrat came along and did something to benefit black people.

We never agreed on national politics, until we both were swept up in Lyndon Johnson's consensus in 1964—he through attending a dinner of Negro publishers at the White House and I more cheaply. LBJ reminded me of Roosevelt.

5. A Family Affair

It was good to be working regularly. I had been out of work for eight months since I had been obliged to leave my job with a New York magazine and return to my home state. Sometimes in that dark period I had feared I might never work again, but the whale had beached on some shore after all.

My wife Susan, with our infant son Michael, had moved in with her parents. I was sleeping in a rented room next door. Susan had found a secretarial job with the International Typographical Union.

My pay at *The Clarion* was a dollar an hour, and I gradually stepped up my time until I was working about forty hours a week. Practically everybody there, aside from Mr. Talbott, had a working wife who was earning more than he was. Bill Whitcomb's wife worked in a factory and drew United Automobile Workers wages. Lehman Scott's wife was a teacher. Harold Pierce's wife was a social worker. These couples had complicated railroad-schedule arrangements and their family cars to get everybody to work and home on time. Susan and I didn't own a car—in New York, we hadn't needed one.

It was quite a sight to see Lehman's wife pull up for him at the mildewed *Clarion* office in the big Chrysler, every evening between five and six. You might say he was in society on his wife's side.

The Clarion was first of all a family enterprise. Mr. Talbott, of course, was editor and publisher. His wife was also on the payroll, more or less doing something of a clerical nature at home. His older sister, Mrs. Edna Talbott Lewis, functioned as the office business manager. She and her husband were separated, but her son George later came on as the firm's business manager.

Mr. Talbott's younger sister, Luvenia Talbott Weyhouse, and her husband George came to *The Clarion* from Detroit a few years after my arrival. George Weyhouse sold advertising, and Mrs. Weyhouse shared the duties of Mrs. Lewis. An older brother, George W. Talbott Jr., who had been destined to head the firm, had died young of the family ailment, diabetes.

There was also an aunt, Mrs. Charlotte Hill McPherson ("Aunt Lottie"), who was the widow of an African Methodist Episcopal bishop and edited the church page. There was an uncle, universally called "Old Top" (I think his name was Claude Talbott), who made collections for circulation. And there was Lehman, who was married to the sister of Mr. Talbott's wife.

Mr. Talbott's sons, George and Cassius, were small boys when I went to *The Clarion*. Before I left the paper, George had been installed as city editor. "Cashy" worked there several years but didn't like it and got himself a factory job. However, he still came around and pitched in at odd hours. He also made compensation to the family by bringing into it through marriage the star female reporter, Marguerite Woodson.

To fit all the relatives into the newspaper's framework, Mr. Talbott sometimes had to shove the square family peg into the round *Clarion* hole. He didn't hesitate. His philosophy was that people could do anything if given a chance and shown how. Bill Whitcomb complained that he thought "writing editorials was no different from cooking hamburgers." Mr. Talbott was not a writer himself, and it was true he had the disdain for fancy qualifications that are upheld by many of society's outsiders. I was reminded of the sequence in the Soviet movie *Chapayev*, in which the guerrilla fighters are preparing to shoot a captured veterinarian because "he won't make a single peasant a doctor." Mr. Talbott wouldn't have made anyone a doctor, but he wasn't above making a brother-in-law an advertising manager.

That is, I believed it was Mr. Talbott who made these decisions. But we non-family staffers were of course not privy to the proceedings of the Talbott clan away from the office. We frequently got a whiff of internecine wars, combinations, and alliances. The actual head of the family and the newspaper's owner of record was Mr. Talbott's mother, a frail lady in her seventies. It was her disapproval that was given as the reason for finally breaking up the poker game, for instance. But I thought she must function like the queen in England, voicing decisions that were arrived at through the family battles.

The contending parties were, nearly as I could make out, Mr. Talbott on the one hand and Mrs. Lewis and later her son George on the other. Where the other members came down, I had no idea. Not a word disclosing the substance of the disputes was breathed in the office, although the family was loudmouthed in its quarreling. Mrs. Lewis, who Bill Whitcomb said had the most native ability of any of them, was especially subject to long ranting fits. I remember one that she ended by shouting to Attorney Peckham—he was on Mr. Talbott's side—that she wouldn't consult him "on behalf of my dead dog if I had one!" But it was a family trait. Ms. Weyhouse wasn't far behind, and Mr. Talbott, though ordinarily self-possessed, was no mean shouter when aroused. The various individual families lived near one another on the north side, some of them in a double house for a time, and the family members usually came to work by the carload. It sometimes happened that a fight that had begun at home or in the car would rumble away like dying thunder as the group came in the back door and through the composing room to the office. At such times, the non-family workers standing by would turn to one another with smiles and head-shakings.

But to tell the truth, most of them were shouters too. I have heard Bill Whitcomb and Mr. Talbott go to it by the half-hour, in voices that resounded throughout the building. Striding repeatedly to the water cooler and spitting out mouthfuls of water, Bill, to show his badness, would bring up the time he dived into the Green River and got his head stuck in the mud, the time his brother was shot by his side so that his brains fell out on the porch, and other bloodcurdling stories. Sometimes he would take a bullet out of his pocket and gesture with it. (He kept the gun in his car, or said he did; I never saw it.)

Mr. Talbott would roar back at him—he wasn't above needling Bill, and sometimes would start a yelling match in jest, become serious, and then be overcome by laughter before it ended.

With such a collection of nervous, frustrated people—and I made another one—it seemed that hostility was the very atmosphere of *The Clarion*. Take, for instance, the exchange of presents at Christmas. It was the custom for the firm to place in each pay envelope an extra five-dollar bill, while the employees would collectively bestow a gift on Mr. Talbott. The latter ceremony took place at the end of the day on Christmas Eve, in the front office. The workers gathered slowly—some still completing jobs, others like George Brown with a glint in his eyes from an early start on the holiday merry-making. When a good number of employees had arrived, Mr. Talbott was not to be found. I wondered whether he disliked the practice, by which he lost so heavily in the balance.

By the time he showed up, usually about half the employees had gone off somewhere. And then Bill Whitcomb, as spokesman for the staff, would make a speech—it varied little from year to year—that I found amazing. It consisted for the most part of a recital of grievances against Mr. Talbott: he had done those things he ought not to have done and left undone those things he ought to have done. And, indeed, all this was spoken like a prayer, in a formal voice. Then at the end he threw in, in contrast to what had gone before, that this was a time for fellowship of all who worked together, and he presented Mr. Talbott with his gift. Mr. Talbott said, "Thank you," or made no reply but simply took the gift and opened it. Everyone departed for home simultaneously, and that was that for another year.

And yet, it will be seen that if such expressions could be made, the workers must have felt a basic freedom as far as the boss was concerned. There was no need to comfort oneself, as Bill Whitcomb put it, "with your head bowed down like a Chinese schoolboy." It was said that Mr. Talbott had never fired anyone in all the years he had been in business. Certainly he never did during my time: he shouted at them, he swore at them, he traded threats with them, but he did not fire them. Years later, I heard that he had fired Robert Hancock, the linotypist; if that occurred, it was the exception to the rule.

This record was all the more remarkable because he had in his employ so many alcoholics. Smitty Smith was the most notorious of these; when he was city editor he would go on a spree every week on the night before press day. Apparently, it was the approach of his day of responsibility that set him off. Finally, Bill, whose drinking seldom interfered with his work, was made city editor and Smitty was put to reporting.

When drunk, Smitty could be expected to go roaring on the town, and then be heard of only intermittently for a few days. Robert Hancock, on the other hand, kept a pint of whiskey on the floor by his machine, and nipped from it silently all day long. I could tell in my proofreading when the booze had gotten to Hancock: his normally clean galley would become pocked with errors. He was the kind who waxed philosophical under the influence, and launched interminable discussions. His small face worked a frozen smile, but he spoke from the deep angers of a quiet black man. He would buttonhole me with a seemingly innocuous question if I came by, or he might go directly through the office to Mr. Talbott. He sought the sources of power: in my case, the white people; in Mr. Talbott's, the boss.

George Brown was another who drank invisibly, until suddenly he turned up in the middle of a busy day, smiling foolishly, teetering a little at the side of a room, and saying tentatively to people who passed by, "Hey . . . hey. . . ." He might go straight to Mr. Talbott and with a heavy scowl demand his pay, saying he was leaving. The conversation would be something like this:

"Mr. Talbott . . . Mr. Talbott . . . give me my time."

"You'll get your pay like everybody else, on Friday."

"No, goddammit, I want it now. I quit! Give me my money!"

"You're drunk, Mr. Brown! You're drunk in working hours! Goddamned niggers!" said Mr. Talbott, walking away from him.

"Who's drunk? Who says I'm drunk?"

"You're drunk, and you know you're drunk. Now if you're not working, punch out! Goddamn you—don't get drunk on my time!"

"For y'r inf'mation, Mr. Talbott, I can get another job any time I want one. Now if you don't think so, just pay me off and see. I asked for y'r time—give me my time, man, just like I asked for!"

"I don't have to give you your time just because you asked for it. My God, man! You get your time on Friday, just like everybody else. Now if you ain't going to work, punch out!"

"Who says I ain't going to work? I do my work, man!"

"I didn't say you didn't do your work. I said if you're drunk and ain't going to work . . ." And so on.

I must have heard a thousand such exchanges between Mr. Talbott and various employees. At first they frightened me—I feared they would end in violence. But after listening to a number of them, I realized they were ritual combat, something like:

"Just step over that line!"

"I don't have to step over it! You drew it—you step over it!"

George Brown seemed nearer to violence than any other man on the staff, but no matter how drunk, he wasn't going to assault the head of the paper. And Mr. Talbott, no matter how provoked and how angry he became, wasn't going to commit murderous assault on another man by taking his livelihood from him. It wasn't his business to fire people, but to get them to work.

Thus, underlying all the angry yelling and shielding its participants from consequences that might have been expected to follow, was a foundation of mutual loyalty such as I had rarely seen in the white world. There was something of almost feudal fealty about it. Whatever the workers might boast in excitement, practically there was no other place for them to get jobs at their trade and everyone knew it. They were bound to *The Clarion*. And on the other side, if you were born into the Talbott family, or married into it, or went to work for *The Clarion*, or aided its projects or did it a courtesy, or took an ad in it, then *The Clarion*, and specifically Mr. Talbott, would hold up your hand. Your life was your own: you might be called a Communist or arrested for larceny (as one of the part-time reporters was), or get a reputation as homosexual or psychotic, and it made no difference—you were "*Clarion*."

It was a time before I came to appreciate this. Along with Whitcomb, that born rebel, I offered passive resistance to Mr. Talbott's directives. We turned down the corners of our mouths and withdrew our eyes. When Mr. Talbott had left the room, Bill would say acidly, "Nobody gets bigger than the boss," and with heavy hearts we would start to do whatever we had been told.

I was suffering not only from anti-boss syndrome, but from the advantages of a college education. I had always been a detail man. My difficulties in this respect began when we were still across the street, and I was reading proofs for the Victory Edition. What should I do when I came to a galley that was full of author's errors, faulty grammar, and misspellings? I could hardly let them pass without disturbing my white middle-class conscience. And yet when I marked them, I was bringing out the resetting of practically entire galleys. This was prodigal of time and money, both of which I knew were grievously short.

The corrections should have been made, by somebody, before the articles were set in type. But except for Robert Morgan, there was probably no one who could have made them. Bill Whitcomb, who wore such matters in his expression "as a loose mantle," wouldn't have taken the trouble.

This being said of the editors, what difference would it make to the readers? Would there be one in five thousand who would know where the comma should go, or how to spell the words? Wasn't I forcing a mandarin mold on a language that was satisfactory to the people? And wasn't this an arrogant and insensitive thing for a white man to be doing in that situation?

I flipped and flopped. Meanwhile the linotype men complained that the heavy marking of their proofs made them look bad, when all they had done was to follow copy. This was especially irksome to Robert Hancock, who could set type better when moderately drunk than most men could sober. But the boss, without investigating, might jump him for a "dirty proof."

And then, Lord preserve us, Hancock now and then took it into his head, as a way out of the difficulty, to correct the copy as he set it. But he was a printer and not a writer—and then I would be obliged to correct his corrections!

This was good for at least an hour's conversations, beginning as he approached me with his false smile. "Well, now, Mr. Preston—what do you want me to do? It kind of looks like I'm damned if I do and damned if I don't! Begging your pardon, but now you are white—do you think a black man would know how to set type?"

"Mr. Hancock, it has nothing to do with black and white," I would attempt.

"Oh, but it does! Oh, but it does!" in the most gentle cordiality, but with that simmering anger beneath it.

After such a rebuff, he would go to the opposite extreme and "follow copy out the window," setting the word "shit" if someone mistakenly had typed it for "shirt."

I decided that in principle it was wrong to overlook errors on the grounds that our readers were Negroes. I should give them the very best proofreader I was capable of being. This was in line with the Communist dictum that "nothing is too good for the working class." I devised a system of using a blue pencil for typesetter's mistakes, and a red one for editor's corrections of the original copy. Thus the linotypists could not be blamed for what was not their fault. I even found some handy pencils with one end red and the other blue.

Sometimes, overwhelmed by the volume of semi-literacy, I would make red-pencil corrections only in lines that also had blue-pencil ones and let the rest go. This had the disadvantage that a word might appear in the paper spelled one way in one line and another in the next. But it served to appease (a) my middle-class conscience, (b) the typesetter's demands for justice, and (c) the boss's necessity to cut down on resetting.

A campaign that Mr. Talbott carried on with us of the newsroom, with little avail, was that *The Clarion* should devote more space to local news rather than national stories. This now seems to me a truism of the newspaper trade, but Bill and I resisted it for years, with looks and coldness. For one thing, working up local news requires more effort than pasting "takes" from the Associated Negro Press. That wasn't how we saw it, of course. We thought we were trying to weigh the problems of the world, while he was concerned only with putting Reverend Dingbat's name in the paper.

Mr. Talbott frequently said that people on white newspaper staffs worked a lot harder than we did. He usually gave the small-town *Harrison Weekly News* as an example. Since none of us had been there, we couldn't refute him, but we glared. We continued to maintain a pace fit for human beings, with time to reflect on the passage of the stars.

With this single exception, I moved at some point—I could not tell you when it was—from opposition to Mr. Talbott into feeling deep respect for him. I became a veritable Jesuit of local news. During these years, I was also a Civil War buff, and it occurred to me one day that Mr. Talbott, in his unpretentious, dogged determination, bore a resemblance to Ulysses S. Grant.

Extending the fancy, I imagined Bill Whitcomb, fiery and impatient, as William Tecumseh Sherman. Since the generals were two of my favorite Americans, it seems that I felt I was home at last.

6. Every Day but Sunday

The Clarion office was open every day but Sunday. Mr. Talbott was a man diligent in his business. His life was *The Clarion*. Not only didn't he put on the dog socially, but he served on no civic committees. He went to the office at eight in the morning, and there he remained until eight or nine in the evening. Mrs. Talbott brought his lunch to him, and sometimes his dinner.

People came to him—politicians, businessmen, cronies. Except for the bank, he rarely went out on business. He did not attend publishers' conventions or the like, but he would sometimes drive a hundred and fifty miles to the state prison, several times with the boxer Archie Moore, who went to entertain the convicts. He became a member of the State Parole Board—the only public office he ever held. Out of all the members of society, his heart was with the prisoners.

The printers also came at eight, and the rest of us about nine and usually went home between five and six. Thursday was press day; everybody put in a heavy day and usually a long one, since the paper was never ready until hours after the ostensible deadline of 5:00 p.m. Many of those who had completed their work would gather round the printers, who were working away to make up the final forms—page one last of all. It was a great time to shoot the breeze, sometimes until ten or eleven at night. Mr. Talbott, and later his sons and George Lewis, might pitch in to help make up the forms, but the rest stayed strictly away from this work of the printers. (I have seen Bill Whitcomb do it when directed by Mr. Talbott on a particularly late night.) Nerves needed relaxing after the long day's work, a few drinks might have been nipped, jokes and stories were told. Some of the men saw, for the first time, as it lay in type, what the editors had prepared, and wisecracked about it. With Harold Pierce and George Brown hammering in the leads to tighten the forms, while conversations on every conceivable subject ran on all around them—in which they joined without looking up—it was the most exciting and sociable time of the week.

Meanwhile, the ragged carrier boys were gathering in the front office. They took over the place, sitting at the desks, fighting, rolling on the floor, and as the hours went by, they too grew more and more excited. Various adults would go out once in a while to restore order by shouting commands. If it got too bad, Mr. Talbott would bellow threats at them. Neither he nor anyone else ever sent one of the boys away, however, since *The Clarion* was dependent on them to sell the papers in the streets. For this reason, the disciplinary admonitions, while fierce in tone, were somewhat lacking in content. The kids (there were some girls, too) recognized this, and weren't really frightened. They would become quiet for a while, and when the adults went away, it would start up again.

Stout white men from Hoadley's stood by while the forms were being completed, waiting to carry them to their truck. This was the signal for the staff gathering to break up. Some men would head out for a drink or two before going home. During the halcyon five-year period of the Thursday night poker game, at this point the tables and chairs would be set up in the newsroom, and Lehman would start shuffling the cards and selling chips as the men moved quickly into their accustomed places.

In about an hour, the printed front sections began arriving from Hoadley's (the back sections had been printed earlier in the day). The boys stuffed the sections together with incredible speed. Then Mr. Talbott would yell, "Holler the headlines! Holler the headlines!" and they would take off into the streets.

After this hectic climax, Friday morning always came cool and peaceful. *The Clarion* did considerable job work, printing tickets, handbills, church programs and so forth. Much of this work was done on Friday—although no job was ever refused, and if necessary, it would be crammed and jammed through on any day of the week, even when the newspaper was going to press. The supervising of these jobs was one of the reasons why Harold Pierce, as composing-room foreman, was the hardest-working man in the place. He equaled Mr. Talbott in the amount of time put in—and worked unremittingly.

So Friday morning clopped along with the jobs and the wrapping and storing of last week's copy, that sort of thing, and then the pace more or less slowed for the rest of the day. There might be some tinkering with the machines, and in the afternoon there would be the leisurely setting of a few galleys of features already received for next week's issue, but there was no hurry. There was seldom a quarrel on a Friday. Mr. Talbott handed out the paychecks at his desk starting at four o'clock, looking at each one before he gave it to the employee. I never learned his reason for this practice, and at first resented it, thinking that he was suspicious of our overtime and perhaps was reminding us where our pay was coming from. But I got used to it, as I did everything else, and then it seemed to me a good, straightforward way of doing business. If Mr. Talbott was out or tied up in a bull session with one of his friends, you could sometimes get your check from the bookkeeper, Miss Daisy List.

When they had their pay, the workers departed, often with the exception of Pierce, who might still have some job work to do. The family cars took off about five o'clock. Lehman Scott and Bill Whitcomb waited for their wives. Bill would have been socializing all afternoon, talking a blue streak. Robert Morgan didn't come in at all on Friday except to get his check. Smitty was another who seldom showed up until Monday. The circulation people were the only ones who were really busy on Friday, making their collections from the carriers, who came in to pay, and from the newsstands. That's not to count Miss List, who worked all the time, but so humbly and quietly that she was taken for granted.

I thought all this was wrong. I had a theory—I suppose it was the Puritan ethic—that a weekly newspaper on a five-day week should do a fifth of its work each day. On Fridays I would write editorials, or, when I was sports editor, send out about one-fifth of my copy to the printers. Like any good Puritan, I had an itch to impose my way on others. I pointed out my views on the subject to Mr. Talbott, and he heartily agreed with me. But I never saw a reform movement fall so flat. Nobody else would have any part of it. It was contrary to the collective will. Bill Whitcomb would open the ANP envelope (the "wire" news came by air-mail special delivery) and mark enough features to "hold the printers," but that was all. Then he would relax, read exchange newspapers, and talk for the rest of the day.

On Saturday, the printers were off (unless Pierce was in on a special job). Bill and I worked until noon, preparing copy for the printers to set Monday. The business side of the paper might also be in until noon. That was one day when Mr. Talbott might not arrive until ten o'clock. But he was there all afternoon, in the summertime sitting in a chair on the sidewalk, its frame tilted against the building. That was the time the people rolled by like a mighty stream. A stream of poor colored people, rolling up from the Deep South toward Chicago—as the saying had it—till their money ran out when they had got only as far as our town. It was the day of the street people. A good lot of them had been drinking since the night before. Mr. Talbott, although he never drank, was there talking with the people. The white bill collectors and salesmen and meter readers were gone, and so usually was the "crazy peckerwood at *The Clarion*," as somebody had dubbed me. It wasn't much of a time and place for whites. The times I did go by, the Avenue had a more friendly, festive air. Often St. John Ashley was standing on the sidewalk leisurely chatting with a group of men.

In the winter, Mr. Talbott was inside with his feet propped on his desk talking with Luke Landrum, the barber to governors and rich men, or some other crony of his who could come by only on Saturday afternoons. The talks went on for hours, and I had a feeling they were about more interesting things than ever got into the newspaper.

Some of these cronies, for example, were waiters at the Athletic Club, the Union Club, or the downtown hotels. Disregarded by the patrons as a part of the accessories—like the tablecloths and silver they supervised—they had eyes, ears, brains, and memories. They thus acquired a great deal of expertise on the business and political happenings of the city and the state, not to mention personal happenings of a certain type. They were an "in" group whom the white people, blinded by prejudice, did not realize were in.

Thus qualified, and having also acquired for the members of the power structure a contempt bred by familiarity, the waiters would have been well able to govern the city if a turn should come. One of Mr. Talbott's friends, Remus F. Hazelwood, had been a waiter for years. In midlife he completed his courses at the state university law school, passed the bar examination, and hung out his shingle. After practicing for several years, he was appointed to a big Washington job with the U.S. Civil Rights Commission when it needed a Republican Negro. That lasted two years, and he came back and continued his law practice. It was early in the 1960s. Our city's bipartisan system of excluding Negroes from the City Council foundered on the reality that blacks now constituted one-fourth of the population. Each party slated a Negro candidate, Hazelwood being named by the GOP and a young minister, Reverend John D. Carroll, by the Democrats. Ironically, due to the very workings of the "gentlemen's agreement," which was not operating in reverse, both were elected. It was at once apparent that Remus Hazelwood was the most competent member of the council, with the best knowledge of what made the city tick. He would have been a natural for mayor if he hadn't been a "nigger."

These attributes were even more possessed by certain barbers. Luke Landrum, a thin, light-complexioned man who was a boon talking companion of Mr. Talbott, had operated a barber shop for thirty years in the downtown Crone-Housman Building. His establishment was patronized by the great and the wealthy, and Luke himself was the barber to the governors and senators and the men who made them and broke them.

Luke's personality, as I came to know it, was a variant of the court jester or "crazy nigger" type. That is, far from showing deference to his prominent customers, he would assail them with a rapid stream of insults and bad language. His audacity at first might be startling, but soon the patron would realize with a glow that he was being treated not as a stuffed shirt but as the fallible and even evil man he knew himself to be. Moreover, by accepting it with a smile, he was showing that he was democratic.

The prominent man patronized Luke for the same complicated reasons that white men cruised at night along the Avenue looking for Negro girls. He felt that Luke's services were not just a haircut, but "something special"; at the same time, he knew that Luke was not exactly a person, and thus there was no danger if he should unburden himself of some shady matters. Luke wouldn't tell, and if he did, who would take him seriously? Less than a century earlier, a person of color could not testify in court in our state. Practically speaking, in the court of public opinion, he still couldn't.

Three decades of this no doubt had their effect on Luke's character. Standing with his shoulders bowed from leaning over the barber's chair, dressed in the silk suits and impeccable shirts of the wealthy, he reminded me of a debonair, mad Satan as he poured forth a stream of foul-mouthed chatter that reduced public affairs to their lowest common denominator. Meanwhile, he lived in a big house and was putting his son through medical school.

Sunday at *The Clarion* was entirely set aside for worship and rest, as the Lord our God had decreed. Then Monday rolled around, and we banged our time cards. Smitty turned up sober and shaking. The family piled in. Robert Hancock and Harry Martin sat at their machines, rapping out the lines of type. The old building began to hum as we launched on our four-day week. Four days to shake up the world.

7. An Old Family, a New Family

Susan and I, after considerable searching, found a house for sale on the west side, on a block that was threatened with the arrival of Negro residents. The owner, a recently divorced young man, was leaving town and had a problem of sorts with the disposal of his property. To be precise, it was at 3006 Stilwell Avenue, the second house north of 30th Street, which was a main traffic artery. The Negroes were expanding rapidly northward on that side of town, but for the time being, the real estate people were holding them south of 30th Street. When they were finally permitted to jump this barrier, it would be not haphazardly but all at once, as the real estate interests opened the neighborhood to them as far as 34th, the next cross street that was somewhat wider than the others. It was generally believed, although I never heard it proved, that this land-rush system was plotted and managed in the offices of the Real Estate Board, for the obvious effect of higher profits in house sales.

In this situation, Mr. Drogue could not sell his house to a Negro, at least not through a realtor. Even in a private transaction, despite his desperation he probably wouldn't want to be the "first" to do so; at least, the generality of white settlers hesitated to take this step, which they saw as disloyalty to their neighbors. Color was thicker even than money. But it was practically impossible to find a white buyer, with the anticipated "change" of the neighborhood poised visibly across the street. Therefore, he was overjoyed to come across us (actually through Mr. Morton, a Negro real estate man whom Susan's father knew), and he let us have the property at quite a reasonable price. We borrowed the down payment from Susan's father, and bought it with a mortgage. It's an ill wind.

It was an old-fashioned frame house, the likes of which neither of us had lived in since childhood. We were less than a mile across town from Susan's parents, Mr. and Mrs. Berge Avakian, and her sister and brother-in-law, who lived above them. We, too, had a second-story tenant, William Partemeyer, a bachelor who came with the house and was an office employee of General Motors.

My widowed mother was a high school teacher in Winette, a town thirty-five miles away, where I had grown up. We visited back and forth by bus. Her sister, Mrs. Iva Roush, and her brother, Felix Bridges, were both well-fixed and living in our area of the city—the Roushes actually only a few blocks away, but on the solidly white side of town. I thought it would have been interesting, though uncomfortable, to hear their comments on my new job. We saw them on family occasions, but no word was uttered on the subject. I supposed that my aunt, an aristocratic lady, couldn't think of anything polite to say, and that her husband George, who was a banker, simply considered it beyond discussion. Once, long ago, we had all been Republicans together. My mother had veered away at the time of Al Smith's candidacy, and during the Depression she and my younger brother Harry and I all had offended the family by adhering to Roosevelt. Then, George and I had a famous drunken argument in his ample living room one Christmas Day, during which I expressed some of my Marxist views. It ended in a formal reconciliation to keep peace in the family (he had offered me to the keys to his car, and I had respectfully declined them), and after that our relations had been cool but correct. And so I now assumed he was horrified at the idea of a relative, even by marriage, going to work for *The Clarion*.

I supposed he was; and yet if it's wrong to stereotype Negroes, I have since also learned it's a mistake to stereotype white men in their attitudes toward Negroes. Especially if someone, by an action such as I had taken, presents them with a challenge. My neat classifications of white men as "reactionary capitalists" and "progressive-minded workers," while perhaps true in a wholesale sense over a long period of time, didn't pan out when it came to individuals on the race question. I was forgetting that George was a graduate of an Ivy League college, that he had been a fierce admirer of Mencken, and had scorned the Ku Klux Klan when it overwhelmed our state during the 1920s. I was also forgetting that he had no use for the publisher of the two dominant newspapers, whom he regarded as an upstart who had debased conservatism, and he would read the pseudo-liberal one instead. In short, he was that patrician who was above vulgar prejudice, and had his hair cut by Luke. And while he never mentioned *The Clarion* to me—my mother said he feared having to support his impecunious relations—I found him several times telling me of something he and Iva were doing. It wasn't much, but it was unusual for his class at that time. For example, he was having dinner with State Senator Robert Lee Bancroft and his wife now and then.

The senator, a courtly black gentleman from Virginia, who was regarded by the power structure as having a first-rate, level mind, also spoke warmly to me of George when we met.

My mother's grandfather, William Bridges, was the squire type, with large land holdings and a house as nearly resembling an old Southern mansion as you will find in our state. But Mother said that whenever Old Sam came on his rounds to this farm, a chicken was killed and he was invited to have dinner with the family. It seems to me there is a connection, if only one could trace it, running from Old Sam, the guest of honor at Bill Bridges's, to Senator and Mrs. Bancroft dining with the Roushes.

My Uncle Felix and his wife Emily had befriended me when I was ill, taking me on a three-week jaunt to Florida. After we returned, I had spent the summer convalescing at their show-farm home west of the city.

One day, Felix appeared at *The Clarion* and asked me out for a talk. It was a difficult thing for him to do. He was a Hemingway character, a true representative of the Lost Generation, and in personal relationships he affected to be a tough guy. He had always been the wild one of the family. He used to tell me, when I was staying at his home looking for a job during the Depression, that he had wanted to be a beachcomber but didn't know how to become one, so he had drifted into the position of president of a fence manufacturing company. Now this man of the Twenties—he was only that much older than I—was called on to dissuade his nephew of the Thirties from a course that was in many ways straight from his own code. I saw him wriggle, and I thought Emily must have put him up to it. She was a Christian Scientist, and saving people was more in her line.

Our conversation wasn't long. He made no references to my situation, but inquired whether I might like to take a job with the county seat newspaper near his place. "I know the editor, and I could speak to him," he said. I stammered a reply—I suspect I forgot to thank him—that I didn't want to "spend my time writing about what happened to Farmer Jones's cow." We clasped hands and that was that.

There were others who tried to rescue me. I think the most bewildered of them was Papa Avakian. As an Armenian youth, after undergoing incredible hardships, he had escaped from Turkey and come to this country, started penniless and built a prosperous Oriental rug business. The Depression wiped him out. But he kept his faith in the American Way of Life, that extreme conceit of the foreign-born. He and I often debated politely, he for the merits of the greatest country on earth and I for the opposition.

Papa had become such a good American that he had even acquired an anti-Negro anecdote, which he wore like an ill-fitting suit of clothes. It seemed he had once been riding on an excursion train to somewhere and a lower-class black woman had seated herself beside him, whereupon Papa had handed the conductor a note reading: "This is supposed to be a pleasure trip. Do you call this pleasure?" And the conductor had found him a seat in another car.

He knew he couldn't, as his nature prompted, set this straight with a command. But he thought he might accomplish something by the use of reason, Unitarian-style. He would sit dissimulating in a smile his obvious wrath and throwing out hints that were either too blunt and drew laughter or too farfetched and failed to be understood at all.

One Sunday afternoon, long after I thought everyone had written off the belief that I might be persuaded to change my course, I realized that Papa was addressing an unusual statement to me. It was a summer day, and we were sitting on the porch of our home.

"Charles," he was saying diffidently but with an underlying determination, "you know, Mr. Hoadley [of the printing firm] is a good friend of mine. I see him every week at the Scottish Rite Temple. I had a certain talk with him."

Michael was playing at our feet. I pulled him back so he would not stumble off the porch. "What about, Papa?" I said mildly.

"We had a certain talk," Papa said. "Not interfering. . . . He said he would be glad to see you . . . about . . ." He threw apart his hands in a gesture. "He has proofreaders' jobs, you would be good at that, unh? It's a big firm . . . a sound business . . ."

Poor Papa! I made as nice an answer as I could, and took Michael to ride his tricycle.

These men did not understand that they were trying to pull me back from a new life, a whole new world. Although I had been living in New York, the city of my dreams, and held interesting jobs, had my little family and our friends, read *The Daily Worker*, attended meetings and demonstrations, plays, foreign movies—even while all this was going on, an indifference to this society had been mounting steadily within me. As I look back, I think this was the nature of my illness. I wouldn't have said it, I only halfway realized it, but at bottom I did not care, I felt it was all a show of nothing. Even as a Communist pledged to a new world of the future, I had lost my touch and my taste for the world out of which it should be born.

What an experience, then, to discover that in this world of the black people I was interested in everything! In every man, woman, and child, every conversation, every trivial happening. Not a dark sparrow flitted or fell, but I had to know all about it. And many things of which I had long spurned the counterparts in white society—in such events as the establishment of a luncheon club or the elections in a lodge—these too I now felt a compelling interest, because they were the affairs of the Negroes with whom I was identified.

It was, in a way, as if I had found again the long-lost big country family of my boyhood, the family of my father's parents with whom I used to spend my summers and Christmases. Never mind the frowns of white people, the low pay, the dirt. In fact, in the humble physical surroundings of *The Clarion* I believed I felt an echo of that unassuming, intimate life.

My mother would have none of this version of my childhood. But in vain she pointed out that my grandfather was a doctor, and that his wife had toiled patiently to keep a clean and "respectable" home. Where I was wounded was in the loss of that unity, embracing all the relatives that had made life meaningful. And I believed I had rediscovered it on the scale of twenty million people!

Mrs. Ruth Reynolds, the black community's fiery-hearted battler for freedom, once was canvassing the sidewalk for NAACP memberships in conjunction with a sound truck cruising the Avenue. She approached an obviously enthusiastic, white-haired tatterdemalion who told her: "I don't have to join the NAACP, child. Every colored person is born into the NAACP."

Mr. Talbott, it was true, ridiculed the notion that Negroes stood together in practical affairs in some kind of Irish Republican Army. "The nigger is the most disunited, backbiting man in the world," he scoffed. "Any time a nigger starts to get a leg up, some other nigger will pull him down—to curry favor with the white folks, or for no reason, just for the pure hell of it. It doesn't make sense!"

But Mr. Talbott also used the expression "My people! My people!"

Looking back, it is entirely likely that I was more impressed by the fellowship of the Negroes than the bitter, often violent hostilities among them. No one who spent time in the ghetto could escape the hideous fact that black people faced harsh reprisals for even giving the appearance of attacking whites but could murder their own kind practically with impunity. Thus, the power structure turned the Negroes' very defenses in on themselves, creating that continual human slaughter that sold so many copies of *The Clarion*.

My connection with *The Clarion* gave me entrée to the offices and sometimes the homes of prominent Negroes, who were desirous of a good press, and who were at the opposite pole of our constituency from Eddie. Among these were Lewis H. Fielding and his wife. They were at the very top of the black heap, socially speaking, and even had a certain standing in the white community. He was a highly successful lawyer in the criminal courts. He had the reputation of charging high fees, but his clients—really I should say, "and therefore his clients"—had the utmost confidence in him. He was one of those Northern lawyers known to Negroes of the South and made frequent trips to Alabama, his native state, for the defense of blacks. I would not be surprised to learn that they also paid a high fee. There was nothing cheap about Attorney Fielding.

What did surprise me—because I wasn't prepared to link "success" with devotion to the freedom struggle—was the extent of his civil rights activity, dating back to the early 1930s. He claimed, for instance, to have authored in the state legislature during the Depression "the world's first fair employment law." It had to do, he said, with hiring on state-contracted highway building and other construction jobs. He wasn't noted for modesty, and I suspected that was a whopper, until I looked into it in the library. I found that except for some legislation in Sweden, he was about right.

Mrs. Fielding, an articulate, good-humored woman of light complexion, was prominent in liberal circles, and served on such bodies as the governor's and the mayor's human relations committees when the Democrats were in office. She was later active in the movement around the integration of Northridge High School, where in the committee meetings she and I rubbed each other the wrong way. She was integrating with well-to-do whites while I was integrating with poor blacks, and our dreams interfered with each other. To tell the truth, the Fieldings were a cut of liberal that I didn't feel comfortable with. They used to go off to institutes at a Quaker college in Ohio, where the agenda would include fellowship, peace, and whatnot. Later on I got into the peace movement myself, but I didn't attend things at colleges—not, at any rate, until the militant college movement of the 1960s.

I don't think the Fieldings were the richest Negroes in town, but they had the kind of social connections that enabled them to "jump" north several years in advance of the orderly progression directed by real estate people. For a long time, in our part of town, the Great Wall of China was 38th Street. South of it, the dwellings were modest houses that were "ripe" for selling off to Negroes. North of it were three distinct areas: a community on the west where Negroes had lived for decades, but from which no one was permitted to move east of Washington Place; then a buffer strip of three streets, inhabited by middle-class and lower-middle-class whites; and finally, starting abruptly and extending to the east, a section of large homes and even mansions owned by some of the wealthiest whites. The Fieldings bought one of these and moved into it at a time when no other Negroes had even crossed the boundary into the buffer zone.

Susan and I once had the pleasure of dinner with the Fieldings. Their house, a chateau of white stone with blue trim, was on a hillside set back from the street, from which it was hidden by a grove. It was reached by a drive that wound through the trees. We had cocktails, and then were summoned to dinner by a maid. It was summer, and Attorney Fielding was resplendent in a white suit that set off his handsome, ginger-colored face and hands. After dinner we sat out on the stone patio and enjoyed the stars.

I don't remember what we said—as I recall, he wanted to interest me in something he had going, and I was duly attentive. Otherwise the four of us chatted, I suppose, about matters having to do with The Question. I reflected that the Fieldings' establishment was far more lavish than those of my wealthy relatives.

8. What's in a Name?

Before coming to *The Clarion*, I had been imbued with sufficient understanding to address black people, no matter how closely I was in contact with them, by Mr., Mrs., or Miss and their surnames, unless they indicated unmistakably that they desired otherwise. This point was of crucial importance, because, of course, white people had for so long robbed them of adult status by withholding this simple courtesy. There was a black man in our state whose legal name was Mister, let us say, Mister Smith. *The Clarion* used to carry items from that town, "Mr. and Mrs. Mister Smith motored to Elliottsville on Sunday." I thought that man's parents had fixed the white folks good—when they tried to call him by his first name, they had to call him Mister.

Among the Negroes themselves, first names were not much used, although the Mr. might be dropped—"Pierce," "Hancock," etc. Even this was not done if the occasion was serious, or if the name was being called across a room in public. Smitty Smith was a special case, because he had taken legal steps to have his Christian name changed from Clarence, and he desired to be universally known as "Smitty." Then there were a number of people around town, of whom "Old Top" was a representative, who were so widely known by colorful nicknames that their real names had disappeared. There were mostly people of the street: "Jitterbug," "Treetop," "Johnny Cool." It was this practice that St. John Ashley tried to capitalize on in signing his column "The Saint." But it wasn't quite the real thing, and most people who knew him called him "Ashley."

My fellow workers in turn called me "Mr. Preston." When the time arrived to be less ceremonious, they dropped the "Mr." and I was generally known as "Preston" or for short, "Pres." In fact, when I had my sports column, it was headed thus: "The PRESton Box."

There was, of course, a special difficulty with my Christian name, even if the people had been disposed to use it. You don't call a friend "Charles" but "Charlie," and that (or "Mr. Charlie") meant The Man, otherwise known as "the white man." Nobody in the black community ever called me Charlie. Actually, my nickname at home was Chuck, and in the latter years of our working together, Bill Whitcomb got to calling me that. And now Chuck too had become a (perhaps even more contemptuous) designation for the blue-eyed devil.

On the other hand, from our first meeting, Robert Morgan called me Charles, a form of address he picked up from Penny Parker, and I called him Robert. It seemed to me that when black people did use the first name, they were more inclined than whites to use it undiminished, as a matter of respect. With them, it would be Thomas, Richard, and Harold.

A stupidity I wasn't tempted to commit was to address a Negro man as "boy." You would do better to call him son of a bitch. Yet, I didn't appreciate the extent to which this applied, and slipped once. The Talbott sons in their early teens had taken to serving as copy carriers, and it popped into my head to bellow out for fun the familiar city-room cry, "Boy!" I will never forget the shocked expressions that came onto the faces not only of Georgie and Cashy but of Mr. Talbott, who was passing through the room. I never did that again. With my ears opened, I noticed that Negro male children called each other not "boy" (except in insult) but "man." Even girls were called "man."

My friend Claudio Tubman, whom Susan and I had known in the Reed Club and who now wrote a tennis column for the paper, was one who was particularly sensitive on the "boy" question. His life illustrated why it was so. He was by nature an intellectual, a lover of poetry, who should have been perhaps a college teacher; but like so many such Negroes, he worked to the end of his days as a postal clerk. And for that matter, from his appearance—light skin, straight nose, thin lips, straight black hair—one would have been hard-pressed to swear in court that he was a Negro. But he was, and that was that. He used to draw himself up to his full, robust six-foot-three height and say, "Boy? I asked him how big men got where he came from." It was so much on his mind that when the NAACP staged its satirical revue, "The Dark Side," he wrote the line into his part.

Without false modesty, I must say that it was evident that most of the Negroes at *The Clarion* were refreshed by my arrival. It was something different; it was another of those twists that made it interesting to work there. And as Mr. Talbott said, they were curious about white people, and welcomed the opportunity to observe one close up. Thoughts about white people dominated their lives, but they hadn't previously had a chance to know one on a daily man-to-man basis and see what he was really like. My advent had something to say about The Question. Times must be changing if a white man would walk in and go to work for *The Clarion*. They were proud that *The Clarion* "had a white man working for it." That showed the color line wasn't such-a-much, at least in the minds of sane people. As for my civil-rights proclivities, while they didn't exactly share them to the point of joining in action—these were old stuff to them, and they looked on me as something of an enthusiast—nevertheless, it was good to see somebody taking up these causes, and they encouraged me. Maybe white folks, who ran everything anyway, could succeed where black people had failed.

In eighteen years at *The Clarion*, I don't recall ever being subjected to an unfriendly word. And yet, even after Mike Gale had signaled the end of my "probation," I became aware that such a man as Robert Hancock still held a measure of distrust for my white skin. It was a baffling disappointment. If we could come so far, if we were genuinely fond of each other so that our faces lit up with smiles (and he too finally got to calling me Chuck on occasion), if we enjoyed each other's minds, why did there have to be this ultimate barrier?

Hancock told me his story one afternoon. I led into it by making some remark favorable to unions.

"Huh-uh!" said Hancock, shaking his head vigorously.

Then calmly, in his way of speaking that was meticulous—like his typesetting—he drew me aside and said, "When I was a young man, in Dayton, Ohio, I had a job in a white printing plant. That's not usual for a nigger, begging y'all's pardon. But I got in, and I was setting a little type. And taking home white pay, if y'all will accept the expression. Y'all see, I say y'all. All us darkies does."

Hancock looked at me quizzically, through his wire-rimmed glasses that he once showed me were trifocals. Still quietly, he went on: "The union came and made them fire me. Lord a' mercy, I tried to join the union, I pleaded and begged but it wasn't no use. And since then,

I have been working twenty-three years in nigger shops like this one."
His gaze went around the room, and he concluded: "Taking home
nigger pay, living in a nigger house, an' my son going to nigger schools.
Unions—huh-uh!"

Hancock was not only forever anti-white, but he was even broken off from solidarity with his fellow black workers. He was a
loner. The men dropped little indications that Hancock was not to
be trusted, vis-à-vis the boss. You often hear such things around a
shop, and I admired him so much I thought it incredible. But it
could have been true.

Hancock and I got along well perhaps because we were both
"detail men" in the use of words. He rivaled Bill Whitcomb and
George Weyhouse in his command of the rich folk language from
"down home," and he used to instruct me in it. I told him one day of
threats that had been voiced in an NAACP meeting to picket Lauter's
supermarket, which had black patronage but refused to hire Negroes.

"Humph!" snorted Hancock. "That's talkin' at the big gate!" Then
he explained: "On the old plantation down South, y'all have two
gates. There is the big gateway out by the road—anybody can talk bold
out there. But if ya'll go in all the way to the little gate, which is by the
house, that's where y'all will meet the Man. An' that's different!"

Or, if he was in a good humor, he might call out when I came to
work, "Hello, Pres! What's on the rail for the lizard?" This expression, he said, came from the habit of lizards in the Southland stretch-
ing themselves on fence-rails to bask in the morning sun. It amounted
to "Good morning, what have y'all got for me?"

The Clarion possessed three linotype machines, bought secondhand but serviceable, sitting in a row. The one nearest the office was
"Hancock's," the far one was operated by Harry Martin, and the middle machine was used only when one of the others broke down.

Martin had two distinctions: he was a part-time preacher, and he
was the only man on the regular staff who had served time. The latter
had resulted from a passion for children. His favorite expression was
"Dog my sister's cat!" with a sort of giggle. One occasionally saw waif
girls of the neighborhood gathered about his machine, which was near

the back door that was left open in mild weather. There was also a pre-
cocious-looking, shining-eyed boy who ran errands for him. I never
knew Martin well. He traveled by bicycle. He was close-mouthed
about his private affairs, and we fellow workers learned only by roundabout courses that in his spare time he had become the pastor of a
storefront church. He gave off an odor of corruption—he enjoyed
other people's misfortunes, and nothing so much as two other men
fighting—but with it all he had, or put on, a genial disposition.

Hancock and Martin sat still, while the rest of *The Clarion* traffic
flowed behind their backs, to and from the parking lot. Pierce and
George Brown moved back and forth in the composing room. Once a
day, without saying a word, each of them would go out somewhere
nearby and buy a number. Pierce was tall and dark; Brown was short,
light and heavily muscled, with a tattoo of the American eagle on his
arm. He smoked cigars. He was continually involved in family dramas,
of which the principal scenes took place elsewhere than at *The
Clarion*, so that we saw only the resulting appearances in the shop of
his wife and his sister, both of whom were very good-looking women.
They came and stood tautly and said nothing, waiting for Brown or
waiting for his pay or whatever their business was. We men noted
them with our antlers up like buck, and found it necessary to visit the
water cooler or take copy to the machine so as to pass by them.

Pierce was in many ways the antithesis of Brown; I thought perhaps
it was the orphan's home that had left him tamed, civilized. He and his
wife Betty had what appeared to be a happy marriage. With two salaries
and no children, they were able to buy a small new house in a decent
neighborhood, with green lawns and fresh air. They did some socializing and card playing, and Pierce—even Betty called him that—had his
nights with his men friends, when there would be friendly poker and
drinking. Pierce enjoyed his nip but one seldom saw him drunk, hardly ever during working hours. Between him and Betty there was a very
good understanding, involving a smiling recognition on her part that
Pierce might play and stray a bit, because it was fun. As for Betty, she
would jive with you in a lighthearted way, but make no mistake, she
knew a good thing when she saw it, which was her life with Pierce.

The work that Harold Pierce has done in his lifetime! Sometimes when I looked at him, I seemed to see in his background slave forefathers, the strongest of the strong, bred to that strength by a process of unnatural selection. He was constantly on his feet, from early morning till late at night—no chairs were assigned to him and Brown. Pierce even marked copy standing and holding the paper on a waist-high ledge, as Ernest Hemingway is reputed to have done when he was writing. What this finally got Pierce was varicose veins in the legs. Even then he didn't change his habits—the doctor wrapped his legs and he carried on.

A number of other workers came and went during my tenure. One who stayed to become "*Clarion*" was a short, black-skinned, quiet young man who assisted Pierce and Brown. His name was Virgie Wilson. He was the poorest of the poor; he was the thinnest of the thin; I think he was the most unassuming little man I ever met. He looked so much like a teenager that he was called by his first name, although he was married and had three children.

Virgie was another man in motion who had no place to sit. One day I found him leaning on the bank, his face twisted with an expression of pain. I asked what was the trouble, and he replied with a sort of stammer: "I . . . it's . . . don't feel well."

"Are you sick, Virgie, what is it?" I asked.

Holding his hand to his chest, Virgie at last gulped out, "It's my heart."

"Hadn't you better sit down?" I suggested, but Virgie mumbled with an air of embarrassment, "I'll be all right."

All I could think to say was, "Have you been to a doctor?" and he answered, "Yes, oh yes."

In a little while he recovered, and went about his work, but he was dragging his weight. And there was many a day he dragged through after that. It got to be an accepted thing, Virgie's illness. It was sad because everyone was fond of him, but what could you do? People looked at him with a speculative eye, as they often do with a heart patient.

This was before I was entirely won over to Mr. Talbott, and I was inclined to blame him for—I don't know what—for the fact that Virgie was working in such a frightening condition. It reminded me of what Bill Whitcomb said about John Kay Hamilton, a gentle man in his sixties who was doing editorial work when we were across the street with the Victory Edition. He had been with *The Clarion* for many years, wrote a column, and was well thought of in the community, but now he was ill with vascular disease. He was obviously uncomfortable, but he went on working. And then one day he didn't come in, and the next day he died. Bill used to speak of Mr. Talbott "standing over John Kay Hamilton and making him work while he was dying."

I'm happy to say that Virgie's condition improved over the years. He got to taking a drink or two, and joked and laughed more as his personality blossomed. I particularly remember one Easter when I met him, wearing a neat dark suit, with his family on the way to church. He looked pleased and relaxed. Whatever was wrong with him seemed to have turned out, at least for the time to be, in his expression, "no big deal."

Besides playing the numbers, the anodynes among which *The Clarion* workers chose from were dreams, drink, and women. No given man, however, was addicted to more than one or perhaps two of them. We always had quite a few daily drinkers, some gin, some whiskey, some whatever came along. And why not, when in one block of Illinois Avenue there were seven liquor stores, all owned by whites. Not to mention the taverns, also white-owned, in which, the saying went, "you could lose your life for stepping on a man's foot." One of these, across the street from us, was the Green Lantern. It was owned by a Hungarian woman and notorious for its homicides. I should say that these slayings started inside the tavern, but would end up on the pavement outside it. Mr. Talbott said that the proprietress, Rosa, made certain anyone injured in her establishment was carried out, wounded or dead, and deposited on the sidewalk before the police arrived. Journalistic ethics, otherwise known as the fear of libel action, prohibited *The Clarion* from reporting that such a killing had taken place in, or even in front of, the particular tavern. One shuddered to think of the connections—starting with the patrolmen in the squad car and reputedly working up to the state Alcoholic Beverage Commission—that enabled Rosa to stay in business.

The staff's champion drinker, Smitty, was a preacher's son. Indeed, his father had been a bishop in Philadelphia of the African Methodist Episcopal Church. How Smitty got from there to here I don't know. People tended to regard him perennially as a young man, although he was far from it. He was a sort of unofficial ward of the Talbotts and lived much of the time at their home, where his duties sometimes included doing the laundry and washing the windows. Otherwise, his private life was a mystery. I never knew him to have an address of his own, not even a room, nor did I have any idea what circles he traveled in outside the office. He too was a loner but a roving one, who was known throughout the city, by whites as well as blacks. The thought of Smitty would instantly bring a smile to one's face. It was generally believed, by police as well as civilians, that to mistreat him would have been bad form and might have brought bad luck.

I once was obliged to mistreat him, however. After I began covering the Braves, our city's professional baseball club, one night Smitty came staggering along the catwalk to the press box. In that room you were not allowed to sneeze, much less speak out loud during a play. That baseball was dying in our town didn't help the edgy atmosphere. And here's Smitty at the locked door, raving drunk, hollering, "Hey Pres, lemme in, I wanna see the God-damned game." Hunching their shoulders and trying not to listen to him were Ed Parker, the scorer, who wrote for *The Tribune*, a thousand years old (both *The Tribune* and Ed), and the other sharp baseball writers, who already looked down their noses at me. "Lemme in Pres, I'll pull the Braves through this mother-fuckin' game." I cast a look at him as he pounded on the glass of the door and rattled the knob.

It was a hard moment. I didn't know if I should just tell him to go away. By now even Gil Proser of *The Post*, who had a considerable sympathy for Negroes, was scowling at me. He was in somewhat the same position as me: the more sympathy you had the more scowling you would do. And so I got up and stepped outside. Smitty was at first clamorous, but after we talked a while he calmed down and went off into the night.

Smitty never said a word about his comedown from a bishop's family. I thought it was significant that his favorite exclamation in the poker game, when confronted with a straight flush overpowering his full house, was, "Well, kiss my go-to-church!" And something was indicated by his specialty, when boozed to the right point, of placing phone calls to the world's great—the presidents and senators and the like. "This is Smitty Smith," he would announce to whoever answered. He once got the governor out of bed at two in the morning for a rambling philosophical chat. Another time he tried to call Stalin in the Kremlin, but the Russian operator wouldn't put him through. He had better fortune with Uncle Dummy, a soothsayer of Grand Rapids, Michigan, with whom he was a soul mate via telephone. Smitty would call him, or he would call Smitty and give his predictions for the coming year—war in Asia, a hurricane in Mississippi, and so forth. These stories went over big with the readers, and we played them on page one. It took Smitty to do them just right.

Smitty was a real journalist with a good news nerve, but as is sometimes true of such men, he wasn't cut out for desk work. He was one of *The Clarion*'s series of police reporters, whose copy was put together in such a raggedy way that the printers often refused to set it until somebody typed it over. He paid no heed to their complaints. It was like his drinking, a part of his personality, and nobody's business but his own. He had a strong belief in his own powers. Once he went on the wagon for the better part of a year, just to show he could do it; having made his point, he returned to booze. Because of his color, there was no Alcoholics Anonymous for Smitty, but if there had been one I think he would have given it a hard way to go.

Quite the opposite in his habits was another man on the staff whom I might as well call Jones. He was intelligent and enterprising, and discharged his *Clarion* duties with vigor. He was the kind of man who always had something new going: he took up color photography (*The Clarion* couldn't use it for mechanical reasons) and eventually had an exhibit at the YMCA; he took up jazz in a serious way, gave talks with records before clubs, and discovered that Huddie White, an old-time great guitarist, was living broke in an alley near the Avenue.

Jones brought Huddie a guitar and arranged for him to cut a record, which sold well nationally among the cognoscenti. Before he was through, he recorded Huddie's playing for the Library of Congress. Huddie was always pawning the guitar to buy gin. Jones would redeem the instrument and chew Huddie out in down-home language. Huddie would grin sheepishly, and when he got thirsty enough would pawn the guitar again.

To give another example, Jones was good at Spanish. So far as I knew, he had studied it in high school and then picked it up more informally at every opportunity life presented him, which you wouldn't think would be too many in our Midwestern town. The next thing you know, he had a special certificate in Spanish and was teaching it in night school at Dunbar High. Then the Council of Churches established a mission to improve conditions for the Mexican migratory workers who harvested crops in our area. Although he had no relation to churches that I ever heard of, Jones got the post as director of the mission, because of his Spanish and I suppose because he was brown-skinned. It was a temporary project, and Jones added it on to his *Clarion* responsibilities. He would take off in his big new car—he somehow acquired one every two years while his employer, Mr. Talbott, continued to drive what was commonly described as "a load of junk"—for the mission on a Friday night and return on Monday mornings. He would drive there another evening or so during the slack part of the week.

And even with all this, Jones was a womanizer.

He was one of those men who give such a picture of their relations with women that they seem to be describing a different society than that in which most of us live. My Uncle Felix used to sardonically define a nymphomaniac as "a woman who has the same amount of sexual desire as a man" (part of his Hemingway complex), but that wasn't Jones's story: for him women tumbled like tenpins. He once told me that, while working as a house-to-house insurance collector, he had laid nine women in a day.

I knew it was standard to discount such talk as psychologically motivated boasting, but in the case of Jones I was inclined to believe him. For one thing, I saw evidence in the face of his wife, a little round-eyed woman who showed up at *The Clarion* from time to time, ill at ease and looking as if she might have been crying. Although she always worked and brought home a salary, she wore rather poor clothes, especially when one considered his gleaming car. Their home was a run-down place on the east side.

And I saw more evidence.

There was a girl about half his age—I was told she was eighteen and preparing to go to college in the fall—who got to dropping in to see Jones. He was teaching her color photography, but one look at her lovesick expression said something else. Jones was on good terms with Walt Evers, who was the staff photographer at the time, and Jones and the girl spent much time in Evers's darkroom on the second floor. Jones was not at all reticent on such matters and soon told me all about it, describing the various odd positions (she on a high stool and he standing, etc.) in which they made love in the cramped quarters. Of course, they had other rendezvous, such as lovers' lanes and shaded streets where they went into the backseat of his car. But I had the impression the darkroom was their favorite place, because it was safest from detection except by *The Clarion* people, whom Jones didn't care about.

The affair worried me on Jones's behalf. The girl was underage, she was obviously in love, and it became clear she was not going to college if she had her way. If I understood Jones aright, he didn't use condoms but just thrust his dick in and banged away.

Jones said that he was worried himself, just as he was after he stuck his dick into some woman whom he suspected of venereal disease. And while he was screwing the girl, he was also, of course, knocking off such other pieces as fell into his path, not to mention (one presumes) his wife. But he didn't panic, the god of lovers protected him, and he paid no penalty for his amours. In fact, the teenager abruptly disappeared. Jones's domestic story eventually took a turn much like that of Virgie's illness. Whether Nature had slowed down Jones or something else happened I can't say, but with the passing years he and his wife apparently reconciled, Mrs. Jones dressed better, smiled, and talked with more self-possession; she altogether changed into a woman who either was happy or gave a good imitation of being so.

Old men shall dream dreams and young men shall see visions; Bill Whitcomb did both. He was a fool and a sage. He was a prophet. He was a mute inglorious Milton. Long before young people began demanding the teaching of black history, Bill was telling us of his forefather, a black king in the highlands of Dahomey ... he was also telling us of another forefather of his, Thomas Jefferson, who "sired seventeen babies by black slave women."

Through his genes from these two ancestors, Bill was able to cover a lot of ground. If he was so minded, he could send a spider to kill you. When majestically angry, he revealed that he was "the seventh son of a seventh son," although I otherwise never heard of more than one brother, who had been shot dead in a ghetto battle in his youth.

His talk, and there was plenty of it—Claudio Tubman said he had been "vaccinated with a phonograph needle"—at times resembled *Bartlett's Quotations*, so studded it was with lines from the classics— from Shakespeare, Byron, Shelley, the *Rubaiyat*, and the *King James Bible*. These came to him naturally. He was widely read, and at some early stage must have gotten much from Julius Haldeman's *Little Blue Books*. He neither lived nor thought in prose. He pronounced some of the words— for example, "sub-SEE-quently" and "tur-BU-lent"—as a man who has made them out with his eye but has never in his life heard them spoken. Didn't Penny Parker, with the advantages of Ward Belmont, name her dog Ishmali "after the character in *Moby Dick*"?

Bill also had a stock of expressions he had picked up from popular comedians: "That's a revoltin' development"; "Funny the things a man sees when he hasn't got his gun"; and so forth.

Bill, my dear friend and comrade, I am tired of waiting for the seven books you are going to write once you acquire the five-thousand-acre ranch in South Dakota. So far as I know, you haven't even started work on "Flowering Weeds on a Back Road," or is it to be "Cabbages in the Jimson Patch"? I understand you will do it someday, when the conditions are right, but meanwhile I must draw my breath in pain, to tell your story:

You grew up a dark-brown youngster in Christian County. You and the other boys of your gang played on the southern Kentucky hillsides and went swimming in the Green River, where the celebrated head-in-the-mud incident occurred. Also the incident where the five-hundred-pound boulder rolled down the hill and passed over your foot without hurting you. It became apparent that something was watching over you, which explains why you have never since been afraid of anything but a snake, and in particular of a Gawd-damned white man. In this matter of fear and fearlessness also is the explanation of your refusal to take an anesthetic when having a tooth extracted. Of course if anyone, white trash or nigger, calls you "boy" or insults the memory of your mother, you are ready for both of you to die and go to Hell in a minute, but I think that is maybe a result of your being a Kentuckian in the first place.

A sensitive youth, you went to Hopkinsville's "Jim Crow high school that was no better than a good grade school." But meanwhile you discovered, through a remarkable Southern white man at whose home you were sometimes employed, the world of books. Or was it a remarkable Southern white lady? I have forgotten, although I also know you were introduced at an early age to the world of men and women.

In your family there was no money for higher education, but you did enroll in a correspondence course at Springfield YMCA College and kept it up, never mind how long. You worked for a railway express in some lowly capacity, and you worked for Revenue agents who were hunting bootleggers.

But what in hell is this? The short and simple annals of the poor? As Langston Hughes would say, you have known the rivers, Bill Whitcomb. Yes, and you have known Pharaoh Ahknaton, Queen Nefertiti, Hannibal, the Emperor Honorious, Benjamin Banneker, Alexandre Dumas, Pushkin, and Christophe. You have known Harriet Tubman, Sojourner Truth, Frederick Douglass, Victor Hugo, William Lloyd Garrison, and John Brown. You have seen fallen empires and empires falling every afternoon; isn't one of your favorite sayings "It was great to be a Roman"? You won't ever come to a Communist meeting, though you've accepted my invitations, but you wouldn't be fazed in the slightest by a revolution or two. Now that I think of it, you will get your ranch, possibly of fifty thousand acres, and write your seven books. Or, at least, you could.

9. The NAACP Was the Ship and All Else Was the Sea

My own dreams require more of an arena than was provided by *The Clarion* alone. As a Marxist, I wanted to take part in overturning society. It had borne in on me that the American proletariat seemed to show little interest in such an enterprise, but the Negroes were ready, willing, and at least able to make a try at it. Though they didn't identify their struggle as Communist, I felt that it was the same great revolution.

For various reasons, including the circumstance that they had been in this struggle all their lives and were somewhat bogged down, the Negroes at *The Clarion* were content with their journalistic—so to speak, propagandist—role. But for me, who had come fresh on the scene and was bursting with newfound enthusiasm, this wasn't enough. I soon got my chance to join the ranks of the active fighters.

As I was walking to the bus stop one winter night, I caught up with a tall young man on crutches, a polio victim. This was Holmes Mellett. He had been serving for a few weeks as a volunteer executive secretary of the NAACP. Our city's branch couldn't afford to pay such an official, and therefore didn't usually have one. For this reason, it lay dormant for long periods, awakening spasmodically as some individual got the spirit. Holmes lived in a room at the Congress Avenue YMCA, and, as far as I knew, was able to devote his time to the cause by being unemployed, or rarely and partly employed. Perhaps some individual was giving him some small help. I was reminded of the Communist organizers during the Depression who "slept around" and ate when food appeared.

One day Mellett asked me point blank: "How would y'all like to get into the NAACP? I don't mean join it, because that y'all have got to do, but come to meetings and be active?"

I was somewhat surprised, because I was used to asking Negroes to join my left-wing organizations (and having them politely agree and then not show up) rather than the other way around.

I went to the next meeting and didn't miss many in the years that followed. I was "accepted," or thought I was, if for no other reason than the organization's activities would be generously reported by *The Clarion*. For the reasons already mentioned, I was the very man to do it.

The NAACP has come to be called a middle-class organization, stigmatized amongst radicals. In our town and at that time, it was—to borrow Booker T. Washington's description of the Republican Party—"the ship, and all else was the sea." This was before the SNCC, the SCLC, CORE, the Muslims, and the Panthers. Within our branch, I discovered that the atmosphere among conservatives, moderates, and militants was basically so respectful and friendly that, while there were sharp disagreements, you could hardly speak of factions. Indeed, it was recognized that the differences in viewpoint came in handy, as many approaches and tactics could be used in the all-encompassing struggle for freedom.

Thus, I found that the epithets "Communist" and "Uncle Tom" were not hurled back and forth. I was glad of this—"Communist" for obvious reasons, and "Tom" because it seemed to me that with few exceptions it was really undeserved and its use was just another form of blacks fighting each other that Mr. Talbott so deplored.

As for "middle-class," if there were NAACP branches whose members were more concerned with status than with activity, then ours was not among them.

After some years of mulling over The Question, I developed a theory that it was precisely because our state and city were somewhat small potatoes on the national scene that their protest organizations showed such solidarity and vigor. For one thing, the reactionary white folks with whom they contended were a bit old-fashioned, and didn't take Negroes very seriously. They looked on the NAACP as a band of noisy children that might as well be ignored, or even humored a little, and it would go away. In part, they didn't want to get a reputation of being against "colored people." There was the time Winifred Thompson, a white spokesperson for the Communist Party, was given a very cordial reception at a legislative hearing in the statehouse. Our politicians were firmly against "Communism," but they didn't connect it with this local woman, a perky blonde, having her say.

And not only the reactionaries, but the high-powered national liberal organizations also had little time for us, as they considered our state hopelessly backward. This was a mistaken opinion, but in some ways it was a blessing in disguise. The branch only sometimes paid attention to the rules and written directives of the national NAACP. When a national representative did come to visit and realized our branch was on the maverick side, he may have been disturbed but had more important things to worry about. The question came to a head once, in 1948, when the NAACP national leadership was for President Truman and forbade activity on behalf of Henry Wallace. But Wilbur D. "Pat" Johnson, then state president of the NAACP, was a leader of the Wallace campaign and quite a few others were in the thick of it. At the NAACP state convention that year, the national staff representative, John Wooster, was very upset and strove mightily against the tide, but in the end he had to let the group go its own way.

The members of the state NAACP felt beholden to no one, and even took a certain satisfaction in the odds against them. It was in those years that I became fond of historical axioms, such as: Benjamin Franklin's "Where liberty is, there is my country" and Thomas Paine's "Where liberty is not, there is mine." If you want to be happy, go to a provincial place and take up the cause of liberty. There must be enough kindred spirits for a meeting, enough to march, with knees trembling and picket signs wavering, around the Civil War monument. But there will never be so many that you will fail to look at each other, individual by individual, with delight. You will forget, in those gatherings, the terms moderate, militant, Communist, Trotskyist, even Republican. I observed in particular that the word "liberal" shifted its meaning in action. In theory and on the national scale, I wouldn't have permitted myself to be called a liberal; I was a radical, and nothing else. But to be understood by your fellow members, you had to be a liberal *or* a conservative. God knew, there were few enough "liberals" already. So you took your place.

In the NAACP and at *The Clarion*, of course, it was even simpler and more direct: you were either pro- or anti-Negro and nothing else mattered.

The first big question to come before the NAACP after I joined it was the case of Donald Dallas Wright. This was a bloody killing of the worst kind. A white woman, the wife of a corporation executive, was found slain in a bedroom of her posh north side home amid signs of violent struggle. Wright, a young Negro who worked for the city streets department, was arrested two days later. In due course, or perhaps short order would be more accurate, he was indicted on the charge of first-degree murder.

The evidence, made public at the time of the arrest by the daily press (it was their turn to sell newspapers), was circumstantial. Wright had been driving a truck to the city garage, and was an hour late in getting there. His course would have taken him near the Stanton home. He had allegedly told conflicting stories to explain the time lag. And then a few days later, a police spokesman was quoted as saying that his jacket, stained with blood, had been found in his locker. The blood reportedly was Mrs. Stanton's type.

I thought he was likely guilty, though perhaps of second-degree murder rather than first, but I didn't find one Negro among my *Clarion* and NAACP associates who agreed with me. Mr. Talbott, Walt Evers, Pierce, Hancock, Bill Whitcomb, Ruth Reynolds—an NAACP activist who could overturn the state legislature with one speech—vehemently insisted on a frame-up. So I decided to hold my tongue. I reminded myself that Wright's defense hadn't been heard yet, and in the atmosphere of hysteria that had set on the city, he was going to need all the help he could get.

My coworkers, who discussed the case from morning to night at *The Clarion*, discounted the bloodstained jacket as a plant by the police. They declared Wright had been drinking beer at the home of a friend—some said a woman friend—who would come forward in due time. They made much of the behavior of the slain woman's husband. He was quoted as saying he had come home from his office and, finding the front door open, had become alarmed and had not entered. Instead he had gone to the home of a neighbor, who had returned with him and accompanied him into the house.

"Now what kind of a tale is that?" asked Evers. "Y'all mean to tell me y'own door is open, and y'all don't go in and find out what is happening? Why did he run off and get the man across the street for a witness? Hell, he knew what was in that bedroom!"

Mrs. Reynolds, who among other things was a patron of young people, told me that she was acquainted with Wright, and that a few years earlier, when he was just out of high school, he used to come to her house to talk. "He's not like that at all," she said. "He was a good student, you know, intelligent, serious. He wanted to make something of himself. This is the most vicious thing that ever happened in this town, Preston—it's vicious!"

Wright's parents employed a big white law firm for him. Our local NAACP branch asked the national organization to enter the case because of the massive prejudice displayed. A member of the national legal staff came to investigate, and immediately another form of hysteria became evident: this was on the part of NAACP members who were in a panic because their organization was being "identified" with Wright. The grumblings, by word of mouth and telephone, rose to such a volume that a special meeting had to be called, so the national man could explain that the NAACP wasn't proposing to defend Wright, per se, but the procedures of a fair trail as exemplified in his case. The disturbed members who gathered were mostly rather inactive people who were concerned with the NAACP's "good name." Some were prominent in the city, but there were also some "silent" people who supported the organization financially year in and year out.

Having adjusted myself to keeping silent on my own doubts, I was totally taken by surprise by this development. And it wasn't gratifying—it gave me a start to realize that my *Clarion* and NAACP friends could be thus insulated from a section of their customary supporters.

These people had been swept off their feet by the anti-Negro terror that followed the crime. Many had vivid memories of personal experiences with lynch rule in the South. And these worked in two opposite ways. They helped to explain the militancy of Abraham Jackson, whose family had fled southern Tennessee when he was a young boy while their home burned behind them. But the trauma also lingered on in uncontrollable fears.

Most of the waverers steadied after hearing the NAACP's explanations. But even so, it was winter, and the darkness that fell so early each day accentuated the civic gloom. The police and prosecutors soon pushed matters beyond all reason, as word spread that they were attempting to pin on Wright various unsolved slayings of white women, including the sensational Nurse Jones killing outside of City Hospital, and even the Columbia Hotel WAC murder of the Second World War (when Wright was still in high school). These efforts drove Mr. Talbott to the point of fury, and he took an unshakable stand in which he wouldn't tolerate even a question about Wright's complete innocence. I thought his hope was too like despair, but what could he do? The battle had gone far beyond the slaying of Mrs. Stanton, but it was being fought out on that issue.

White people were going about our pleasant old city in mortal fear of, and rage against, every black person. Black people were listening every night for a mob. When the trial at last came it was sent to Harrison, twenty miles away, which didn't have a bad reputation race-wise, mostly because the Jameses, a family of outstanding Negro athletes, came from there. Miss List lived there and commuted to *The Clarion*, and it had other Negro residents, none of whom, however, got on the jury.

Of the trial, I remember only that the prosecution called a very shapely blonde, a sort of liberal of the League of Women Voters variety, who testified that Wright had once forced his way into her home and she had escaped by running into the street naked. I think this was allowed on the ground of motivation. Otherwise, there was nothing that hadn't already appeared in the press. Wright's rumored alibi failed to materialize, and he was found guilty. Attorney

Fielding, who represented the NAACP, took an appeal on constitutional grounds, and in a landmark decision the U.S. Supreme Court overturned the verdict because of the exclusion of Negroes from the grand jury panel. Wright was again indicted and tried, again convicted, and was put to death in the electric chair at the state prison. Mr. Talbott still upheld Wright's innocence. And if you will go to our city today, you will find numerous black people who remember the case as a legal lynching.

Because I didn't share their belief in Wright's innocence, the case opened my eyes to the abyss across which Negroes looked at the white man's justice with total cynicism. I remember an incident a little later, in which the NAACP undertook to help a young man who was wrongfully arrested on a charge of larceny and then brutally beaten by the police. Since he had been "punished" in this fashion, the chances were serious that he would be convicted of larceny, in order to make the police smell better. And yet there was no doubt that he had been in California at the time.

The young man had only slight knowledge of the NAACP, and at the committee meeting he appeared apprehensive. Finally, Pat Johnson said to him: "Don't worry now . . . we're going to get you a fair trial."

The young man seemed alarmed. He looked at Pat with dubious eyes. "I don't want a fair trial," he shot immediately. "What I want is a fix."

These legal affairs, while the best-known phase of the NAACP's work nationally, were only a small part of the local activities. Except for Johnson, the lawyers did not usually attend the meetings. Not that they were indifferent; I was surprised at the extent to which the black attorneys were "on call" for the NAACP and other civil rights organizations. You often heard complaints of the inactivity of the preachers, but never of the lawyers.

The week-to-week stalwarts, however, were working people, housewives, a few small business proprietors, one or two ministers, a couple of teachers, and a social worker or two. Not many turned out at a given time: twenty-five was a pretty good meeting. The annual membership drive would be launched with fanfare, with a goal of two or three thousand (in a city of perhaps eighty thousand Negroes) and would stagger to its end several months later with at best around a thousand persons having signed up for one dollar (later raised to two dollars). Even that achievement was due in good part to the work of a special citywide campaign organization, through which the sparkplugs of the Congress Avenue YMCA and other community organizations pitched in to put the NAACP across. In these drives, the branch usually employed the services of a national staff worker for several weeks.

At a meeting, one man decided to take a lifetime membership, at $500, but the secretary had neglected to put it into the minutes. He was then and there prepared to pay his first annual installment of $50, and did so with an indignant flourish as he signed the check. Whether he ever paid the second installment would be interesting to know.

In this particular type of absentmindedness, this man was not alone. The situation became "too much," in the words of Dorothy Wendell, one of the regulars, when the very same thing happened on the election of the next president, where the secretary failed to document another lifetime membership. The lifetime membership campaign had been launched at a YMCA "Mammoth Meeting," a thousand members were in attendance, and Attorney Fielding made his rousing pledge. It was just the needed gesture, and it brought down the house. Years later, I heard that collecting even the first installment was proving to be difficult.

"My people," sighed Mr. Talbott. But I would explain to him my belief that it was entirely a matter of conditions, of resources. In the sit-down strikes of the 1930s, I had seen the unions in their revolutionary days and then I had seen them with their closed shops and dues check-offs become something like insurance companies as far as the workers were concerned. But the NAACP had to keep going to the people, with its appeals and also its goofs and scandals, and the result was that it was alive for them.

I pointed out that small as it was, the NAACP attendance was as good as anybody else's in town, including the Republican and Democratic parties, and at mass meetings, usually better. The people of our town were not going to meetings. (For one thing, of course, they were sitting in front of their new television sets.)

One obstacle to rallying the poor people together was the city's wretched public transportation system. Bill Whitcomb was fond of saying, "Evil communications corrupt good manners." The poor bus service in our spread-out blob of a city corrupted the civic spirit of those who did not own automobiles. There very well might be as good a turnout in a small town like Winette, where the black people lived in one ghetto and could walk to the meeting, as in our metropolis of disconnected neighborhoods. It must have been very tiresome, after working all day in the white woman's kitchen, to go out and stand waiting on sore feet for one of the infrequent buses or trolleys, not to mention getting home after the meeting. There were a few hardy souls who did it, but generally the members came in their cars, and this tended to cut the organization off from important sections of the community.

The crosstown service was especially bad. Bill said that it had been planned that way so that anyone who wanted to cross from the east side to the west side had to go via the downtown area, where he would see the department store windows and get the idea to buy something. The Vesper-Congress route was crescent shaped so that it connected the east side black community, the department store area on Lincoln Street, and then, swinging far north again, the black west side. Geographically, it made no sense whatsoever, but its ethnic rationale was apparent at a glance. There were no white people on those buses but the drivers, for the company at the time refused to hire Negroes. It was this long, strung-out route that the NAACP members had to take to reach a meeting at the YM or YW.

But despite these difficulties and countless others, the members met and wrestled with the many-headed hydra monster: lack of day-care centers, segregated schools, "Jim Crow" hospital mistreatment, refusal to employ Negroes, confinement to broom-pushing jobs, frame-up of black GIs on charges of raping white women, refusal to serve chocolate sodas to chocolate patrons, separate toilets for coloreds, racist propaganda in newspapers, in KKK leaflets, and in college textbooks, police brutality, denial of constitutional rights, bureaucratic abuse of black welfare clients, housing segregation, white-referees-only in high school basketball games, banning of Negroes from public swimming pools and semi-public bridge tournaments, segregated cemeteries (including a pet cemetery where a black man couldn't bury his white dog), and a thousand other issues.

They protested with telephone calls, letters, telegrams, delegations, and press releases. There were lobbies at the City Council, School Board, and State Legislature. They circulated petitions. They demanded, deplored, denounced, pressured politicians, and played one against the other. They honored good deeds, led boycotts without calling them that (they were said to be illegal), carried on an election campaign under another name (the NAACP was nonpolitical), and staged a satirical revue. They gave fund-raising social affairs, held institutes, state conventions (the State Conference of NAACP Branches was organized under Johnson's leadership and had its own schedule of activities), and attended regional and national conventions. They brought to the city national speakers, including eventually Dr. Martin Luther King, Jr.

The branch was not yet—as the national movement at large was not—at the stage of picketing, sitting-in, and the like. But some of the members were edging toward it. There was a group, of which I was a member, called the Public Accommodations Committee (PAC). At that time, all the downtown restaurants and hotels denied service to Negroes. The policy was so well known that it was rarely tested—only when some New Yorker, so to speak, came to town. There was a state law, enacted after the Civil War, forbidding such discrimination. It was ignored by the restaurants, and, of course, could not be enforced unless somebody brought a complaint. The group resolved to go in an interracial body, seat itself at a table, and start the ball rolling.

The committee was small in number, but unable to resist the demands of an idea whose time had come. There was Archie Cinq, a Redcap, small and benevolent. There was Irene Roberts, a soft-eyed young social worker, who couldn't afford to risk her job because she was supporting a bedridden mother but who also couldn't live with evil. There was Johnson, son of a former city councilman, Harvard Law graduate, a captain in the Judge Advocate-General's Department in the Second World War and groomed to be the town's top Negro, but he had come to the conclusion that he didn't want to go up without his brothers. There was Mrs. Rochelle Worth, Alabama born and raised, churchified and conservative, but faithful unto death. There was Ruth Reynolds, angry and resolute. There were a handful of white social workers, Communists in my Party organization, who came quietly and put their careers on the line (later, in McCarthy days, they saw them destroyed). Who else were there? Not many. Honor to them.

One morning in September—I remember the tang of the air, the bright sunshine—we came by ones and twos to Stegel's Restaurant, feet refusing to work properly, terrified, but borne along as in a dream, to do what no one had done before. I remember the dragging minutes; I remember thinking how did they rope me into this; and we laughed together foolishly, and went in.

What happened then? That must have been the day we waited forty-five minutes, with hard white eyes of hatred on us, until Pat and I sought out the manager and he ungraciously relented. Later came the day the waitress said she would serve us because she had to, but it disgusted her. And the day the manager saw us coming and had us served with amazing promptness. And the day we were asked to move to another table, which turned out to be behind a screen. We refused, of course. And the day they served Negroes but not the whites—that was much later.

That first time, when we got our lunch and were eating it, we were already beginning to feel like new people, and loved each other and ourselves. It was never so hard to begin again. So we systematically put in other appearances around the town, and other managers and waiters conferred in far corners, and some white customers glared but more looked straight before them. Some of them had heard about us. There wasn't a thing you could do about it, and it wasn't any of their business anyway, and they might somehow get in trouble and the best thing would be, don't move a muscle. Or, how did we know which man or woman was saying silently, "Well, I always did think it was wrong to keep colored out of restaurants, they have to eat don't they, I always thought I was the only one but maybe not, there are white people eating with them." Or at least, in a muffled conversation, "Harry, now don't stare, don't show your ignorance." "Who, me, why I ain't prejudiced, if niggers clean up and act like decent folks, I would be the last man in the world to be against them. Don't judge me by this overgrown hick town! Listen, when I was in San Francisco that time. . . ."

And remembering my country childhood, I imagine there were others, especially in the Smith's Bus Terminal Restaurant, who said, "Look son, there's some niggers. Those folks with dark skin. They live here in the city."

Ephraim Center, the Dunbar High School athletic director, told me the basketball team once played at Jefferson, a town isolated in the hills. When the Dunbar players came onto the floor their hosts greeted them with a well-meant cheer: "Hello, Niggers! Hello, Niggers! Niggers, we say hello!"

At any rate, nobody knocked anybody down, or stalked us out, or even called the cops on us. (We called them once, but they wouldn't make an arrest.) There were a few places catering to working-class people that put up signs: "We Reserve the Right to Refuse Service." Some of these signs had to wait until there were governmental Human Rights Commissions, and I have no doubt some are waiting still. But the campaign as a whole was successful. After half a dozen visits by the group, as if by agreement, all the principal restaurants capitulated except the one at the bus station. The owner, Smith, was a diehard, with hatred in his heart where a dollar sign should have been. The committee went to the prosecutor's office, swore affidavits against Smith, and was sent to talk with a deputy prosecutor who wasn't familiar with the provisions of that particular law but would look it up right away, and so forth. The committee demanded to see the prosecutor himself, issued press releases, and brought it up in the next political campaign, but Smith was never prosecuted. He just went on refusing Negroes, mostly bus passengers from out of town.

There were a few other dedicated race-haters like Smith in town. One was the owner of Lakeside Amusement Park. Singlehandedly, he kept generations of black children from enjoying his rides and swings, despite laws, statements issued by the Mayor's Human Rights

Commissions, and a little later, demonstrations. I remember as a small-town boy on a visit to the city having the signs posted throughout the park indelibly impressed on my mind: "Patronage of Whites Only Solicited." For some reason, I was even then shocked by them but at the same time made to feel an insidious satisfaction at being white. This was about my earliest lesson in the doctrine that niggers were not human beings. The signs were still there forty years later, but then the Mayor's Commission, with Mrs. Boatner demanding action, finally got them down.

It was also around 1960, and under similar pressure, that Smith's Restaurant at last buckled to integration. An idea whose time has gone is powerful too, as powerful as a dying turtle, but only until sundown.

By then, the big hotels had discovered what every Negro knows—that there's no spender like a black spender. The Elks of the World, the Prince Hall Masons, the Kappas, and the Alphas were admitted to the downtown hotels and started giving lavish affairs that made bellboys remember the glory of tips, and the managers forget the competition of motor courts. Negroes from time immemorial had been associated intimately with the glittering life of hotels and restaurants. Now it seemed that they, the modern urban people, were coming to the rescue of these great urban institutions. The managers met them with open hands, but I never heard of a hotel manager contributing to the NAACP.

10. The Mammoth Meetings

In a life such as I have been describing, between *The Clarion* and the NAACP, what do you do with your Sundays? Although Susan had been a member of Everyman Unitarian Church since her youth, we didn't attend in those years. But in the wintertime, once a month and without fail, we went to the Sunday afternoon "Mammoth Meetings" at the Congress Avenue YMCA.

This was a lecture series featuring well-known black speakers, and occasionally a white. It was said to be the oldest such series sponsored by a Negro institution in the country. Despite its name, adopted in a more naïve time, its cultural level was high and its speakers generated more interest than the majority of those brought in on the white side of town. There were often a number of white liberals in attendance. The series had been opened annually, since its beginning thirty years before, by the president of Howard University, Dr. Mordecai W. Johnson, whom the people affectionately and reverently called, as if he were a biblical prophet, "Mordecai." Other speakers included such men and women as: Dr. Benjamin E. Mays, Dr. Mary McLeod Bethune, and other college presidents; church fraternal leaders; prominent civil rights spokesmen Walter White, Thurgood Marshall, and Adam Clayton Powell; foreign dignitaries; and popular heroes like Jackie Robinson. Mrs. Eleanor Roosevelt came once. The site shifted to the white Masons' Temple downtown for that occasion.

The Congress Avenue YMCA, I found, was a great deal more than the institution in which I had played basketball and shuffleboard as a boy in Winette. It was that too, as well as home away from home and a number of other things, but in presenting the Mammoth Meeting speakers, it was acting in its capacity as one of the centers of the Negroes' freedom struggle, what was in fact, although it was not so called, the black revolution. That it was a revolution—the same one that had been going on for three-and-a-half centuries—wasn't immediately apparent, because those were years in which revolutionaries tried to look like everyone else and dressed in their Sunday best for meetings. (This conservative mode of dress, in fact, was continued into the time of the Black Muslims and Malcolm X.)

I found this revolution all the more meaningful because it wasn't shoved down your throat; you had to find your way to it, listening with both ears, so to speak. The arts of the speakers, I supposed after hearing a number of lectures, were basically those developed by Negro preachers during slavery, by which, through religious parable and indirection, they roused the slaves to resist the masters, while giving the masters no excuse to come down with power. The peerless practitioner of these arts was Dr. Johnson. He played marvelous platform games, in which he seemed to be—almost—agreeing with the power structure, took off suddenly on great forays that brought his listeners up cheering, touched base again for safety's sake, clowned a little, then called for the Almighty's intervention, and ended by welding two thousand people into a single force. And yet, Dr. Johnson pleaded each year to the Dixiecrats for funds for his publicly financed university, and at that too he was eminently successful. As they say, "Cunning as serpents, and harmless as doves."

To me, in my political situation, all this was tremendously thrilling. It was the thrill of conspiracy (for a good cause), carried out in public, on a grand scale, and with brilliant deviousness. I had never thought I would be listening to a college president or minister as if he were Daniel confounding the lions in the very den.

In addition to the speakers, each Mammoth Meeting featured a great deal of singing by the church choir, the introduction of committee chairmen and champion membership solicitors, and the identification of oldest persons present. The meeting was a community. The collection speech might be given by Senator Bancroft or Attorney Fielding, but the rest of the program was according to the hierarchy—not wealth or civic prominence—of the Y itself.

Sitting at one end of the stage and ruling despotically over the proceedings, to the extent of interrupting the chairman and even the speakers, was the veteran executive secretary of Congress Avenue, E. F. LeFever, "The Skipper." He was then in his early fifties, a giant of a man, and half-white. I had known him since long before I came to *The Clarion*—he had attended Reed Club meetings and sometimes joined in the bohemian social life that went along with them. That might have seemed a rather unusual thing for a YMCA executive to do, but it was satisfactorily explained by his interest in "politically advanced" cultural matters—and a certain reputed interest in sexual integration. One of our female comrades said he made a downright nuisance of himself one night in her apartment, accusing her of white chauvinism when she said no. She said he became ugly, and she was afraid of him.

It was only when I saw him in action on his home turf, at the Y, that I realized he had an insatiable curiosity about every Negro and especially every interracial group. Half-white and tormented by The Question, it seemed a basic part of his personality. It was also the method by which he maintained his dominating position in the community and the revolution. The Skipper was the outstanding example in our town of those men, like Dr. Johnson, whom fate had placed between the two camps—as Bill Whitcomb said, "between the white people who built the orphanages and the Negroes who provide the orphans"—and yet maintained their credibility with the black people. He had access to powerful industrialists, to university presidents, and trustees. He could approach them on terms of familiarity, in order to drop a quiet word that would advance a move for integration or abate a crisis where some Negro was in difficulty. Or, knowing the Skipper, the word was more likely a gruff one, like Luke Lewis's in the barbershop but on a higher level.

His work made him risk being called an Uncle Tom, but the Skipper was too angry and outspoken a foe of discrimination for that. When he was in a meeting on a civil rights issue, woe be it for the timorous black woman who should counsel moderation. The Skipper would tear her to pieces, possibly even referring to her as "that little woman there," rather than by her name. He tolerated no breath of second-classism in his citadel. And despite his hobnobbing with the rich, he had for me—and Susan and Penny and Winnie—a special, intimate tone of voice, a particular look as it were, could the truth be told, for all Communists.

It seemed to me that if he was at home with white millionaires and black sweepers, the manner in which he compelled you to stand still and smile while he took you down a peg was testimony to that. I thought that if some could play the serpent-and-dove role with aplomb, for the Skipper it was the all too real act of rending himself.

He knew many of his visiting speakers personally, and they stayed at his home. On Sunday evening after the meeting, he and Mrs. LeFever would entertain a gathering of thirty or forty Negroes and white liberals, maybe one or two power-structure people, all of whom would have the pleasure of an informal discussion with the day's notable. There were soft lights and courteous, reasonable voices. I felt that these sessions played a part in "shaping the climate" of the community.

At this time also I became a member of the state board of the NAACP and state editor of *The Clarion*. When the sale of cars was unfrozen after the wartime shortage, Susan and I bought a little Studebaker, shaped like the turret of a tank. I would drive to a town where news of interest was happening, and I rediscovered my old home state from an entirely different point of view. For instance, I went to Greenville to cover a situation in which some black railroad laborers had gone on strike and had been barbarously thrown into the county jail. This was a town to which I already had a twofold relation. In the first place, my father's family had lived there from the 1840s—he had been born there, before my grandfather moved to the country—and there were still some old families whom I knew. Secondly, I had gone to college there. And now I came in to a little area of Negro homes, which, in both my previous incarnations, I had hardly known existed, and I saw the whole place from the black people's view. I didn't, on this occasion, visit the fraternity house, or call on my old professors. I really should have done so, but I simply lacked the gumption to pull these worlds into focus.

There was one person whom I knew on all three levels. Mrs. Mona Barkley, a by now elderly black woman, had worked all her life for the Delta Kaps. She recalled my father when he was at Ashley; when I had been there, she was the cook at the house and I waited on tables. We had been great friends. I went to see Mona and we had a nice little talk, but I'm afraid she was mystified as to what I was doing with my life.

When I was at Delta Kap, I had not known our cleaning woman, Mrs. Julian. I think I was dimly aware that she had a son who was doing graduate work or was an assistant in one of the science departments. At the time, Ashley had no Negro undergraduates. The next time I visited Greenville on behalf of *The Clarion* was to report a testimonial dinner given by the university on behalf of this man, Dr. Percy L. Julian, who had become one of the nation's best-known biochemists for his part in the discovery of cortisone and had then set up his own drug manufacturing corporation and become a multimillionaire. He had bought a large farm near the town for his agricultural experiments.

At this event, I looked straight into the eyes of my former English professor and gave no sign of recognition. Away from my customary black haunts, I felt hostility toward these people; I felt like a nigger.

Years later, when I paid a third visit to Greenville, the rupture in my mind had become so complete that I didn't even drive through the campus. I went straight to the AME Church, took part in the meeting, did my task of installing the officers of the local NAACP branch, and then drove straight home. On another occasion, returning from a convention with a carload of Negro friends, I detoured from the National Road to show them my family's plot in the cemetery, but without going into town at all. The people in the graves had been the generation of the Civil War, Union supporters if not exactly abolitionists, and a couple of them had actually fought against the Confederates. It was there in the moldering, gloomy graveyard, I guess, that I found the whites of Greenville with whom I thought I had more in common than my former professors and fraternity brothers.

My development of "*The Clarion*'s Race Relations Honor Roll" (later changed to "Human Relations") stemmed from these trips and other state editor duties. This was a feature published across the top of page one in the first issue of each January, consisting of the pictures and citations of eight to ten people who made "signal contributions to improved race relations" in the city or the state during the previous year. The project, of course, wasn't original; various newspapers did something like this in order to strike a positive note for New Year's, before returning to 364 days of murder and mayhem. But I thought most of these features had a phony air, as they played on the vanities of stuffed shirts, who, in return, might do the newspaper some good. I resolved that ours would be fresh, honest, and real. The person honored must actually have done some deed of goodwill or courage, and not merely sat on committees or made speeches. There was to be a mix of prominent and ordinary persons.

To uphold these standards, I asserted myself and kept the selection tightly in my own hands. I did not trust my fellow workers to stick firmly to my criteria. And indeed, as soon as the idea was broached in the office, St. John Ashley began coming around with, "Say, why don't we put so-and-so on? I mean, he's a big man," and so forth. I foresaw endless arguments and delays. And so, I held this project close to me as my "baby." You could do that at *The Clarion* if you'd been around for a while. After making my list, I would show it to Mr. Talbott. He usually suggested one or two changes, which I accepted.

Thus, among the honored was a Negro ditch digger who had risked his life to rescue a white child from a cave-in, and a white house-wife who had taken a collection for a black family whose home had been burned. Ruth Reynolds was honored for her legislative lobbying, and Governor Burton when he sponsored a fair employment law. One year, the list included Pat Johnson for his leadership in founding the State NAACP, and Attorney Hamish Chesterfield of Greenville, a notorious former Klan member, who, nevertheless, had gone out of his way to free the railroad workers.

The Honor Roll was an instant success. The dailies reported it each year, bringing *The Clarion* a lot of favorable publicity. I don't think anyone outside *The Clarion* was aware that a white man was making the choices. Inclusion in the list took on a status value. One could fairly feel the waves of indignation coming from Attorney Fielding and the Skipper when they failed to make the first one. But within a few years both had been on it, and they changed their tunes.

Then one year I was out because of illness, and somebody else edited the Honor Roll—I guessed Mr. Talbott and George Lewis had worked it up together. When I saw it, I was aghast. In place of my eight or ten pictures, there were about twenty-five. And what people! It seemed that every Republican politician in the county was there, side-by-side with rich white businessmen and conservative, but influential, black preachers. That was catch-up year for plain old hustling. Mr. Talbott avoided my gaze for weeks.

One morning around that time, a poorly dressed youth of eighteen or so years came into the office and related an account of a night of terror in Mississippi. We sat him down in the newsroom and as he began to tell his story *The Clarion* workers silently dropped in until there was a throng of a dozen. When I think of him I tend to think of

Emmett Till, the Chicago teenager who was brutally murdered by two white men while on a visit to the Magnolia State.

He said his name was Orley Walker and he had lived with his family in a cabin that we all could picture in southwest Mississippi. Besides his parents, there were three sisters and a small brother, "Little Pete." One day, his father had a quarrel with a white man over a pig that had strayed into their potato patch.

The next night, Orley awakened to the smell of smoke. The house was on fire. He managed to get out, but by then the crackling flames, leaping into the sky with a "swush," were devouring the building. He heard the cries of the others and tried to go back in, but the flames drove him away. And then he noticed a small cross burning in front of the cabin.

Orley said he ran and hid in the cotton field, watching the house as it burned to the ground, and that no one else came out. Then, in mortal fear, he made his way across country, heading north, stealing food or begging it from colored people, until after about two weeks he reached St. Louis. After staying there for five days, sleeping in deserted buildings or wherever he could, he got to Chicago, and then had hitchhiked to our city.

Most of *The Clarion* men were deeply moved. St. John Ashley, who often declared he would never travel south of the Ohio River, shook his head, "My Lord. My Lord." Hancock, when the story was finished, returned to his machine, where I heard him give one short, sharp laugh to relieve his feelings.

But Mr. Talbott and Smitty cross-examined the youth professionally. "Now where did you say your place was exactly? Couldn't you run and get help from somebody? How old were your sisters? Didn't you even go back to look at them?"

Although I realized that this was proper procedure, I cringed to listen to it.

"Have there been any newspaper stories about this?" asked Smitty.

"No suh, it wasn't in no papers at all, not none that I seed."

We men looked from one to another in horror. Only in the South, could a thing like this happen and not even be reported!

I was assigned the story and before I began to write it, on Mr. Talbott's instructions, I called a well-known man in Mississippi who was the publisher of a Negro newspaper, as well as a leader of the NAACP. He seemed to take a considerable while to get back to me, and when he finally did, his voice was dry, matter-of-fact. "No, we haven't heard of anything like that. So-and-so county? Nothing at all. Walker? That's a common name. . . . As far as I know, nothing like that happened."

I replaced the phone hardly satisfied. Had I detected a note of irritation? "As far as I know." Was he trying to tell me something without saying it? I vaguely remembered hearing a rumor that he was an "Uncle Tom" (it was either that or just the opposite). Could he, too, be covering up the slaughter?

In the story, I pulled out all the stops for Orley, burying the publisher's dismissive comment at the end. The community responded with its dark memories of the Southland, its fear and hatred of the savage Southern whites. St. John Ashley took Orley under his wing, and Womley Sherwood, a hotel proprietor, gave him room and board and bought him a nice set of clothes. For three weeks he was the talk of the town, making appearances at churches and lodge meetings. The NAACP asked the national office to take up the case.

Then, one Friday, the *St. Louis Argus*, a well-known black newspaper, arrived among the exchanges and was opened by Bill Whitcomb. "Say, looky here!" he shouted. "Say, Mr. Talbott, here's a revoltin' development!"

Several of us gathered around Mr. Talbott and read over his shoulder a story headlined: "DIXIE YOUTH EXPOSED AS CON MAN." Orley had indeed been in St. Louis, and his story had enjoyed the same success there as in our city. It seemed he had hit some other places before that. I was sickened. Mr. Talbott laughed and said, "He's a smart little tricker!"

As soon as the news spread around town, Orley Walker departed for points unknown. I had been given a lesson that my white man's ready sympathy did not stamp me as morally superior to Mr. Talbott and the Mississippi publisher, as I had thought, but as a journalist capable of doing a poor job of research.

And yet, I continued to be trapped by a benevolence that was essentially pride. A man who said he was a taxi driver came into my office one Tuesday. Distraught, he told me of his predicament: he had a wife and eight children and they were going to be evicted from their home the following day. If he only had ten dollars, he thought that he could stall the landlord until Friday, when he would be paid. He had always been honest; he paid his bills; but he had had medical expenses for two of the children. He would surely repay this ten dollars on Friday, without fail. He had not been able to find another house, and if he couldn't raise the money, they would be in the street.

George Weyhouse and some other men stood looking without moving a muscle. I, however, found the man's appeal irresistible. The thought entered my mind that they probably didn't have money this long after payday, as I did. I couldn't otherwise account for Weyhouse's callous expression. I forked over the ten dollars, and was thanked profusely, embarrassingly so.

We never saw the man again.

That was a small payment to make for getting some more of the noblesse oblige out of my system. I began to listen more closely when Mr. Talbott told his stories of the struggle for survival in a world where all the doors were closed. For instance, he told me about Johnny Martin, an ace pickpocket. Johnny's get-well day was the same as that of the downtown hotel-keepers and merchants—the annual races that drew several million dollars from across the continent into our town.

Mr. Talbott said he saw Johnny on the eve of race day, and he was dead broke. "I'll have money tomorrow," Johnny said.

"You won't have any money tomorrow," Mr. Talbott said.

"Oh, but I will!" Johnny retorted.

Johnny stood by the racetrack gate watching the patrons take their tickets out of their wallets until he noted a white man with a large amount of currency. Then he followed that man all day. When the races were over and the man got on a bus for town, Johnny got on the same bus and stood beside him, with his topcoat folded on his left arm. Every time the bus would stop, Johnny would bump into the white man. Seven times he did that, and the eighth time he took the man's wallet. Then, he pulled the cord and got off. He took another bus back to the racetrack and got on one of the trains that also ran into town. He knew that the victim and the police might be waiting downtown for the buses and trains, so he dropped off the train as it was going slowly through the west side, and turned up on the Avenue with eight hundred dollars.

Once, Mr. Talbott said, a victim who knew the town headed for the Avenue and, by sheer good luck, saw Johnny and had him arrested. Fortunately, Johnny had stashed the money in the floor of a wino's hangout. When they reached headquarters, a police captain told the irate visitor: "This man? Why this man doesn't do that! Now there is a little nigger does things like that," and he pointed at another young black man in the lineup. And, since all Negroes look alike, the white man himself became confused as to whether Johnny was the thief.

That might have just been civic spirit on the captain's part. The whole town made common cause in screwing the race visitors who, after all, were going home the next day.

Mr. Talbott said black people who engaged in such occupations were only following the examples set on a larger scale by the most prominent white men. He asserted that some political campaigns were nothing but personal fundraising forays. In particular, he ridiculed the notion that white politicians bought Negro votes. "Sure, they raise money on the excuse of paying off niggers," he said, "but they don't pay 'em off. They pocket that money themselves. Shit—not one-tenth of the money raised for nigger votes ever gets down here."

He cited as an example "Honest Tom" Blakely, a recent Republican candidate for mayor. He said Blakely, never intending to win, had collected a war chest of $100,000. Three months after the election, Mr. Talbott said, "He built a $60,000 home on the north side."

Mr. Talbott loved such muckraking stories, and I didn't know how far to believe them as literal truth. I can attest that one candidate for mayor walked through *The Clarion* plant and handed every one of us a five-dollar bill. I thanked him and thereafter had a kindly feeling toward him, though I didn't vote for him and doubt that the others did either.

11. Red and Black

I resisted, and still do, the fashionable saying that the Negroes spurned the blandishments of the Communists.

The Party, on its side, never lost sight of the importance of "the Negro question." The members were sincerely and vitally concerned with the Negroes' situation, and they made every effort to break down the color line and join with and aid in the struggles. When a member committed an action or even made a statement reflecting "white chauvinism," he would be severely criticized and if he failed to mend his ways, would likely be expelled from the Party.

The Negroes I knew were certainly not inhospitable toward the Communists who came among them. I don't mean that they embraced Communism, nor did they believe that this tiny band of white people had a chance of attaining its goals. But once they realized that these were outsiders, pariahs like themselves who were fighting against discrimination, the walls tended to come down. It was for this reason that so many Party meetings and social affairs were held in the black community—it was friendly territory. (Another reason was that Negroes seldom came, especially at night, to gatherings in white neighborhoods.)

This was also the reason why the Communists, when we had petitions that needed large numbers of signatures, made a beeline for the ghetto, usually on Sunday as church was letting out. There we obtained the signatures in short order, without anyone punching our noses or telling us to go back to Russia. I heard many times the same criticisms and self-criticisms: it was exploiting the Negroes, and thus was a form of white chauvinism. But it was only human nature, and nothing could stop it until black people started saying the same things.

Needless to say, the Party didn't have much success in recruiting Negro members at the time. If one wants to play the numbers game, there were at most forty Communists in our city, and of these not more than eight or ten were black. We considered this paucity of our numbers discouraging but not fatal; as Evers Thompson, Winnie's husband and the district organizer, used to quote with a wry smile, "When three men stand together, the kingdoms are less by three."

Winnie was widely known in the black community, because she had been so active for such a long time. She and I often went around together. Winnie's acquaintances were mostly poor people, or at least people whom I didn't customarily meet at *The Clarion* or in the NAACP. I prized her friendship, among other reasons, for bringing me into touch with "the masses."

With the more politically vocal Negroes, however, the Party member who was in closest touch was myself. I wasn't inclined to be, nor did the Party consider me, an agent of the Communists among the Negroes. Who wanted to pose as a white "Negro expert"?

In the black community, I think that after I became known as "Preston at *The Clarion*," there wasn't much interest in my politics. Most Negroes had more important things to worry about. There was interest at police headquarters, because a black policeman told Mr. Talbott that the Red Squad had a file on me, "as long as your arm," Mr. Talbott told me. He told the policeman he didn't believe I was a Communist. And he really didn't. I was sorry to deceive him, even tacitly, but I had to let it go at that. In a very important sense he was right, in that I never tried to "smuggle Communist propaganda" into *The Clarion*. The views I expressed in my writings were legitimately those arising out of the Negro community itself and not my politics. Except for the fact that a Communist thinks as a Communist, just as a capitalist thinks as a capitalist, my Party activities were carried on in my free time, and not on the time of *The Clarion* or, so to speak, of the NAACP.

On one occasion, I reviewed a book about labor that called for a more explicitly Marxist approach. Claudio Tubman reported that his father, who was a veteran member of the postal clerks' union, said after reading the review that he understood for the first time what made me tick.

The Party made extraordinary efforts to get Negroes to its meetings and to recruit them into its ranks. Bill Whitcomb never came, but Ruth Reynolds, a Republican, actually attended a couple of meetings; she would sup with the Devil himself if he was against segregation.

In the time of McCarthyism, most of these people went through the double hell of persecution as Negroes and as Communists. One member was placed in a state mental institution where, I was told, he affirmed that he was the commander-in-chief of the Red armies of the world. Another was blacklisted and passed interminable years in the filthiest poverty. Another man, a community leader I used to refer to as "Adam" (of the Bible), told the FBI agent to get away from his door and stay away, and he wasn't much bothered after that.

The point used to be made that America's black people, through the centuries of wars, had always been loyal to the United States and in particular that they didn't join the Communist movement— assumed to be the agent of a foreign power—in overwhelming numbers. It seemed to me in those days that most Negroes did love their homeland while abominating its evils, just as American Communists did. If more of them didn't join, I thought, it was because they were so bound in an elementary struggle for existence that they couldn't bring themselves, in the words of the *Communist Manifesto*, "to comprehend theoretically the historical movement as a whole."

12. Challenging the School Board

While *The Clarion* did not shy away from sensational stories, I knew that our readers' hunger for equality demanded deeper and more serious fare. The community's top priority was on integrating the schools. Many a man and woman were resigned to stand it all for themselves, but when it came to their children's rights, they were ready to fight.

The city had a segregated system, the exception being a handful of integrated elementary schools in poorer neighborhoods. These schools, incidentally, had been integrated ever since the years following the Civil War, when Negroes were first allowed to enter the public schools. All the Negro youngsters were assigned to Dunbar High School, where they received, or so their parents thought, an indifferent and inferior education with little stimulus toward college except for the "talented tenth"—typically the economically and socially favored few, especially if gifted with the lighter shades of skin color.

Susan said that when she was a child, the grade schools were integrated, and Mrs. Weyhouse had been a classmate of hers at Northridge High School. I, too, had had Negro schoolmates in Winette, including a basketball star and a youth with a fine singing voice who was the pride of the town. But the KKK era in our state had turned back the clock, as far as it could be done.

The School Board members of our city were elected on a "nonpartisan" basis, off at a corner of the voting machine. Like the city councilmen, they were all elected at large (it was the perfect system for disfranchising minorities), but the councilmen at least had to live in the districts they presumably represented. The School Board members didn't represent districts. To do so would have brought them under the accusation of speaking for "special interests." In practice, the majority of them lived in the upper-class north side areas. I once wrote an editorial sarcastically asserting that the chairman could muster a quorum by walking to the homes of a few neighbors.

The "candidates" for the School Board were nominated by a self-established, self-perpetuating organization called the Public Schools Committee. Its nominees had always been elected since it was founded in 1927 (the same year Dunbar was built); only once had a candidate even run against them. It had never nominated a Negro.

The committee was not prejudiced, however, and to prove it, four Negroes were sprinkled among its approximately one hundred members. They were Senator Bancroft, Pat Johnson, Ruth Reynolds, and an eccentric old man named Joseph Barnett, who was so far to the right that he was still parroting the line of the isolationist America Firsters.

For the Negroes seeking redress of their school grievances, however, the tinsel had long worn off the committee and all its works. Parents, PTAs, and the NAACP had gone to Superintendent Kleindienst (he was a liberal, too, by the way, and a Quaker) protesting incidents of discrimination, and had almost never received satisfaction. Delegations, with overflow crowds backing them, had alternately spoken softly and shouted at School Board meetings and had been rebuffed with the curt answer, "The Board will consider your petition in executive session. We will now proceed with regular business." *The Clarion*, along with an interracial group of respectable citizens that went in person, had urged the Public Schools Committee to nominate a Negro, either of its own choosing or suggested by a community panel. And for our pains, we had been allocated with the denomination "pressure group."

Reverend Jonathan Bigbee was a pastor in the Black Methodist Church. His home was two blocks away from a white school. While his twelve-year-old daughter, Linda, was being bussed to a colored school two miles away, she was injured in a collision. Reverend Bigbee had sued the School Board, but his suit was thrown out on technical grounds.

Wherever the black people turned, the answer was "no." They were without representation, and, it seemed, without recourse.

It occurred to me, one July afternoon in 1947, that candidates should be run in opposition to the Public Schools Committee. I broached the idea at once to Pat Johnson, for the election was less than three months away, and he agreed enthusiastically. We brought it up in the next meeting of the NAACP, and thus the People's School Group was born. The NAACP, according to national bylaws, couldn't take part in election campaigns, but that was easily gotten around. The NAACP would hold its meeting first, and then the branch president— I believe it was Ruth Reynolds—would trade seats with Pat, who would call the People's School Committee to order.

Winning was out of the question, but the group thought that the mere fact that somebody was challenging the Publics would stir half the town. If we put up only two candidates, a black and a white, and could get the Negroes to engage in "bullet voting," we stood to make a good showing. I had public office fever, and now and then entertained the fantasy that our people might be elected. Sometimes it gave me pause. I would have to attend all those dull School Board meetings, and pore over the prices of trucks.

For I had easily been persuaded to be the white member of the ticket. Finding the Negro candidate turned out to be harder. For various reasons, the other NAACP members were not available. The best bets were ministers, whose income derived from their congregations. We finally settled on Reverend J. P. Arthur, a leading Baptist who was strong on civil rights although not active in the NAACP. He accepted.

The next steps were to get the petition signed and to raise some funds. We needed only seven hundred or so signatures, and as soon as the word got out, thousands of black voters were ready to sign. There was a bit of a problem with the timing. It was August, quite a few people were on vacation—most of the middle-class folk at Wolf Lake, a black resort in Michigan—and the deadline was September 3. But we made it, with three hundred extra signatures to take care of any chicanery.

The money was another thing. W. D. W. Killens, an energetic promoter type, was appointed campaign director, and we went about soliciting funds. All of us coughed up according to our means, and so did people like the Skipper and Hatteras Thompson. We even got $50 from a Public Schools Committee liberal, an elderly Jewish merchant, who was outraged by the Negro-baiting and Red-baiting. He said acidly, "I didn't understand this before. Of course there should be Negroes on the School Board!"

Yet all we could manage was $500. When it was over, I went to the courthouse and looked up the filed financial statements. From the money angle, our challenge had been the best thing that ever happened to the Publics. At long last they had something to alarm their contributors. They raised and spent $17,500 on that campaign; the city's three daily newspapers generously donated their services. They employed an executive director, an attorney who happened to be an old Delta Kap brother of mine, at several thousand dollars. We had *The Clarion* barking at the top of its voice once a week, Killens, at a salary of $50 a week if he could raise it, and unpaid volunteers at the polls.

Another handicap for our committee developed early in the campaign. Word sped around town that a Communist was running for the School Board. Between this and other pressures developed by the Public Schools Committee, many of whose members had ties in the black community—such as maids or cleaning women, or even fellow-members of interracial church councils—some of Reverend Arthur's congregation became disturbed and served a demand on him to withdraw. He would have done so, but fortunately for us, it was found that the deadline for withdrawing had already passed. All he could do was to pledge from his pulpit that he would take no active part in the campaign.

We had on our hands a Negro electoral struggle without a Negro candidate.

13. People's Politics

Reverend Arthur, after his statement to his congregation, said no more one way or another, but since his name was still on the ballot, his personal absence was little noticed. Ruth Reynolds worked tirelessly, lining up Negro women's groups. The word got onto the street, and such men as Womley Sherwood and Reverend J. V. Simpson, "The Avenue Preacher," began plugging our cause. The nonpartisan aspect of the School Board race added to our benefits, for it meant that the Republican and Democratic political machines were unconcerned with this part of the election. Thus, the Negro ward heelers of both parties could support their respective slates and also tell their followers to vote for the People's candidates. They snapped up the issue: "Y'all pull this first (or second) lever and then y'all be sure to pull these two little levers over here for Reverend Arthur and Preston that works at *The Clarion*. They're runnin' against Jim Crow schools. Now y'all understand me? Lemme show y'all again."

Alarmed by our threat, the daily newspapers outdid each other in backing the Publics' ticket. But they didn't want to bring out the race issue, and so never specified why the Publics' election was so important that particular year. This must have been mystifying to white readers who didn't know what was going on. The puff stories they ran everyday for the worthy cause appeared to be merely the sort of thing the newspapers would do for the corporation executives and retired bank officials who were on the Publics' slate.

The Clarion's readers, on the other hand, were as explicitly informed as we could make them, and the more boosts for the Publics they saw in the daily press, the angrier they got. Why should the other party, those seven rich white folks, get all the publicity? But who would expect those papers to tell the colored people's side? And so they phoned neighbors about it, spreading the word informally.

Thus, just as we helped the Publics to raise money, the city's white newspapers helped us to line up votes. Another accretion to our voting strength was made up of white people around town, independent or disgruntled spirits, who didn't like the Public Schools Committee or "the power structure" for reasons of their own. The figures later showed that we had received votes in every precinct of the city. Since most of the city relied on the dailies for information, they may not have known what the issue was. Come to think of it, we may have got some Klan votes.

Then, the Publics ran into trouble in their own ranks. Pat Johnson and Ruth Reynolds resigned from the committee, and Senator Bancroft sat out the campaign in a cold silence. This disturbed some of the white liberals. In an effort to make sense of it without attacking the opposition in print (which would have been considered partisan), some of the Publics' leaders began spreading the rumor that a Communist was running against them. This upset the liberals still more. It seemed highly unlikely that a real Communist was running for the School Board, but they were familiar with the wild Red-baiting of Judge Masher. He had called so many people Communists that they didn't believe I was one.

By coincidence, one of the Publics' candidates was named Prescott, and in the alphabetical listing on the voting machines and sample ballots, my name was directly beneath his. This, of course, was confusing: which was the eminently trustworthy power company executive and which the interloping Communist? Some of the Publics had become a little paranoid, and I heard that the similarity of names was considered somehow an instance of our Machiavellian plotting. (In the outcome, Prescott led his running mates, which may have been due to extra-careful instruction of the voters.)

I didn't have many speaking engagements, but I remember one before the PTA of a Negro school in which I had a confrontation with a mild-mannered retired businessman of the Publics slate. It was pitiful. These mothers were thirsting after integration, and the man gave them only platitudes about economy in the schools and reminiscences of his work in the Boy Scouts, which incidentally, like everything else in town, the Negroes were struggling vainly to desegregate—but he didn't know it. Everybody was relieved when the program was over, but perhaps it did some good because the Publics man's wan smile showed that he had become aware there was something wrong.

I learned a lot through such meetings. I learned that our enemies were not brown-shirted Nazis but good Germans who hadn't the faintest conception of the lives, sufferings, and aspirations of their Negro fellow townsmen. This knowledge wasn't necessarily comforting. The Nazis of my imaginings presented better targets.

Then, a full two weeks before Election Day, I had to drop out of the running. Every crusader is vulnerable: Achilles had his heel, and I had my rectum. I took to my bed with *pruritus anus* and there I lay, reading long books such as *And Quiet Flows the Don* and *Ulysses*, emerging from my home only every two or three days to visit the specialist, who treated me with X-rays and the gentian violet solution that dyed the sheets atrociously but seemed to be the only medicine my skin could stand. A psychiatrist might explain that I had developed this condition to excuse myself from the remainder of the campaign. I wouldn't argue the point, for the person who was going through these experiences was only human, all too human, and if I don't write about the fears and tensions of a man who had changed sides in society, it's because I didn't recognize them, instead pushing them down somewhere whence they returned as a sore colon or an itch. Nevertheless, I got up on Election Day long enough to cast my vote. A few days later, I had recovered.

Meanwhile, Killens came to my home on the night after the election with the glorious news that Reverend Arthur had received 24 percent of the vote, and I 22 percent. With such a showing, the black people had burst open the door that shut them out of public life. The

People's School Committee, having served its purpose, disbanded. The Public Schools Group entered on a drastic shaking up, which was intensified with the revelation that the committee had spent thirty-five times the amount of its lowly opponents. The process continued, until, at the next election, it nominated a Negro itself. Superintendent Kleindienst retired, and the man who replaced him began the process of desegregation, in advance of the Supreme Court's 1954 decision. And it all came about without Reverend Arthur losing his church, or me having to serve on the School Board.

That was a year of people's politics. The postmortems on the School Board race were hardly over when the Progressive Party campaign of 1948 arrived with a bang. The election had been in November, and the first Citizens for Wallace meeting was held in February of the following year. Pat Johnson and I went together.

It has always seemed to me that the Henry Wallace movement was forgotten more quickly and thoroughly than it deserved. The principle of that forgetting was, I suppose, Bill Whitcomb's aphorism: "Nobody follows a losing horse to the barn." But despite the electoral flop, there were achievements. The former Vice President, who was trying to halt the Cold War policy at its inception (and what a difference if he had!), was also the first national figure to personally challenge segregation in the South, making himself the moving target of tomatoes and eggs. And his running mate, Senator Glen Taylor of Idaho, was arrested in Birmingham for entering a church through a door marked "Colored."

In our town the first large public affair was an appearance by Paul Robeson. It was held at the National Guard Armory, which was one of the city's bigger meeting places. The colonel in charge was sticky about renting it to left-wingers, and the Civil Liberties Union had to make a fuss before he would do so. The evening was a stunning success, drawing about seven hundred, including numbers of university faculty and the middle class. The *Daily Sun* couldn't get over the fact that all those people paid their entrance to a political rally.

Robeson's address and singing brought cheers from the audiences of usually undemonstrative Midwesterners. We were all highly encouraged. We didn't dream that the rest of the course was to be downhill. The bright brains and lovely smilers had come out with a puff of hope that earth might be fair, but daylight revealed college presidents and chairmen of boards and influential neighbors screwing up their mouths, and that was another matter.

Although Gideon's Army lost the ten thousand who bowed down to drink, it still had the three hundred (well, maybe seventy-five) who pressed on. The Negroes, I would say, responded in about the same proportions as the white people—that is, in very small numbers. Johnson became state secretary of the Progressive Party and its candidate for Congress from our district. Since he was also Mr. NAACP, the national NAACP's ban on Progressive Party activities did not run in our state. But the air became so polluted with the Red scare (Wallace's coalition included the Communists) that the same result was achieved. Abraham Jackson was a teacher, Ruth Reynolds was the wife of a prominent Republican, Irene Roberts was a social worker; they couldn't take the risk to support us, but I thought their hearts were with us in the Progressive endeavor. The Negroes didn't come right out and say it, but they were reluctant to desert the party of Roosevelt and Truman for what looked like a sometime thing. At Pat later put it, "They thought we were too good to be true." Mr. Talbott, on the other hand, was for the party of Lincoln and Dewey, and to Bill Whitcomb's great disgust had a paperback in the office entitled *Why Dewey Wins*. Bill got the last laugh on that one after the election, especially in view of the *Chicago Tribune*'s premature announcement of a Dewey victory.

Even so, the Progressive organization (as distinct, perhaps, from its following) was the most strongly integrated in town. Besides Pat, there were a number of working-class folk. A thin, wry black man named Ralph Rovere was quite active, but he didn't talk much about the issues. What was impelling him? I sometimes found myself thinking, was Ralph Rovere a narc? If anyone had planted spies among us, and we assumed that at least the FBI had, it seemed such sheer foolishness we could only laugh. As Pat said, "You've got to be glad; they swell the crowd."

The Negro masses, although not planning to vote Progressive, were ready enough to sign the election petitions. As it turned out, the party got on the ballot throughout the state with little difficulty. It only required something like 6,000 signatures and twice that many were gathered. More to the point, the State Election Board consisted of two Republicans and a Democrat. It was believed that the Progressive votes would come from people who would otherwise vote Democratic, and so the two Republicans shot the petitions through like lightning. One of the press services even carried a story that "forces close to" our Republican Senator, who was up for reelection, were contributing money to the Progressives. There were certainly no funds, but he wasn't putting any obstruction in our way.

At the last minute, the Dixiecrats also tried to benefit from the smart politics of the GOP. They came to town all the way from Alabama, and in little more than a week collected as many signatures, or so they said, as the Progressive statewide organization had in two months. Since they too were likely to draw from the Democrats, attorney Fielding challenged the election and a hearing was held. It was quite a circus as witnesses read off misspelled names, nonexistent addresses, and the signatures of persons who had changed residence to Forest Park Cemetery since the last city directory was published. It was too much boloney, and they were sent back to the Southland empty-handed.

14. Important People

The Progressive movement brought some outstanding personalities to our town, but I'm afraid they weren't met with the hospitality that was its slogan. Wallace came to speak at a luncheon, and the former Vice President was denied accommodation by both the leading hotels, just as if he had been black. He held a press conference at the apartment of a liberal artist, addressed the luncheon, and then went on to his next stop.

Robeson returned in July. The Progressives managed to get a union hall for his address, but what I remember most was an impromptu concert he gave while making a tour of the ghetto. The place was an area of sticks and trash and dog houses, and people's homes that seemed also made of sticks and trash, and were only a little taller than the dog houses. There the world-renowned Paul Robeson climbed onto a wooden box, threw back his mighty head, and began to sing. There was hardly any audience when he started: no professors now—only the poor black people who had come out of the houses. The word spread swiftly through the neighborhood, and soon a crowd gathered, including Hancock, Brown, Walt Evers, and then others from *The Clarion*. Trucks rumbled by, and the drivers looked out wondering what was going on. It was over in half an hour.

Sometime during the Progressive's second and less-publicized effort in 1952, the city was honored by a visit of Robeson's wife, Mrs. Eslanda Goode Robeson, a charming and very intelligent personality in her own right. I had the privilege of showing her the sights in the Studebaker. I remember pointing out to her the statuary group, including the slave with broken chains, around the base of the Civil War monument.

One Saturday morning, I made my way to the Trotter Coffee Pot, the restaurant in the basement of the Trotter Building, where about fifteen persons were gathered for a breakfast. The guest of honor was a slight brown man with a goatee: Dr. W. E. B. DuBois. He was about eighty and was in the city for personal reasons—he had married, or was about to marry, Shirley Graham, who had relatives in our town where she had been well known as a YWCA worker. DuBois had taken the occasion to spur on the little band of Progressives. We savored his courteous manners, which seemed to mark him as a visitor from another planet, and even more his keen observations.

Meanwhile, back in the 1948 campaign, the Progressives held interminable organizational meetings, scratched for funds, and quarreled among factions and personalities. Besides Pat Johnson, Negroes on the ticket included Ralph Rovere and Lucille Jackson, a woman from the working-class Stilesburg district. I ran for state senator. About twenty from the county organization were delegates to the National Convention, held in Philadelphia beginning July 23. It was a splendid convention. I was strongly impressed by the powerful, dignified keynote address given by Charles P. Howard of Des Moines, a Negro attorney who had formerly been a prominent Republican. In the after-session activities I saw some of my old friends from New York and made new ones from various places.

When we returned home from the convention, we carried through the campaign and in the outcome received a crushingly small number of votes. Some of the members contended that we had been "counted out" by the major parties, because we had only a few poll watchers. I admired their spirit but couldn't share it; people's politics had lost.

It was just then, when something like that took the last gasp of air out of you, that Howard Haverson dropped in from Timbuktu or Tibet to put you among the living again.

A tall, lanky, and truly unique man, Haverson linked the black community with the rest of the world: with Nigeria, Germany, and India. I thought it was because of him and a few others that Negroes couldn't properly be described as simply poor, dark-skinned Americans; they were rather a people with many of the attributes of a nation, including relations with other countries, but condemned to do it all without money.

Some, of course, had a certain amount of money. The Trotter Company, Pat Johnson told me, had a foreign trade department, dealing mostly with Latin Americans. Then there was Dr. B. B. Robinson, a chiropractor who had come from British Guiana and kept in close touch with Caribbean politics. He was always impeccably dressed and wore a carnation boutonniere. He was a dark, cheerful man with a British accent. I never learned the source of his wealth.

Howard Haverson was nominally, in his career, a representative of the United States (or at times of the United Nations), rather than of its black people. But, in practice, it was more complicated, as I shall try to make clear. I wrote many stories about him before I ever met him and he became my friend. *The Clarion* sometimes styled him the "Globetrotting Diplomat," but that was journalese; when he walked down the street the people of his age group greeted him familiarly as a "brother."

Howard had an unusual childhood, which Mr. Talbott explained to me. He was brought up in the home of the superintendent of schools, where his mother was a lifelong housekeeper. On Dr.

Canaday's death, the house, in a white neighborhood, of course, was left to Mrs. Haverson, and she continued to live there through my time. I got to know her during one of Howard's visits in the city between assignments—she was a tall, dark woman, self-contained and poised. The neighborhood was then at long last "going Negro."

I thought Dr. Canaday must have been a remarkable man for our town, and I longed to hear more of the story, but Mr. Talbott left it at that. It remained in my mind as a glimpse of another America that is little known, but all the same is somewhere there to be reckoned with in the future.

Howard's heredity was questionable; I never heard of a Mr. Haverson nor saw a photograph of Dr. Canaday. It was a matter of much interest, because of his unusual appearance. Indeed, I thought his appearance must have been one of his strongest assets in working for the State Department and United Nations. Like Claudio Tubman, he didn't represent any nationality except possibly mankind five hundred years from now, assuming that the program Mr. Talbott called "fuck 'em out" shall have been followed in regard to eradicating ethnic differences, and also, in regard to creating a biological superman. Howard stood six-feet-four, had been a Negro All-American football player at one of the Southern colleges, and he still looked it, because he was impeccably trim and fit. His color was a light brown, and his features were something like those of an American Indian, with a sharp, aquiline nose and thin lips. I used to speculate that wherever the diplomats sent him in Asia or Africa, the native people must have identified him as certainly not an American but some kind of strange, colored giant in whom they could place their confidence.

By profession, Howard was a social worker. I was told he had been on the staff of a settlement house in Elliottsville for several years. Then somehow he got a position in the diplomatic service. He worked alternately at the State Department and the United Nations Relief and Rehabilitation Administration (UNRRA) for the rest of his life. It was said he was the first American representative allowed into Communist China, in connection with an international food mission during the civil war. The mission proved abortive, but it gave Howard a chance to meet the people. Later, he sent me long letters from West Germany, excoriating his superiors in the U.S. occupation for lording it over the Germans. He was utterly heedless of the consideration that his mail was surely being scrutinized. In fact, in the very same letter he would indignantly relate that personnel were being hounded and dismissed from the service for the same sentiments he was expressing.

I was alarmed on Howard's behalf, and took care to write him totally innocuous replies. But it finally dawned on me that his charmed life was due precisely to the attributes that made me fearful for him: the combination of his color and his outspoken democratic radicalism. Somebody smart among the imperialists—and it must have been somebody rather high up—had recognized that this sort of man was not only useful but required by the times. A man without a country, he didn't think in terms of government or nations or political movements, but of the condition of the people wherever he had landed.

Early in our acquaintance, I witnessed an excellent example of Howard Haverson's undiplomatic rendering of the truth as he saw it. My wife Susan and I had taken the lead in forming an organization called the One World Forum, for the discussion of foreign affairs from an "internationalist" point of view. After a couple of years, we had succeeded in persuading the Reverend Dr. W. T. Bentley to take over as chairman. Dr. Bentley was president of a Protestant missionary society that had its headquarters in our city. He was eager to combat the Cold War through support of the United Nations, church peace work, and the diffusion of understanding among the peoples.

The organization counted itself fortunate when Howard came home from China and agreed to address a meeting. For the occasion, we forsook our usual quarters in a dusty loft and hired the downtown YWCA. There was a turnout of fifty or sixty people, many of them Negroes. Dr. Bentley, of course, was in the chair.

Howard wore a khaki outfit with a sports shirt open at the neck. He was obviously not a professional speaker, and for that reason his words were all the more convincing, and were soaked up especially by the blacks in the audience. Howard, as was his way, had mingled with the Chinese peasants, and that evening he told us many things about them.

It seemed to me that he waxed strongest on their feelings for missionaries. "The people hate the missionaries!" he said passionately and
without qualification. "They hate them and they ought to hate them!
The missionary doesn't live with the people, doesn't share their poverty and hardships. The missionary goes out there—usually a man or
woman who would have a hard time making a living here at home—and
in China he lives in a big house on a hill! The Chinese people live in
huts, they starve, and the missionary on his American salary dines like
a king! Then he hires them as servants and pays them a few cents a
week. Put yourself in their places—what would you think if foreigners
came into your country, preaching Christianity and acting like that?"

He went on and on, with no leavening of humor or finesse, throwing out generalizations like a Soviet propaganda statement. But this
was sheer Howard Haverson: crude indignation and straightforward-
ness. The radicals lapped it up, but Susan and I cringed as we
watched Dr. Bentley. He fidgeted and frowned, and his round face
flushed red under his white hair. After the talk, Howard was entirely
unaware of the currents he aroused. He hadn't grasped who Bentley
was, but if he had, it likely would have made no difference.

Needless to say, we had to find a new chairman for the group.

Whenever Howard came to town on furlough, he and I would have
good long talks. I think it was after his tour in Nepal, where he was
helping villagers build water systems, that he told me what a revolutionary impact was made by his simple habit of riding up front with
the driver.

"They're used to Americans getting in the back seat and saying,
'Drive on, my man,' but you know, Pres, I don't live like that. I jump
into the front seat and say, 'Let's go, man.' It's not a stunt I thought up,
it's the way I feel. Hell, these guys aren't any different than the cats I
run with on the Avenue, understand what I mean?"

Howard Haverson never changed. Through his last assignment he
continued to ride with the driver and castigate the "ugly Americans."
There was some thought he might marry, for he would have been an
excellent catch, and while at home for a six-month stretch he had
some dates with Irene Roberts. But you can't domesticate an eagle. In

the end, he soared right off the earth. He died at the age of thirty-nine in a New York hospital of an esoteric disease he had contracted in some faraway place.

15. Road Stories

My work brought me into contact with Negroes from whom I went home every night, and indeed at lunch, to my white wife and white child, to my white home. It was not until I began a series of trips, chiefly to NAACP conventions, that I advanced into more intimate relationship with my black companions.

The first of these journeys the Studebaker was called on to make was to the 1949 Midwest regional convention in Des Moines. The delegation set out, with Ruth Reynolds, Irene Roberts, Dorothy Wendell (a gay-hearted young woman), Pat Johnson, and myself at the wheel. It was a holiday group, joking and singing, and underneath, apprehensive about the fortunes of the road. Let the white American reflect on how he would feel speeding along the highway if, in addition to the hazards and stresses he is accustomed to, he faced the ever-present chance of his woman companion and himself being refused service at some luncheon-place, and maybe arrested and beaten for good measure. Bill Whitcomb had told me of his experience when he tried to find a place for his party to stay, late at night, in Buffalo, New York, after they had been denied service at a roadside restaurant. It was a harrowing account. I tried to write a short story about it, but my imagination couldn't do it justice.

Since Whitcomb's experience was common knowledge, I am sure the expedient solution of a shoebox lunch had crossed the mind of every member of our group, and then had been rejected as unthinkable for an NAACP delegation. And so, when we crossed the Mississippi into Iowa, we pulled up at a place, walked in boldly and seated ourselves at a table; and we were served.

While the others were still eating, I went out to get the car serviced. The man who handled the gasoline pump asked whether we were "show people." Someone thought he might have been misled by Ruth's colorful headscarf. His question provided a great deal of laughter that afternoon.

It was dark when we reached Des Moines. The host housing committee, instead of directing us to a hotel, gave us the addresses of local Negroes we'd been assigned to. That let us down a peg, because it smacked of shoebox style, but I drove on to the home where Dorothy Wendell was assigned to lodge. She went in, leaving her luggage in the car. In a few minutes she came out and said it wasn't her idea of a convention, and she wasn't going to stay there.

"Preston," said Ruth Reynolds, "go back to the housing committee."

When Ruth was furious, she talked in machine-gun sentences. She stood in the line before the housing chairperson, and then rapped out, "What is the situation in regard to the hotels?"

"Well, I—," said the thin, fortyish woman, and hesitated. That was enough, though she continued vaguely with "Most people prefer to stay in private homes" and "We have a small branch here."

"Have you checked with the hotels?" Ruth demanded. When the woman didn't answer at once, Ruth went on, "What's the name of your best hotel here? Where is the telephone?"

The chairperson began to say something about "The committee," but before she got very far into it, Ruth was calling the hotel. I wondered if she would tell them she was Negro. She did not. She said, "This is Mrs. Ruth Reynolds and I'd like to have a room with twin beds for tonight and tomorrow. The other person is Miss Dorothy Wendell."

Ruth replaced the telephone and said matter-of-factly, "That's arranged. Miss Wendell and I will be staying at the — Hotel. Preston, can we go now?" But, as we started, she turned, went back to the chairperson and put her arm around her. "Honey, you must think I'm terrible," she said, "but everybody gets bold when they're away from home. Y'all will have to come over and integrate that old Jim Crow town we live in, and we ain't doing nothing about." And they had a laugh together.

In the end, Pat and I stayed in our assigned home, where we had a good bed that we didn't intend to spend much time in anyway, and all three of the women went to the hotel. The woman responsible for housing assignments spread the word that the hotel was "open," and soon delegates from other places were checking in. By the next day, an entire floor had been turned over to the NAACP.

That was for me a memorable convention—even more so than the Progressives' national. It seemed to me that our branch made a better showing of both militancy and unity than some of the others. We were still flush with the People's School Committee triumph and its fruits, and during some discussion I took the floor and reported on it. The delegates, who were tired of listening to panels of experts, woke up and cheered at this fresh note of action. The differences over the Progressive campaign had receded into the background during the past year, and Pat Johnson was given a prominent place on the program.

The out-of-session activities were great too. Our group visited Henry Wallace's farm just outside of town. We made facetious remarks about the interbreeding of black and white chickens. And then six of us found ourselves, about five o'clock on Saturday afternoon, sitting and drinking whiskey in the law office of Charles P. Howard. There was Winnie—she and Evers had moved to Chicago, and she was an alternate delegate from that branch. There was Pat, and I don't remember whom else—some people who had been in the Progressive campaign, and who felt like boozing. I was drawn to Charley Howard at once, and not because he had been a great Progressive keynoter but as a friend. He seemed to be paying for his part in the Progressive effort. His affairs were going badly. A great husky man, like Robeson, a onetime noted athlete, he looked out the window at the streets and the courthouse where he was so well known—and poured another drink. He was also the publisher of a weekly newspaper that was then, he said, being put out of business because the printers had gone off to St. Louis and he couldn't find replacements.

Nor was that the only price he was paying. As the whiskey got to us the conversation deepened and he went off on a self-cursing jag as to what he had done to his wife and children. When history records in a footnote (or doesn't record at all) that a man or woman stood up and boldly challenged all the reigning evils, and lost, somebody should come along and add that in the quiet days that followed they were often stripped of their livelihood, identity, and sometimes home and family. As for Charley Howard, shortly after that convention, he moved, alone, to a hotel on the south side of Chicago. Later he went to Africa and for years wrote a syndicated column on the emerging black nations. To the end of his life I kept, from afar, that affection for him that had sprung up after a few drinks.

He seemed to show the same instant feeling for me. When I reflected on it, I thought he had a perceptive and warm concern for the white antiracist in the room. Maybe it was because in Iowa, which had a small Negro population, he had associated a great deal with white people. It was a warming and rather rare experience for me. As I look back on my years in the Negro community, I realize it is hard for me to name a truly intimate friend. But Charley Howard took one look at me, and I was suddenly reminded that I too was a person.

My next destination was Chicago. I had visited the Windy City surprisingly seldom in my life, considering that it was only a few hours away from most of the places I had lived.

Winnie arranged a luncheon at her and Evers' apartment, and after we had eaten, I drove with Nancy, a woman I had a "fling" with in Des Moines, to the Lake Michigan shore. We sat in the car watching the waves lap in. It was nearing Memorial Day, but the weather was still quite cool. Our feelings for each other were the same as in Des Moines, but I soon realized she did not want the problems of taking a lover. I drove back to Winnie and Evers' place and Nancy took her departure. I never saw or heard from her again.

After she left, the three of us sat and boozed. Evers and Winnie knew what had happened and tried to keep up my spirits, but it worked the other way—I went on a wild crying jag. About the next thing I remember, I was on the Outer Drive, alone, and driving like a maniac. Somehow I wound up with Charley Howard in his hotel room. As we downed drink for drink, I told him about the Nancy affair from beginning to end.

"I'll get you a girl," he said.

I thanked him but said I didn't want one. We kept on drinking and Charley, who couldn't stand watching a friend suffer, kept on insisting. I kept on declining. At some point he must have called anyway, because a very pretty brown-skinned girl showed up, but I apologized and sent her away. To use an old-fashioned expression, the hunger was not in my pecker but in my heart.

Charley and I slept what was left of the night in his double bed, and in the morning, he was still asleep when I dressed and left. As I was going through the lobby with my bag, the clerk at the desk challenged me. He looked surprised to see a white man apparently sneaking out of the hotel. But I said, "I stayed with Charley Howard," and he nodded.

I went to Chicago quite often after that. There was a peace conference that I attended with Tom Clare, an elderly white man who had been the Progressive candidate for senator. After one session, I offered to drive the Soviet delegates to their hotel. The political level of the discussion between these Communists of the U.S.S.R. and the U.S.A. was such that, while we were traversing Michigan Boulevard, I asked them what they thought of Chicago, and a slim young man said he found it rather frightening. I replied that I had been born a hundred miles away and had always found Chicago frightening. I never went there without being afraid of its police, its stockyards, its south side, and, I guess, the gangsters who had always been in the news when I was an adolescent in the 1920s. It seemed to me that even its traffic was typically Chicagoan. There were a great many four-way stop intersections (at least on the south side), and I observed that the rule appeared to be: "Everybody stops and the baddest man goes first."

Tom Clare and I took a stroll one day, to see a crumbling hotel where he had been a clerk during the race riot of 1919. He told a hair-raising account of his part in it. A mob had chased a Negro youth into the establishment. Tom said he hid the youth under the counter, drew a gun, and ordered the pursuers to halt. When they vacillated, he fired a shot that broke a door window over their heads. Then, he said, the members of the mob knocked each other down getting out. He showed me the window.

A couple of years after Des Moines, it must have been, the NAACP regional was held on the south side. We stayed in a twelve-story Negro hotel, a "representable" place in Bill Whitcomb's word. It was like being in a fortress, I thought, from which you would dare to venture only in good-sized groups. In front of the marquee, litter blew about on the filthy sidewalk. Across the street was a large, begrimed building that must have been the world's most sinister appearing church. And a Chicagoan who took several of us in hand for an afternoon walk explained that I couldn't possibly park overnight on the street but would have to go into a garage. "In this neighborhood y'all'd be lucky if they left y'all the horn," he said.

Inside the hotel, at the bar, were several of the best-looking unaccompanied young women I had ever seen. They were Negro girls— but one could hardly tell that of some of them, for they were light-skinned and made up white. They were each impeccably groomed and dressed like a class of model or entertainer you didn't see in our town. They toyed with their drinks in what I supposed was an inviting way. They were enough to make one's john go stiff upon first sight. I was a married man on the loose, but I wouldn't even venture to think what the outcome might be if I should make a move. Not in Chicago.

My Negro companions weren't oblivious to all this, but with them it was overridden by the fascination of Chicago as the great black metropolis, the Harlem of the West, the free and swinging place. After all, it was none other than Jack Johnson who had said, as quoted by Bill Whitcomb, that he "would rather be a lamppost on State Street than the mayor of Paris." Harold Pierce, explaining that he was "a city man," would take his vacations in Chicago.

There was the story told by Walt Evers about the white man who drove north from Alabama with a black chauffeur. They came to a city and the Negro asked, "Boss, if y'all please, what place is this?" "Boy, this is Nashville, Tennessee," the white man replied. When they came to another city the question and answer were repeated, except this time it was Indianapolis. They reached the outskirts of a third city, and the white man said, "This is Chicago, boy," to which the Negro responded, "Motherfucker, who in hell you callin' boy!"

Before we left the regional convention on Sunday, some of us had breakfast in the apartment of Pat Johnson's cousin in a low-rise housing development. Here everything was quite the opposite of the city outside: cheery, friendly, and relaxed.

Nevertheless, with my fears about Chicago, it may have become obvious to the others that I was an unusually apprehensive person. For all my identification with Negroes, I didn't plunge with abandon into the night and street life of the city. Even in our own city, I always approached a meeting at night in a black neighborhood with circumspection. I tried to find a space to park from which it would be a short walk and preferably under streetlights to the meeting place. On more than one occasion I drove around the block a few times weighing the relative dangers of the spots available. When the meeting was over and the lingerers had dwindled to two or three holding a conversation on the sidewalk, I became impatient, for I liked to go directly to my car and then, if the truth be told, to roll up the windows and lock the doors. And when obliged to walk in such a neighborhood at night, I kept a sharp lookout in all directions and often crossed the street to avoid meeting an oncoming figure.

This gave me a rather poor opinion of myself until I realized that, when not totally enraptured by Chicago, most of my Negro friends were similarly wary. The robbers and violence-wreakers operating in the ghetto would as soon jump a Negro as a white. In addition, they had a special fear of being in a white neighborhood at night, where I felt relatively safe.

In the newsroom one afternoon, Mr. Talbott and Bill got to recalling their hell-raising days. In the midst of the conversation, Mr. Talbott started ribbing Bill.

"I'll never forget the time you quoted Shakespeare to that whore," he said tentatively.

"Oh hell, man, I never done no such a God-damned thing!" Bill retorted.

"Shit, Bill, you did, you know you did. Why do you always deny what you know is the truth?" said Mr. Talbott. "Preston, I'll take my oath on a stack of Bibles that Bill Whitcomb quoted Hamlet to a whore instead of screwing her."

Addressing a third party was a trick of Mr. Talbott's to keep his victim on the run. Bill at times seemed aware of this, but couldn't control himself. Taking a bullet from his pocket, he said hoarsely, "If I was to jump out an' get what goes along with this, we'd find out who's tellin' the goddamned truth!"

"Shit!" said Mr. Talbott. "You ain't gonna shoot nobody, Bill. The only person you ever shot at was that old woman next door who got after you with the broom. You blew your top, man. Shot up the neighborhood in an argument with an old woman over a piece of shrubbery. Right out in the street, in the 3200 block of Clairwood Avenue." He turned to me. "May I be struck dead, if the cops didn't take Bill down for shootin' at a woman in her eighties."

Even Bill smiled at this point. "Oh, pshaw!" he said. "She wasn't over sixty. You're lyin' like a goddamned preacher."

I had heard of this incident, a truly grim neighbors' quarrel. As a result of it, Bill had no use for Senator Bancroft, who had been the woman's attorney. He wouldn't even write straight news stories about the senator.

"Bill, she was eighty if she was a day!" said Mr. Talbott. "Everybody knows she was in her eighties. But this other thing," he turned to me again, "we had these two whores out in my car, parked out by the reservoir. I was fuckin' mine in the front seat, because I'm shorter, and we was squashed under the steering wheel and couldn't see what was goin' on. But we kept hearin' Bill in the back seat, talkin' about Romeo and Juliet and destiny in the stars an' all this Shakespeare." He laughed till he had to wipe his eyes. "That whore didn't know what was happenin'. She wanted to get screwed and Bill talked Shakespeare all night long I swear to God he did!"

There came into my mind a picture of the young Bill Whitcomb that, while I too laughed, still made my heart ache. "Hell, man!" Bill said in a parting shot. "There wasn't nobody in that front seat would know Shakespeare if they heard it! Was it Hamlet or Romeo and Juliet, now answer me that!"

And when Mr. Talbott had gone, Bill stood over me and whispered excitedly for twenty minutes, turning to glance at the door now and then to make certain the boss wasn't coming back. He told me stories of what a ne'er-do-well Mr. Talbott had been in his youth, how he had flunked out of college and worried his father into the grave, until at one point the entire family had given up on him.

And yet I thought the exchange had served a purpose—the teasing, bantering, and playing the dozens was a form of therapy. At that time, Negroes seldom went to psychiatrists. Moreover, in our city there were no black psychiatrists. A good many Negroes, it is true, became patients at the state hospital, but I never heard of anyone being in treatment by a private psychoanalyst.

Suicide was another practice in which Negroes rarely indulged. This was evidenced not only by statistics but by our experience at *The Clarion*: we reported many homicides, but hardly any cases of self-destruction. So uncommon were black suicides that a sort of prestige was accrued to one young woman who drowned herself in a love affair. It was felt that in so doing she had made an advance into yet another formerly all-white activity.

George Weyhouse told a joke illustrating this situation. "The figures show that 287 white people have jumped off the Golden Gate Bridge," he said, "but only three Negroes—and two of them were pushed."

16. How We Became Non-Exploitative Landlords

In my life, the time had arrived for several "strategic retreats." One of these was related to the Cold War atmosphere, which was heating up toward Korea and at home with Senator McCarthy. Communist leaders and Hollywood writers were going to prison. The Party anticipated widespread jailings, and there was considerable "going underground." Some members, like Evers and Winnie, were moving to other cities and getting new jobs. I knew someone who also changed his name.

Under these circumstances, Joe Devine, the local Party organizer, came to me at the office one day and we went outside to have a talk. As we strolled, he asked me whether I felt I could move away. I said that I didn't think I could or should. Then he said, "Because of these practical difficulties we foresee, the Party has decided that members can either stay in or drop out as they think best for protective purposes. That is, without any political connotations—in order that they can best carry on the fight."

It was thus that I became a nonparty Communist, if there can be such a thing.

Susan and I were thinking about moving. We had lived at 3006 for four years, where our son Michael had grown from a baby to a boy of six. First, one black family had moved onto the block, then a second and third, and then the exodus of whites began in earnest. The block became half Negro, then three quarters. "The wicked flee when no man pursueth," quoted Bill Whitcomb. The young couple across the street, who had a daughter and a son with whom Michael played, moved all the way to a small town twenty-two miles north.

Eventually, we too found ourselves succumbing. Principles aside, when your neighbors are all moving, you begin to look around, realize you are living on a shabby street, and find your thoughts drawn to something better. One autumn day I was on a bus bound for a football game at the Carlton University Bowl and we passed School 34 with the leaves sifting down around it. That was a neat-appearing school in a well-kept neighborhood—and it was the school Michael would attend if we moved north of 38th Street.

As it was, he attended kindergarten and began the first grade at School 23, a huge, unsightly structure dating from the 1880s. Penny Parker said she had gone to elementary school there, but with the "white flight" that had since taken place in the neighborhood, it had become a Negro school. A few other white children lived in its geographical district, but the school administration honored the pretexts their parents devised for transferring them to schools farther away; that is, to white schools. Or, in some cases, they went to Catholic schools, which were interracial. At any rate,

Michael was the only white child in his kindergarten and first grade classes.

That this was "revolutionary" was even recognized by Michael's kindergarten teacher, a modern young woman who, judging from the look in her eye, would have made a good NAACP member. She always had a brightly special smile for Susan and me. For years after, whenever I saw her at various functions she always inquired after Michael's progress, and I understood at last that she was cheering us on.

Michael, as far as I could see, made no distinction between whites and Negroes. When Susan first went back to work, we hired a young brown-skinned woman, Mrs. Lucille Fields, as a housekeeper through the daylight hours. She remained in our employ until he was in college. Now that he is a grown man, Michael has told us that as a child he was quite confused by the arrangement by which he had "two mothers." One evening while he was still in kindergarten, he asked Susan, "Is Lucille colored?" He said a boy at school had said she was. As further evidence that he knew little of race, I recall an incident a couple of years later when he was playing softball at Meredith Park. I stopped by the park for a few minutes after work to watch the game, a pickup affair in which boys, teenagers, and even men were taking part. At dinner that evening Michael told us about it and said, "Our pitcher, Al Jackson—he's a Negro!" What I had observed, however, was that all the players except Michael were Negroes, the pitcher being a very black one.

While unfortunately I can't testify that from growing up without prejudice Michael took a strenght that made him a happy man, I can report that his difficulties were not with Negroes. To my knowledge, the only "racial" fight he was ever involved in took place when he was still very young, about five years old. I happened to look out the kitchen window and saw that something was amiss on Thirtieth Street. Michael was standing on our side of the street yelling across at a Negro boy a size or two larger who was on the south side—the Negro side—and who was yelling back.

The first thing that impressed me about Peter Starr was that he stood his ground when I approached. "That little boy threw a rock at me!" he charged.

"He took my scooter!" Michael countered. And indeed, Peter was standing at the ready position with the new scooter, a Christmas gift from Michael's aunt and uncle.

It was an occasion, however, for peacemaking: the three of us went to draw a truce over cookies and Kool-Aid. On the porch, Peter said forthrightly, "He's got so many things, and I ain't got nothing!"

Michael and I looked at the things—fire engine, tricycle and other vehicles—the veritable motor pool of a child with too many fond relatives. I had a feeling that Michael himself thought, it was too much, and that the scooter was expendable.

Through Peter's open shirt I saw he had something Michael didn't—an umbilical hernia.

On the spot, and without moralizing, the scooter was conferred on Peter. Michael and I went with him to his home, a decaying, gloomy frame house, to assure his grandmother that this had been done. A few days later, I had to go over there again. A policeman had apprehended Peter on suspicion that he had stolen the scooter. How else would he have gotten it?

Peter Starr was the first of many black youngsters I would get to know as Michael's father. After we moved from 3006, I lost sight of Peter until, about ten years later, I heard that he was in Greene's Institute for Delinquents. I didn't know whether it was his penchant for direct equalization that got him there, but whatever it was, I wasn't too surprised. But then life showed another of its twists, and Susan and I saw him at work in the supermarket where we shopped. We would stop to chat with him whenever we went there. He had become not only a great strong young man, but, in personality, it was as if a pathway of clear and good sailing had opened before him. He was the most cheerful, courteous, and diligent employee I ever saw in a supermarket. He said that his hernia too had been repaired at Greene's. The company rather rapidly promoted him, and he could be the manager now for all I know.

What finally clinched our decision to move from 3006 was the first law of nature. To attend School 23, Michael had somehow to be got across Congress Avenue and Thirtieth Street, both of which were heavy traffic arteries, with no stoplight at their intersection—and it had to be done four times a day, since he came home for lunch. The lack of traffic signals at the approaches to the school was then and for years to come a sore point in the community. The school administration was repeatedly charged with neglecting the problem because the children were Negro. It took a long campaign to obtain the appointment of adult crossing guards.

As one stood at the corner and watched the cars and trucks speed by, it seemed hardly likely that all the efforts of Daddy and Mommy and Lucille combined would prevent Michael from becoming a traffic statistic in a matter of months. That settled it.

We borrowed some more money from Papa Avakian and bought, with a mortgage, a sun-drenched bungalow, also on Stilwell Avenue but ten blocks north (and in the School 34 district). This area was in the same situation as had been the other neighborhood when we moved there—all-white but threatened with the coming of blacks at any moment. We used this as a lever again to get favorable terms: the owner, an insurance man, was in a frenzy to move to the suburbs but as a matter of principle didn't want to sell to Negroes.

Selling 3006 Stilwell turned out to be not so simple. Susan and I were determined not to sell on contract. Buying on contract was the black people's common way of obtaining a home in our town, but it was a living horror. Under it, the buyer was permitted to move in without a down payment, and then to make monthly payments (and keep up the house) while the seller retained the title. Under this arrangement, the buyer amassed no equity. If the day came when he could not meet a payment, the seller was entitled to repossess the property at once. The buyer might over a period of years pay $6,500 on a $7,000 purchase, and then due to some bad twist have some trouble paying the rest and be set into the street, with his family and furniture. We reported on such cases in *The Clarion* from time to time. We decided to put the house up for rent at the same fifty dollars a month we were paying on the mortgage. That made us landlords, but we thought at least we were not exploitative ones. In the Devil's country you too will grow horns, regardless of your intentions. Downstairs tenants were easily found, and Mr. Partemeyer stayed on the second floor. On the first day of October, the moving van, with Michael perched by the driver, made its way across Thirty-eighth Street to the land of the lower-middle class.

17. The End of an Era

It was the following June when I drove the Studebaker away from 4032 Stilwell for its longest trip, to the 1950 NAACP National in Boston. I picked up the other delegates: Irene Roberts; Lois Madison, a quiet young married woman who was secretary of the branch; Pat Johnson; and Reverend Bigbee. Irene and Reverend Bigbee were going on to other destinations after the convention, while Winnie Thompson planned to take a train from Chicago to Boston and then to ride back with us.

Incidentally, that was one occasion the branch treasury felt it could make a contribution toward the delegates' expenses. Usually, our local NAACP representatives paid their own way, but for the Boston convention the five-member delegation was voted a grand total of $125, or $25 each for the ten-day trip. This was a gesture toward covering the costs of gasoline, registration fees, and "housing." It was ludicrously inadequate, but we had grown so used to paying all our own expenses that we felt we were traveling in style.

We made it the first day to Cleveland. As always on such trips, with the world locked out of the moving car, there was a chance for relaxed, probing talk that didn't ordinarily get done. I remember, for instance, that Irene or Mrs. Madison voiced the idea that Negroes had a tremendous amount of backwardness to overcome. Pat and I rejoined with the view that blacks had as much to contribute to integration as whites. The discussion went on and on, quietly dying away at points, and then reviving. I sometimes thought the most valuable parts of conventions were these conversations we had en route.

In Cleveland, I dropped the women at a settlement house where they had made reservations, and the men stayed at a downtown hotel.

We were off bright and early the next morning, and the drive turned out to be a long one, something over six hundred miles to Albany. There was no stopping at a highway motel for our group; it was thought best to get to a city. Then Albany gave us trouble. We were so hungry that we had dinner at a roadside restaurant, and by the time we sought accommodation, it was late and dark and we were exhausted— and of course strangers in a strange town. We finally found the YWCA for Irene and Mrs. Madison, and there we made our first mistake by inquiring as to where a mixed group of men could stay. We should have had Ruth Reynolds along to hold us to our principles. At any rate, we were directed to a certain establishment. On the way there, we passed a first-class hotel in the business area; we discussed the question as to whether to check in there, and we were aching with fatigue, but we went on.

The place that had been recommended to us was near the Hudson River; it was a waterfront flophouse. Too tired to care, we took a large, dirty room where Pat and I had a double bed and the Reverend a single.

We quickly went to bed. Within ten minutes the Reverend was loudly and prodigiously snoring. Pat soon chimed in with a steady drone. The room was bright from the lights of the street, which a poorly shaded window failed to hide.

I was in the grip of insomnia. The long day's traffic ran through my mind. I was nervous about the day to come, when we still had the width of Massachusetts to go and plans to arrive for the opening session in the early afternoon. I twisted and turned, got up and smoked a cigarette. There was nothing to read. Bigbee's snoring reached new volumes.

About an hour and a half went by in this way. A thought entered my mind, but it was a desperate remedy. Soon I was wrestling with it. How could I leave my brothers and go to a luxurious room in a hotel that might not have admitted them? What kind of solidarity would that be? On the other hand, how could I lie awake all night and then drive to Boston? Or, what the insomniac really asks, how could I remain there and endure those assaults of sensations, thoughts, lights, smells, and sounds?

In the end, I dressed silently, wrote a note, took my bag and went to the other hotel. My car was in a garage and there were no cabs in sight; I struggled on foot carrying the heavy bag up the hill to the hotel we had passed by earlier. In addition to a bad conscience, I arrived suffering from grievously aching arms and legs.

But I slept the rest of the night. I think it was the abolitionist Theodore Weld who said something to the effect that if the rich, the eloquent, and the able had taken up the anti-slavery cause, it would not have been left, as it largely was, to the poor, the inarticulate, and the neurotic.

The way it was, I was more a chauffeur than a delegate to the Boston convention. For one thing, I stayed with friends from my New York days, Donald and Barbara McShail, in their home at Concord. The theory was that I would drive to the sessions in south Boston every day, and I did for the first few days, but I didn't find them very interesting. Lately I had been developing more and more of an interest in history—1950 was a pretty good year for "progressives" to fall in love with the past—and there were many sights to see in Concord: the reconstructed bridge of the Embattled Farmers, Emerson's home, and an integrated cemetery where Barbara and I found the tombstone reading:

> Born a free man in a country of slavery,
> He died a slave in a country of liberty . . .

The verse went on to say that he had gone to a better world where all men would be free together before their Maker.

Another day, Barbara and I drove to Salem. We saw the field at Lexington on the way back. And one afternoon we visited Thoreau's Walden, littered with trash all around.

I was all the more willing to indulge myself in historicizing because I had caught wind of something else that was happening at the convention. The National Board had seen fit to sponsor an anti-Communist resolution, barring members of the Communist Party from holding office in the NAACP. It was an attempt to appease the witch-hunting spirit of the time and had little if any practical meaning. There were very few Communists in the organization, and some of these, like me, were no longer members of the Party. At any rate, you can't decapitate a Communist (by such methods) if he won't put his head under the axe.

All the same, it was sickening to watch the organization do this mean and petty thing. "Freedom is indivisible" is something of a slogan, but even black people can make certain small gains when Reds are being persecuted. It's the spirit of freedom that is indivisible after all.

The resolution was bound to pass. Communism had a bad name, and the overwhelming mass of the delegates were concerned to show that the NAACP was not Communist, Communist-controlled, nor a "Communist front." But about seventy-five out of more than a thousand delegates insisted on standing up to be counted against it. A dozen or so paraded to the microphone and spoke, and then in the interest of time, the rest agreed to register their names. I was among the protesters, as were Winnie, Pat, and Reverend Bigbee.

It was when the resolution passed that I—not in protest, but with a sort of loss of interest—drifted out of the sessions for good. I spent the rest of my time with the McShails.

The McShails had a Negro maid. On the morning after my arrival, Donald whispered to me at the breakfast table as the maid stepped into the kitchen, "If you don't mind, Chuck, it might be just as well if we kept the NAACP out of it. She doesn't know about you."

I looked across the table and saw that Barbara was tense. I nodded, and throughout my stay never mentioned the NAACP within hearing of the maid.

The irony of the situation was that the McShails held as strong views of integration as I did, and certainly were not afraid of the NAACP. In fact, when Donald was leader of the Progressive Party he made national news by taking a bold stand before a legislative witch-hunting committee. At the time I was visiting, he was the target of a Red-smearing attack, with front-page headlines in the Boston press that would derail his career for a long time to come. It was understandable that Barbara and he were nervous.

In those days, such upside-down relationships were not rare. I have been in several homes where the white radical employers and the black servants did not communicate on these matters. I have even been in homes where the black activist employers lowered their voices on certain topics when in the company of the black maid. In my own house, there was no concealing my job and my interracial activities from Mrs. Fields—as I conscientiously called her for about ten years until to her apparent relief, I began calling her Lucille—and on principle I wouldn't have wanted to. She was no civil rights fighter, but a broken woman from Tennessee, struggling to raise her family in poverty. I don't know if Lucille ever joined the NAACP. In later years, she seemed to develop, and to express the lines of liberation. I wondered whether her children might have helped her understand these things. Or maybe she did all along. To tell the God's truth, the master and the servant face each other through a glass, darkly.

This time, only Lois Madison, Winnie, Pat and myself were in the car, heading for New York. Winnie read the newspaper stories about the Korean outbreak aloud. I thought it might be something that would blow over, but she gave a puff out one nostril to clear her sinuses and said crisply, "No, it's a major development. It's a war! It'll change everything. Now we're going to get a taste of real repression."

We had gotten a late start and instead of going in to Harlem, decided to try a small hotel in Yonkers. The manager said he did not cater to colored guests. We put up an argument, and at length he produced a new wrinkle. "I could take the lady," he said, "but not the man. Absolutely not."

Pat said there was an old school friend he imagined he could stay with; he made a phone call, and it was arranged. Such was our experience with chivalrous Jim Crow.

We got a piece of our own back the next day on the Pennsylvania Turnpike. When we went into a Howard Johnson's, we took care to pair off blonde Winnie with Pat, and Lois with me. As we anticipated, this drew thunderbolt stares from several white travelers. We enjoyed it so much that we stopped at two more restaurants.

Late that afternoon, I pulled up at the swank George Washington Hotel in Washington, Pennsylvania. The black doorman's face was a study as we halted under the marquee; of all things, he seemed to fear most that we would hesitate. He had our luggage out of the trunk before we were even out of the car. Then he said, "This way, please!"

The white room clerk also was ready for integration, but it took some time for him to comprehend in what form it was approaching him. He assumed that we were a white couple and a Negro couple traveling together. Pat and I had to explain to him that, while we were all married, in fact, none of us was married to any of the rest of us.

We suggested a double room for the women and another for the men, but the clerk went us one better: he gave us a suite of two double rooms with a connecting door. I guess he thought that whatever was going on, that ought to take care of it.

Shortly after our return we found that Pat's presidency was going to be challenged at the state NAACP convention to be held in the autumn. This was apparently another development in the Red hunt, and some of us thought it might have been cooked up behind the scenes in Boston.

It reminded me of an election I once attended at the Co-op Community League, which was led by Clarence Bailey. This was an organization in the Stilesburg district, and its members were working class.

The meeting was held in a shed in Clarence's backyard. Clarence was a molder in a steel plant when he was not being blacklisted, and he held the chair. First he announced that he would not be a candidate for reelection as president. The members were flabbergasted. An effort was made to draft him, but he rebuffed it. Then he explained that he would run for executive secretary. Since this meant he would continue to do the work, there was a collective sigh of relief.

"Then we don't need no president," said one of the workers.

"Oh my, yes, Brother Sampson, we got to have all the officers," replied Clarence in his reedy voice. "It don't seem to me that would be right at all, no indeedy. And besides, I ain't even executive secretary unless I'm elected. There has got to be two candidates run for every office."

There weren't enough members present to nominate two for each post but this was solved by taking votes for the offices one at a time, and having some of the losers run again. When the voting came to executive secretary, Clarence was elected by acclamation, but he said, "No, I done told y'all that can't be did! I think I'll just nominate y'all."

When the voting got down to assistant treasurer, it seemed the meeting was stumped, for the previous losers by now had all either been elected or refused to run again. Even I had been elected second vice president. Finally, a woman was noticed who wasn't a member, but had come with a friend. Her name was put up, and the election was concluded.

It was a satisfying experience for all involved. I have often reflected that if only the Soviet Communists had practiced Clarence's stubborn adherence to workers' democracy, the history of our century might have been vastly different.

Pat's challenger, Booker Washington Stoker, was a good-looking, light-brown man with a gray mustache. He was an eloquent speaker, a Democrat, and held a good city engineering job in North City, which had a reputation as our state's most liberal town on the race question. It was just this pleasant picture that troubled the supporters of Johnson. There had never been any question that Pat's base was in the Negro community. His livelihood was principally in the Trotter Company, of which he was being groomed to succeed Senator Bancroft as general manager. He, too, had had entrée into the worlds of white politics and liberalism, indeed far more than Stoker, and spokesmen for these worlds treated him halfway respectfully. If at any time he would go over to the Democrats, he could write his own ticket, as far as "Negro" positions were concerned—even, probably, the token City Council membership his father had held. I wouldn't say that Pat threw this entrée away, but he made it clear that he must be accepted as his own man, and more so, as a man of the black people. When he joined the Progressives and associated with Communists he was simply maintaining his independence.

For this, he paid a price. The people in the street knew that he was "hot." His wife was fired from her job in the federal government's

General Procurement Center, which was in our town, simply because of Pat's activities. Pat tried to keep this incident quiet, because it would be frightening to ordinary folk, but the news got out. Some Negroes started to stay away from him.

As Pat said, he had never intended that his presidency of the state chapter would last forever but he didn't want to be voted out in these circumstances; and particularly not by Stoker. He feared the roaring young tiger of an organization might be turned into a kitten on the leash of the Democratic Party and such liberal groups as Americans for Democratic Action.

Ruth Reynolds was more emotional about it. "Stoker just wants a title to put after his name," she said, "and we're supposed to tear down the NAACP to give him one." She added, "Those North City people are too thick with the National Office." But signs appeared that the disaffection wasn't confined to North City, and a coalition was being formed. The state's second city, Mercer, was said to be in it. The branch there, led by Mrs. Lillian Cummings, a large and rough-spoken woman, had developed a stepchild syndrome. The problem was really one of geography: Mercer was stuck in a far corner of the state and for that reason alone tended to be neglected. Word spread that Mrs. Cummings was going on Stoker's slate for vice president.

Most of the smaller branches had a loyalty to Pat for services he had rendered them during his founding and leadership of the state chapter. All the same, a tide was creeping in. In our city branch there was Walter Rowland. A neat, soft-spoken, well-educated young man who had moved to our city from Cleveland, Walter was in real estate, a Republican, and a son-in-law of Senator Bancroft. He worked as hard and as systematically for the NAACP as he did for his business. You couldn't call him a Tom, but he had an image in his mind of a more acceptable NAACP, one that might play its part in civic affairs with such organizations as the Junior Chamber of Commerce and even the Real Estate Board (of which he later became the first Negro member). I thought Walter an example of the adage that the good is the enemy of the best. He was a personal friend of Pat Johnson, but a political opponent, who sooner or later would have to be reckoned with.

A new element had entered the ranks during the membership drive of the previous spring.

A small brick building across the alley from Jose Stanton's place served as headquarters. At a meeting there one night, I was surprised to see four new white people, two men and two women, all in their twenties. They were what would now be called beautiful people.

After the meeting, I was introduced to Stephen Caron, his wife Kitty, his sister Elizabeth Caron, and John Thompson. The two men were lawyers. Elizabeth Caron was a graduate student at the state university extension in the city.

I recognized the Caron name at once, for theirs was a distinguished family. Their father had been a well-respected federal judge, and an older brother was already making a name in the District Attorney's office. Their mother was a well-known author of children's books.

Stephen Caron was a tall man, and with the bright wit of his Irish descent was engaging and charismatic—a sort of blond Pat Johnson. His sister also was tall, good-looking and well dressed. Kitty was a petite redhead.

The group was candid and relaxed in their approach to Negroes. What they represented was the first bonus to the branch from the NAACP work that had begun a few years earlier on the state university campus fifty miles to the south. In the meetings, I had eyes for Elizabeth, and once had thoughts when she was so courteous as to give me a lift home in her car. Her Mona Lisa smile no doubt was due to my age, although I could also sense that she didn't like my politics, or I should say my political reputation. At any rate, she soon married Thompson.

I was to enjoy the friendship of Steve Caron for many years. After he dropped out of NAACP activity, our association was in the Civil War Round Table, where we went together on many a caravan to far battlefields. We had a bond in secretly wishing we had lived during the Last War Fought between Gentlemen. In fact, it reached a point where our wives sometimes said we did, with Kitty referring to herself as "the only living Civil War widow." With the Round Table, Steve and I expressed, or sublimated, our contemporary enthusiasms by being the most outspoken pro-Unionists and the only really pro-Negro men.

Steve continually and boldly brought up the Negro question, which otherwise, as if by tacit agreement, was totally ignored in this interest group devoted to the war against slavery. He even did this when he once addressed a Round Table composed of scions of the Confederacy in Montgomery, Alabama. I sometimes thought I would have been shunned if it hadn't been for our friendship. Actually, we had our differences. In contemporary politics Steve was an adherent of Americans for Democratic Action, while I of course was a Marxist. In the Civil War period, Steve was a War Democrat (he once gave a talk defending Stephen A. Douglas), and I was a Lincoln man.

We were both very much aware that there was a precedent for our alliances in the war itself, which was one of the things we liked about it. No less a figure than Grant could be described as a War Democrat; and I once read a paper on Brigadier General August Willich, one of the original German Communists, who came to the United States and commanded a Union brigade. During the discussion, Steve revealed that Karl Marx and the First Workingmen's International were among Lincoln's heartiest supporters. He got a bang out of shocking the retired military men and Republicans who made up a large part of the membership.

In our relationship, Steve and I were trying to make a refuge of humanity above the harsh lines of politics. We were noblesse-obliging each other. Perhaps it was because we had both lost our fathers in childhood and had been brought up by literary-inclined mothers. If his code encompassed a tolerance toward my pariah status as a Marxist and a Negro-lover, I didn't hold it against Steve that he was in the powerful law firm of Franklin, Snow, McCleod, and Baker.

Within the NAACP, the Carons and their friends lined up with Walt Rowland. These views, with their tincture of anti-Communism, were pretty much those of the national NAACP. Steve stood up for me as a Communist in the Round Table, but opposed me as such in the NAACP. I think Steve hadn't the least idea what he was getting into when he ranged himself against Pat Johnson.

After a branch meeting one night, I drove Ernest Cinq to his home, which was in a Negro area a short distance west of our new house. He asked me in, and we settled down with beers. "Say, look here, Preston," he said, "what do y'all think of these young people, anyway? What are they up to?"

I replied that their politics was what might be expected of them, and that I thought they would be helpful in broadening the organization's influence.

"Well, yes," said Cinq, his polite way of saying no. He lit his pipe and drawled, "But that Franklin, Snow runs the town, Pres. What they messing around with us for?" His face wrinkled in a smile. "Don't y'all think we'd maybe ought to beware of Greeks bearing gifts?"

In the rest of the conversation I tried to sketch out for Cinq the social developments, as I saw them, that were impelling young people like the Carons into the Negroes' cause. And he, who was the soul of benevolence toward individual human beings, kept agreeing with me and then stubbornly disagreeing.

Mr. Talbott's views went in the opposite direction. He saw the Carons as a new generation of the white power structure who could make a better place for Negroes in the city's life. "Back 'em up!" he admonished me. "The niggers wouldn't be ready for Jesus Christ if he turned out to be white. It doesn't make sense!"

The convention was held at the YWCA on a sunny weekend in October. There was a pre-program on Friday night, with a panel discussion on housing integration, and then on Saturday morning, the out-of-towners began arriving. Here came Stoker with all his geniality, and his North City people. Among them was Attorney Harry Mills and a silent young white woman who always wore an expression of doing her religious duty but who, according to report, went where Stoker went.

In came another "white woman," Mrs. Morley of Sheltonsville, who later was the cause of a joke on me. Unlike the North City woman, she overflowed with a fiery enthusiasm. When she made a speech, with her alabaster face set off by coiled raven hair, I wondered what could have roused this farmer's wife to start campaigning for black people in her tiny community. It was after I put her on the Human Relations Honor Roll that I found out: she was Negro, of course.

Next came the delegates from Mohegan, headed by quiet, ginger-colored Raymond Duke and his wife. They too had confused me when I first saw them at a state board meeting. A sheet of paper had been passed around to record the attendance, and I noticed the names from Mohegan: Mr. and Mrs. Raymond Duke and Mrs. Bergdorf. Looking at them, I took it for granted that the short, Slavic-appearing white woman was Mrs. Bergdorf, but Ruth Reynolds told me after the meeting I was mistaken—that was Mrs. Duke. Mrs. Bergdorf was the coal-black woman.

Mrs. Bobbye Willie Rishards arrived from Elliotsville in her shiny new Cadillac. She had Southern charm as thick as the scent of magnolia. She was an enterprising woman on her fourth husband, and she owned oil land in Texas. She was in the Johnson camp. Also from Elliottsville, but driving by himself, was Sid Millstone, a young Jewish lawyer I had heard much about. He had been active in Wallace's campaign, even while those who supported Wallace were getting beat upon by right-wing unionists in Elliotsville. Sid stood high with the black people in his community. They said he carried on a running one-man battle, in court and out, against segregation.

The delegates converged until eighty-some were present. The last to arrive were the delegation from Mercer, led by Mrs. Cummings, who no sooner stepped out of the car—I happened to be in a group getting a breath of air on the sidewalk—than she began complaining, "Why do we always have to have the conventions here? Don't y'all know they's other cities in this state?" The session opened, the program proceeded through the reports of officers and branches, the "workshops" (a term to which Smitty Smith strenuously objected), and the election of committees for resolutions and nominations. The delegates threw themselves wholeheartedly into these matters with that collective split personality enabling them to concentrate first on the united crusade against discrimination, and later on their internal politicking.

Not that there wasn't a discreet conversation here and there during the day. I was among those elected to the nominating committee, and at lunchtime, Pat and I had a quiet ten minutes in his office.

"Chuck, they're coming on like Gangbusters," said Pat with a smile and a shake of his head. I quoted Bill Whitcomb quoting Napoleon to the effect that "ambition has killed more men than arms."

Pat asked me whether, for the good of the organization, he ought to step down. "God knows I'm ready," Pat said with, for him, a rare display of weariness. "But I can't run out under this Red scare. Only Stoker's not going to like it," he laughed. "Maybe we ought to put Stoker up for first vice, and next year he can have it. To stop all this foolishness."

But his heart wasn't in this either. "Mrs. Cummings should be vice," I said. Pat ruminated. "Yeah, I think so too," he said at last. "They'll nominate Mrs. Cummings for first vice, and let's not oppose her. Then I'll appoint Stoker director of branches or something, and next time they can fight over it."

At three-thirty, the nominating committee was excused from the floor of the convention to hold its meetings. The committee was three to two for Johnson: Bobbye Willie, who was chairperson, Raymond Duke and I voted against Mary Jean Hollis (the North City white woman) and Ben Holter of Mercer. There could be no agreement, and the Stoker pair said they would make a minority report. They were surprised when we didn't put anyone up against Mrs. Cummings. They went out and huddled with Stoker and when they came back, said they would not oppose our candidate for second vice, Mrs. Morley. The issue was drawn.

The voting session took place after dinner. There was an atmosphere to the room, packed with delegates, that was at once thrilling and unhappy.

It was my sixth year at *The Clarion*, and four years had passed since Johnson launched the first steps for a statewide NAACP. Pat Johnson, who had once told me I was not wanted—by the process of working together, striving, hoping, rejoicing, and despairing together, battling and balling together week after week and year after year—Pat had seen my inspirations and my failures, my bursts and enthusiasm, and my remaining weakness and whiteness. He was used to me. Pat and I had come to sit side by side (Attorney Mills was in the chair, because Pat was a candidate), waiting to see whether this organization we loved would endure or would undergo a change, perhaps into something like its opposite.

Ruth Reynolds stopped by and leaned over to Pat; she was brilliantly made up, stunningly dressed, and I thought she was going to kiss him. She whispered something into his ear. Pat turned up his benevolent cupid's face with a shrewd glance, and he said, "Ruth, everything's gonna be all right."

We were looking out at the delegates. There was Cinq, appearing bemused. There was Irene Roberts, with a wise turning down at the corners of her lips. And at the opposite side of the room there was Reverend Bigbee, tensed up in his chair, staring straight ahead.

I turned my head. Attorney Fielding was standing with the Skipper, who was nodding gruffly. They weren't voting delegates; their presence showed power was at stake. Then I saw Abraham Jackson, impeccably groomed, with the glittering smile he wore on public occasions. By contrast, Clarence Bailey was in a knit sport shirt and old pants.

The meeting began, as the saying went, on "C.P. Time" (colored people's). It was forty-three minutes past the scheduled start time when Attorney Mills banged the gavel. Bobbye Willie gave the majority report, and Holter the minority. But what was this? Steve Caron was on his feet. "Mr. Chairman, are seconding speeches in order?"

Mills showed surprise, for the organization was not accustomed to having speeches of any kind at elections, but he quickly recovered, and said in a bass drawl with a polite smile: "Why, certainly, that would be perfectly in order. By all means. The delegate has the floor."

"Mr. Chairman and fellow delegates," said Steve, "I rise to second the nomination of Mr. Stoker. I do so confident in the knowledge that within this assemblage, I won't be discriminated against on the grounds of race, creed, or color." As he said this wryly, the delegates warmed. The members were always proud to show that although whites discriminated against them, they didn't reciprocate. Steve scored again when he acknowledged, "I am highly conscious of being a Johnny-come-lately here tonight. This is the first NAACP state conference to which I have had the honor of being a delegate. Maybe by the time I have finished speaking, this body will decide it should be the last. I believe my wife thinks so now." The delegates laughed and turned to see Kitty, who was hiding her face with her hand.

Steve went on to note that he had been active in the university chapter—another popular point—and said that the North City branch, and Book Stoker in particular, had given the students valuable assistance. I looked questioningly at Pat, and he said *sotto voce* with a shrug, "His son was in school. He went down there and helped them get started. . . . Strong speech," he added.

Then Steve highlighted Stoker's ability: "While never losing sight of the objective, to work harmoniously with all fair-minded groups so as to put the maximum possible gain for integration." This, he declared, was the kind of leadership the state organization needed.

Pat and I exchanged frowns. Steve continued, "I have also the greatest respect for Mr. Stoker's opponent, the incumbent who has held the presidency for four years. As a man and as a leader of the freedom struggle . . ." (he had the acuity not to say "Negro leader"), "Mr. Johnson has few equals. And yet, much as I regret the necessity of raising this—I think is a time to speak frankly—Mr. Johnson's activities in connection with the Progressive Party have tended to alienate many people of whom I have knowledge in this state. It goes without saying that he has every right to choose freely his political course, and I for one honor his courage in doing so, although I don't happen to agree with him. May the day never come when Mr. Johnson or any other citizen of our state can't stand up for the party of his choosing!"

"But what unfortunately had resulted is that the public is confused," Steve said reasonably. "The people are asking whether the NAACP and the Progressive Party are one and the same. Mr. Johnson knows this is not the case, and has never pretended otherwise, and we know it. But we have to make it crystal clear to the people. And that's why, without criticism of the founding president—with all credit to him for a job tremendously well done—I nevertheless urge you to cast your vote for Booker Washington Stoker."

When he sat down, there was a stir. "Long time coming, but it finally got here," Pat said to me. "Real soft shaft, too," I replied. Sid Millstone jumped up asking for the floor. It wasn't like what I had heard of him to make speeches in the NAACP, but I guessed he thought a white could take on a white. He was furious. His nose quivering like a rabbit's, he demanded, "What is all this reviving the ghosts of political parties?"

Walt Rowland spoke next. He calmly limited his talk to an endorsement of Stoker without mentioning Johnson. His quiet words had a shattering effect, because it was unheard of for a man's candidacy to be opposed from within his own branch, among his own friends. One could fairly feel the votes shifting toward Stoker.

For a half-minute it seemed there would be no more speakers. Mills raised his gavel. Then Ruth Reynolds called for the floor. She came down the aisle and turned to face the delegates. I realized I had never seen her so angry. "Now we're being asked to get rid of Pat Johnson, in favor of a man who is harmonious with all groups," she said in cold sarcasm. "I'm not going to say anything about Book Stoker, except if I know what harmonious means, he is it—at least he's about one hundred times as harmonious right this minute as I am. Y'all are here, and I reckon y'all know how you done came to be here. I'll say one thing—it wasn't because Pat Johnson was 'harmonious with all groups.'"

"I have nothing against Mr. Stoker for wanting to be president," she went on. "If that was all there was to it, he might as well be. Maybe he will be some day—I might even vote for him. We need all kinds of colored people."

She paused, and I stole a look at Pat. With his head bent down, he was gazing at her intently. And suddenly, a flood of words poured from her. "What I don't reckon even Mr. Stoker realizes is that he's being used by white folks here today. Here we are, black Negro people—I ought to say niggers, that's what we're best known as—and we're tryin' to build up a little thing of our own. We've done been four years makin' it, without any money, just us, meetin', meetin', meetin'. Drivin' around the state, tryin' to get the Negroes together. Old women, poor old women, are prayin' for us! And we finally got the thing on its feet. The big white folks looked over and said, 'Hey, the niggers done got that little organization goin!'"

She choked, began to cough and Mills got up and took a glass of water to her. But she couldn't drink, her hand was trembling so that the water spilled and she shook her head and thrust it back, saying, "I don't want it." I thought she was going to cry, but instead she shouted in a deeper voice, "Who are these white people that want to elect Mr. Stoker! They came into our branch all at once a few months ago, and what are they doin' there? They're watchin' everything we do, and they're takin' it all back downtown, because who they are, if you want to know, is the Chamber of Commerce! They're the same people that are slum-clearin' the Negroes' houses away from 'em, and keepin' our children in Jim Crow schools, and keepin' Negroes pushin' brooms, and burnin' Donald Dallas Wright in the electric chair because a white woman got killed by her husband! Only these are the young, smiling, pleasant ones that come into our meetings!"

Mills was looking down; Ruth's rage was too strong to face. Many delegates were frowning. All were listening. I caught a glimpse of Steve, studying his hands, "I'm not talkin' against white members, y'all know me better than that," Ruth said, and she whirled and pointed straight at me, shouting, "There's Preston, and he's a Communist! An' what does he do, he comes to our meetings and tells us what the white folks are up to. If he goes into the Chambers of Commerce, he's spyin' on them for us. You go around with him, he never loses a chance to make his point about Negroes—and the white people treat him like one. That's all I've got to say, now let's vote."

Nobody else asked for the floor. It had been brutal for Steve, and I was sorry for him. I felt I ought to protest her contrasting the two of us. I believed he was no more a conscious agent of the "Chamber of Commerce" than I was the fearless crusader she had pictured. Under the circumstances, there wasn't a word I could say.

Pat won the election, forty-five to forty-one. Even so, it was the end of a time in an out-of-the-way place when the road ahead had seemed clear, straightforward, and joyous. No more Victory Editions, People's School Committees, Progressive Parties. The world was not to be overturned just yet. Not that the organization, even though its edge was momentarily blunted, ceased to fight; Johnson's party, to our betterment, discovered that there had been vanity in that fear of ours; that will never be, as long as people called Negroes are persecuted. The next year Pat stepped down, and Ruth was elected for one term. Then Stoker came in and was president for, as I recall, two years. Later, Mrs. Cummings held the office, and still later, Abraham Jackson.

As for Steve Caron, I never heard him say a word about the speech. He and his friends stopped coming to NAACP meetings, although Steve kept up his membership. And the following January, he was named to *The Clarion*'s Honor Roll for his contributions to improving race relations.

PART TWO

To understand Harlem, one must seek the truth and one must dare to accept and understand the truths one does find. One must understand its inconsistencies, its contradictions, its paradoxes, its ironies, its comic and its tragic face, its cruel and its self-destructive forces, and its desperate surge for life. And above all one must understand its humanity.

—KENNETH B. CLARK

18. Sports Mania

The Clarion was in need of a new sports editor, and as had been the case with the NAACP, I was the only candidate available for the job and I moved in.

Those were the years when the freedom movement was taking its giant strides not in legislative halls or factories, not in churches and colleges, but on the baseball diamonds and football gridirons. Our "Negro leader" was Jackie Robinson, and through the gap he had opened in the national pastime, black people could see themselves beginning to move into the national consciousness. It was a revolution in which nothing in particular was at stake—not jobs, not houses, not day-care centers, not citizens' control of police—but a revolution that encompassed it all.

In our state, it might be said that cleanliness was next to godliness, but high school basketball was ahead of both. The ordinary citizen well could have lost hold of life to the point where he was in various stages of indifference to his job, his marriage and family, his church, and his country—but he likely took his hometown's high school basketball team very seriously.

In my new job as sports editor, I was privileged to be a close observer, almost a participant, in this revolution. And as such, I found myself in greater harmony with the men of *The Clarion*, and with thousands of the black masses of whom they were a part, than I had ever been through my civil rights activities. They had always looked on these activities as well meaning but of dubious value. Basketball, on the other hand, was a recognized, legitimate field of battle in which one could demonstrate his manhood fairly and squarely, and the white people would have to come round and accord equality to Negroes without a lot of bickering and trouble. And that, I had come to realize, was exactly what Negroes wanted.

Although white America tended to see the appearance of Negroes in sports as the arrival of Superman (delimited to the physical), in my experience it was not that simple. At the time I came to *The Clarion*, the black youths of the city were languishing; with few exceptions, it was the result of a long period of segregation and neglect. The Dunbar High School teams were strictly nowhere—a fact that both reflected and contributed to the Negro community's status of inferiority. It was from Claudio Tubman, his eyes gleaming with excitement before a game, that I came to understand that the black community, like any other "town," considered Dunbar its standard-bearer in the sports arena. I used to go with Claudio to the odd game and the basketball tournaments, but it was just "home town" reporting: for all the enthusiasm one could work up, and all the cheering the scarlet-and-green-clad girls might lead, it was perennially obvious that Dunbar had a mediocre team, and could count its season a success if it won a single round in the tournament.

What else could be expected? Ever since the black high school's founding, its athletic directors had great difficulty in finding opponents to fill the schedule. The city's white high schools refused to play the Lions. Consequently, the schedule was made up of an odd assortment of teams: either their coaches were old college chums of the Dunbar athletic director, Ephraim Carter, or the coach, Anderson Lancaster; or they were small-town schools in remote regions that also had problems in lining up opposition. There were even religious motives—Carter was a Catholic, and the parochial Memorial High School was the first white school in town to play Dunbar.

For football games, Dunbar, Lincoln High of Mercer, and other Negro teams were sometimes obliged to travel to other states in order to take on other black schools, as far away as Arkansas.

Not only did this rejection deprive the Dunbar players of competition with their peers under decent conditions, but every one of these transcontinental wanderings, and every game with Smallsville or Dart's Crossing, was, in itself, a humiliation. Under such conditions of second-class sportsmanship, the Dunbar teams were beaten before they began, and the season was a matter of going through the motions. An air of inconsequence hung heavy over the school's gymnasium, and even the coach, as he offered perfunctory congratulations to his conquering opponent in the tournament, gave a sigh of relief that another year was over.

Dunbar's perennial defeat aroused contempt in white fans of the game and, among the more liberal, an odd sort of pity. Dunbar was looked on in much the same way as the State School for the Deaf, as a group of handicapped youths who deserved polite cheers for their efforts. In fact, the High School Athletic Association (HSAA)—a self-constituted organization (like the Public Schools Committee) that controlled the games and conducted the annual tournament—at first had excluded the four Negro schools in the state, along with the Catholics and the Deaf School. It had taken a hard campaign, in which I was told the Skipper was a leading figure, to get them all in. The Association leaders had resisted until Senator Bancroft introduced a bill in the legislature to place all high school athletics under the State Department of Public Instruction. This was regarded as a desperate remedy, because it meant putting the unimportant (politician-educators) in charge of the all-important (basketball). It posed sufficient threat to cause the HSAA to admit the outlaw schools. Senator Bancroft, who had no desire to rip apart the state's very way of life, but only wished to be included in it, then withdrew the bill.

By this dispensation, any of the white schools that desired to play Dunbar, or the School for the Deaf, could do so without itself being cast out of the Association. It was like Anatole France's right of the rich to sleep under the bridge.

Dunbar continued in the doldrums into my time as sports editor. True, there were signs that something was happening among the young Negroes. The Lions, who now played one or two city schools in addition to Memorial, could give you a good game before they lost. The last year he coached, Lancaster had a noticeably sprightlier collection of players who actually won two games in the tournament.

It was the following year that John Elliott came to *The Clarion*. John was a sable-skinned young man from a poor family—the Talbott women never ceased to "signify" the hue of his skin as well as his father's delinquency—and he was intelligent, capable, and full of drive. He was working as a general reporter, but toward January he went on his own to see Dunbar play.

"Pres, you're missing something," John told me the next Monday morning.

"How so?"

"Dunbar. They're out of this world." He then described a team that he said was fantastically skillful, and bound to win at least the Sectional stage of the tournament.

I nodded. I had heard hometown basketball patriotism since my own high school years. But I attended the next game, and came away a believer. Soon the daily sports writers, too, were taking notice.

A conjunction of developments had brought a new and wondrous thing into being. Lancaster, tired out with the years of losing, had been reassigned as a physical education teacher. His place as Dunbar's coach had been given to Paul James, a suave, younger man, who had been a college star and semi-pro basketball major. He led by example: he could do it himself and showed his team how to play. The boys idolized him.

James had been coaching in a black junior high school, and had moved up to be Dunbar's freshman coach the previous year. Moving along with him were several of his players, a new breed of Negro youngsters who seemed suddenly to have caught fire in sports. Two of these were to make instant basketball history: Willie Hempstead, a coal-black stripling of six-foot-six, who at the age of sixteen handled the ball like a professional, and Hallie Thomas, a lissome guard who possessed moves and shots our basketball-crazy state had never seen.

From the vital standpoint of height alone, the Winged Lions, as they were soon dubbed to distinguish them from their predecessors, were phenomenal. At forward, Hempstead (though six-foot-six, he was usually described as six-foot-seven and sometimes up to six-foot-nine, but when he was called for the Army draft, I got a tape measure and found he was six-foot-five and a half) and John Harding six-foot-four; at center, Bob Garnett, six-foot-five; at guards, Thomas, six-foot-two, and a couple of six-footers who alternated, "Tee" Taliaferro and Bennie Baker. Sitting on the bench was a six-foot-two forward, DeJuain Mann. And for contrast, there was a little sophomore named Bailey Bentley—another of James' boys—who was a deadeye shot.

Youths of this size, even without ability, would have given the opposition plenty to worry about. But these were graceful, superb ball-handlers, who could perform Harlem Globetrotters tricks, and they were excellent shots. They had a way of doing things with extra fillips and in contempt for established procedures, which demonstrated their utter mastery of the sport. Harding, for instance, who might have been expected to use his rugged height to grab rebounds under the basket, specialized in shots from far out on the floor. Thomas fired his long shots flat-footed, which was the hard way, as if he could afford to give himself a handicap. Hempstead, or "Dill" (or "Deal") as he was nicknamed, was the first high school player in our city to "stuff" a shot, that is, to leap up with his hands above the basket and ram the ball forcibly down through it. Then Garnett and Harding began doing it in the warm-up drills before the game. Sometimes the players of the opposing team, instead of concentrating on their own drills, would turn and watch the Lions in fascination. Their coaches would upbraid them for this; it was now they who were defeated before the start.

Dunbar won all its games but one that season; Wells High School managed to catch the Lions on a cold night. The city had cynically built the Dunbar gymnasium with a tiny spectator section by prevailing standards, and it had always proved ample until now. The interest among fans of both colors became so great that Dunbar took to renting other high school gymnasiums for its home games, and finally Carlton field house itself.

The tournament came at last. The countrywide Sectional round started with sixteen teams and proceeded by elimination of the losing team in each game, until the last two played for the Sectional championship. Thus, you had to win four games in a row, over the space of three or four days, to become champion. The same thing was going on at sixty-three other Sectional centers, although not all had sixteen teams. Every one of the 765 high schools in the state, from the smallest to the largest, was entered in the grand design. Was this the American Dream pathetically expressing itself in the "nothingness" of sports?

It is beyond my powers adequately to describe the excitement—aptly called "Hardwood Hysteria"—with which the public became involved in this affair of schoolboys. My mother once joked that Hitler took over Czechoslovakia in March because the eyes of the world were on the state basketball tournament. From bankers to ditch diggers, the whole nation turned its frenzied attention to the tournament. All the seats in Carlton field house and the other gymnasiums were sold out in advance; indeed, measures had to be taken to reserve a number of them for the high school students, lest adults grab them all. Among the adults in the communities, season ticket holders were usually honored first, or a town-wide lottery might be held, and "politics" of various kinds played their part. It was a mark of status to attend the tournament. The institution of "scalping"—mostly with students selling their seats to adults at inflated prices—was a perennial problem.

Meanwhile, the rest of the populace was glued to its radios, with all stations broadcasting play-by-play accounts, or to its television sets for the climactic games. I don't mean just the sports fans, but the entire population, including old ladies in nursing homes. Every listener was highly partisan. "Who are you for?" was a universal question. The listener would shriek with joy when "his" team scored, groan and curse when the opposition tallied, and challenge the calls of the referees, often booing them, despite the fact he was listening to radio and couldn't see the play.

"There he goes again, the son of a bitch, every time we start a rally he blows his damn whistle!"

"How in hell do you know, you ain't there, for Christ's sake!"

"Yeah, I've seen the bastard work before, that's the way he is. He ain't only no good, he's crooked. They hadn't ought to assign him to the tournament. Boo!"

"Yeah, well, I think it was a good call, because that team's always fouling, it's the dirtiest team in the state. They ought to put 'em out of the Association. Hurray!"

Into this maelstrom of primal emotions came the black team, for the first time a factor, and even the betting favorite. They were bigger than "our" boys, and much better too. Dunbar had a new song, strongly rhythmical, the beat accented by clapping hands, which resounded through the field house packed with fourteen thousand sports lunatics.

> Oh, Wells is rough,
> And Wells is tou-ough;
> They can beat everybody,
> But they can't beat us.
> Hi-de-hi-de-hi-de-hi,
> Hi-de-hi-de-hi-de-ho-o,
> Oh, skip bop beat 'em,
> That's the Crazy Song.

The sound was massive and irresistibly exciting. Sitting in the press box and frantically scribbling notes, I would stop a moment to join the singing and hand clapping.

> Oh, they scored some points
> Right over that li-ine
> But we never did mi-ind—
> They were so far behind.
> Hi-de-hi-de-hi-de-hi. . . .

The Winged Lions soared through the four games, getting revenge over Wells in the process, to win the Sectional. It was an undreamed-of thing, the world turned upside down. While it was happening, the bulk of the white people were against Dunbar on racial grounds, but by no means all. The liberals and the underdog backers came out of their holes and cheered, and they were joined by numbers of sportsmen who knew a good team when they saw it. At *The Clarion*, we heard funny stories from among the common white people, like the elderly woman who said, as she settled before her television, "I just love those nigger-babies!"

Walt Evers reported a white man listening to the radio who became incensed at the call of a foul and shouted, "Goddamn it, it ain't fair! He just called that on him because he's a nigger!"

It seemed, the beginnings of a new interracial consciousness, far more profound than anything protest and politics had been able to bring about, was being assembled.

On the other hand, there was a character who sat beside me in the complimentary seats and kept yelling, "Get that black boy! Stop that nigger!" and so forth, until I leaned over and told him off. He had a red face and boozy breath. A young white man leaned from the other side and said to him, "And that goes for me too, Buster!"

The Negroes were in seventh heaven. When it became apparent that Dunbar would win, girls fainted and adults wept. I remember one fat black man, his face transfigured, who cried out to some glum white people around him, "Why don't y'all yell for me—I'd yell for y'all if y'all was in it!"

At the end, the white fans largely behaved with sportsmanship, or at least a semblance of it; many found their hearts conquered and became Dunbar fans. The tournament and city authorities saw to it that the rites and ceremonies belonging to a champion were scrupulously afforded to Dunbar. Trophies were presented, and a ladder was brought onto the court so the players could cut down the nets and wear pieces of them draped around their shoulders while the television men interviewed them. Next was a ride for the team on a city fire engine to Monument Square, a trip around it the wrong way (traffic-wise), and a huge victory rally in the heart of the city. Ominous forebodings had been rather widely expressed during the previous week,

usually in the formula, "If they win, there'll be no holding 'em," but as
it turned out there was nothing to "hold" but "their" joy. A good number of white people took part in the celebration, mingling in the crowd
and joining in singing "The Crazy Song." It was a novel situation for
the police, who found themselves at midnight with thousands of
"niggers" yelling and no reason to arrest any of them. They, too, were
infected by the general spirit.

During the next three weeks, while the higher stages of the tournament were being played, an aura of racial benevolence settled over the
city. The mayor led the way, with an appearance at a rally in Dunbar
High School auditorium in which he proclaimed that the entire city was
backing the Lions in their quest for the state title. As it happened, no
school from our city had won the crown in almost forty years of the tournament's existence; now "we" had a good chance. The red-hot basketball fans dropped their prejudices, in Emerson's phrase, like Jacob his
cloak in the hands of the harlot. In fact, they got into arguments in which
they reproved people mercilessly for raising the color question. The
downtown store windows were festooned in scarlet and green, and the
Lions, looking unfamiliar in their Sunday suits, were guests of honor at
civic club luncheons. The daily newspapers published editorials con-
gratulating Dunbar and embracing the Winged Lions as their own. The
daily sportswriters, some of whom had been snide before the Sectional,
now pounded out reams of copy glorifying the Dunbar team and claim-
ing that they had been the first to recognize it. *The Clarion*, with its one
issue a week, was left somewhat in the shade.

Sixty-four teams were still alive in the tournament. The next
Saturday was the Regional round, a competition of four-team tourneys
at sixteen centers. It brought Winette's powerful team to the Field
House, and two smaller schools that had won the Sectionals in rural
counties. The Winged Lions and the Winette Chiefs dumped the
small fry in afternoon games and then played for the Regional championship at night. I was in a peculiar position, because it was my alma
mater versus my adopted alma mater. I found there was no doubt that
I was "for" Dunbar, but, at the same time, I couldn't quite get up the
requisite hostility toward Winette.

The Chiefs proved to be of championship caliber, faster and with more drive than anyone the Lions had met hitherto. The game was a screaming rollercoaster from beginning to end, with first one side and then the other taking the lead. Dunbar at one point was ahead by twelve, but Winette surged back for a fifteen-point advantage. But here came the Lions again. As the scoreboard clock, with its electrically lighted figures, went into the closing minutes, the lead flipped back and forth on a one- or two-point margin. A call for his fifth foul sent Garnett to the bench and he was replaced by Bailey Bentley.

Winette was leading 80–79, with three seconds to go, and Dunbar had the ball out of bounds. The pass went to little Bentley, far in the corner. He put up a one-handed shot that hit the backboard just over the goal. The buzzer sounded to end the game as the ball dropped through the net. It was victory for Dunbar!

Dick Nelson took a photo of that scoreboard, shining forth "81–80," and we published it in the next *Clarion*. I think some of us will go to our graves with those figures in our eyes.

There were now sixteen teams left in the running. Elliott and Walt Evers and I were thoroughly convinced Dunbar was the best of all, but anything could happen. Most of the black community was living in a fever. I remember how odd it struck me when a filling-station attendant, an old man who obviously wasn't with it, said in answer to a cheery observation of mine, "No, I reckon Saturday is about the farthest they'll go. That's farther'n they usually goes."

They went through Saturday handily, defeating two more opponents with ease, in contrast to the grueling Winette game. That brought them to the Round of Four, the very pinnacle of prestige. An atmosphere of reverence settled over the scene. Walt Evers heard that the principal of Dunbar, Dr. Rhodes, gathered the team and lectured them: "Now boys, the whole state will be watching you. You must conduct yourselves like gentlemen, and reflect credit on Dunbar High School and the Negro race. I don't want to see any sassing of the referee, or unsportsmanlike actions toward the other team. And another thing, be sure to take a shower before the game" he looked dubiously at the coach, "or the night before. Be sure you are clean, and get your hair cut, and put deodorant under your arms."

It wasn't Walt's idea of a preparation for victory. "Old fool!" he said, and never forgave him.

Dunbar's afternoon opponent was Fields of Elliottsville, a good team—all the "Final Foursome" were good—but not, in general consideration, up to the standard of the Winged Lions. But the Lions didn't get off the ground that day. After ten minutes, they were slipping behind. There was something about the Fields' coach, while scouting Dunbar, having discovered a fatal flaw; at any rate, a short, husky guard kept driving down the center, while our boys were too much in the corners. Or, was it the grandeur and solemnity of the occasion, with Dr. Rhodes' talk on top of it? Harding, who was older and maybe less impressionable than some of the others, kept firing his "bombs" from outside, and Willie Hempstead made a good showing under the basket. But the team fell apart. Taliaferro, for instance, a notoriously poor shooter (he actually had poor vision; I once heard a young fan yell at him, "Get some backboard, man! If you can't score, at least get some backboard!"), took great long shots instead of passing the ball to sharp-eyed Thomas, who was open and calling for it.

With two minutes to go and Dunbar twelve points down, James conceded defeat by putting in the reserves so they could have the thrill of playing in the Round of Four. After that game and after he had gone with the boys to the dressing room, James came back smiling and took a seat in the stands to watch the next game. It was a gallant gesture I hadn't seen many white coaches make.

Though the dream bubble had burst, a tremendous amount had been achieved. The black team had risen to the very top rank of basketball, with all that that carried with it, and was to remain there for years. With Hempstead, Thomas, and Bentley having two more years in school, it seemed a foregone conclusion that Dunbar was the team to watch in the future. As it happened, those particular boys never got back to the Final Foursome, but the second-class years were over. Now every school wanted to play Dunbar—for a good game and to sell all the seats in the gymnasium.

19. All Around the Sports Beat

Taking up sports was like my coming to *The Clarion* had been in the first place: a whole new world opened before me. I made it my goal to publicize the exploits of every black athlete in the city or who came to play in the city. It was a big order, and it kept me busy. The state tournament ended always on the Saturday nearest March 21. The next day was spring, and the high schools turned to track and field, as well as to baseball, tennis, and golf. I concentrated on track, in which Dunbar usually had a fairly good team, and in which tan athletes around the state figured prominently. Mercer Lincoln won the state championship five times and Mercer Hamilton, which was largely Negro, three times.

Meanwhile, the professional baseball season opened in April. The Braves, our city's entry in the American Association, the top minor league, acquired their first Negro players in the early 1950s. From then on, I covered them regularly, often taking Michael with me as he grew into the baseball years. We watched stars who were down from the majors such as Luke Easter and Harry Simpson, and youngsters on their way up like Willie Mays, at the time a Minneapolis center fielder who was hitting for an average of .551.

The only player I got to know at all well was Dave King, who rented a house a few doors from us. Unlike many ball players, he was a modest, almost morose, family man. He was black as the coal he told me his father had mined. Dave was with the Braves three seasons, and was their top slugger, but he was a little small for a major league outfielder. He was also a little old, especially by the time he was called up to Chicago. He injured himself crashing into the right field fence his second week there and was sent back to the Braves on the way down, with the sands of his time running. I used to reflect that if baseball had ended Jim Crow sooner he would have had his shot. And I wondered, what does a black ex-ball player, who hasn't made the big money, do with the rest of his life? It was Smitty Smith who rebuked me: "I can't get sorry for athletes—what do most black men do?"

Negroes had always patronized the Braves, even when they were lily-white. They now did so in somewhat greater numbers, but they didn't turn out in mass unless somebody famous like Easter was appearing. The Braves' management used to hover on the verge of complaining about this, but I said I knew of no law of gratitude that compelled a man to go to a ball game. The club was reaping the harvest of a half-century of discrimination, and with its all-white staff hadn't found the knack of pleasing the Negro fans. Even so, Mr. Talbott felt that support of the integrated club was a proper civic duty for *The Clarion*, and might even improve its image among the ever-elusive advertisers. Not that he had any illusions about the management, which had played him a particularly rotten trick in connection with the baseball clinic for boys held annually at Liberty Field. *The Clarion* had sponsored the first clinic, and it was an outstanding success. The next year the Braves' management took it away from *The Clarion* and gave it to the daily *Tribune*. Mr. Talbott got angry and talked in a loud voice every time he thought of it.

Something of what was missing in the Braves' approach to black fans became clear during the summer, when the Braves were on the road and a night of Negro baseball came to Liberty Field. This would be the Kansas City Monarchs versus the Birmingham Black Barons, or other touring clubs, with two or three clowns for entertainment. I must admit that for a long time I was hostile to this event, thinking it smacked of Nigger Night. The teams, highly touted by their promoters, usually displayed a flashy but ragged brand of baseball, committing frequent errors. Partly this was due to their condition, traveling by bus sometimes several hundred miles between games. By this time, I reflected, the great days of Negro baseball were over, with the talented young players already picked up by "organized baseball." Some of the fellows in these games were too old—not a little too old like Dave King, but much too old. Overall, it was a garish atmosphere of alcoholic hilarity that I didn't think accorded with the sedate sport of baseball.

But the fans, almost all black (except when whites came to see Satchel Paige pitch three innings), turned out by the thousands—far more than the gate at most of the Braves' games. As was the case with so many things during my life in the black community, I hung around and appreciated what was going on: a community festival of baseball, very near in spirit to what the town games must have been in my father's youth, before the sport was totally professionalized. Then I discovered that, when viewed with a friendly rather than a hostile eye, the baseball didn't seem so bad either; or rather, mixed in with the over-the-hills were a number of gifted youngsters who could be the Jackie Robinsons and Willie Mays of tomorrow. Major league scouts in the stands were probably seeing more of this potential than I.

The truth was, I supposed, that like everything segregated it was almost impossible to judge. The men at *The Clarion* held as a tenet of faith that in their prime, old-time black stars such as Paige and Josh Gibson had been fully worthy to rank with white immortals like Ty Cobb and Babe Ruth. "Organized baseball" is finally saying the same thing by starting to admit these men to the Hall of Fame, albeit in a Jim Crow corner.

The Clarion also covered as best it could, although not in the sense of supporting them, the annual automobile races. Since there were no Negro drivers, it might be thought there was nothing to write about, but where there are black people, there is black news. And wherever there are crowds of people in America, there are black people.

In the first place, the very absence of tan drivers was something to write about. We started off protesting on principle. Then I got into it deeper, discovered that the problem was the exclusion of Negroes from the lower ranks of auto racing—it took years to prepare a driver for our town's races—and learned who were some of the black men in the United States who were making a try of it. We revived the legend of one sepia speedster who, according to legend, had almost made it, or at least had gotten higher up the ladder than anyone else. From the drivers, we worked down to the pit crews and mechanics, where there might be a Negro or two. If there wasn't, we asked the race management why.

With a similar purpose, each year before the Kentucky Derby I ran a story about Isaac Murphy, who rode winners in 1884, 1890, and 1891, and other Negroes who were victorious before the Jim Crow barriers on jockeys were lowered at the turn of the century.

In connection with the auto races, besides the out-of-town visitors in the stands, there were black high school bands and other participants in the parade, and there was Negro society folderol paralleling that of the whites. Among the events ancillary to the races was a tournament that brought in the Professional Golfers Association. On the tour was the lone aging black pioneer of golf, Charlie Sifford.

I interviewed Sifford every year, in the private Negro home where he was staying, in contrast to the white pros and their elegant hotels. Chewing his cigar, he struck me as a man who had cut out for himself an almost superhuman assignment. You could see that he had the authentic fire, and his scores were in the pro class; but he was bone-tired. He told me the story of his career, starting as a caddy in Georgia, and also explained the endorsement of balls, clubs, and other equipment that the professionals depended on for a good part of their income. Sifford had some endorsements, but not so many and none so lucrative as the glamorous white stars. He complained that Negro golfers weren't holding up his hand by buying the equipment. *The Clarion* gave him what help we could by publicizing this situation.

Otherwise, Sifford had to win prize money, and he wasn't good enough to be certain of a proper income but was too good to quit. He must have faced discrimination and hostility everywhere he went, but I could hardly get him to speak of that; he preferred to dwell on the newly occurring examples of fair treatment in tournaments in the Middle South. I couldn't tell whether that was his nature or he thought it prudent for a "pioneer" to avoid racial controversy. He would turn the subject aside to the lumbago or similar ailment that had struck him.

The Clarion also reported on the Negro golf associations that had been built on the basis of exclusion by the whites. These included the national United Golfers Association and, in our city, the Washington Golf Club. In every sport, as in other aspects of life, the black people had established parallel groups of this kind, with tournaments, national championships, and even country clubs near the larger cities. In tennis we had the Capital City Tennis Club.

There were a few other standing sports events in the summer (in addition to the big boxing matches that came along infrequently). In mid-June there were the Muffin House Games, a day of track-and-field competition for the younger boys and girls from the city playgrounds. It was held on Dunbar's poorly maintained athletic field, and seemed to me all in all a dreary affair: I thought it was conducted more for the prestige of Muffin House than the enjoyment of the children. At any rate, it was a chance to put lots of youngsters' names and pictures into the paper, and so we covered the games and didn't charge Muffin House for the photos, although Mr. Talbott would have liked to. Another thing the event had going for it was that, for some reason, Negro girls of a certain age were more involved than boys in track, and this was one time in the year when they could get on the sports page.

A little later in June came a pair of All Star Basketball Games in which the outstanding graduating seniors from our state met a team from the neighboring state to the south. These events were played at the Carlton field house in extreme heat and humidity. (At the other end, they had air-conditioning.) The games were the grand and glorious finale of the basketball year, and the state once again rallied its forces.

It was my habit then to judge everything by a single yardstick—how it affected the "race question"—and at this the All-Star Games came off pretty well. In the year of the Dunbar "Big Team," Bob Garnett was named to the squad and comported himself well in the games; in the following years, the lineup always included a player or two from Dunbar, as well as other Negro boys from around the state and several on the other state's team. Early in the series, I had feared we were going to have trouble with our Southern neighbors, but it wasn't too long until they were embarrassing us by integrating faster than we were. A "Star of Stars" was chosen by the sportswriters covering each game; on only one occasion did I feel that a sepia player— my friend Jumpin' Jack Hudson of Winette—was "robbed" of this award on color grounds, and that took place in our city, as our writers fell all over themselves trying to be nice to the South. Otherwise, I thought the writers were scrupulously fair. In 1953, Hallie Thomas, in a game played on the enemy's territory, carried off a last-second one-man play to defeat the home team and was overwhelmingly voted the kudos. Later it went hands down in both games of the series to the incomparable Oscar Bentley of Dunbar.

Thus while church, state, business, and labor fumbled at the challenge of desegregation, two dozen youths on basketball courts, with a number of underpaid hack writers in sports shirts, were achieving it without looking twice, from the Great Lakes to far below the Mason-Dixon line. The black community's adoption of the basketball way of life gave rise to a unique sporting event, the Johnson Dust Bowl Tournament. This meet took place each August on the outdoor basketball court of the James Weldon Johnson Homes, a large housing project lying west of the Avenue. Regular and pickup teams from throughout the city and state would participate, and the fame of the event began to spread even as far as Chicago. The players were a scrambled collection of high school stars, a few college players, sometimes a pro or two, and neighborhood youths who weren't on the high school team. The teams were white and interracial, as well as all-black. Such a mixture must have horrified the HSAA officials, but I think for once they chose to look the other way, out of a curious mélange of motives including not wanting to tackle Darktown.

That was the spirit of the Dust Bowl. There were youths who, for one reason or another, had missed the guiding hands of Coach James and everybody else, and yet had blossomed into fine basketball players in the alleyways of the projects. They got their day at the Dust Bowl. There was one youth who was known as Bo-Diddley, a great favorite at the Dust Bowl. He didn't go to school, and God knows how he lived in the streets. He would take off with his self-perfected shuffle and his incredible faking shots and match them point for point.

The crowd loved Bo-Diddley and the other alley players who kept up with the stars. It proved something deep in their hearts. There was quite an audience at the Dust Bowl tournament, made up of older residents of the projects, as well as the young fans. The tournament was managed by Lieutenant Sam Hicks, the Police Athletic League's officer-in-charge. He borrowed folding chairs from Negro funeral homes, and they were placed around the court. Since it was a city playground, admission was free (although a hat was passed), and the people came and took seats and watched the games all day long, fanning themselves or shielding their heads from the sun with handkerchiefs. The court had lights, and play went on into the evening hours.

Some fortunate residents could watch the tourney through the windows of their apartments. Robert Hancock was one of these; he was then living (he was later expelled for earning too high wages) in a building not fifty yards from the basketball court. One day when I was reporting the tournament, I went to see him, and he graciously invited me into the kitchen where we sat, with cool drinks, on stools and watched the players running back and forth.

For sheer quality of the game, I found that the Dust Bowl left the HSAA's annual extravaganza in the shade. There was more genuine appreciation of skill; as at a first-rate tennis match, the spectatorship was both more expert and more sociable.

After Labor Day, the football season opened. Ours was not a football town, and Dunbar emphatically was not a football school. Even the students didn't attend the games in any numbers. I did it in the line of duty. I was rewarded one year when Ephraim Carter, who was the football coach, came up with a four-star backfield that enabled the Lions to win all but one of their games, but it was back to normal the following year. It seemed so futile, and was so expensive. Now and then a boy was seriously injured, so that finally I wrote a column advocating that some unnamed schools should substitute soccer for football. I had seen a couple of soccer games and thought I had some points, but that campaign fell flatter than Dunbar football.

Black players on the other high school teams, and so their games, had to be reported. In fact, both Steel High School, in the south side slums, and Northridge, the erstwhile elite school into whose district Negroes were flooding, soon fielded predominantly black teams. Nor could Vo-Tech on the east side or Jefferson in Stilesville be ignored. This rapid dispersal of *The Clarion*'s constituency kept me very busy as the one-man sports desk. I was tearing out to two or three high school games a week, plus a college game on Saturday afternoon, and, in later years, a pro game at Liberty Field on Sunday night.

I was also still reporting on the meetings of the NAACP, sundry other civil rights organizations and committees, as well as occasionally the City Council, School Board, and other public bodies. It left me little time to ruminate on where it was all carrying me and my family. I only knew that I was happy, and I supposed it would last forever. Susan and I led a quiet social life, what used to be called a "movement life." We kept up with the foreign movies and a few radicals and old friends. We never got into the black social whirl.

We were no longer, at that time, quite so poor. Mr. Talbott had given me a small raise, and with the adding on of overtime for all the games and meetings, my weekly envelope was beginning to contain sixty-five or seventy dollars. Susan was making eighty-five, and there were always the two rents from 3006.

At the same time, something came along that increased my cost of living.

20. Deal Those Cards

> I'm a bettin' man
> From a bettin' land
> With my bettin' money
> In my bettin' hand.
> —GEORGE WEYHOUSE

I don't recall just when or how Lehman Scott started the great four-year poker game. I know it was the smartest thing he ever did, enabling him to double his income. Which made it only proper that it was the most expensive for the rest of us at *The Clarion.*

Many years before, when I was a young white man fresh from Winette, my first experience with Illinois Avenue had been in connection with gambling. Late one Saturday night, two white friends and I, made bold by liquor, had decided to try our luck in an Avenue crap game. We found one in the back room of a store, but then the difficulty that developed was in getting away. The oldest of us, a man named Bertie Smith, ran into a streak where he couldn't lose. With every throw of the dice, he raked in more money. We were three whites in the company of a dozen blacks who were growing hostile; we couldn't leave until Bertie got rid of his winnings, or at least reduced them, but luck clung to him like an unwanted fever. We were finally saved by a police raid. The white cops questioned us as to what we were doing "down here," and then made us walk off in three different directions. In the excitement, Bertie's stack of bills disappeared, and from the vantage of experience, I would guess the cops split it with the house.

In *The Clarion* game, winning was not my difficulty. The poker game was played every Thursday night, after the forms went to the printer, on one of the sawhorse tables in the newsroom. There would be five to eight men in the play at any time. The game was five-card stud, nothing wild but the players. White chips were a nickel, red a dime, and blue a quarter; there was a blue chip limit on a bet or raise. It was a friendly game, but you could lose your week's pay. Lehman was the banker, and I can see him now, shuffling the cards loosely, wearing a smile from which he tried his best to erase the traces of the fox in the poultry house.

It is easier to list who didn't take part in the game than who did. Mr. Talbott and George Lewis never played, because they were management and also because Mr. Talbott's mother was sternly opposed to all forms of gambling on religious grounds. Robert Hancock would stand watching the game but rarely joined in; St. John Ashley and Harry Martin also didn't indulge.

The regulars, besides Lehman, were Smitty, Bill Whitcomb, Walt Evers, George Weyhouse, Pierce, Brown, and myself. Mike Gale often came in off the street, but "outside" players were discouraged. "Senator" Johnson, during the period he was with *The Clarion*, sat in from time to time. Robert Morgan once in a moon got into the game, took some losses, and got out. Bill Baxter, in a hurry because he was circulation manager and soon would have duties with the carriers, could be depended on to drop—or just possibly, win—a large amount in the hour or so before the papers arrived.

Lehman deals the cards, one face down to each player, one face up. Bill Baxter, with the king of clubs showing, is high man and says, "Shit; Kings open for a white. I'm gonna build me a pot."

"I'll see one card," says Walt, tossing in a chip. George Weyhouse folds, chewing on his toothpick. George Brown, slightly drunk and with a jack up, leers at Baxter. "Hell, man, you ain't got kings," he says.

"Only cost you a white to stay around and maybe you'll find out," says Baxter primly. "C'mon, stay in, help build me a pot."

"Shit, I'm gonna find out right now!" says Brown. "Red up."

"All right," thunders Baxter, and taking a red and a blue chip from his store, makes as if to raise the bet, but then says, "Oh, it ain't my turn. Excuse me."

"I'll see," declares Pierce, putting in his white and red. He has a ten-spot showing.

I also ride along, and Bill Whitcomb, with the five of clubs up, says, "A bunch of goddamned hustlers. I ought to raise it a blue because I've got the best goddamned hand right now. Well, I'll just see, and when I hit this other ace you'll all be cryin'."

Lehman stays in with the seven of spades. It is Baxter's turn, and he again takes a blue chip in his hand, but then says, "Let it go around one more time."

On the next card, nobody improves and Baxter, still showing high, bets a red. Evers stays, but Brown throws in his jack. "No indeedy!" says Pierce. "There's somethin' goin' on. I have nothing and also give up."

"I'm still bound to hit this ace in the hole," says Whitcomb, staying. Lehman looks at his hole card, meets the bet and Evers says, "Goddamn! Lehman's got a pair!"

"Shit!" says Lehman. "I'm tryin' to fill a straight. I shoulda been gone long ago."

"You shit!" says Evers, and Lehman retorts, drawing it out in a way that had become a byword, "Shi-i-it!"

On his fourth card, Whitcomb gets his ace, "Gawddamn!" he says, but Lehman has a pair of sevens. "Well, let's shake out the shoe clerks," he says. "I'll bet a blue."

Without hesitating, Baxter cries, "Give up!" He looks Lehman straight in the eyes, and adds, "Shoe clerk yourself." They exchange a smile. "Shi-i-it," says Lehman.

"Lemme outta here," says Walt, throwing in his hand. Bill Whitcomb jumps to his feet. "Now I warned y'all," he shouts, "I ain't afraid of no kings, and no measly pair o' sevens. I done warned y'all and now y'all got to pay. Blue up!"

"Blue up?" says Lehman. "You tryin' to rough the game?" But he stays, tossing in the two blue chips it costs him.

Baxter also stays, and on the last card, he gets a pair of fives showing, with his king and a four. He hums and Lehman, who must bet first because of his pair of sevens, stares at him. "Looks like you got kings and fives," says Lehman, unblinking.

Baxter picks two blue chips off his stack and holds them in readiness. "Looks like it," he says.

"Two pairs," says Lehman, still staring at Baxter. He bends up the corner of his hole card, peeks at it and goes on, "Maybe I don't believe it."

"That's your business," says Baxter, grinning widely.

"Well, I ought to bet a blue," says Lehman. "I have the best hand showing." He holds out the chip but doesn't let go of it. "Huh?" he says to Baxter.

Pierce looks at me knowingly and, shaking his head, walks away as one would from an execution.

Lehman lets his chip fall on the table, and Baxter immediately yells, "Blue up!" But Whitcomb says, "You done reckoned without the host. Blue up on you!"

There is a nice pile of blue chips in the pot. And now Lehman, who has two sevens, the queen of hearts, and a trey showing, says quietly, "Blue up."

"Whooee!" cry those who are out of it, and George Brown walks across the room and kicks a table leg.

Baxter, although he had only the pair of fives to his name and was beaten on the board by Lehman's sevens, was quite capable of bluffing Whitcomb, whose good luck was overpowering. It might become one of the famous pots. But let's just say Baxter threw in, and Whitcomb called. It was then Lehman turned over his third seven. It was a "mortal." Anyone who knew Lehman's style of play should have known it was in all probability a mortal. Pierce and Brown, out of the hand, had known it. But Bill Whitcomb, jumping to his feet again after the showdown, and spitting repeatedly in the direction of the gas heater, couldn't contain himself. "Gawddamn it, I don't know what it takes to win in this Gawddamn game! You see that? I hit aces, and they don't win! There's something wrong with my luck! Gawddamn it, shoulda run you out on the second damned card! I ain't gonna let you motherfuckers hang around for a dime no more, that's what I'll do! You watch me from now on!"

"Shi-i-it!" said Lehman, but softly and with a smile. He wasn't one to rub it in on Bill. He wanted to keep the game together. "Deal the cards," said Bill Baxter, in the deepest register of his bass.

Lehman did his share (the winner's share) of losing pots, and particularly of getting out when he didn't have the cards. Evers, on the other hand, was usually a "stayer" and a "plunger." With Baxter, it sometimes seemed a downright compulsion to see every card and raise every bet, so that he could lose thirty dollars in half an hour. At the other end of the table, Pierce also would bet rather recklessly while he lasted, but after he had lost about ten dollars might drop out for the evening. I had the feeling Betty had talked him out of it.

I imagined most of the men had talked it over, so to speak, with their wives, for, of course, they could ill afford to lose these sizeable sums out of their meager pay. I looked with horror on Bill Whitcomb's large losses week after week. I knew that Mr. Talbott, although he said nothing against the game, was unhappy about its effects on Bill. But the quick financial blotting out of Smitty, for instance, was a matter of indifference—Smitty was due to be blotted out somehow shortly after payday, and he had no wife and dog (it was the Whitcombs' surrogate for a child) to bear the brunt of it.

Except for Pierce, the players were in no way slowed, however, by such considerations. In the great poker game, the black man gambled gloriously, defying fate without a qualm, and then taking his pain at the end without a whimper. Nobody was going to put him into the class of second-rate bettors!

Lehman alone respected the percentages, threw in poor hands early, bet high on good hands, and above all played the psychology of his opponents. I didn't know where he had learned the game, but he had the temperament for it. His attitude toward the "wild bulls" was altogether that of the pawnbroker three doors south of *The Clarion*. And he had no difficulty, either, with my WASP brand of playing too close to the chest; it only took a different way of setting me up to knock me down. It was this that led to the only instance of violence in the poker game, and who do you suppose was guilty?

I had been keeping a balance sheet in a little black notebook—not a very good idea, if you're going to play poker in the first place. I was some $350 behind the game, and I was brooding about it. I wouldn't have wanted to be ahead, but—I said to myself—there was the family. I felt guilty. On this particular night, I was down twenty dollars by the time it turned midnight. I was in a showdown with Lehman, and he was needling me.

"Look out, Pres, you're gonna have to sell back that new house," said Lehman.

I had a pair of jacks. Lehman had a king showing. Did he yet again have a king in the hole to beat me? Or, if I quit to preserve my dwindling pile of chips, would he "carelessly" flip over a three-spot and let me know I'd been had?

Lehman bet a blue chip, and it was up to me to call or fold.

"Take my advice, Pres, respect this king," said Lehman, tapping his hole card. "You done lost more than you can afford tonight. Ain't no use losin' another one. You gamblin' away the groceries."

It was more than I could stand. Suddenly I threw my cards in his face, and he was on his feet shocked and angry, raising his fists as if to hit me. The other men leapt up breathlessly, and George Weyhouse said in a shaky voice, "Now, calm it down, here."

I quickly realized what I had done. I apologized to Lehman, said I would settle in the morning, and went home.

The next day, I gave Lehman my check, begged his pardon again, and he readily accepted my apology. "It ain't nothin', Pres," he said.

Late in the afternoon, George Weyhouse pulled me aside and said, "You lucky, Pres. Ain't every man do that in a spade game and live." He laughed, cheering me. "Reckon you done turned into a spade yourself. Was you ready?"

I had thought of that, but it was an old white thought and I had brushed it away in self-disgust.

"Mess with Pres and he's ready! What you carry, a blade or a razor?" said George, jiving but in a quiet voice. And that was the last I heard of it.

Mr. Talbott shut the game down a few weeks later. When I asked him, he said it had nothing to do with my incident, but that his mother had raised objections. I imagined news of the affair had reached her ears. There was no objection by the other men to closing the game. It was as if my frenzied act had broken some spell.

Lehman and I had always been good friends, and we continued so. On Saturday afternoons, when his wife didn't come for him, I used to drop him off on the way home. Often he got into a monologue, and after we reached his home, he would be unable to stop, sitting in the car for a while and then maybe standing outside and leaning in, with his elbows on the door. His burden in these talks, perhaps because it was the end of another week and a kind of summing-up time, was always the same: the backwardness of *The Clarion*, the shiftlessness of Mr. Talbott, the dirty office; the progressive things black newspapers in other cities were doing, their new, modern buildings and the like; and again, Mr. Talbott's slipshod ways and the fact that nothing could be done about our situation because of them.

I also heard these sentiments, of course, from Bill Whitcomb, from George Brown, Pierce, and the rest of them. They always ended resignedly, "Nothing we can do about it." And from Mr. Talbott, I heard the same things about the workers: lazy, incurably hostile, they were sabotaging him at every point. I realized it was because I was white that I was the recipient of this constant stream of mutual abuses. This made me unhappy, but there was "nothing I could do about it."

In his daily work, Lehman was entirely loyal to *The Clarion* and, for that matter, to Mr. Talbott. And yet he was obliged to pour into my ear: "No, Pres, if I had it to do again and went into that office for the first time, I'd turn around and run away—not walk, I'd run! Faster'n a fuckin' jackrabbit. Shit, man, Negroes are makin' it these days! You ought to be at *The St. Louis Argus*—it's a business place, you can meet advertisers there. But the other day, a couple of guys from this new supermarket came into the office. They saw Talbott, and I swear to God, they thought he was the janitor!" Lehman laughed uncontrollably and then, suddenly sobering, concluded, "Well, ain't no use in talkin' about it. Like pullin' up a circus tent, stand by and take a line. Can't do nothin' with that man."

Among Lehman's duties was driving a truck with the printed papers far into the night to the newsstands and carrier stations. Now and then, I went with him for company. *The Clarion* trucks were usually in poor repair, and often as not went dead on some lonely street, sometimes in a heavy snowfall. After cursing the night, the truck, and Mr. Talbott's negligence, Lehman would have to make his way to a phone—or I would—call the office, and get somebody there to come out and start us with battery cables. But if any street people were out, he might commandeer their help. I remember one night when the engine died and he said to me, "I'll just see if those thugs will give me a push." He made reference to a group of young men who were standing across the way. Then he shouted, as if he were a policeman, "Hey! Come over here and get this thing started!" To my surprise, instead of calling him motherfucker and beating us both up, they did so. When the engine caught, he called out, not "Thanks," as I would have done, but "All right! That's enough!" Then he pulled away without giving them anything for their efforts. And when we were on the next block, he smiled. "That's the way to handle 'em," he said, "if you're so scared of 'em until you're shitting your pants."

21. Integrating the Little League

As I was receding into games—the games of youth, the games of men—I met another life on the way up. Meredith Park was a glorious large area with plenty of grassy space. It had good-sized trees, a baseball diamond, and two softball diamonds. It became Michael's second home; in the long days of summer, it often seemed his first. At the age of eight he showed talent in softball. That is to say, he could catch the ball, and for that reason was installed at first base. In a year or two, it became evident that he was unusually quick and a sharp-eyed hitter—in short, a born athlete. This talent had skipped a generation. My father had been a player of considerable renown, but though I had been passionately devoted to sports, I was a dub at them. Thus, to me, the sirens were singing what is one of the most dangerous songs heard by man: the one they address to a duffer whose son is a star.

When we arrived in the neighborhood, the park was held by the whites. A pimply-faced young recreation worker conducted softball leagues for the boys, and Michael played on a beginning team. I was standing by this worker one day when a Negro youngster asked to join.

"I'm sorry, sonny," the worker told him. "The league is full."

I guess that ranked as a white lie.

In a short time, I became the coach of the Roosters softball team for boys of the third and fourth grades. That step was to prove a fateful one.

In the second year of softball, one day I saw Michael and another agile little boy throwing a "hard ball," as they called a baseball. Later, Michael came home and sat on the porch swing, not looking in my direction.

I couldn't make out what was bothering him. After dinner, Susan told me he had come to her, as he did in such cases. The boys wanted to play "hard ball," and he was afraid my feelings would be hurt because I was the coach of the softball team.

Thus began the saga of Junior Baseball at Meredith Park.

At that time, Little Leagues were flourishing throughout the upper-class white areas of the city, with their commercial sponsors who provided uniforms and their hosts of parents to coach, raise money for equipment, keep records, and cheer the youngsters on. My brother-in-law, Joe Barrett, was a very active Little League manager on his side of town. But in the black and poorer white neighborhoods, there were no sponsors to donate uniforms and few parents with the drive and assurance to carry on leagues. A charitable organization, Junior Baseball, Inc., in cooperation with the City Recreation Department, conducted a program in the parks. The organization provided balls, bats, and catcher's equipment, kept the diamonds in shape, held brief clinics once a summer, and employed umpires for the older boys' games. It also sponsored an All-Star Game at Liberty Field, and conducted championship playoffs at the end of the season. The teams provided their own uniforms, if they had any, and the boys were supposed to furnish their own gloves. Fathers and other men of the neighborhood, if available, served as managers—in several of the parks in poorer districts, officers of the Police Athletic League filled these posts.

I decided to launch a Class D (for ten- and eleven-year-olds) baseball league at the park, using one of the softball diamonds with its shorter distances between the bases. I obtained the authorization of Junior Baseball and the parks department. The next step was to get the boys—I assumed the interested men would come along with them.

At this point, a great change was wrought in Meredith Park, behind the backs, you might say, of most of the white parents. Knowing I was white, they took it for granted I would uphold the unwritten "whites only" policy. But when Michael and I had procured the mimeographed application blanks, the first place we headed was to the black side of Washington Place. There, Michael, running out ahead of me, deposited leaflets in the hands of two Negro youngsters, Wilbur Van Buren (poor boy, who by reason of his build was fated to play catchers, when he always wanted to be a shortstop) and Roger Munson, a tallish, thin-shouldered boy with the look of a cat that had been caught in the rain. And then, we went on to give applications to the numerous other black boys in the streets. At that time, they were being bussed to a segregated school two miles away, but later the bars were lowered and they were assigned to School 34, thus becoming Michael's classmates as well as teammates.

At the same time, of course, we distributed the forms to the white boys in the neighborhood and left some with the physical education teachers at School 34 and School 40, which then included all the boys who might be expected to patronize the park.

A strange thing happened that day when we got home after handing out the applications. I looked out the window and saw Roger

Munson come quietly along the sidewalk, as quietly as a leaf stirs on a tree. Our block was then still white, and it wasn't usual for Negro boys to come along it. When Roger reached our house, he came and sat down, not in the swing and not even on the porch, but on the top cement step. He sat there and looked across the street.

Susan and Michael and I held a conference in the living room, and Michael was sent to entertain Roger. Michael said "Hi," and took his place in the swing, and they sat together as two boys will. Roger gazed across the street for about ten minutes and then got up and went away toward the black district without saying anything.

At the appointed hour on Saturday morning, Roger was at the park, along with more than a hundred other boys. Half a dozen fathers were also there, and we went to work organizing the league. I got the balls and bats out of my car, and Larry Harris, one of the black fathers, began knocking grounders and flies to the boys. Then I went to work signing them up. According to the rules, they couldn't be over eleven, which caused some disappointments; but it was necessary to draw a line in fairness to the little boys, and it was up to somebody else to organize a Class C league for the twelve- and thirteen-year-olds. Unlike the Little Leagues, which demanded birth certificates, we took a boy's word for it unless he was a great big fellow, in which case we might go and inquire as to his school age.

So eager were the over-age boys to get into the league, that some of them employed guile. Two youngsters new to the neighborhood were in line. The first was Jackie Thurmond; he was eleven and his birthday was August 17.

The next was Bill Thurmond. "How old are you, Bill?"

"Eleven."

"You're eleven too. And when is your birthday?"

"October 28."

"I see." They looked alike, except that Bill was larger. "Are you boys brothers?"

"Yes, we're brothers."

"But you're both eleven? And Jackie's birthday is August 17 and yours is October 28?"

"That's right." "Maybe they're twins," suggested Larry Harris's son Johnny.

I tried to think of all possible contingencies. "Do you have the same mother?" I asked.

"Yea, we do."

There was nothing I could do for Bill Thurmond, who shortly afterward admitted he was twelve, except to appoint him assistant manager in charge of picking up equipment.

That first year, there were about seventy-five white boys in the league and thirty Negro boys. That was enough for six teams, with the Junior Baseball limit of eighteen to a team. Each team had an adult manager from among the fathers.

As with *The Clarion*'s Honor Roll, I peremptorily kept the assignment of players to teams within my own hands, having in mind a sort of creeping integration that I thought had the best chance of success in the community. To begin with, I divided the boys into six groups based on their residential areas. This resulted in one all-Negro team, one all-white team from the School 40 neighborhood, and four teams that at the start had a sprinkling of Negro players. One of the predominantly white teams had for its manager Larry Harris, who was the best baseball coach of us men, with an outstandingly pleasant, patient way of working with boys. I also took a team.

Then, as new boys came into the league, they were assigned to teams on the basis of their ability and the standings. That is, a good player would be assigned to a losing team and the contrary. As it happened under this guideline, no occasion arose to integrate either the black team or the white team.

It was a conservative-radical course, designed to get the thing going with a little something for everybody. The boys and their fathers were aware of my operations in this regard, especially the black boys. As I had expected, it was from some of the white parents that the guff came. I shall never forget a scene one evening in the opening week. A slender towheaded boy on Larry Harris's team—the Yankees—was batting with two runners on base. He was wearing a plastic helmet. The league had bought half a dozen of these to protect the batters, and they used them in turn, so that Negro and white boys were wearing the same helmets.

It seemed it was this that drove the mother of the towheaded boy out of her cotton-pickin' mind, so to speak, for I later was told she was of Southern origin. She was also the wife of the swimming coach at the Town and Country Club, a suburban recreation club that turned away Negroes and had a quota on Jews.

What with the din that accompanied one of our games, especially with two men on base, no one knew she was there for a while, but it eventually pierced our consciousness that she was parked at the curb about a hundred feet from home plate, shouting to her son to "Come here this instant!" He, however, already had too much on his hand—he had two straight strikes—and after throwing her an anguished look, he stayed in the batter's box and kept his eye on the pitcher. The woman, a blonde, then got out of the car, strode across the intervening area and, coming upon the boy from behind, seized him by an arm and tried to pull him away. He refused to go, crying pitiably, "No, Mother!" "You are not going to play here! Take that thing off!" She tore the helmet off his head and threw it aside. "Now you come with me!"

He tugged furiously, "I'm batting!"

Players and spectators, boys and adults alike, looked on with horror. The spindly boy for the first time in his life had made a team. He had a position to play and a glove, and a gold-dyed T-shirt and cap, which comprised the uniform of our Yankees. And now he was even at bat, and although he hadn't hit the ball yet in his short career, he intended to; and his teammates were yelling encouragement to him. And in the very fulfillment of his dreams, his mother had gone insane and was pulling him away from it all. The boy had no idea of the reason for his mother's action. We men, black and white, knew, and looked at our shoes; and I felt that the black boys, wise beyond their years, knew, and some of the white boys.

The mother dragged the screaming boy to the car and finally half pushed, half threw him into it. I suppose she told him the reason after they got home. He never came back.

Most of the white parents accepted the situation and allowed their sons to play as long as they lived in the neighborhood, which wasn't any longer than they could help. Each spring, the league registration also registered the neighborhood turnover. That is, I signed up approximately twenty-five fewer white boys, twenty-five more Negro boys, until the whites were reduced to little Marsh Jarman and Michael, and the next year Marsh moved away. There was one family that stayed on but found a way to beat the system. These were a couple whom I had known in college and who lived in the man's large family home, which they were loath to leave, kitty-corner from the park. Their son Lewis played on my team for two years, a left-handed shortstop—if you can imagine it—who had to pivot to throw to second. And then one spring, he didn't show up. Some time later, Michael said he was playing in a Little League about twenty blocks north. This was hard to believe, because the Little Leagues were strict about their area boundaries. Yet, it turned out to be true. I had occasion to call at Little League headquarters one day, and I saw the roster of the team on which Lewis was playing. He was registered from a false address! I wondered who was worse, the woman who had dragged off the tow-headed boy or the father who had conspired with his young son to lie for the same purpose.

Among the boys themselves, if there was any racial incident in all the years we played, I didn't hear of it. It is true that I inadvertently almost cooked up a mess myself one time, but I managed to cook myself out of it. This was on an evening when, due to the absence of other men, I was obliged to function both as manager and umpire.

The games were scheduled to go seven innings, but many times were cut short by darkness. In the later innings, the question would arise as to how dark it was growing. The team that was leading would complain, "It's too dark to play. We can't see the ball," hoping to be declared victor on the spot. But the team that was behind would snort, "It's plenty light. Come on, batter up!" with the thought that it could forge ahead in one more inning.

There was no reaching a consensus on this matter of how dark it was, and the umpire had to bear the full responsibility of the decision.

Another rule involved in this particular game was that the losing team is entitled to the same number of innings at bat as the winner (or one more). If darkness ends the game before the team behind gets its last bats, the score reverts to the previous inning.

In these fair and harmless rules lay a danger I didn't foresee. My team, the Indians, was playing the all-black Dodgers, whose manager, Milton Sanford, had to work overtime. The Indians took a 6–1 lead early in the game and were still ahead by that score after five innings. Daylight was beginning to fade, and my own boys set up the cry, "It's getting dark, Mr. Preston, call the game," to which Wilbur Van Buren retorted, "What you talkin' about, man! You just tryin' to cheat!"

I glanced at the sky. It wasn't really all that dark, and if the sixth inning passed as the previous ones had, with the Dodgers going out in order, we should be able to get it in; we might even be able to play the top of the seventh. It wouldn't be necessary for the Indians to take their last bats, since they would still be ahead. It wasn't likely the Dodgers would catch up.

I didn't want to call the game with my own team winning, and plenty of light at the moment. "Play ball!" I shouted.

The Dodgers went to bat and, perhaps inspired by this minor victory over fortune, staged a rally. Instead of going out, they got hits and walks and, profiting from Indian errors, paraded around the bases. Don't ask me the gory details. To the accompaniment of great excitement and cheering, before the third Dodger could be put out, they had gone into the lead, 7–6.

All this action, of course, took much more time than it would have for them to come up and go down in their previous orderly fashion. Perhaps half an hour. By now it was really getting dark. A boy might be hit by a pitched or batted ball he couldn't see in time.

"That's all, boys," I said. "It's too dark to play. Game called."

The Dodgers set up a mighty cheer. But the Indians came storming at me. "We didn't get our last bats! Come on, Mr. Preston, there's still light!"

I replied that the glimmer of light remaining wouldn't be enough to finish, and I added, "The score reverts to the previous inning. The Indians win, six to one. That's the rule."

Now, the Dodgers exploded. Robbed of their glorious victory, they roared, moaned, threw their caps and equipment on the ground and yelled at me, "You cheat! You cheated for your own team! You're a cheater!"

The forlorn group of black boys took a long time to disband. They refused to pick up the equipment, kicked the catcher's mask in the dust, and Wilbur shouted "Cheater!" at me as they finally wandered toward home.

The next day, I made the only "sociological" ruling in the history of our league. I announced that on Saturday afternoon we would gather at the park and play the remaining inning-and-a-half of the game. That was not in accordance with the rules of Junior Baseball, and it was technically unfair to the Indians. They were entitled to the victory. But they made no objection, maybe because it meant playing more ball—and maybe because they too felt it was the fair way out.

The playoff took place on a sultry afternoon. This time it was the Indians who went quietly. There was no further scoring, and the Dodgers had their triumph. "Now," I said quickly, "everybody over to the supermarket for Cokes on me!"

As the black boys and white boys drank their Cokes together, the affair seemed to have ended to everyone's satisfaction, and harmony resumed her reign.

22. Tales of the Hardwood

The Winged Lions, in their second year, were indeed a super-team, as Walt had said. They lost only one game all winter long and were generally picked to win the state tournament. But disaster could pounce from many a hiding place in the tournament. By a quirk of the draw, Dunbar was one of the very few teams scheduled to play twice on the opening day. In the morning game, Northridge put up an inspired battle that pushed the Lions to the limit. At night against Memorial, they ran out of steam after the first quarter. It was soon apparent that instead of four weeks, they hadn't survived twelve hours. The Dunbar fans raged that there had been dirty work by the HSAA officials who made the schedule and put the Lions into this predicament. With an ever-ready cynicism toward the conduct of lotteries, they were unimpressed by the fact that six white men, watched live by five white reporters, had sat around a table and drawn slips of paper bearing the teams' names out of an opaque drum. "Humph!" said Hancock. "That's how it's done."

Oh, well. Wait till next year.

But next year, in spite of another super season, brought its misfortunes. The mightiest of the Lions was Willie Hempstead, but in his checkered past was the fact that he had entered Dunbar before the others. On a complaint filed, it was rumored, by the Northridge coach, the HSAA made an investigation. It found that although Willie was still in high school and had played only two years, he would "exhaust his eligibility" at the end of the first semester. Willie was lost for the tournament.

It was a stunning blow, because it was entirely unexpected—every schoolboy thought he knew Willie's "eligibility"—and because it was based on such an obscure technicality. But Hallie Thomas was in his prime, and he led the Lions to the sixteenth round. There they had a cold game, such as the best of them can suffer in a given thirty-two minutes, against a Caruthersville team that was playing over its head. Even so, it seemed that Hallie had pulled it out. With a few seconds to go and Dunbar one point behind, he hit a great long shot, but he crashed into (or was blocked by) the boy who was guarding him. The referee—a white man, of course, as they all were—called Hallie for charging, nullified his basket, and awarded a free throw to Caruthersville. That was the game and the end for Dunbar.

Coming on top of the two-game day the year before and the sidelining of Hempstead, the defeat was a stinger. Could Negroes play basketball after all in the white man's league, or were they simply "spooks"? And at the same time, shit, man, you believe they ever gonna let Dunbar win it? You saw the man take that score away from Hallie? You sound like a fellow that plays with himself, damn if you don't.

The fury, as far as it was turned outward, was concentrated on the official who had called the foul. I was in it with the black people, mean and angry but impotent, because there was no going into that man's mind. I had felt that way as a boy, when Winette was upset in the tournament. And then it occurred to me that for the first time in my life, there was something I could do about it; there was a way of getting into his mind. Recently, I had become aware of the State Officials' Association (SOA), another self-constituted group, from whose ranks the tournament referees were chosen. I felt it was important that the fury be directed outward. And so, I telephoned the president of the organization and asked him whether it had any Negro members. He said, "No, we don't."

"And would you take qualified Negroes into your association if they applied?"

It always struck me as odd how readily people in such positions answered such questions put to them by *The Clarion*. Were they *so* insensitive and so behind the times that they didn't realize the implications of what they were saying? And thus I got a whiff, like the startling odor of tear gas, of what it must mean to be black and surrounded by an overwhelming throng of such idiots. I reflected that I could not have survived a day. But in some cases—and I thought the president of the SOA might belong in this category—they spilled the beans in an effort to dissociate themselves from their organizations. Not that in reality they were any better; they simply lacked the loyalty of thieves. (Sometimes they had the naiveté to think that I, as a white man, would sympathize with them and so it was not necessary to conceal the truth from me!)

The president could easily have sidestepped my question by saying, "I don't know, none has applied during my term of office," or "None has ever applied," or "We would consider them on their merits," and so forth. Instead, he said amiably, "Well, it would be up to the membership, and I don't think they would. You see, we have social affairs, and the fellows bring their wives."

I said, "And what social affairs do you have?"

"Well, we have the annual banquet."

For a moment, I thought he was trying to make a crude joke, but his voice was dead level. I thanked him. We printed the story on page one, under two lines of wooden type, the largest in the plant: "REFEREES' PREJUDICE ADMITTED BY PRESIDENT OF ASSOCIATION."

That was, of course, misleading, because the readers still had in mind the foul called on Hallie, and at first sight believed the headline referred to that incident. But so what? It was the only way you could get hold of the officials' racism, and it was a solid, good hook.

With this exposé, a campaign began to integrate the officials in high school athletics, principally basketball. I loaded my *Clarion* pepper-gun and fired away. It was more difficult than one might suppose. After we spread the president's story, the referees were defensive and angry. They thought they were fair, I suppose; their idea of being fair was to put aside one's dislike of blacks while judging them in a sporting event. This was an effort for which one should be praised, not knocked off balance by accusations and open talk about race. Where had I experienced it before, this feeling that there is no bigot so fanatical as the man who thinks he is not one, so that his prejudice rages without even the control of his awareness? The Citizens School Committee! The first step with the white referees, as with the Citizens, was to get them to admit that they weren't gods but white men, presiding over the competition of white youths and black youths. But it was just this step that they viewed with loathing (and I am talking of the "best" of them, the most dedicated to the strange role of a sports official), as if it had been obscene.

I was therefore surprised as well as encouraged when there came small opposing signs that the campaign was making itself felt. What I had overlooked was an early and unpremeditated expression of the factor that since has became known as Black Power. A number of the referees—perhaps not the "best," but mere human and ambitious types—were eager to work the crowded and widely publicized games Dunbar hosted, and for which all the hiring was done by Carter and James. They had the idea of all white people that Negroes were a monolithic mass, and in particular that *The Clarion* spoke for every one of them. These referees didn't want to get down wrong with *The Clarion*! There was one man, as it happened another of my old college acquaintances, who had seen some Dunbar games and who never missed an opportunity to impress on me his disgust with the racial backwardness of "those other guys." He came around *The Clarion* office gossiping like an old woman, making himself a valuable source of information as to what our opponents were doing.

The next thing we knew, I was invited to take part in a panel discussion of newspapermen at a meeting of the officials' association. Afterwards, I went on to a meeting of the NAACP board. We were all close comrades there, and when I reported that "I was the only Negro present" at the officials' meeting, we all had a good laugh.

The Clarion's crusade awakened a response from the black referees. There was John McClain, a postal worker beginning to show gray hair, who had long been fighting a lonely battle. He was a basketball and football referee. McClain was aggressively vocal about the gradualism that was eating away his time on earth. He "wanted flowers while he could smell them," in the popular Negro phrase. He often came around to stir me up when he thought my writings weren't being disagreeable enough.

McClain got some Dunbar games because of his race, and some Memorial games because he was Catholic. When *The Clarion*'s campaign began to bear fruit, he picked up some small-town games because of his availability. He would take off from his duties at the post office and drive to any out-of-the-way corner to work a game. He badgered the Dunbar people to give him more assignments, and when they refused (James thought he was a poor referee), he tried to sic me on them as race traitors. He, too, had a dream, although he lacked the eloquence of Dr. King in voicing it. It was to officiate in the state high school basketball tournament. He was the first Negro to submit an application to do so, and that was probably his mistake. Although he was by then working as many games as any white man, the HSAA silently passed him by and, year after year, kept passing him by. And he kept standing up in his cantankerous way and blasting them for it.

John "Will" Wilson, a mild-mannered man who was a junior high coach, took another approach. He got together a group of about twenty athletic young men who met at the YMCA and trained themselves scrupulously in the skills of officiating. It was called the Capital City Officials Association. Although Will and I never discussed the matter in so many words, a situation developed in which he and I (and he and McClain) were the rabbit catcher and chaser. In my column and sports articles and even in editorials, I gave the white folks hell, calling them everything but children of Satan (as of course did McClain). This made them angry but also put them on the defensive. And then along came Will, extremely polite and respectful—he was a man with whom one could find no fault whatever except that he was black—and gave them a chance to get off the hook by hiring one of his well-qualified protégés. Then they could say, "See, that radical from *The Clarion* and loudmouth McClain are all wet about us; we're perfectly fair if approached in a gentlemanly way by Will Wilson."

I must admit that at first I had my doubts about Will, tending to consider him an Uncle Tom. Fortunately, Mr. Talbott had trained me so thoroughly to recognize the obsequious Negro as a man "making the white folks believe he is doing what he wants" that I soon realized Will and I were in business.

I wrote up a letter, which *The Clarion* sent to every high school in the state, asking whether it would employ Negro referees. We received a dozen or so favorable responses, several of them from remote country schools where many of the people had never seen a black person. An added attraction to them was that some of the men we listed were famous athletes in their own right. Jack Hudson, after breaking up the high school tournament, had gone on to set a national scoring record at Winette College, and then had been the first Negro to play in the annual College All-Star Professional game. Bill Winslow had also been "Mr. Basketball" in the high school tourney, and then at the state university had become the first Negro to play in the Big Ten. These men, in the basketball dream world so prevalent in our state, were legendary folk heroes. At these remote schools, as many fans would turn out to see Hudson and Winslow referee as they would to watch the game. If they playfully took a shot or two during a time-out, the customers' satisfaction was complete. And some of the glamour brushed off on the young high school coach, who, in his own playing days, had come to know these gods personally, so that it was easy and natural for him to bring them to the town. (We found that this camaraderie of former teammates or opponents frequently played a part in getting assignments.)

Between Dunbar and the questionnaire schools, Wilson, Hudson, Winslow and some of the others began to obtain contracts for a respectable number of games. During the season, black referees were coming to be accepted; I thought the mark of it was when they were razzed by irate fans, just like the white referees. I heard more than one Dunbar follower split his lungs yelling, "You damned Uncle Tom!" when Wilson or McClain made a call against the Lions. And the white fans also seemed to be taking them as a matter of course. But the increase in their numbers was painfully slow, and still the HSAA held out against assigning them to the tournament. Every mid-February, on the day the tournament plans were announced, Walt and I would scan the early editions thinking, "surely this time," and it would not be this time. Even when Dunbar met Lincoln in the state championship game, so that all the players, coaches, and waterboys involved were black, even then the referees were white. Our campaign went on. And then one year, toward the end of the 1950s, Walt opened the paper, and there were the names of Will Wilson and two out-of-town men. It was over. Shortly afterward, the State Officials Association also dropped its color bar.

As it often happens with successful crusades, there was a casualty. On the basis of his experience, John McClain should have been the first Negro to officiate in the tournament. But if the dinosaur had to yield, it wouldn't do so without lashing its tail. While "less controversial" men came to be admitted, as if the door had always been open, McClain never got a call. Bitter and unyielding to the end, he finally heeded Father Time and retired. I wondered whether in the Halls of Fame there shouldn't be a corridor for him and his kind, with the inscription: "Because They Fought the Fight, They Were Denied the Prize."

As I write, I am looking at the only trophy I ever received. At the base is engraved: "Outstanding Journalism in Sports"; my name; and "Capital City Officials Association." Will Wilson presented it to me in the halftime of a basketball game.

As for Willie Hempstead, despite the efforts of bureaucrats, he amassed a collection of trophies, like a true artist, in a very short time. I hope he now has a place to display them.

Over *The Clarion*'s strenuous protests, after the tournament, Willie was ruled ineligible for the All-Star games. The committee in charge, comprised of white newspapermen from the sponsoring *Sun*, held that you couldn't play in the Games if you hadn't played in the tournament. The year before, Willie would have been ineligible because he was still in school. Everyone knew he was the best player in the state, but it was necessary to uphold standards, one of which was that you should enter and be graduated from high school at the proper time, like a white boy. Short shrift to the "shiftless," even if he was only a teenager.

The coach of our state's All-Star team, perhaps sensing that things had gone too far, appointed Willie as manager. So he sat on the bench and provided towels. Hallie starred in both games. He singlehandedly won the away game by stealing an in-bounds pass and scoring an incredible twisting shot with three seconds to go. I don't suppose the fans of that other state would have believed that we had a better player handing out towels.

But Willie continued to make news. I used to visit his home, a rotting shack on the bank of the canal. Although it was near the heart of the city, the house was reached by driving half a block along the canal on a dirt road, which was little more than a pair of tracks made by earlier automobiles. Willie might be "Dill" to his teammates (I was still puzzled by it, and wondered whether it might come from "dill pickle" because of his height—or was it "Deal" after all?), but at home he was a correct and proper Willie. His relationship with his mother, a tall, dignified woman who bore a different family name, was close and tender. There was no man in the home. It struck me one day that "Dill" Hempstead, that awesome scourge of the basketball courts, was a mama's boy.

That autumn, Hallie went to the state university on a basketball scholarship, and Bailey Bentley went to Central College, where he kept "bombing" and eventually broke Jack Hudson's state scoring record. The exploits of college stars weren't for Willie: he went straight to the Globetrotters.

The Trotters called him Wee Willie, and he was quite a drawing card as a kid out of high school holding his own with the veterans. I was told he sent most of his pay home. In a couple of years, his mother and younger brothers and sisters said goodbye to the canal and moved into a respectable house on the northwest side.

It made a happy success story, as the people put it: "Dill with that Globetrotter bread done put his mother into a nice home." I won't claim prescience, but I wasn't quite so sanguine. I knew another side to the Globetrotters. I had gotten into a quarrel with Abe Saperstein, the owner of the team, by writing about it in my column. You saw those carefree black athletes laughing as they performed their stunts but did you ever take a look at their schedule? They played every night, sometimes twice in twenty-four hours, and traveled in between by plane or bus. Organized baseball did something like that (with less-frequent travel and better conditions), but basketball isn't baseball. Basketball is a running sport, a killer. The professional basketball season was eighty games, but the Globetrotters played the year round.

Jack Hudson had been with the Trotters, and I had gone to interview him once when they came to town. It was at the Congress Avenue gym, where they were to practice before playing that night at the Field House. As they filed into the gymnasium, every man headed for a chair. They were bone weary. "Hell, man," said Jack. "This is a crock of shit."

This splendid young athlete—"Jumpin' Jack"—took a seat and talked looking up to me. "I'm telling you, Mr. Preston" (my mother had been his teacher at Winette High School, and he always called me "Mister"), "there's no money in the world can buy this. I'm going to quit and get a job at the General Motors factory." And he did that. The next year, he turned up as the coach at Steel High School in our city.

But for Willie Hempstead, it was the big time. After two years with the Trotters, he was drafted and assigned to the Army. He wasn't sent to Korea, but just went on playing basketball, only now for service pay. The team he was with won the Armed Forces championship. When his hitch was over, he was signed by the New York Knickerbockers. That was almost unheard of, a player without college experience going into the National Basketball League, but Dunbar fans were serenely confident "Dill" would show even the pros a thing or two. And they were glad that at last the years of poverty were definitely over for the Hempstead family.

Then came the sickening news. Before the first game, he was in a New York hospital for study after a checkup. The doctors said Willie had at some time suffered a "silent heart attack." He protested that he had never felt a pain, had no idea when such a thing could have occurred. The doctors couldn't help him there. It might have been in high school. Basketball as it was played in our state was sometimes declared to be too strenuous for growing boys, especially those like Willie who shot up rapidly. It was said that of the Hanover 1927 state championship team, all the five starting players were dead within twenty years.

What the doctors told Willie was that he never could play basketball again—certainly not with the pros. His life would be in danger every time he went on the court. The Knicks canceled his contract.

Willie Hempstead came home. He was twenty-two. He felt fine, he said with that smile. Disregarding the doctors' orders, he played in the Dust Bowl games. His form was sharper than ever. He hung around watching the high school practices.

Willie had no way of earning even a bare living. He had never learned anything but basketball. You can't coach without a college diploma. He was six-feet-seven for sure now and looked strong and healthy—he told me he didn't know what a symptom was. Once a year for a while, he had a new electrocardiogram taken, but they always read the same.

The last I heard of Willie, some men were planning to raise a fund to set him up in a dry-cleaning franchise. They came to *The Clarion* for a write-up, three ordinary sports fans, not too sure of themselves. I gave their project a plug, but I fear it fell through. Black people had other uses for their money than to give it to a former basketball player. Willie wasn't news any more.

Meanwhile, back in the time Willie was at Dunbar, Negro youngsters all over town had taken to imitating him and the other members of the Big Team, and in a foretaste of things to come, they swiftly seized dominance of junior high school basketball.

This was a level of play to which the press had until then not condescended; but Walt Evers tipped me off that the fans were interested, and when two all-black schools met for the city championship, I covered the game.

It was a closely matched contest, but one team held a narrow edge largely because of a gawky fourteen-year-old. He wasn't as tall or husky as some of the other boys, but he played with a scowl, as if impressing his will on everyone else in the game. With the end of the first half near, he dribbled into a corner and stood there, bouncing the ball for half a minute and shielding it from his guard until only two or three seconds showed on the clock. Then he shot, and made it.

At the end of the game, although the opponents were frantic to get the ball, he did exactly the same thing. And he continued scowling even through the presentation of the trophy.

I knew where he got that knack for shooting from the corner. He was Bailey Bentley's brother, and they called him "Little Flap." His idol was Willie Hempstead, Walt told me. His name was Oscar.

23. A Friend Leaves, a Friend Dies

Basketball, baseball, and poker, undoubtedly, were the opiates of the people. Watching the thrilling play of "Dill" and later Oscar, or seeing a third king fall in front of you, made you forget the dirt, the debt, the humiliation. I observed that when one of the Winged Lions shot the ball, leaping off the floor, many of the seated fans would unconsciously raise their right foot a few inches in identification. But in evaluating these various activities, what did "opiate" mean? It was my opinion that Karl Marx's famous dictum on religion was only half understood. Marx said religion was the people's cry for justice, as well as the stifling of that cry that it was "the heart of a heartless world." At any rate, it was the opium of the people; and unless one could free the people of the need for painkillers, how could he stand above them?

How? And then, one of those people bestirred himself, in an effort to break away and find a greater measure of justice before the heartless world closed in on him again. He took his opiate with him, but moved for a time in spite of it.

I'm talking about Robert Morgan. He wasn't interested in sports, and if he was interested in boys it wasn't for baseball. I thought it odd, because of his intellect, that he was interested in religion.

Robert was an Episcopalian. He was organist at St. John's Church and a committed participant in its liturgy. His service as organist brought a small addition to his income, besides enabling him to express his musical bent. At first I supposed it was just that, together with the pageantry that might appeal to one with artistic tastes. But as with Mr. Talbott and the Republicans, I learned that I was mistaken, and that Robert's religion—or perhaps I should say his denomination—meant a great deal in his life.

Occasionally, in the newsroom we used to drop our work and get into lengthy discussions of philosophical or, more rarely, theological matters. I found myself face to face with a stereotype that was true: to the last man, they had an uncontrollable fear of the Almighty. Once while a thunderstorm was going on, I made a joke about God, and it was all Bill Whitcomb could do, with an involuntary glance skyward, to keep from leaving the room. After that, Mr. Talbott, as if showing he had the nerve to engage in this white man's heresy, told a funny story of how, as a teenager, he had attended a revival meeting in a tent; resisting the preacher's exhortations that he testify to being "saved," he had got up to leave. The preacher shouted after him, "Boy, you'll pay for your sins!" As he reached the edge of the tent, there was a loud thunderclap, and he turned around, ran back in, and fell on his knees.

But if my friends didn't care to trifle with the Lord Almighty, they had no such respect for the mundane affairs of churches. God might have been a white man, but the preachers were just so many scalawags. Bill, with his secondhand radicalism and in part to show off his knowledge of history, would tease Robert about the founding of the Anglican Church: "Why man," he'd say, "Henry the Eighth wanted a divorce and the Pope wouldn't give him one, so he started his own church, everybody knows that. That's how y'all Episcopalian Church got started, the King of England had a hard-on!" and so forth. Sometimes I would join in.

"Rave on, O ye ignorant ones," Robert would reply with a shrug. Or he would retort with a disquisition on church history that, while it may have been sectarian, put us to shame. One realized then, from his earnestness, that it was serious business with him. At the same time, it couldn't be denied that there was more than a touch of snobbery about his being a member of St. John's rather than the Baptists or ethicists. St. John's at that time had a white pastor and was under the same diocese as Trinity Church, to which some of the richest whites in town belonged.

It was through the church that Robert got his chance for escape from being a society editor at *The Clarion* and its miserable wages, and above all from the desuetude of our town, where nothing challenged him to a creative life.

Somehow he received an offer to serve as organist at a monastery in New York City. He would have much free time to work on his own music. The news that Robert was going to leave *The Clarion* for the Big Apple struck us all speechless. It was as if the denizens of Hell had learned that one of their number, and an old resident at that, was moving to Heaven. George Brown smiled broadly every time he looked at Robert. After they recovered from the blow, Pierce and Whitcomb dwelt seriously, almost with reverence, on Robert's talents, which he would now have a chance to develop. Mr. Talbott took the lead in making up a purse to which we all contributed, and which eventually reached two hundred dollars, for traveling expenses.

Robert went about the office smiling embarrassedly, feverish with anticipation but not wanting to admit it. He sold his things, including his record collection, and those things he couldn't sell he gave away.

He was living at the time in a rather decent rented house near 38th Street; he had only to choose among a whole lineup of people who wanted to take over the lease on the place. On his last Thursday at *The Clarion*, Pierce proofed a false page, at my suggestion, bearing the headline: "MAD MONK FLEES CITY." In a spirit of merriment, we bade Godspeed to Robert Morgan.

Five days later, Mr. Talbott received a telegram from him, asking for money to come home.

Robert walked into the office the following Monday and quietly went to work. Most of us didn't have the will to question him, except Smitty who, arriving late, dropped his jaw in an exaggerated expression of surprise. "You!" he said.

"Yes, it is I," said Robert, trying a bit of his old facetious hauteur.

"Well, kiss me all over!" said Smitty. "But for God's sake, why?"

"Just so," Robert shrugged.

I never learned what had happened. Pierce told some story of Robert being obliged to get out of bed at six in the morning and kneel on cold stones; with Robert's night living and irregular habits, it seemed likely he would find this difficult. But Pierce wasn't very sure about it, and at last he said, "Hell, Pres, I don't know, that's what somebody said." And he looked round at the grimy wall.

"That's right," George Brown nodded soberly. "Gets in your bloodstream, it don't never let you go."

Which would be a good place to end the story, except that about a year later Robert stole away. Without telling anyone this time, he picked up and departed for an eastern city. He wrote that he had a job as managing editor of a Negro newspaper. As far as I know, he is still there.

On a Friday morning, with Bill Whitcomb settled back to read the exchange newspapers, we heard the single buzz that meant a telephone call for him. "That's a revoltin' development," he said. The buzz came again, insistently. At the same time, he heard Mrs. Weymouth's shrill voice from the front office: "Whitcomb!"

"Damn people out front never take care of nothing," Bill said. "I don't want no fuckin' phone call this morning." But Mrs. Weymouth appeared in the doorway with a mouth full of words, "Mr. Whitcomb, will you answer the telephone! D' y'all think we haven't got anything to do out here but hang on to the telephone for you? You been drinkin' that gin already! We tryin' to run a business establishment, and you sittin' back here readin' the papers. I'm gittin' sick of it. Why don't you do your work!"

"Woman, stop runnin' your mouth and get out of the newsroom," Bill shouted. "You Gawddamned people out front wouldn't know a Gawd damned business establishment if one sneaked up and bit you!" And he wheeled on the telephone, yelling into it, "Hello!"

The phone conversation I heard, of course, from Bill's end alone. "Yes, madam," he said, politely but severely. "Well, madam, likely the funeral director didn't get it to us in time. What was your mother's name? Madam, I'm tryin' to tell you, if the funeral director didn't get it to us, there wasn't anything we could do about it. . . . We'll just have to run it next week. Maybe he told you that, madam, but we didn't receive it. . . . We couldn't print what we didn't receive, madam. We're running a newspaper here!"

There was a long pause. I could tell that Bill was beginning to think we had received the obituary, but somehow, perhaps through an oversight of his, it hadn't got into the paper. And as he did so and the woman went on and on, and he was prevented more and more from reading the exchanges, his fury mounted until finally he bawled into the phone: "I know the funeral will be over, but what do you want us to do, print 'n extra! We've got fourteen deaths in the paper this week, and I done told you the undertaker didn't bring it in! And as for your mother, madam, nobody cares if your mother died! She was just another person! This newspaper is read over six states and parts of the South, and we published a 196-page Special Edition that is on file in the Library of Congress! If your mother died and the undertaker didn't bring it in, that's just another person dead and like I done told you, we'll run it next week!"

That got rid of her, but Bill's nerves were so shaken that he jumped up and, after spitting several times on the gas heater while he denounced the bereaved woman, the funeral director, and the people in the front office, went out for a drink of gin.

Mr. Talbott too was a nervous man. A good part of the time, he was a nervous wreck—this was especially so when his troubles were complicated by his diabetes, which often was exacerbated by his utter refusal to heed the dietary proscriptions. For one thing, he drank Cokes all day long. The result was that he was periodically quite ill, though nothing could keep him away from the office even for a single day. He had the most severe case of hay fever I have ever seen, and one year he came to work for almost two weeks wearing a grotesque mask to filter the air. It had been ordered for him by a prominent allergist who treated him for free, it was said, out of sympathy for the Negro cause.

Mr. Talbott usually held his temper under control, but when it broke loose, it was fearsome. And while Bill would take out his wrath on whoever was handy, Mr. Talbott tended to harbor deep hostility for a few individuals. One of these was Attorney John Sherman. I have forgotten the origin of their grudge, if I ever knew it, but I well remember one night when it flamed into action. While working a bit late in the newsroom, I heard Mr. Talbott shout in the front office: "You're a goddamned liar!" Then there was a crash as if an article of furniture had been hurled, and the sound of scuffling.

I rushed to the office. Mr. Talbott and Attorney Sherman were wrestling like two boys on the floor. Over and over they rolled, working their way around the room until their heads were under one of the desks while their legs stuck out. They grunted and swore. Looking on were George Weyhouse, Lehman, and George Lewis. Occasionally one would mutter, "This is disgusting," shake his head and turn away. "Come on, break it up, you guys," said George Weyhouse, but half-heartedly and without effect.

After about twenty minutes, they stopped, got up, and stood glaring at each other, two middle-aged men puffing and blowing. Then Attorney Sherman took his departure.

Such were the leaders of *The Clarion*. Part of their makeup was a murderous violence, which by the arrangement of their lives was directed against other black people. Even when this did not break into insult or injury, it enveloped us like the dirty walls—a constant disparagement of everyone and everything black. For example, people in the newsroom, or coming into it, criticized the teachers at Dunbar and black teachers generally, as ignorant, backward, and incompetent. One day, I could stand it no longer and burst out: "Listen! I grew up among white teachers, and I can assure you—ten percent are superior, ten percent are hopeless, and the other eighty percent are in the middle. Everything you are saying about Negro teachers, I have heard said about white teachers."

After a moment's pondering, Mr. Talbott said: "I hadn't thought of that, but I expect you're right. It's true, we don't know about the white teachers."

It was this same nervous drive, when turned in the other direction, I thought, that was responsible for the vigor of the NAACP's crusades and for the élan with which *The Clarion* people, in the face of insuperable obstacles, brought out a lively newspaper week after week and also carried on their other activities, such as raising thousands of dollars to give to the poor at Christmastime.

Another project into which the office's energies collectively poured was the annual *Clarion* Carriers' Picnic in August, which the children shortened to "*The Clarion* Picnic." This had been conceived as a means of rewarding the newsboys and girls, as the dailies did their carriers; but by my time, these terms had proved impractical. You would understand why if you ever tried to explain to a child who was not a carrier that he couldn't attend. At any rate, it had grown to include just about ten thousand Negro children. True, you had to have a ticket; these were provided to the hundred or so carriers and their brothers and sisters, and secondly, they could be obtained through any Sunday school—a brilliant idea of Walt Evers that brought all the preachers into support of the venture. It would have to be a most unenterprising youngster who couldn't get a ticket under these circumstances. Poor black children weren't unenterprising, especially when they hadn't been out of town all the hot summer long.

Everything we needed for the picnic was begged from the white folks. Who else? They had it. The camp where it was held we got from the Boy Scout Council, which because of its segregationist policies was in no position to refuse. The hot dogs were begged from meat-packers, especially Weitzel & Son, whose president wasn't the worst fellow in town to Negroes—he patronized black athletic teams and advertised in *The Clarion*—and the buns were begged from the bakeries. The buses to carry the children to and from the camp, which was seven miles north of town, were begged from the City Railways Company.

There had been a time when I would have turned up my nose at all this "begging," but no longer. I remember that early in my tenure at *The Clarion*, Mrs. McPherson once asked me to buy some tickets for charity, and I replied crisply, "I don't believe in charity." This was a point of view she had never heard of and couldn't comprehend. I was unable to explain it to her at the time, and in a few years, I too had shelved my lofty principle before the realization that in our society begging is one way of bringing about the transfer of goods from those who have them to those who die for lack of them.

The picnic also featured entertainment by well-known Negroes. One year Ezzard Charles, then the heavyweight champion, came from Cincinnati to give a boxing demonstration. Black combos and singing groups performed, and there was even a talent competition with small prizes for the youngsters themselves. The Dunbar Winged Lions (flouting the HSAA) played exhibition basketball games, and once, Walt Evers got the Naples state champions, all of them white country boys, to provide the opposition.

Despite this planned program, the nature-starved children amused themselves chiefly by running through the woods, swimming, and eating. Feeding the multitude was by itself a tremendous problem in organization. Under the direction of the circulation manager, at first Bill Baxter and later Walt Evers, *The Clarion* staff devoted its day to the project. The Talbott family turned out in force. On hand also were a number of women of the Christmas Cheer Fund, as well as women of various churches, dressed in their white nurses' uniforms. Black PAL Club officers, in their police uniforms, made up the constabulary. Dr. Guy Sherman, a close friend of *The Clarion*, headed the picnic's medical staff in early years, but later Walt "begged" University Hospital to set up a first-aid tent. The Reynolds Brothers Funeral Home loaned its ambulance.

Except for certain sports events, there was nothing else in town, black or white, on such a massive scale. It took the little old *Clarion* to bring about this day for thousands of poor children. I couldn't help thinking that for all that our daily papers yelped about free enterprise, most of the freedom, and at least an equal part of the enterprise, was headquartered at 518 Illinois Avenue.

Speaking of Reynolds Brothers, I remember one morning when I arrived at the office there was a hush over the place. Mr. Talbott told me, "Bill Baxter died last night."

Bill must have been in his early forties, and he had died of a heart attack. A picture flashed in my mind of him throwing his money into the poker game. That money would be missed now: he had a wife and three or four children. In the black community, the death of the bread-winner was an economic catastrophe. We took up a pitiful little collection and gave it to his wife.

My coworkers avoided talking about Bill and his death. Running off the funeral programs on the job press, Pierce said guardedly, "I don't know what he did wrong—he was superintendent of the Sunday school." And he added something about when your time comes.

"Baxter was too heavy," said Lehman, with a downturned mouth, like a judge reluctantly pronouncing a severe sentence. He was probably thinking that he was on the heavy side himself.

Bill Whitcomb said he didn't like funerals and wouldn't attend "to hear eight jackleg Baptists preach Bill across Hell on horsehair."

Pierce and I went together. Before the afternoon was over, I found that Bill Whitcomb was exaggerating as usual—by actual count, there were only seven preachers. None of them said anything about Bill Baxter. It was a hot day, and the people stirred the air with the Reynolds Brothers Funeral Home fans. The mother and little girls and eight-year-old William Baxter Jr. sat in the front row.

We decided not to join the procession to the cemetery. "That's the first one out of the poker game," observed Pierce as we left the church and headed back to work.

24. A Boy and a Game Teach Me a Lesson

Since the boys' baseball organization was such a success, I decided that winter to form a basketball league. This required a gymnasium. I was able to obtain a somewhat small building but with basketball goals at both ends of its floor on Washington Place. It was called the Rutter Hut, and it had a story of its own. It was the property of the neighborhood white Boy Scout troop, or rather its adult council. There was also a neighborhood black Scout troop, but it didn't own a building and wasn't permitted to meet in the Hut. I guess it met in private homes. As a matter of fact, Michael, at the behest of a white schoolmate, joined the Rutter Hut troop, but he didn't take to the Scouts and soon dropped out. Whether he disliked the segregation that upset what might be called "the boy ecology" of the neighborhood, or whether for other reasons he thought the Scouts were "square," I really couldn't say. On such matters, he and I had entered the generation gap.

At any rate, as the neighborhood "changed," most of the white Scouts had moved away, and there weren't enough left for a patrol, much less a troop. At this point, I was on a delegation that asked the adults to turn the building over to the Negro troop, but they wouldn't do that either. The chief of the District Scout Council said that it didn't own the building and thus couldn't direct the whites to give it to the Negroes. The Hut sat Scoutless while its owners tried to sell it (they did eventually, to a Negro church). It was during the time of its vacancy that we used it on two or three Saturday afternoons.

We soon made a better arrangement to play our games, at night in the ample gymnasium of Elementary School 40. The school was still then almost all-white, and I can't say the School 40 people were happy about our coming, but some of their youngsters were in our league. We never had any trouble, except one night when Richard Morton sneaked into the physics laboratory and broke some equipment.

Richard was a boy whom I had taken on my team in both baseball and basketball. He wasn't much of an athlete and the other boys didn't like him; partly for that reason, but mostly because of his neurotic personality. His parents, although rather poor, were among the few conscientious supporters of our progress. His father was a part-time preacher, a very courteous man. Anyway, his teammates wouldn't pass the ball to him, and once when he was to throw it in from out-of-bounds, he looked this way, looked that way, and then kept it himself, dribbling down the floor. (If you aren't up on basketball, that isn't allowed.)

I thought I knew Richard well, but I was surprised by the laboratory exploit. The boys were not supposed to go into that part of the building. The league paid for the trifling damage, shielding Richard's identity.

That year, the basketball league was won hands down by the Trotters, an all-black team coached by Larry Harris.

Then came the summer when the Little League was reduced in numbers to one team, which represented Meredith Park in a Junior Baseball "Class C" league covering an area of the city. As the boys approached junior high school, the greater part of them decided baseball wasn't their dish, and we had left just enough players to round out a squad of eighteen.

We moved from the small diamond, the scene of so much community drama and excitement, to the full-scale baseball field on the east side of the park. I remember being apprehensive that the thirteen- and fourteen-year-old boys wouldn't be able to make the throws on the man-sized diamond, and that we'd have to work out a system of relaying the ball to home plate. But the first day of practice showed that I hadn't noticed how they were growing.

Unlike the players, the adults got into something of a riffle over who would be manager. Four of the previous coaches stayed with the team: Larry Harris and Milton Sanford, who were Negro, Marsh Jarman and I, who were white. There was little doubt that from the point of view of baseball savvy, Harris should have been the manager. I think, that is, I know damned well the boys would have chosen him. And they would have had a better team than they did.

But men will be boys. Sanford and I had caught the fever and had no intention of withdrawing. We mutually fell back on a sort of theory that the amateur spirit was best for boys' baseball, while Harris would be too much of a "winner." (Jarman wasn't in the running for the top post.) Because I had been the founder of the earlier league, the decision was mine.

The end result was a kind of co-management, I suppose the worst possible arrangement for a baseball team. Sanford was the nominal manager, but I was also there putting in my oar, devising lineups and batting orders, selecting relief pitchers and pinch-hitters. I kept complete statistics on all these things. I must say that I did make polite suggestions to Sanford, who usually accepted them. I don't believe we ever quarreled. As for Harris, he took it with a good grace and devoted himself to training and developing the players. One year, for instance, when both our pitchers had lost their stuff, he discovered and brought up a new boy named Albert Branham, who proved to be the team's salvation. Occasionally things worked out that Harris got a chance to run a game. When he did so, he would make lineup changes that he hadn't said anything to us about.

Harris was divorced. One year he acquired a new wife and with her a stepson, Robert, who was of team age. About that time, Michael, who had always played second base, was slipping in his ability. There was a night that Mike and I arrived late to the game, and found that Sanford wasn't there and Harris was managing. His stepson was playing second. That was all right, except I assumed that since Michael was now there, Harris would put him into the game at his regular position. An entire inning went by, and Harris just left his stepson in, while Michael sat on the bench. It got to be more than I could stand—I was always tightly wound at the games—and I yelled to Harris, "Come on, put him in his position!" Harris gave that laugh he employed so effectively as a substitute for showing anger, and waved Michael into the game.

As long as he continued to live in the neighborhood, Jarman hung around and coached first base. He hadn't even the prestige to keep little Marsh in the first-string lineup—the boy was too much of a butterfingers. He and Michael were now the only white boys left. We all were pleased one evening when, in a tense contest with Arlington Presbyterian, Little Marsh was put in as a pinch hitter and rapped the single that won the game.

The team played together for four summers. Sanford and I never were able to establish much discipline—for instance, we couldn't get the boys to bunt when the situation called for it. They wanted to try for long base hits, and did so in spite of anything we said. In the same way, we never got most of them to slide—they were afraid to, and refused, preferring to be caught out. As a result, the team's progress was limited, but there was a year when we won all our league games and swaggered with dreams of glory. Then, in the first round of the city playoffs, we were slaughtered by a well-coached and disciplined suburban team.

But for all that, "the team" was a very meaningful thing in the lives of this strange group of men and boys. There was our star player, lithe, hard-hitting Jimmy Daniels, a sure-fingered first baseman but a wild left-handed pitcher, who didn't like to pitch because he was afraid he would hit the batter. Tony Madison was a great little fastball pitcher at the age of ten but lost all his speed by the time he was thirteen. We put him at third base after that for the sake of his past glories. Johnny Harris, whom we never knew where to put, could play catcher, short-stop, and the outfield better than anyone else. Tom Bleacher was the team's cutup; he was too old for the team, I felt sure.

There was our rivalry with the all-white Arlington team. It was from the church a few blocks to the east that maintained a super athletic pro-gram—and had turned Negro boys, including Johnny and Tony, away. For years, that team always defeated us, until the day Marsh got his hit. For years thereafter, we always defeated them. The power had changed hands. As we became a team playing on a full-scale diamond and trav-eling to meet well-outfitted teams from other parts of the city, it was no longer endurable that our players should be garbed in the old home-dyed T-shirts. But we had no money and no sponsors, such as the busi-nesses and institutions that paid the bills for the Little League teams. Then, I learned that Mrs. Meredith, the eighty-five-year-old widow of the author for whom the park was named, was still living. I wrote her a letter, and she responded with a check that enabled us to buy eighteen uniforms of pinstriped gray flannel, bearing a red gothic "M" on the front and numbers on the back.

The uniforms, however, remind me of an incident involving Roger Munson and myself, and perhaps this is the most fitting story to remember us by. It was during a game in the summer before we got the uniforms. Roger was down to play third base, because the pitcher was sick and Tony, our regular third-baseman, was going to pitch. Somebody else was visiting his relatives, and Roger was the only substitute left who could throw the ball from third to first. That's a pretty good throw.

Something had kept Sanford and Harris, and I was the sole manager. What with so many people being absent, including Roger, who had not yet shown up, I was in a sort of mood.

Three of the substitutes rushed at me across the diamond, all shrilling at once, "Mr. Preston, Roger isn't here! Can I play third? Please, Mr. Preston!" I frowned at them and bit my tongue. Not one of them had ever been known to field a ground ball cleanly. Not one of them could make the throw from second, let alone third. "Shut up," I yelled. But they immediately fell so silent and small that I went over and sat on a bench under the crabapple tree to simmer down. I saw that I was getting manageritis; I ought to be glad the attendance was down because the substitutes would have a chance to play, after hanging around week after week. Sanford and I still followed, or tried to follow, a policy that every boy who was present got into the game, regardless of race, creed, color, or inability to catch a pop fly. With these three, it was usually in the last inning, as pinch-hitters or in the outfield, with a prayer that nothing was hit in their direction. Let them play, and to hell with your ego. But what fun did they ever have?

Jarman came up, wearing his red cap. "Hi, Chuck," he said. "Who's gonna play third? Roger ain't here."

I turned away, answering over my shoulder, "We've still got five minutes." I walked to my car, opened the trunk, and handed out the bats, helmets, and the catcher's equipment. And there were little Troy and little Mitchell, both looking wistfully for the "team glove" we had bought in case somebody couldn't provide his own. It was bad enough that we hadn't been able to get uniforms like the other teams, only these T-shirts that the mothers had dyed various shades of red. It made us feel like niggers—all of us—before we even went on the field. And here were boys whose families, in all the years we had been playing, hadn't even bought them a miserable glove!

I handed the glove to Troy and went to meet the St. Philip's manager and the umpire, who were standing at home plate. It was clear that Roger wasn't coming, and I would have to let Adams play third. I thought, gloomily, that despite everything we would lose the game. We would lose and we would be "mired," as the baseball writers said, deeper into the cellar of the league standings—beneath the teams with baseball shoes and the teams that barred Negroes and the teams that played to win. We would be mired so deep that we would lose all hope.

I took my place in the third-base coach's box. It didn't help my mood when Troy and Harris struck out. I felt an actual dislike for the St. Philip's players, with their uniforms and their rubber cleats and their brand-new gloves. I told myself that I shouldn't, but all the same, I couldn't help hating Joe Woodson for striking out Troy and Harris in their faded T-shirts.

I kept brooding about Roger. It was Michael who had told me there was another side to him. Michael said that when Roger was with the boys, he was as mischievous as any of them and in school he was even something of a "bad boy." That was hard to square with the youngster who didn't say anything but "Yes, sir" and most of the time not even that. But after Michael said that, I noticed that Roger had a way of getting into the sideline wrestling matches instead of taking his turn at batting practice. Of course, the substitutes often got to doing that, because they played so little they lost interest. And sometimes when I called to Roger as he was fighting or throwing crabapples, he came with a smirk that, had it belonged to another boy, might have made me angry. On him it seemed more like a smile that was afraid to be.

In the first year, Roger had been one of the most inept players. At bat, he stood at all angles like a scarecrow, and even wearing a helmet he was afraid of the pitch. He swung around weakly and awkwardly, after the catcher already had the ball.

But as he grew, he got pretty good height on him and long arms; and one day when two other players had muffed easy grounders at third, we put him in there. The batter lashed a grass-cutter down the line, and to everybody's surprise, Roger got his glove on it. Then he threw to first on the fly, in itself an achievement.

From then on, Roger was the backstop third baseman and utility infielder—when he showed up. He managed to get in front of a percentage of grounders, and he caught flies even though he didn't look good doing it. When a game was over, and I checked the book, I would often find that Roger had figured in several plays.

In the games he started, I batted him seventh, and he came around at the plate too. He didn't often get a clean hit, but he developed the ability at least to put wood on the ball. That was much better than nothing, because in our league you could always count on the opposition for errors.

What Roger really thought of all this I couldn't tell. I knew all the phrases about keeping boys off the streets and saving them from juvenile delinquency, and when we needed support in some circles, I even used them, but I couldn't actually see much difference in Roger. He would come to a couple of games and miss a couple. And it might turn out he had been loafing on the corner with a group of older boys. When I asked him about it, he looked away, and his timid voice disarmed me. But I noticed that nearly always after I talked with Roger on the street, he would turn up at the next game.

But where in hell was Roger today? St. Philip's took a 2–0 lead, and then in the third Johnny Harris hit a triple with a runner on and pretty soon he stole home and it was tied. They went down to the top of the sixth that way. St. Philip's loaded the bases but there were two out and it didn't look too bad until this little redheaded kid poked one toward third. It was a ball Roger probably would have stopped, but it went through Adams' hands and into left field, where Billy Sanford threw the ball away. Three runs came in, and the batter reached second, and it was the same old story. Our wrong-side-of-the-tracks team was whipped again. It was just a matter of taking our last bats.

Jarman came up to me glowering. "Where's Roger?" he muttered crossly.

I shrugged. "It took a bad hop," I lied. What I was thinking was that now we were as mired as Roger was in his home. I had gone there many times to get him, for "going and getting" was the lot of a manager of Roger. It was an old, white folks' hand-me-down house, a rambling thing set back from the street in a bare and dusty yard. It had a wooden porch that was falling to pieces, so you had to be careful not to step through a rotten board.

Dogs and children made a kind of welcoming procession when you went to see Roger. Vague adults moved in the background, but mostly it was teenaged girls and little girls and a pair of tiny boys who looked as though they had stayed in the world by accident.

If you went at night, in basketball season, you stepped through the doorway into a room with only the eerie light of the television set. The room was filled with children sitting on the bare floor. There might be a light in the kitchen, and you would hear adults' voices, but nobody came. When you asked for Roger, a whole flock of children began running through the house calling for "Butch," which was the nickname they had hung on that gentle boy.

Roger would come down the stairs, smiling a little and looking for his gym shoes. The children all would begin looking for them in the dark. Roger's application form had been signed by a Roger Sr., but I never met him. Roger's mother was a fleshy woman who smiled too easily and too much. Her smile had Deep South and welfare and the cheap parts of pork written all over it; and it also had written on it "I give up."

Roger's parents were not my favorite Negro couple. They made me think of Shaw's line: "I hate the poor and want to abolish them." I thought also that a visit to Roger's home would be good for these Little League managers in the suburbs. It might teach them some humility to have a team full of Rogers, whose parents didn't keep score and make lemonade, and who didn't drive the boys to the games, and above all, didn't contribute money. I had never seen a thin dime from Roger's parents. If there was a spare thin dime in that family, I imagined it went for gin by the half-pint, or wine to get through the day, or a numbers ticket that would hit for the price of a Cadillac to make you forget this dirt and those cheap parts of pork. As for Roger, he was given up to me.

We went to bat in the last inning, and there was little Troy striking out again. Now, if it were Roger. . . I was getting fed up with thinking about Roger. I shouted to Troy, "It only takes one to hit it!" while I knew full well that Troy would never hit anything.

Troy struck out, Harris dribbled one to the pitcher, Tony Madison popped one to the second-baseman, and it was over. I congratulated the St. Philip's manager. Jarman and I began taking up the bases. The boys were downcast, and I was hot and tired; it was then that I saw Roger.

Roger was in the grassy space behind the crabapple tree and he was laughing as he threw crabapples with some little boys who were not on the team. And he was wearing a baseball uniform! It was white with green trim and green socks and a green cap. It was clean and practically shone in the late sun. It made Roger look like a genuine Little Leaguer on the first day of the season.

"Well, I'll be goddamned!" said Jarman.

I crossed the diamond in quick strides. "Roger!" I shouted as I passed the pitcher's mound. I yelled again at the baseline. The boys who were leaving stopped and turned to watch. Jarman was right behind me. Roger was looking at the ground.

I halted in front of Roger. "Well, look who shows up now that the game is over!" I snapped. "Look who we've been waiting for all afternoon and here he is! Tell me one thing, Roger—did you have fun watching us lose?"

Roger didn't answer, and it all boiled up in me, all the telephoning, all the "going and getting," and all the faded T-shirts and the losing. I thought about Roger's parents buying him a uniform, and blacks buying Cadillacs when their children needed shoes, and as Bill Whitcomb said, white people building orphanages and Negroes providing the orphans, and I lost my temper all the way and sneered, "And aren't we fancy in our new uniform! Not a boy on the team has a uniform, but Roger has to get one! But where was Roger's daddy when we took up the collection to buy the T-shirts?"

There was a gasp from someone, and then a dead silence for a few moments. It was so quiet you could hear the insects chirping in the trees. And then out of the silence came Troy's small voice!

"He didn't buy the uniform, Mr. Preston. It's an old uniform from the Little League. The people his mother washes for gave it to her."

Roger looked up from the uniform. There was no smirk on his face now, and for an instant I saw all the misery of the world in his eyes. In a flash, his expression seemed to harden and suddenly I saw Roger standing on a street corner, in another year or two, with Tom Bleacher and a gang of young thugs, loud-talking, blocking the sidewalk, and flashing switchblades, then piling into a car to roam across town in the night.

And I saw other things. I saw a slave ship en route from Africa; a brown mother sold at the auction block; plantation cotton pickers; and unpainted sharecroppers' huts in Alabama. I saw the frenzied eyes of a lynch mob. I saw black people cleaning latrines, and pushing mops, and bending and picking up and carrying. I saw a black man walking along a street where he could not eat or sleep or get a drink of water or knock at a front door. I saw the men piloting the slave ship, and selling the slave, and running with the mob, and sitting in the personnel office, and looking coldly out a window at the man on the street. Jesus Christ! I saw myself.

25. The Civil Rights Movement and the Changing of the Guard at the NAACP

There was no longer anything to keep Walter Rowland out of the NAACP branch presidency. The Progressive Party disputes had long ago receded into the past, and the radicals and moderates trotted along smoothly together. Then occurred a more fundamental change. Beginning with the Montgomery bus boycott, the stirring of the Southern Negroes cast up the leadership of a new breed of militant ministers, notably Dr. Martin Luther King, Jr. Following this pattern, our branch's presidency went to three preachers in a row.

This meant that we middle-class secularists of the previous decade had to adjust to new ways of working. With the preachers came the masses, which was the good part of it. It was what we had all along been striving for, and we found that public meetings became bigger and more eloquent. At the same time, something was lost: the details of committee work, of carrying through after decisions. The preachers were inclined to hold a meeting, raise a shout, and forget the follow up. But there were two things they excelled at: they "lifted" a good collection and they avidly took advantage of the new interest in Negro affairs that was being publicized by the media to garner a lot of coverage.

I never ceased to marvel at this utterly sophisticated and dynamic relationship between the preachers and their followers. There was, for instance, Reverend Watford, one of the fiercest presidents we had in my time. His home was in our city, where he was a teacher in the public schools. His church, however, was in Highland, seventy-five miles to the west, and he preached there every Sunday morning. He also worked in the post office during the school's Christmas vacations. And with all that, he had no hesitancy in becoming NAACP branch president and two years later state president.

Reverend Watford, or "Henry" as Ruth Reynolds called him, was an excitable militant. A short, fleshy man with a stutter, he affected a clerical collar, which wasn't customary in his denomination. I thought perhaps he did it because less of a "Christian" never lived! Reverend Watford emphatically did not turn the other cheek, much less do good to them who used him. Quite the contrary, he fought hard and unscrupulously.

With all his hats, Reverend Watford had to slight something now and then, and quite often it was his school. I heard a rumor that he was in trouble with the school authorities. True to his nature, he met the problem with a fierce counterattack. He spread the word that the principal had it in for him because of his civil rights activities. There was a day when the NAACP held a march on the statehouse, to support passage by the legislature of fair housing and employment bills. It was the first street demonstration the statewide organization had conducted. Starting early in the morning, members drove in from all corners of the state until about five hundred had arrived. The staging point was the church of Reverend Barton, who had been Reverend Watford's predecessor as president. The members formed ranks and marched with placards down Illinois Avenue, around the Civil War monument and to the statehouse steps, where a mass meeting was held. One could look up from the assemblage of Negroes, most of them well dressed in coats and hats, and see white faces peering furtively from windows of the legislative chambers at this new thing under the sun. We were told later that the oratory, singing, and praying had brought the proceedings inside to a halt.

Reverend Watford, of course, "took off" from school that day. I was standing by him on the steps when he was interviewed by one of the television reporters. The first thing he said was, forcibly, and with glittering eyes: "We have been given to understand that some of our teachers who are attending this great civic meeting have been threatened with reprisals by the school administration. This is a legal and nonviolent legislative gathering, very important to the future well-being of our state. It is the first duty of each citizen—every citizen—to support with his spiritual and physical presence this mighty outpouring to bring about a new day of brotherhood and harmonious race relations. I want these un-American tyrants to know," his voice grew shrill, "that I have received a telegram from Roy Wilkins in New York, the executive secretary of the National Association for the Advancement of Colored People, pledging the full resources of that powerful organization for the defense of any teacher they attempt to victimize in this dastardly fashion!"

Nobody else had heard of any attempts to victimize teachers. When I asked Ruth Reynolds about the telegram from Wilkins, she just laughed. But the Reverend's warning was broadcast far and wide, and, as it turned out, not a single teacher was penalized.

When Henry stepped up to the state leadership, the local presidency went over to Reverend Sanford Black, a Baptist who was pastor at a large, bleak church in the east side slums. Reverend Black was not someone I would call an excessively pious man. He was about Pat Johnson's age, and resembled him a good deal. Like Pat, he usually wore an amiable smile, almost a happy-go-lucky one. Although I never saw him at it, he was even reputed to play around. Whether he actually did or not, the point was that this anti-Puritan image was the one he deliberately projected: when that sort of subject came up, he would merely smile knowingly, as if to say, "of course, as a minister I can't talk about it, but I get around."

In contrast to the members of his congregation, Reverend Black lived in a swanky brick house on "Sugar Hill," six blocks to the north—that is, the rich direction—of us. Reverend Watford and some other ministers had also been among the first to integrate that neighborhood. One might have thought the poverty-stricken church members would object, but here again the white Protestant ethic didn't apply. The Negroes had enough misery in their own lives; what they wanted in a pastor, as the subjects of monarchies want in a king, was a man living out their dreams of affluence and happiness. Their only bright light in a week might be Reverend Black's merry smile as he got out of his long black Cadillac and ascended the steps of the church.

Besides his cheerful personality, the important thing Reverend Black brought to the NAACP was his church connections. The two earlier preacher presidents were, respectively, of the Colored Methodist Episcopal and African Methodist Episcopal Zion churches. Reverend Black was of that most numerous denomination, the Baptists. Henry Watford, because of his out-of-town church, was considered something of a maverick among the local ministers. Black possessed the solid standing to rally the city's other pastors into the civil rights movement. The atmosphere was ripe for such a development, with the continuing news from Dixie of the people's struggles headed by Dr. King and his Southern Christian Leadership Conference (SCLC). The ministers welcomed the opportunity to come out. Indeed, after Reverend Black got his interdenominational breakfasts and luncheons going, you would think, to hear them talk, that these ministers had invented civil rights, instead of being notoriously absent from the movement. At these affairs, which I attended as a reporter, there was much observance of protocol; the exchanging of "Doctor" as a courtesy title; and much fulsome praise, in order to commit the target of it to take an NAACP collection at his next Sunday service. There was also fulsome counter-praise and sometimes very quick thinking by the target in the hopes he might get out of it. In short, we were in preacher land. Never before did I have an opportunity to appreciate the practical side of the Negro minister's calling. I now saw him as a borderline entrepreneur who had to think twice, and three times, before giving away his revenue, the collections, or his stock-in-trade, the confidence of his congregation. It was for lack of understanding this situation that we secular people had never been able to enlist the clergy. Maybe Reverend Black could pull it off.

Reverend Black had been educated in the South. Through old friendships from those days, as well as his current activities in his national Baptist organization, he was in touch with the young ministers of SCLC. Indeed, he frequently dropped the word that he was a personal friend of Dr. Martin Luther King, Jr. I was inclined to take this with a grain of salt, until he announced that Dr. King would come to speak and spend a day or two in our town.

Dr. King's visit gave a priceless boost to the NAACP. There was a highly attended ministerial luncheon and various other events, including a scheduled television session at which both Dr. King and Reverend Black did not show up. Our inner circle surmised that they had been out and about. The principal affair was a mass meeting, which filled every seat and every corner of standing room in Reverend Arthur's new church. I don't recall just what Dr. King said on that occasion, but I remember that his eloquence roused an enthusiasm like that of spectators at a championship basketball game.

I reported all these events and after the luncheon, in Reverend Black's church office, I had the privilege of interviewing the Greatest American of the Twentieth Century. But the interview somehow didn't click. Dr. King was taciturn and seemed ill at ease; perhaps he was distrustful of me. Throughout the two days and during our conversation, I had had in mind one question, which I did not ask. I was curious to form an opinion as to whether he really believed in nonviolence as a way of transforming society, or privately considered it, as I did, a tactic, a good approach under the circumstances. I certainly couldn't conceive that this rather tongue-tied young man was another Gandhi. I concluded that I had been right about his nonviolence. It was only later that I came to believe I had been vastly mistaken: that like the other Negro ministers but on a more perfect scale, he was at the same time the most profoundly revolutionary of prophets and the merest of mortals.

For our local preachers, Dr. King's visit proved to be the high-watermark of their crusade. Most of them fell back to the cultivation of their own churches, and the NAACP returned to the care of Reverend Black and the activists.

Meanwhile, I was pursuing my interest in Negro freedom in another direction—into the past—as I traveled with Steve Caron and our comrades from the Civil War Round Table to the battlefields of Gettysburg, Antietam, Chancellorsville, and eventually to Vicksburg.

Steve and I knew there were those who thought the Civil War was over, but it seemed obvious to us that what was signed at Appomattox was only an armistice. And, if the black man needed his history to build his future, it was no less true that the principled white man had the same need, and one of the few places he could satisfy it was on a Civil War battlefield. Of course, this motive, with its pro-Negro ramifications, wasn't shared by all our buddies.

I drove the Studebaker with four of us south through Kentucky and Tennessee. There are two sets of feelings a Northern white American has as he enters the South, and men vary as to which they exhibit more of. One of our party, a retired insurance executive, was an extreme example of the type of Northerner who savors Dixie hospitality, cooking, magnolias, Spanish moss, the accent, flirtatious women, and, if the truth be known, having Negroes at one's beck and call. I found him in this respect more offensive than a Southerner. The other men seemed to feel, as I did, the sinking of the heart at the poverty, the backwardness, the ground-down state of the black people, and the vacuous hostility shown by the whites as we went through little towns. We were Northerners, and white ones at that, in Southern America. After a stop or two, we were quite conscious of our Northern license plates, and more than a little nervous. In part, we knew with inward smiles that this was because of our mission, in which like boys we were imagining ourselves the descendants of Sherman. Suppose we should happen to say, as we did, "Civil War" instead of that historical and grammatical monstrosity, "The War between the States"?

This came to a head in an incident at the first town we reached in Mississippi. A husky policeman waved me to "pull over" off the street and onto a gravel runway beside a large lawn. There was a tense silence in the car as I did so. I think every man—including the insurance executive, who may have loved the South only, after all, because he was afraid of it—said to himself, "Now!"

The policeman, however, came to the car window and bellowed, "Welcome to Mississippi!" Then we saw a billboard proclaiming that this was "Hospitality Week" in the Magnolia State. Some high school girls dressed as Old Southern Belles tripped across and gave each of us a cup of punch and a stick of graphite, one of the main items manufactured in the town.

We joked about this incident all the way to Vicksburg. It made a good story when I returned to *The Clarion*, too. Robert Hancock smiled and bobbed his head, saying, "Lord ha' mercy!" My black friends, balefully concentrating on the thought of Mississippi, didn't seem to begrudge me the fact that if I had been driving with them, my reception would have been different.

The Vicksburg battlefield and others near it, such as the secluded Champion's Hill—which appeared to have changed little since the day Grant and Pemberton faced each other there—we found well worth the journey. I was also engaged in a peripheral activity: observing the Negro in the Deep South. I watched bellboys and maids in the hotel as if they were the slaves and I was an agent of the Underground Railroad. I was half-moved to talk with them, to tell them who I was and where I came from. And yet, what good would it do?

I remained silent. It was Steve who almost brought my identity to light through a prank. Our caravan of six or seven cars, tracing Grant's famed incursion below Vicksburg, had halted in the town of Port Gibson. It was a blistering June day, with the temperature in the sun at 110 degrees. Some of us were chatting with the local newspaper publisher on a sidewalk in the town square.

With a glint in his eye, Steve said, "Mr. Preston here is a newspaperman too."

"Is that so?" said our host. "What newspaper is that?"

"*The Clarion*," I replied.

"You don't say." He reflected a moment. "I've been up that way, but I never heard of *The Clarion*. What kind of a paper is it?"

With a squirm I answered, "It's a weekly paper."

You would have thought the publisher knew my secret, for he continued relentlessly. "Well, now, what kind of a weekly paper?"

"It's a community paper," I answered curtly, and added, "Excuse me, I'm just going across the street to get a Coke."

Back at the hotel, over glasses of whiskey, the group had a laugh at my expense as Steve christened my action "The Battle of Chicken-Out Bayou" (in parody of nearby Chickasaw Bayou). I guessed he had got a little of his own courage back from Ruth Reynolds's speech.

Often in our peregrinations to the battlefields—except for Gettysburg in the North—we came upon Southerners who were suspicious of us or downright nasty. There was the year our license plates bore the words: "Lincoln Home." A son of Virginia who was an historian for the National Park Service led us all through Chancellorsville and the Wilderness and into Spotsylvania Court House before he blurted out like a belch: "Say, y'all . . . what's that Lincoln on your licenses?"

Once, the Round Table visited the field of the bloody battle of Franklin, Tennessee. That was the place we saw a plaque at the courthouse listing the county men who gave their lives in the Second World War, with the names segregated into "White" and, below, "Colored." We stayed in a dingy motel. During the night, we were awakened by the sound of sirens, and in the morning we asked the proprietor what they had been.

"It was nothing," he replied. Looking us square in the eyes, he added, "Just a colored house burned down."

From the Vicksburg trip, we brought back another picture of a "colored house." This was miles from the highway, down an unpaved road amidst thick trees and vines leading to Grand Gulf and the river.

Our destination, Grand Gulf, was of importance in the Union operations below Vicksburg. It proved to be a couple of shacks. The road was so dusty that on the way back I lost sight of the car ahead of us at a fork and took the wrong direction so that we lost the other cars in our caravan for a while.

Suddenly we came on a clearing with a house, I suppose, that was no worse than many homes of blacks in the rural South. Several indescribably filthy children were playing, and they stopped to look at us. One little girl, who appeared to be about five or six, had bulging sickly eyes and her arms were covered with some sort of excrescence, like a tree fungus.

We had got used to seeing thin, ragged, and uncared-for black children, but these kids, deep in the delta jungle of the Mississippi, looked as if they were wild. They wouldn't talk with us. One of the men tossed some coins to them, but they didn't hurry to pick them up. They stood as if rooted, watching our cars as we drove away.

As I recall, it was a story in *The Herald*, the afternoon paper that was timidly becoming more liberal, that put me onto Jesse Goode. He was an elderly white man, a prolific inventor and president of the Goode Lock Company, a manufacturer at the edge of the ghetto not far from *The Clarion*. What *The Herald* revealed was his activity in the white supremacist National States Rights Party. He traveled between our state and Alabama and Georgia in his private plane, attending conferences and meeting with leaders of the party. He was actually seeking its vice presidential nomination, to be made at a forthcoming convention. He was assisted in his campaign by his two sons, who were also involved in the management of the firm.

I decided to interview Goode. I set on just going in without warning and identifying myself as a reporter from *The Clarion*, with the hope he wouldn't know it was a Negro newspaper. I walked in, but the receptionist said he wasn't there. I improved the opportunity by engaging her and another woman employee in a conversation from which I learned some curious things: that no one could work for the firm who smoked (much less drank), and that all employees were required to attend a certain fundamentalist church. "Mr. Goode is very strict," the receptionist said.

I said I would call again and went away.

But I didn't have to return. The following day when I got back to *The Clarion* after lunch, I found a strange sight in the newsroom. A circle of the Negroes—Mr. Talbott, Bill, Smitty, and one or two others—had gathered, as they sometimes did, about an interesting caller. In the center, speaking slowly and earnestly, was a very clean, well-dressed, white-haired white man. I soon realized it was Jesse Goode.

"My program is to send all the colored people to Africa," he was saying with precise politeness, looking directly at one after another of *The Clarion* men. "You don't belong in this country; your forefathers were brought here by force; that was aggregate sin on the part of my forefathers. Now America must atone for that sin, and must put things back as God intended them."

"And what do you propose to do in the meantime?" asked Mr. Talbott.

"In the meantime," he replied quietly, "we must establish absolutely total segregation of the races throughout the United States. Not only in schools, in places of public accommodation, in churches, but in all places of employment. This is the only way we can preserve racial purity. The purity of the white race, which is the American race—and the purity of the black race, the African race."

"A little late for that," quipped Walt Evers.

Goode did not smile—he didn't smile once during the hour he spent with us. "What? A little late?" he said. "I didn't hear you, I don't hear too well. You are referring to the fact that some colored people have a certain amount of white blood. They are the victims of the sins of the fathers. Their fathers cohabited with white people."

"Most generally, their mothers," rejoindered Walt, but the visitor answered, "Fathers or mothers, it doesn't matter, they committed carnal sin. They will die out. God is not mocked. They will not generate, we can leave that to God. They will all be gone within a century."

He went on and on, calmly spinning out his theories, and the Negroes sat there enthralled. It was a very courteous session on both sides. It was obvious that he had come fully expecting the Negroes to support his plans, and when he rose to leave, he believed he had done so. He left a copy of a brochure he had published in his quest for the vice presidency.

We looked it over after he left. It was a luxurious printing job, on expensive, coated paper. It had been edited by a former radio personality who was out of a job. He was a man who should have known better. One could almost see him blush as he put his name to it.

None of us could blame the neat old man with his staring eyes. He was being taken, right and left. But it was horrible to think of his sons, his employees, and the men who were in it for the sake of nothing but money, helping to advance his insane schemes.

Jesse Goode's views on interracial sex were not shared by every religious white person. At the time of the Wright case, Walt reported meeting with a white woman who said forthrightly, "If God didn't want the black people and white people to get together, he wouldn't have made the fixtures to fit."

The Skipper, in connection with his attitude toward intimacy, was bothering me more and more. When I was sitting in the auditorium at a Mammoth Meeting, which was where I usually saw him, or for that matter, on any other occasion when we came together, he would drop down beside me and ask in his husky voice, "Say, Chuck, what do you hear of Frances (or Warren, or Shifra, or Aughenbaugh)?"

These people had all been in or near the Communist Party twenty years before, during the Depression. In the movement, such questions were not answered; indeed, they were not asked, except by the police and their agents. In most cases, fortunately, I was unable to answer them, since I had heard nothing of the people involved. But scraps of information might be lurking in my mind, and there was always the danger of blurting them out in reply to these point-blank demands.

"Now Frances, she moved to Washington, didn't she?" We both knew that she had (long ago) and that her husband worked for some government department, where a loose word might bring his job crashing down on him. What should I say? The Skipper had put his question as one exchanged between confidants who were discussing an old mutual friend and co-conspirator of theirs—between comrades concerned about the fate of a fellow revolutionary.

"Well, I don't know, Skipper, I lost track of her," I would answer weakly.

"Lost track?" he would reply with asperity. "She moved to Washington. Joe got a government job. I wonder if they're still there. They were a couple of real people."

I gathered that I was supposed to feel less real. The Skipper's look indicated that he knew I knew where Frances and Joe were. But another thing I noted was that he never went on to accuse me directly of evading a question.

"Where is your brother now?" he rapped out suddenly.

This was different. My brother Harry had never been a Communist, and the Skipper had not known him. The first time he asked me, I was taken by surprise and gave him the correct answer. But still I didn't feel good about it and resolved, since I was having such difficulty declining to answer, that in the future I would lie. And when he asked me again (for he would ask the same questions over), I said quickly, "Pittsburgh."

"I thought you said he was in Dayton," the Skipper observed mildly. "Is he still working for a newspaper chain?"

"We don't keep in very close touch," I said, almost stammering, "but he's in Pittsburgh."

The Skipper gave me a withering look. Obviously I would know whether my brother was working for the chain.

Even after I had talked it over several times with Susan, I never could get ready for the Skipper's cross examinations. My trouble was that I couldn't decide firmly what I was dealing with. My suspicions were strong, but, on the other hand, the Skipper was a highly respected figure in the Negro community, with a place in the "Black Revolution." Even more to the point was his well-known avidity for gossip. He had to know all there was about every person. I had observed that this trait was useful in his dealings with the public, both inside the YMCA and out, but it was accepted as an inherent part of his personality. Other people laughed it off. Were they too trusting of the Skipper, or was I getting paranoid about him?

There was only one person I could take this problem to. Pat Johnson listened, at first with some embarrassment, but with curiosity. He said he was glad I had told him about it, and he agreed we should be as careful as we could. What else was there to say? We always knew that somewhere about us were "the men in black suits," fantastically occupied in making lists of our names, places of abode, and our very conversations. There were also foolish people who didn't belong in this category, although they might do harm by running their mouths. We didn't stop our lives or our work because of either one or the other.

26. Dreams Deferred

The first time I covered the state finals, on a press ticket issued by the HSAA, it was the equivalent in our community to, say, a dinner invitation to the White House. The following Monday I received a call from the Association's Commissioner, M.W. Paulson. We had never met.

"Mr. Preston," he said, "how did you enjoy the Finals?"

"I didn't like the way they turned out," I joked. "Aside from that, everything was fine."

"As a matter of fact," he said, "you didn't go to the Finals, did you?"

I realized he had discovered a white man sitting in the seat assigned to *The Clarion*. From this, he had leapt to the conclusion that *The Clarion*'s reporter must have sold his press ticket—this ranked as a capital crime in our state.

It was the sort of thing Negroes were suspected of doing, and that was why a "respectable" organization like the HSAA generally didn't work with them.

"Oh, but I did, Mr. Paulson," I said. "And wrote stories all over *The Clarion*, if you've read this week's issue."

He was nonplussed, but persevered. After all, he had the evidence. "Are you sure you went to the Finals?"

I decided to let him off the hook and explained that although I worked for a Negro newspaper, I was not a Negro.

The man was mortified and apologized profusely. It wasn't a simple mistake: he had leveled a racist charge, by innuendo at least, and just then—because of fire that was coming at various institutions from pro-black quarters—that was the last thing he wanted to be caught doing. He had formerly been a high school principal in the southern part of the state, and he now spent a good deal of his time declaring that he had never been prejudiced against Negroes. And he knew better than I—so that I didn't have to remind him—that many of the white men occupying press seats were not actually reporting the games, but were editors on whom he relied for a good press, or even big shots who had wheedled their way in with their influence.

This small incident would benefit *The Clarion* and Negroes generally in the HSAA's future operations. M. W. Paulson leaned over so far backward in being courteous to black newspapers that his hat almost touched the sidewalk. My *Clarion* mates were familiar with this kind of situation and knew how to take advantage of it. Walt Evers, Lehman, and Smitty overwhelmed the Commissioner with smiles of affection, extracting from him in return unheard-of numbers of free tickets and parking places in reserved areas. If you let a man make a fool of himself in mistreating you, he will sometimes become your benefactor for life.

For the next three years, the story of basketball at Dunbar, and indeed throughout the state, was principally the story of Oscar Bentley.

When Oscar Bentley was a sophomore at Dunbar, he spent the first couple of months as a substitute. He had grown in the previous two years, and it was apparent he was going to be a good deal taller than his brother Bailey. There was a groundswell among the students on his behalf. "We want Little Flap!" they would chant at games. But the starting five were veterans, and Coach James was waiting until the talented newcomer should, so to speak, fight his way into the lineup.

There came a game when, in the third quarter, things were going badly. James decided to put Oscar in, and the fans sent up a mighty cheer when they saw him report to the scorer's box. As soon as he entered the lineup, the struggle took on a different complexion. The young fans had not been mistaken. He was liquid fire. Dunbar came from twelve points behind to win. Oscar had arrived.

Only a sophomore, his skills hadn't really matured, and Dunbar again was eliminated after reaching the Round of Sixteen. That summer he visited relatives on a farm in Tennessee, and when he came back he had shot up to a sturdy six-foot-three (eventually he reached six-five). There was no holding him, and that year Dunbar finally won the state championship, with hardly a close game all the way. The next year, Oscar's last, the Winged Lions won again, beating Mercer Lincoln in an all-black championship game with a score that resembled the pros. It was after that game, incidentally, that M. W. Paulson told me a fan had called to ask him, "How many Negroes can a team have?"

Oscar then went on to break up the All-Star games and to be named Star of Stars in both of them. His subsequent career at a nearby university and in the National Basketball Association is known to all fans. He is ranked as one of the greatest players in basketball history.

On the court, Oscar had all the shots, all the moves there were, plus some new ones of his invention. I don't know how many records he established. Above these, he had that same ability he had shown in junior high school to dominate the game. After mastering the skill of shooting from anywhere, in fact, he concentrated on his assists; that is, passing to other players so that they could score. This decision was of great value in his career. Shooters, or gunners as they were called, were a dime a dozen in college and professional circles. Bailey Bentley was a gunner, and never had a chance with the pros. But a player who could set up the offense, maneuver it, and then whip a fast and accurate pass to a teammate for an easy shot was a coach's darling. And in these things, Oscar has never been surpassed.

He was shy, and I didn't get to know him well, even though his family moved to our neighborhood and Michael had the thrill of playing with him in alley games. I can't say I was a friend of Oscar, as I was of Hallie Davis, who for years sent me postcards from faraway places where he was appearing with the Globetrotters; or Lavern Howard, the bubbling little star of later Dunbar teams who was his own best press agent, and used to engage me in long conversations.

Dunbar won the championship a third time after Oscar left for college. It was the Dunbar Era. Little white boys hung around the

Dunbar players, seeking their autographs. Fans of the losing team in an early round of the tournament called to fans of the winning team: "Too bad! Now you'll have to play Dunbar!" It seemed there would be no end to the glory. But something major was happening. After many long years of Dunbar being the designated school for Negroes, the city's school authorities "tightened the enforcement of high school integration," that is to say, the assignment of Negro athletes to the neighborhood high school. There was to be no more of the system whereby Negro youths, no matter what part of town they lived in, were to be enrolled at Dunbar. Under the old system, several of the Dunbar athletes had lived in other school districts. Even Oscar had been first in the Vo-Tech district, and then in the Northridge district. Now the white high school coaches decided that was a shame and a scandal. They darned well wanted the district regulations enforced, so they would get their own Negroes! The fans supported them: "Give us our Negroes!" And the School Board obliged. Practically speaking, it was the greatest spur to integration during my life in that city.

At a certain point, Paul James was obliged to assess his situation. He had won all the honors there were, and he stood at the very top of the state's leading "industry." He was universally acclaimed a basketball miracle man as well as "a gentleman and a credit to his race." His protégés were going on to clean up with the colleges, the Trotters, and the pros. Where was he to go?

James wasn't quite as young as he looked. He had a wife, Ruth, and a couple of youngsters. They were living on a coach's salary—and by the rules of the school administration, every coach in town received the same salary, regardless of whether he won the state championship or lost all the games, nor were there any merit raises for exemplifying the best sportsmanship and youth leadership.

In the ordinary, that is to say, the white, course of things, James would have been offered a better-paying position either by one of the large high schools around the state that were constantly bidding for winning coaches (with under-the-table benefits from businessmen reputed to reach lavish figures), or a college. It was just about this time that our state university went looking for a new coach. There was no more logical man for the job than James, and I wrote many a column boosting him for it. I thought he had a chance. I knew, of course, that colleges did not employ Negro coaches, but James had received so many compliments, tributes, awards, and dinners—I didn't believe that was how the people of our state looked at him, so dapper, so winning and so sportsmanlike.

I was wrong, as far as the university was concerned. The appointment went to a white man from another state. James received one or two offers from black colleges in the South, but he didn't desire to move there.

When the news broke it was like a thunderclap: Paul James resigned as Dunbar's coach. He would replace Ephraim Carter, who was retiring, as athletic director, a position which carried a higher salary but in which he would have nothing to do with coaching. Bill Winslow, the young star a few years out of the state university, would become coach.

The people were struck down. Walt Evers was on the verge of tears. James was going to leave the Lions! It was "The Lost Leader" and "Say it ain't so, Joe" rolled into one. It was the eternal story of the black people: something pure and priceless had been theirs for a time, and then somehow it had been destroyed. The fans were bewildered.

"But why?" demanded Smitty, who had been restored for a time as city editor. "The niggers are saying they got to him, or maybe got something on him. Paul James desert the ship? Unbelievable! Why?"

I went to Dunbar and interviewed James. Smitty read my story avidly, then said, "Now that makes sense! I understand that!" Like all the rest of us, until then he had been looking on James not as a man with normal ambitions and needs, but as a sort of King Arthur of the basketball floor.

Because it was a page one top streamer story, the headline was up to the city editor rather than the sports editor. Smitty wrote: "WANT ONLY MORE MONEY—JAMES."

I objected. What Smitty meant by it was "I DON'T WANT TO LEAVE THE DUNBAR LIONS BUT I WANT TO ADVANCE—JAMES," but he couldn't get that into the type space. I tried to point out that the headline made James look like a mercenary, and that a salary increase was only part of the story.

But Smitty, who was sober, was not disposed to give more time to the headline. He had struck it off, and it counted (that is, fit the space). "Hell, no," he said. "Money—that tells the story. The readers understand money. He wants more money, and he ought to have more money. Damned shame!"

After publication, Smitty's headline got me in trouble with the Jameses. Paul said a few soft but unmistakable words, and Ruth was less inhibited. She told me off on the telephone, and was chilly toward me thereafter. I regretted that, but there was nothing I could do about it. Experience had taught me it's a waste of time trying to explain newspaper procedure to laymen when they're filled with indignation.

It was the next year, under Winslow, that the Winged Lions won their third championship, but it was a team that had largely been developed by James. That proved to be the end of the Dunbar Era. The Lions' wings were clipped, and they went back to losing in the Sectional. Winslow didn't appear to have the touch as a coach. Meanwhile, James sat in the director's office scheduling games and ordering equipment, and also took up real estate on the side.

After two years, there was a sequel to the Paul James story. I continued to urge in my column that it would be a significant move for him to become coach at one of the basketball-minded integrated high schools around the state. But I hadn't considered all the angles of their private life. The Jameses had bought a home in Clearview Acres, a suburban development for Negroes northwest of town. Pat Johnson and Walter Rowland had also moved there, as did a good many members of the younger middle-class set. Clearview had all the advantages of suburbia: clean air, sunshine, a good new school, plus the companionship of like-minded Negroes. There was no other place like it in the entire state, and Paul wouldn't want to take his family to some town like Winette, where the black community was sequestered in poverty on the other side of the tracks.

A solution seemed to have appeared, and the millennium Walt and I were waiting for seemed to have arrived, when the authorities of Cedarville High School suddenly made an offer to James. Cedarville

was an old basketball town that had fallen on a losing streak. There
were a handful of Negroes there. It was a county seat about twenty-five
miles northwest of the city, only twenty or so from where James lived,
reached by a four-lane highway that ran directly past his development.

He could live in Clearview and commute to coach in Cedarville; it
would involve hardly more time than it took him to drive to Dunbar in
city traffic.

James told the press he was accepting the offer. The news flashed
throughout the state and seemed to meet a favorable response. Walt
and I were ecstatic: basketball was bringing about civilization, as we
had always dreamed it might. Not only was James receiving a sizeable
increase in salary, but a Negro was getting a chance to show what he
could do with the boys of an ordinary "white" school. We had, of
course, no doubts on two scores: one, that James's teams at Cedarville
would immediately become championship contenders; two, that the
suave sportsman himself would soon be the most popular man in that
typical American town.

And then one afternoon, Walt came into the newsroom and threw
a *Tribune* on the desk. "There," he said, "read that!" and turned to
look gloomily out the window, at the side of the church next door. He
was picking his teeth nervously.

The paper had fallen off the desk onto the floor. I took it up and
read. Groups had been gathering on the downtown streets of
Cedarville and talking excitedly. The targets of their indignation were
the school board and the principal. They didn't want James. They
didn't want, and were determined not to have, the best coach and the
most inspiring sportsman in the state. And the reason for their indignation, although not reported in those days when journalism was less
frank than it is now, was obviously because he was a nigger.

The school officials caved in to the community's pressure and
withdrew their offer. James insisted on a personal meeting so they had
to tell him face to face. Then he went back to his scheduling at
Dunbar. Cedarville went back to white supremacy and its losing
streak. Negroes went back to playing the numbers, which they hadn't
stopped in any case, and how right they were.

27. Father and Son

The year the Meredith Mansions were in the seventh grade, they were among the best in the league. They looked splendid in their new uniforms and their red baseball caps, which, however, a number of them insisted on crushing at the sides and turning the bills up to wear bebop style. Far behind were the days when lily-white Arlington practiced on us; now Arlington was our country cousin. The team won all ten of its season games and went into the city playoffs, where it lost in the first round. I remember I was in such a frenzy that Wilbur Van Buren at one point looked up at me and said, "Mr. Preston, how you're cussing!" I realized I had been shouting things that weren't suitable for boys' baseball. The next year, as Negroes kept moving into the neighborhood, we picked up several new players and again were a contender for the playoffs. One of the newcomers was Officer Whitmore's son, "Dizzy." He was a homerun hitter, and in the presence of several boys, I once complimented him on his play.

"Yes," said Johnny Harris. "It's too bad he's so ugly, ain't it?" He was actually a handsome lad, but as I should have known, in friendly Negro circles you weren't supposed to pass compliments.

The Jarmans had moved to the suburbs. Another white youngster, the son of a professor from Canada who seemed with us on the race question, became Americanized and went over to Arlington after playing with us for a season. Michael was the only white boy remaining on the squad. None of us—not he and I, or he and Susan, nor the whole family together—discussed this situation. Not that Susan and I weren't worried about it. Michael was a teenager, was in the gang stage and approaching the girl stage, and he seemed to be—in contrast to his earlier livewire self—unusually shy. He wasn't nearly as good a ball player as he used to be; his hitting had fallen off to the point where I had to move him from lead man to eighth or ninth in the order. After this happened, for two years in a row he wouldn't go out for the team at the start of the season until I practically dragged him to the park. I insisted, "Just try! Just try it for two weeks, and then if you want to drop out, it's okay."

At the start of the eighth-grade year, he couldn't hit the ball at all. One horrible afternoon at practice, I threw him about fifty pitches, right over the plate, at first fast, then soft and easy. The whole team was watching. My idea was that when he hit one, his slump would be over. But he missed them all. I was overwrought, and finally Larry Harris said to me quietly, "That's not the way, Chuck. Let the boy go."

He stayed with the team through the season, getting by mostly on his glove. He seemed to enjoy it, making me think I had acted correctly. What Susan and I were really worried about was his non-baseball relations with his peers, how they might be treating him, and whether he wasn't tending to withdraw from a social life that must have its rough spots. How was he reconciling loyalty to his father's notorious pro-Negroism (which he too seemed to have totally adopted) with his need for friendship with white boys and girls who had the common prejudice? What attitude were they taking toward him? Junior high school kids can be cruel, and I knew well that the frequently voiced opinion, "Young people have no prejudice," didn't apply, at least not to the race question at that time.

School, the streets, his friends' homes—these were areas into which we couldn't follow him, and we just didn't know what was happening. Michael never brought up the subject. I now believe he may have been afraid to, fearing I would be angry with him for his doubts and vacillations. I used to watch him, wondering what he was thinking, and I suppose he felt the same toward me.

I had never envisioned Michael following in my footsteps. Integrationist, yes; but I had dreamed he could pick up that one quality and go on to lead a "successful" life, in an America hopefully with some improvements, or, if worse came to worst, even as it was. He was a bright child, he had brought home rather high grades from school— and Susan and I, in the quiet of the night, had talked of sending him to Harvard. We thought his blossoming would begin about now, in junior high school. However, while his grades were still mostly respectable, it seemed to us he was hanging around home too much, seeking to remain in that state of childhood where our family group had been warm and intimate. And living, as we now and then got a glimpse, a life of who knew what fantasies in an effort to deal with the wild and enormous pressures he was under. Meanwhile, his only close friend for a long time was Harry Thurman, a good-looking and gentle, extremely shy black boy from a poor family, who was an utter failure in school and wasn't even on our baseball team. Susan and I felt sorry for Harry, who one year suffered the additional misfortune of losing sight in one eye when it was struck by a random shot from a BB gun. It seemed to be the friendship of the lost boys.

As for discussing it all, what was there to say? We had set out on a road, or I had set out and taken the other two with me; and there wasn't any other road, there was nothing to do but go on wherever it led.

On the team itself, they were all good friends and there certainly wasn't any difficulty for Michael. I never heard one slight racial remark from any of the Negro players, nor from Michael. Whatever Michael's situation might or might not be doing to him psychologically, it was preserving him physically as the neighborhood filled with black people. During a period when black youths of the city were committing attacks on whites, he came home one night from a tournament game at Carlton field house after a narrow escape. He said a group of strange Negro boys had been following him, obviously bent on assault. He had begun to walk faster, but they did likewise. In the nick of time, he overtook Tony and Johnny and Jim Daniels, and they called out to the strangers: "Leave him alone, he's all right."

That eighth-grade summer, one of our new players was a wild black boy from the South named Dennis Baxter. He was tremendously strong and hit the ball a mile, but he fielded as though he had never played baseball before.

Dennis was game for everything and somehow acquired a set of spikes, which he wore although he didn't know too much about them. One afternoon at Northwest Park, he slid into second and caught his foot on the bag. He didn't get up. I ran to him and saw his foot turned at a sickening angle.

Having once broken an ankle myself, I knew enough not to move it. Some of the boys helped Dennis hop off the field, where he was deposited in the shade of a tree. As it happened, Joe Best, the white

PAL officer who was in charge of our league, was at another diamond in the park, and I sent for him.

Joe was typecast for the role of cop—he had a long, lantern jaw, bluish cheeks from prolific facial hair, and an expression of stupidity. He arrived and started to take hold of Dennis's leg and foot.

"Joe, you'd better call an ambulance," I said. "It looks like a broken ankle."

Joe considered this, or something, as he stood there. And then I thought I understood what was going through his mind. This boy was jet black and poor. Joe didn't have a radio car and would have to go to the park headquarters and make a phone call. Not that Joe was lazy, but he didn't like the idea of doing it for a nigger. And then the ambulance would have to drive all the way to the park. Was it necessary?

Joe took off Dennis's shoe. Then he started to peel off the tight baseball stocking. Nothing could be worse, if the ankle was broken.

What Dennis needed at that point was somebody who would knock the policeman down. At least I said insistently, "Goddamn it, Joe, call an ambulance—don't fool with his foot, can't you see it's broken?"

Joe didn't answer me, but continued peeling off the stocking. Dennis grimaced and said, "That hurts."

When it was bare, the boy's ankle looked as broken as it had in the stocking. Finally, Joe went off to call the ambulance.

The next time I saw Dennis, he was lying in a swing on the front porch of the broken-down house where he lived, a half-block south of Thirty-eighth Street, with his leg in a cast. I stopped by several times: I was anxious to see how the ankle would work after it came out of the cast. If it hadn't healed properly, that would be it. What had held me back from raising a storm that would have stopped the policeman from his fooling around? Suppose it had been Michael? The season ended, and I got busy with football. I never did see Dennis Baxter after the cast was removed. Wherever he is now, I only hope he isn't limping.

That September, Michael and most of the others entered Northridge High School, and when spring came, several of them tried out for the freshman team. Jim Daniels and Johnny Harris had no trouble making the squad. Michael, however, and Milton Sanford Jr., the son of the manager, went through a weird experience that I don't understand to this day. It has always seemed to me that it bore some relation to the racial struggles in town—but with a twist.

The Northridge varsity baseball coach, Harry Lieder, was a white man and a prominent member of the State Officials' Association. During the summer months, he was the city director of Junior Baseball. I had many dealings with him in this capacity. I wasn't conscious of any particular animosity between us, but I never knew what the white referees and schoolmen were saying about me in my absence. The freshman coach, however, was a Negro, Dick Cochrane, a onetime outstanding athlete at Carlton. He was not a young man. After years of teaching in black elementary schools, he had benefited by the city's integration gestures to become the second Negro coach in a "white" high school. There were only two other Negro faculty members at Northridge.

Michael answered Cochrane's call for freshman tryouts reluctantly, again at my insistence. "After all these years you've got to try," I commanded. "The chance won't come again, and you might regret having passed it up. And besides," I said, "either you'll make the team, or you'll be cut and it will be over."

Milton also seemed like he was in a retiring phase, and I thought his father might have said much the same thing to him.

It didn't work out that way. The two boys went every day to practice, but they neither made the team nor were "cut." And when uniforms were issued they weren't given any. This wasn't definitive, because the team was short of uniforms and one might still be in candidate status. They were waiting for the coach to post a list, or to come around and say, "I'm sorry, but we'll have to let you go." Cochrane never did so.

Mike told me Cochrane was taking only fourteen boys to the games that were played on the Lakeside diamonds. Judging from my own experience, I thought he might be in need of transportation. I called him and offered to carry some of the players in my car. If only Michael and Milton could be regular members of the squad, I thought, it wouldn't matter so much that they didn't get into the games.

I could hear hostility in Cochrane's voice as he said briefly but with courtesy, "Thank you, that won't be necessary." I realized I had made a mistake. He was sensitive toward parents trying to tell him how to run the team.

The season went on and on—Mike went to all the practices—and he was miserable but helpless, caught between his father and his coach. Milton quit after a few weeks, which was more humane. I couldn't interfere again, but I kept expecting Cochrane to do something. Maybe it was a simple misunderstanding that could be cleared up in a minute. Damn it, I was on his side! But nothing ever came, and Mike finished out the season in limbo.

He wasn't one to express his feelings, but I thought he was in agony. I had nothing to say to him because I didn't know what to make of it myself. I had learned in my years of Junior Baseball that men will make war on men through boys. At times, I suspected that Lieder had a grudge against me because of my militant writings and activities, and was taking it out on the boys through Cochrane (who, in his "pioneer" position, could be easily intimidated). Then, I thought Cochrane might have been afraid of my radical reputation, or disliked me because of it, as some conservative Negroes did anyone who rocked the boat. Then I thought the converse, that Cochrane secretly "dug" my activities and thought Michael wasn't good enough for the team but didn't want to cut him because he was my son. Then, I wondered if there hadn't been a breakdown in communications: Michael had been ill one week, and Cochrane might have made the cuts then and forgotten that he never told Mike—in which case he would be as mystified as we were. Or Lord knew what.

It wasn't an auspicious beginning, to say the least, for Michael's high school years. I had long been used to not knowing what certain people, or a given person, thought of me. You can lose your identity that way. I hadn't realized that my sins in defying prejudice would be visited on my innocent and helpless son—that he, too, would never be certain what people thought of his father, and thus of him; and what his identity was.

After school was out that summer, the Manford's had a team, but it wasn't the same. The boys were drifting into other interests. For

Sanders and me, both our sons having lost their touch, it was coming to be a chore. Michael couldn't hit a lick and had to bat last. Milton was worse than useless, for he could no longer even catch a fly ball. A couple of rough youngsters had shown up from around 28th Street. One of them was a boy who had stolen Mike's bicycle. We had gotten it back, and it was forgiven. But it was hard to put him at second base and send Mike to the bench, and yet he played rings around Mike and there was no dodging it.

What little parental support we had ever had was breaking down, and sometimes I was obliged to carry as many as ten players in my car. God knows how they packed themselves in, they were getting so big. I took to making two trips and found it tiresome. One night, we played on the east side, and after the game, I couldn't round them up to start home. They were in a kind of silly mood, throwing clumps of dirt and laughing. They wouldn't get into the car and it was growing dark. Finally, I drove off with Michael and little Troy, leaving the others to fend for themselves. After I reached home, I felt remorse and decided to go back for them. No matter how angry I was with them, I knew they didn't have bus fare.

I drove along the routes I thought they might have taken if they set out walking, but I saw no sign of them. They weren't at the park. I learned later that they had walked all the way home by another route, singing and shouting in the moonlight. What to me was a distance necessitating transport of some kind was a merry stroll across town to them. Their "rebellion" had been a sign that they had no further need of Sanders and me. At the end of that season, we disbanded the team.

Meanwhile, on the small diamond at Meredith Park, what might be called the Second Saga of Junior Baseball had begun. This was an all-Negro league starting out again with the little fellows. The managers were young black fathers whom I hadn't known before. Sanders and Harris and I met with them a few times to help them get started, and then turned over the equipment and uniforms and left them to their own devices. They went through their period of difficulty, but as Emerson said, when half-gods go, the gods arrive, and in four or five years, Meredith was winning city championships. One summer

Michael had a job with the Junior Baseball organization, umpiring the Meredith "Class D" games.

On the east side, the development of Negro boys' baseball took a different course. A black father and former athlete named Larry Dunham was determined that there, in the midst of the city's worst slums, a regulation Little League should be established just like those in the affluent suburbs. While working at his job with the electric utility to support his wife and four children, he labored tirelessly in his spare time to make this dream come true. It took him years. Dunham gathered and held together a committee of people from the neighborhood; obtained the cooperation of the "white" Little League organization, and begged financial contributions from business firms. He persuaded the owners of a foundry to donate some unused land for a baseball field. The committee, with a borrowed bulldozer, then pitched in and performed the physical labor of clearing and grading the site themselves, shaping the diamond with raised pitcher's mound, sodding the outfield, building dugouts for the teams and stands for the spectators, and erecting a fence. It was incredible. They then had to buy complete Little League uniforms for six teams of fourteen players. Since altogether too many boys turned out for one league, they had to form another, for the younger boys. These youngsters played in a city park, and the committee provided them with T-shirts and caps. Then, the committee members discharged all the multifarious tasks involved in conducting this vast organization (it later expanded to one "major" league and three "minor" leagues) all summer long, year after year.

It was a glorious day for the community when the Washington Little League opened in the new park. And after five years of the men and boys getting their stuff together, it was another glorious day when that league won the state championship. As for Larry Dunbar—and his committee—what people there are in the black ghettoes of America!

28. The People's Paper

The people came into *The Clarion* with stories, problems, questions, bills of goods to sell, and axes to grind. They came sober and they came drunk. They came in trouble, because they didn't know where else to turn. Negroes felt at home at *The Clarion* as soon as they saw all those black faces. They might look at me, but I must be harmless; maybe I was a fair-skinned Negro. They came in, relaxed, and told their stories. Mr. Talbott never tired of talking with them, or rather listening to them. He didn't hurry them; he gave them all the time there was. He told them that we couldn't dispense legal or medical advice, but he never brushed them off. They interrupted the work and the workers, but to him they were as sacred as cows in India. You must welcome the people into your newspaper plant, let their children peck on the typewriter, and have Pierce cast a line of headline type with their name for a souvenir; the people bring you the news. Even when they don't, they bring their need for a friend and champion, and if you treat them hospitably, they are loyal to you from then on. Their eyes light up when they see *The Clarion* paper. They buy it just to have it around, even if they don't read it. Even if they don't buy it, they speak well of it. Or at least think well of it. Lock out the staff if you must, but let the people in.

Mrs. Weyhouse calls: "Hey, some of you reporters, come out here, these people have a three-week-old baby that talks."

But the publisher gets there first. "Well, hello, and how do you do, sir? And this is the little fellow. Or is it a girl? And what's his name? And you say he talks?"

"Well, he talked once—just once. Yes, he named Little Robert. He named for he daddy."

"Is that so! And what did he say when he talked?"

"Say, 'Da.' Seem like he talkin' to he daddy. Right at him."

"Is that so! You don't say! Well! He's a fine boy. Call us if he speaks again."

"Yes, suh, thank y'all—we will."

"You do that now! Goodbye, madam! And goodbye, sir! Be sure to come back again!"

That was Mr. Talbott. Another time a dark young couple came to the front counter and the man asked, "Can a chicken live after its head is cut off?"

I was there, and Bill Whitcomb—a little crowd soon gathered.

They had the chicken with them, in a stewing pan with some water. Not only was its head off, it was dressed and ready for stewing. And there—its heart was beating, or something beat in its thorax. Seeing is believing.

Walt Evers leaned over for a closer look, then wrinkled his nose. "How long y'all had that chicken?" he asked.

"Yes'day. We was gonna cook it las' night."

"It's dead all right!" Walt said with a laugh, turning away. But *The Clarion* was nothing if not enterprising, and on Mr. Talbott's suggestion, I then and there made a telephone call to a widely known heart research clinic that was in our town and put the question to a prominent doctor. He, too, asked how long the chicken had been dead, and he theorized, as I understood him, that there could be a "reflex" twitching of the heart muscle.

This explanation sufficed and was discussed from person to person, until Smitty came in. He unceremoniously picked the chicken up and turned it over. The entrails had been cleaned out; there was no heart to beat. He put it back, and the thorax twitched again. Then someone saw that this happened when the pot was moved or tilted, causing the water to swish and force air upward inside the carcass. The air bubble, having nowhere to go, compelled the thorax to expand. Thus ended the mystery of the living-dead chicken.

Not only the black people were welcome at the "*Clarion* station," as some called it, but peripheral white people, young rebels, radicals like Penny and myself, stray cats and dogs—anyone cast out by the power structure. There was a year when Mr. Talbott rented space on the parking lot to a band of gypsies. They lived, not in tents as in my boyhood, but in trailers. First arrived three trailers of them—then eight or nine—and finally twenty-four. I knew that one solid motive of Mr. Talbott was to make some money. But I also recognized, from the way he thrust his jaw out, the motive that gypsies were people and entitled to the freedom of the city. For that matter, though they weren't Negroes, nearly all were rather dark-skinned.

The gypsies obtained water from the old house next to the lot, and they were supposed to use the sanitary facilities there. As often as not, they simply used the lot itself. We saw their turds as we came through the parking lot to work. Mrs. McPherson and the other women shuddered at such habits, but we men, filled with curiosity as to the gypsies' exotic ways, were friendly toward them. There was one gypsy woman who took my eye—a black-haired, red-cheeked young beauty, the wife of a swarthy man who seemed to be the leader. She spoke French and turned out to be not a gypsy, but a French Canadian. We believed her husband mistreated her, for she often looked as if she had been weeping. She was well along in pregnancy.

The gypsies were there all the summer of 1956. They had rented a storefront where they told fortunes; I don't know what else they did to support themselves. They were given to celebrations. One day, Hancock and George Brown went off, upon invitation, to the storefront to drink wine with them on some occasion. Another event, more of a gala, was the wedding of the gypsy prince, a boy of about twelve, and a little girl. Gypsies over an area of several states came to take part in this ceremony and the festivities that accompanied it. We understood it was an important political event.

As time went on, however, *The Clarion* men—Pierce in particular—became disillusioned with the gypsy situation. There were so many trailers that the workers had to park on the street. And while the gypsies were always good for a laugh, there was no developing a meaningful relation with them. After a while, it seemed they were lacking a social chromosome. "They're human, but they ain't people," said Pierce, who was usually the most tolerant of men. I thought the experience enabled me to delineate better what Negroes were, and to grasp the meaning of Mr. Talbott's assertion that black and white Americans were basically the same. Negroes were held at the bottom of society by persecution and poverty, but for all that, it seemed to me, they had the values and aspirations of that society; they had no more in common with gypsies than white people did.

Nor did the gypsies, as true outsiders, show sympathy for the Negroes' condition.

The gypsies' affairs rose to a climax on a day that was a big one for the Avenue, although the gypsies had nothing to do with that. Adlai Stevenson came to town in his quest for the presidency, and his motorcade passed down the Avenue. He was the only presidential candidate to visit our part of the city during my stay at *The Clarion*, although Eisenhower sent Joe Louis, making for an even bigger occasion.

I remember the Stevenson procession because of what Bill Whitcomb did. The cars sped past *The Clarion*, presumably because of its Republicanism, and then slowed their pace in the next block, where there was a Democratic headquarters. A group of us followed them, on the sidewalk. The convertible bearing Stevenson came to a halt. Suddenly Bill darted from the crowd, holding his press card high in the air before him. He made an odd appearance, as if he were bowing. He reached the car, shook hands with Stevenson, and they exchanged sentences. It was quickly over. Bill was happy and smiling the rest of the day. He had found a way for a moment simultaneously to identify himself with the world's mighty and to dissociate himself from Mr. Talbott's Republican backwardness.

Later that afternoon, there was a terrible row in the trailer of the gypsy chief and his wife. When we heard the noise and went to the door of the shop to look, the chief was outside the trailer. The woman was throwing pots, pans, and dishes out the door of the trailer. I had never seen such an angry woman. She was shouting in French. The chief kept ducking the objects and yelling back at her; it was clear that for once he was frightened. He turned and called to us: "She say she throw everything out. What I do?"

It was still going on when Pierce and Brown and I left for the day. We were concerned, for we were afraid he would beat her, if he hadn't already; I thought he might kill her. And she was near her time. "Ought to call the police," said Pierce. But in the end we went our ways.

The child was born that night, in the trailer, delivered by an ambulance doctor from City Hospital. The next morning, the chief asked us in to see the new gypsy. The chief was all paternal pride and solicitude; he even gave us cigars. In spite of the previous night's spectacle, between him and the mother there was the most joyous and tender love.

"You know what we call him?" said the chief. And showing that they too had not been untouched—if somewhat confused—by the great event of the day before, he disclosed, "We name him General Ike."

For obvious reasons, Negroes who could afford it enjoyed traveling outside the United States. One couple who could afford it, what with the poker game added on top of everything else, were Lehman and Bernice Scott. They went to Canada, to Mexico, to the West Indies, anywhere they could taste the heady wine of being treated like human beings.

For a long time they had plans to travel to Europe. At last the time came, all the arrangements were complete, and they set out. They were to drive to Montreal and take a boat from there.

Two days later, Lehman's mother died. As I talked with Mrs. Weyhouse about it, it was apparent she was withholding something.

"Lehman and Bernice can't be reached," she said in a quiet voice. "They are at sea."

Startled, I asked, "But when did they get to Montreal? It's a three-day trip."

She looked down at her desk. "Maybe they drove straight through," she said unctuously. "When did they leave, anyway?"

I guess I stared at her, for she continued, shrugging: "All I know is that they are on the ship, and sure 'nuff can't turn back." (Mrs. Weyhouse used expressions like "sure 'nuff" only when she wanted to add color or vigor to her speech.) "They say they can't be reached there." She went on more quickly, looking at me candidly: "It's too bad, but would you want to spoil their trip? The funeral can be after they come back."

And so, the Scotts continued on their tour of France, Italy, and Greece. It was Mr. Talbott who revealed sometime later in the newsroom, "The Reynolds Brothers have got Lehman's mother on ice."

"And Lehman hasn't been told about it?" I asked.

The men in the room looked in different directions. Finally, Mr. Talbott said, "I'm not sure whether he has or not."

Since he would have been the one to tell him, I took this as a signal to shut my white mouth. The Scotts returned in six weeks, and a few days later the service was held.

Let the living bury the dead.

The town was changing, but to the naked eye it was barely detectable. The hotels and the better restaurants were warming up to integration; some firms were practicing a degree of fair employment; juries and jury venires had been purged of lilywhitism; and other advances had been made. But at least nine-tenths of the Negroes had no dealings in the affected areas—except that their school segregation was now *de facto* rather than *de jure*—and these things meant nothing to them. In their daily lives, they were unaware of the reforms that had taken place, one might say, in another world. They were still black and impoverished in, as Huddie Ledbetter ("Leadbelly") had sung it, a "bourgeois town."

At *The Clarion*, too, little seemed to be happening, certainly in the way of improvement. Despite all the plans and the architect's sketch, the building was a decade older and dirtier, although it had already been so dirty that another decade didn't show. I had become reassured that it wasn't going to fall down, a possibility I had considered seriously in my earlier years. One night, fire destroyed everything burnable in the newsroom, including most of the files. This made a big news story because it was *The Clarion*; otherwise, it wouldn't have been very newsworthy, since two out of three of the Fire Department's runs were to the black neighborhoods, to the rotting old buildings that were rented to Negroes. The writers had to move to the front office for a few days, while the debris was being removed, and then we returned to our quarters, which retained an acrid smell of smoke.

I had also come to understand that, though *The Clarion* kept getting deeper into debt, it was not headed for bankruptcy. The printer's investment was by now altogether too great for that. What had broken out at this time was a struggle for power within the Talbott family. I had assumed that Mr. Talbott owned the paper, but such was not the case. As befitted the organ of a dynasty, its actual owners were Mrs. George W. Talbott Sr., the mother of Mr. Talbott, Mrs. Lewis, and Mrs. Weyhouse. And the old woman was nearing her end. At the same time, Mrs. Lewis's son George was already a married man with two children. He had been given the title of business manager, but in daily practice, Mr. Talbott continued to run the operation as a one-man show.

Whatever else the Talbotts might be, they were ordinarily very closemouthed about the family's business affairs. And so we had to pick up our information of what was going on as best we could. It seemed that Mrs. Lewis was battling like a tiger for her son to be granted an equal share of authority with Mr. Talbott. She charged that Mr. Talbott was diverting business funds to himself and his family. Even more important was the succession that laid between George Lewis and George Talbott, the boss's wastrel son whom he was determined to eventually put into the driver's seat.

In all this—I am condensing what had been developing for years— Mrs. Weymouth held the "swing vote." In a hunch, I surmised that she and her husband had come down on Mrs. Lewis's side. At any rate, Mr. Talbott showed signs of being harried. But everything depended on the terms of the mother's will. There was a rumor that she was leaving the paper to Mr. Talbott until his death, with it then to pass to George Lewis. Assuming this to be legal, which I wasn't qualified to judge, it was hard to know how much credence to put in it. The patrilineal tradition was strong, stemming from the reverence for *The Clarion*'s founder, her late husband; and George Talbott bore that hallowed name, with a III after it. But on the other hand, Mrs. Lewis was senior to Mr. Talbott, and if not for her sex would have been the editor herself. I gathered that she had been a favorite of her father. In her tirades, when she burst through the accustomed caution and accused Mr. Talbott of "robbing" her, she several times shouted: "My daddy didn't start this newspaper so you and your no-good son could run it down to nothin'!"

At length, Mrs. Talbott went to her rest. She was buried in Spring Lawn, the city's most prestigious cemetery, which was predominantly white. The entire family peered after the coffin as it was lowered into the grave, to make certain that the cemetery proprietors didn't somehow defraud them. As for the will, we, the workers, never learned its provisions. Later developments showed that it didn't cut George Talbott out of the succession. My guess was that it divided the company equally among the three heirs, and that the women then served notice on Mr. Talbott as to how things would be. For a time, he appeared in the office as if he had been chastened, and we employees learned that we had two sovereign bosses: Mr. Talbott and Mr. Lewis. (Being female and having no son, Mrs. Weyhouse couldn't aspire to make it a triumvirate. She would not have been able to push George Weyhouse forward—had she so desired—because he was not a Talbott.)

But even if they were now supposed to be equal in the management, George Lewis was no match for Mr. Talbott. The nephew was an agreeable young man, sober and diligent. He wanted to introduce progressive business methods into the firm. This was easier said than done. The only one of his projects I can recall coming to fruition (and that after a good many years) was the changeover to cold-type printing.

That was designed to reduce printing costs and succeeded in doing so everywhere else it was tried, but Mr. Talbott said it increased them at *The Clarion*. In fact, it was from hearing his lamentations on the subject that I became certain it had not been his baby.

Although I didn't believe Mr. Talbott on this score, I found myself sympathizing with him, because I didn't like the new process either. Granted it made a much cleaner-appearing paper, and it especially gave better reproduction to the photos. Still, it seemed to me that a cold-type page had a dead appearance. I thought it made *The Clarion* look somehow like a throwaway shopper.

The truth was that George Lewis was the first of the younger generation to intrude into our settled way of life. It was fortunate for him that under his buttoned-down reasonableness of the "silent 50s" there was a strain of the Talbott stubbornness, for he found himself almost crushed among demonic personalities. Not to mention the rest of us, there was on one side of him Mr. Talbott and on the other Mrs. Lewis. With the passage of years, she had become more frenetic; her diabetes had grown worse, and she suffered from frequent attacks of uncontrollable coughing. Her spells of shouting out hostilities at Mr. Talbott, or Attorney Peckham or another of her numerous targets, had left all bounds of reason. She was a raging woman.

To complicate matters, George Lewis's wife was also a woman with an extreme temper, and warfare without limit had broken out between her and Mrs. Lewis. At first, the three of them had tried to live in the same house, but that wouldn't do and the mother had moved to an apartment. The two women had long since passed the speaking stage. Weirdly, the younger Mrs. Lewis had extended her fury at her mother-in-law to *The Clarion* and its staff. She had laid down a decree that her husband was not to be called at home. (In all this, of course, poor George was helpless.) I shall not forget the night when I felt this arbitrary command had to be violated. We were going to press, and there was some question concerning an ad that only he could decide. Pierce cautioned me, but I overruled him and made a telephone call to George Lewis's home. It was answered by his wife. "Mr. Preston," she began, "I have told you people down there never to call Mr. Lewis here," and she continued for some time. I was tired already, and after only a couple of moments, replaced the phone.

She called back immediately. "Mr. Preston," she said. "You bastard!"

This sort of thing always had gone on at *The Clarion*; it was its element. The paper issued forth every Thursday, dependably late. Pierce had his varicose veins taped and kept on laboring as if he had invented labor; Hancock drank and set type; and George Brown demanded his time. Nobody was fired, workers came and went—from itinerant typesetters and secretaries to the circulation manager. Harry Martin died one night, as surreptitiously as he had done everything else, and then we needed another linotypist. But the new generation, with a few core employment opportunities that their fathers didn't have, also didn't find *The Clarion*'s pay attractive.

It was during these years that the bookkeeper, Miss List, who always resembled a sepia version of the film comedienne Zasu Pitts, had "got down to a dragging bundle of sticks": she had developed an illness. In an expression of the country people among whom she lived, she looked like death warmed over. It was discovered that she had an intestinal tumor and would be obliged to undergo surgery.

It was the first time any of our "family" had faced such a battle with destiny, and the office was heavy with foreboding. Miss List was so polite, and the enemy so powerful and ruthless. In listening to Mr. Talbott, I learned of another fear that had never occurred to me. "Well," he said hesitantly, and not looking me in the face, "rich white surgeons, what do they think about cutting on a poor nigger woman?" I understood then that all my friends had in their minds the same thought, and why not? It wasn't so long since all the hospitals in town had refused to employ Negroes except as janitors, and they were still Jim Crowing Negro patients. *The Clarion* and the NAACP had been fighting them over it for years.

Everyone resisted speaking of anticipated misfortune, but on the day of the operation Pierce could stand no more of it. "Pres," he blurted as he handed me a job to be proofread, "I'm afraid Daisy ain't gonna make it."

Thus, expecting the worst, for three or four days the staff hung on every word from the hospital, as relayed by Mrs. Weyhouse or Mr. Talbott. And then it appeared that a miracle had taken place, and Miss List was recovering. In a few weeks, she returned to work. She filled out, she blossomed like a rose; she even seemed to dress better. Within a year, Miss List, who always had been regarded as a drudge in the corner, had taken on personality and become a figure in the Christmas Cheer Women Sponsors. In the years that followed, the Talbott women accepted her as a kind of auxiliary member of the Talbott family itself. I don't think I've ever known another case of surgery with such body-and-soul felicitous results.

Aside from these events, time seemed to be standing still for *The Clarion* and for me. But, of course, it wasn't; for one thing, George and Cashy Talbott—and Michael, and with them their generation—were growing up. From this simple and inevitable circumstance, Mr. Talbott faced problems he never had known existed. My boat also was getting ready to rock. But it was to be some time before these things worked themselves out.

29. Of Boxing and Bullfighting

The effort to give complete coverage to black sports led me to many a byway and strange place. Since my youth, I had looked down on boxing as brutal and exploitative. But rightly or wrongly, the ring was where many Negroes were, even in our not very boxing-minded town. So I found myself covering the national championship fights—from the closed-circuit screenings or television or radio broadcasts—and also serving on the board of sponsors of the Golden Gloves tournaments for youths.

As far as the big fights were concerned, I had sense enough to rely on other people who knew something about the sport. Mr. Talbott, like most Negro men of his generation, was a rabid boxing fan. I wasn't too confident in his judgment, but he certainly held strong opinions, which I thought served just as well in reporting boxing. He believed that the sport was mostly crooked, and that a great many fights were fixed. However, this didn't dampen his enthusiasm but seemed to spur it all the more. Of course, practically all Negroes swore that Jack Johnson took a dive in losing his title to Jess Willard (as Johnson, himself, said); Mr. Talbott could prove to you that Jersey Joe Walcott's loss to Rocky Marciano was also a tank job. If you challenged his skepticism, he became so excited that he almost threw a few punches of his own.

Mr. Talbott and Luke Lewis in a conversation about boxing sounded like a witches' sabbath of cynics. They went together to some of the big fights, including the Walcott-Marciano fight in Chicago, where they spotted the fix. These were the only sporting events Mr. Talbott attended. He feared the tension of basketball games and didn't even listen to the radio when Dunbar was playing. In that respect, he was like Pierce, who said, "You'll never find me dead in that Field House."

Another knowledgeable boxing guide I turned to was Geronimo Smith, the former longtime trainer of the light-heavyweight Archie Moore. Geronimo was a soft-voiced man, but not much of a smiler. He hung out in a little shoeshine parlor and numbers station a few doors north of *The Clarion*. He came into our office quite often, and when he didn't, I would go there to consult him.

Moore had gotten his professional start in our town, according to Geronimo, and he came to visit now and then, although he didn't fight there in my time. Of all the black boxers, he was the one most heavily penalized by bold-faced discrimination. The white champions of his division refused him a shot at the title until he was around forty, when he finally won it, as he could have done all along. But if there was one man who had a worse deal than Archie Moore, it was Geronimo Smith. Geronimo had been Archie's trainer from the first, when Archie was a kid out of St. Louis. Let's not say he had made Archie, but he had been with him through all the lean years. Then, just as Archie's fortunes approached, Geronimo had been eased out by another, presumably sharper, man.

It was something Geronimo couldn't accept. Far from blaming Archie, he kept bringing up evidence that he was still in Archie's mind and affections. He showed me postcards he got from Archie, and he told me that when Archie came to town he stopped at Geronimo's home. He was always waiting for Archie to call him back for the next fight. And finally he did, although it was only for one. Geronimo went off to San Diego to help Archie train. What happened then, to tell the truth, is unknown. Mr. Talbott and the other *Clarion* men were skeptical about Geronimo's recall. But in the telecast of the fight, we saw him in Archie's corner. Except that, as Mr. Talbott observed, "Shit, he ain't got no place! That other nigger is givin' him orders!" And when he came home from the fight—which Archie won—little was said about it.

Unless hope is addictive, Geronimo was not a man of vices. I never saw him drunk. He was also not a man to rush out and get a job, assuming there were any available to someone of his age and with his experience. It was Mrs. Smith who, by working as a domestic laborer, brought home the family's steady income. "Act well your part," the bard has written . . . and Geronimo's part was waiting for a call from Archie and talking about boxing in the numbers shop. When he talked about boxing, especially about keeping in shape and training, he came alive. He would have made an excellent trainer for a youth club, much better than the easygoing, fat PAL officers, if the youths could have put up with the strictness he had learned in getting Archie into shape for fights. Although Geronimo seldom talked against Archie, I gathered that between the booze and the women, he sometimes had his hands full. But then again, Archie expected him to be harsh about such things—that was what he was for. I didn't think the young boys in our town would stand for it, or that he could adjust to working with them. Geronimo's eyes were on the ring in a way pros have, and he couldn't come down from that. If his waiting for Archie proved vain, it appeared he might be a long time waiting for nothing, along with a number of other broke black sportsmen.

As for the Golden Gloves committee, that was a collection of white men about town and sportswriters who had lunch at the leading hotels to plot how poor black and white boys might make each other bleed in the ring. At any rate, the tournament was run dictatorially by the city's recreation director, Sam Harding. And all the committee did was to rubberstamp his decisions while lunching on expense accounts. I felt that the old revolutionary had risen, and fallen, into some strange company. In a faint way, the interests of the black youths were spoken for now and then by two members of the group—Father Auld, the pastor of St. Anne's Catholic in the east side slums, and myself.

Of course, if I had not been there, there would have been a black man on the committee, probably John Elliott, or maybe even Mr. Talbott. Sam Harding would have preferred that. I can only say in self-defense that I don't believe the interests of the blacks would have been served any better—perhaps not so well. In order to do that, Sam would have had to turn to a different kind of Negro, one who was making things hum in his corner of black amateur boxing. This man in motion was Art Arthur.

Art was youngish, with wavy black hair. He resembled perhaps a Spaniard. He had come our way from Ellettsville, which was more of a sporting town. He was a parishioner of St. Anne's, and soon after his arrival, he took over its boxing program from Joe Stanton, a mild-mannered man who bore the title of athletic director. Art was anything but mild-mannered; he was an enthusiast, a self-promoter, and a scrapper. He had a reputation and impressed one as being "unscrupulous," although I never could put my finger on just why. Maybe it was a reaction to his overpowering push. Anyway, scruples aren't the mark of a good boxing manager. Whenever Art was snubbed, he would come to *The Clarion* and try to stir up a breeze in print. I usually accommodated him, but likely as not, this would cause Sam Harding or whoever had done the snubbing to come down on him still more. I put him on the Honor Roll one year, after his St. Anne's team won the city championship. He so desperately wanted a piece of the action, even though it was only the poor prestige of sport in our backwater town. Of course, he intended to turn that prestige into a living for himself and his family—but would that be a crime? Wasn't Sam Harding living? Weren't we eating lunch? I will confess, I got tired of Art calling me (usually at my home and after office hours) with his complaints, but I got even more tired of the power-structure men who resisted him.

Instead of just shoving his boys into the ring, Art made careful plans and trained them well. It wasn't long until they won the city title and Sam could no longer keep him down. He invited Art to the next luncheon and had him elected to coach the local Golden Gloves winners in the national finals.

After that, we saw no more of Art Arthur at *The Clarion*. He was taking his stories to the daily press.

It was through covering this event that I got acquainted with the ring, filled with swirling smoke and raucous shouts; the foyers, with lines of fight fans waiting for beer; and the men's rooms, with incredible jams at intermission waiting to piss it out. The tigers came, often rather joylessly, into the ring and pounded each other. Because we weren't a fight town, they hadn't trained long enough and weren't in great condition. Most of the teams were thrown together by PAL Club officers a couple of weeks before the fights. The bulk of our local champions were promptly eliminated in the second round of the tournament, although occasionally one who was naturally gifted would fight his way to the quarterfinals. It all seemed to me an exercise in bureaucracy and dreariness, but I did meet a set of young people different from the basketball players, and whose faces lit up as they spoke the boxing patois. It took this kind, too, to make a world.

In our town, we had only one or two professional boxers of even statewide repute. But sometimes Kid Gavilan, the welterweight champion, and other outstanding boxers came to town for fight programs in connection with the races. Young fighters on the make would come through and stop in at *The Clarion* for interviews. At some time or another, in preparation I think for a local pro card, I talked with a white man who managed a number of very young Negro boxers. He was trying to paint himself as a benefactor, but what he said confirmed my prejudices against the sport. He told me all about how he took these youths to Des Moines, and how he "got" white girls for them and gave them everything but sound advice. I disliked the picture of these youngsters having their heads battered for a few years of fast living, after which most of them, not having shown sufficient talent, would be dumped. What would be ahead for them then?

One year, our city hosted a heavyweight championship bout. The champion was Floyd Patterson, and the challenger a young white man from overseas. The match was held in conjunction with the annual races.

The fight did not make boxing history, as Patterson disposed of his man with the greatest of ease. But it did make a couple of good stories for *The Clarion*. The first of these came when Patterson, taking a stroll a few blocks from his training camp, went into a confectionery for an ice-cream cone. He was not recognized and was denied service. I'm not certain whether the dailies didn't learn of this incident, which the ubiquitous Walt Evers reported to me, or whether, in their capacity as town boosters, they didn't see fit to make it public. We spread it all over page one—"CHAMP JIM-CROWED BY EATERY"—and sold out of papers that week.

By the time *The Clarion* hit the streets, the store management was making all kinds of apologies—they had thought he was just another Negro. But, of course, it was too late.

The other story was more complicated. A good many boxing writers were in town and some of them, knowing the importance of the black community as a news source, dropped by *The Clarion*. One of these was a man from the homeland of Patterson's opponent. In covering the pre-fight developments, I had enlisted the services of Shorty Graham, a young man who had formerly been a popular Golden Gloves fighter. Shorty couldn't write very well, but he knew his way around—and he could drink.

One night, Shorty and the foreign writer consumed a good deal of liquor together. Shorty came away with a more interesting story about the fight than had yet been published: Patterson's opponent was managed by the boxer's father, and he—the foreign scribe guilelessly disclosed—was not licensed in his country as a boxing manager but rather as a ring second. He said the challenger was being managed by Gus D'Amato, Patterson's manager! Here was a pretty kettle of fish. And its odor wasn't helped by the circumstance, which was widely known but no one in town was publicizing, that D'Amato was also the bout's promoter.

After we printed as much of the story as I felt we could get away with, Shorty said the foreign newsman was exceedingly embarrassed and told Shorty he had not intended it for publication. We felt that was, in Mr. Talbott's words, "too fuckin' bad." We were used to people expressing indignation after what they told a *Clarion* reporter turned up in *The Clarion*. The story brought a small crowd of the out-of-town writers to the office to buy a paper. What had been going on in town was a more or less open conspiracy to "build" the fight; the daily writers had all gotten the word that they were part of the promotion. As usual, *The Clarion* had been overlooked, and now this "voice from the gallery" had made itself heard. There was no danger, of course, that our story would be read by the hundreds of thousands of white folks who were expected to buy most of the tickets. But anyone who has been through a situation of this kind knows it is felt essential that not one voice, even the smallest, shall speak out and break the illusion.

The Clarion found itself no longer ignored. Mr. Talbott and I promptly received a visit from D'Amato himself and an invitation to the champion's camp and supper with him. I don't know precisely what the manager's intention was but I had the impression of a carrot-and-stick treatment. He was obviously in a rage, and yet he restrained himself except for some sharp looks. D'Amato was a rather formidable figure to us Middle Americans, who weren't used to dealing with big-time fight managers. We also read up on the Mafia. Not that we had any reason for thinking D'Amato was connected with it, except that we shared the common prejudice in regard to persons of Italian ancestry. In short, Mr. Talbott and I thought we might have been offered a one-way ride.

I believe D'Amato had a suspicion that we were trying to shake him down.

Someone said that D'Amato slipped Mr. Talbott a C-note in the interest of public relations. I'm inclined to think he got us on the cheap. And there we were, talking with the champion and sharing his simple training camp meal.

We found Patterson a "nice guy," as everyone had said. He talked freely but modestly of his youth in the Brownsville section of Brooklyn and his time spent in the Wiltwyck School for Boys, which he said was a turning point in his life. He had an air of sadness, almost of moroseness. One seldom comes across such a loner. Hoping possibly to get him on to basketball, I asked whether he had ever taken part in team sports, but he said no. What was his favorite sport at the school, aside from boxing?

"Horseback riding."

Patterson was no Joe Louis in the ring, nor Muhammad Ali out of it. (On the way home, Mr. Talbott informed me that he was naturally a light heavyweight rather than a heavy.) It seemed to me that poverty in his youth had eaten away his spirit and made him humble and wistful. He entirely lacked the "killer instinct," and, indeed, disliked hurting his opponents. Yet no one can deny that he was the world's heavyweight champion for five years (in two stretches), and some of his qualities now appear to be coming into style.

This brush with D'Amato reminds me of a conflict I had with Syd Pollock, a lieutenant of Abe Saperstein of the Harlem Globetrotters. I had written some columns blasting the Globetrotter organization on two scores. One was the physical exploitation that Jack Hudson had told me about. The other was the shafting of Reece Tatum, the veteran comedy star of the Trotters who was nine-tenths of the show and who, after many years, demanded a higher salary because of it. But Saperstein's tricks weren't confined to the playing floor. One of them was always to have understudies ready in case any of the black performers got too big. One could hardly conceive that this went for Tatum, who was an institution on the order of Satchell Paige. He found out it did; he was denied the raise, dismissed from the team, and lived out the rest of his life in obscurity at his home in Arkansas. At one time, he played out the characteristic last gambit of the Negro by launching a team of his own, but despite his great name, it couldn't compete with the famous and well-heeled Globetrotters.

It was about the same as if the New York Yankees in the old days had fired Babe Ruth at the height of his powers and put somebody "just as good" in right field. Except that this was also a throbbing race issue. By my way of thinking, they should have gotten rid of Saperstein.

Besides airing these questions, I continued to rewrite the Globetrotters' handouts, cutting all the promotional bullshit out of them, just as any daily would have done.

These acts brought Pollock down on me, by mail, long-distance telephone, and, the next time the Trotters were in town, in person. He let me know in strong language that he was very angry. He started routing his material through St. John Ashley, and he cut *The Clarion* out of his advertising budget for a while.

These men in the professional sports world were accustomed to battling for their interests. But I think they wouldn't have battled quite so abusively if we weren't a Negro newspaper. They seemed to have a feeling of outrage that we would dare to be independent and talk back. Taking my cue from Mr. Talbott, I continued to do so. There is a freedom in having little to lose, if your courage is in hand.

I met another sad professional athlete, sadder even than Patterson. He was a tall man, café au lait in color, with a long face and with the corners of his mouth turned down. He was tending bar for Jose

Stanton, because that was where he had got stranded. But in addition to being sad at heart and broke, he was ambitious. Even imperious.

It was Walt Evers on his circulation rounds who first ran into him, as Walt came across so many novel and interesting people. Walt took me over to meet him. The young man had a story for *The Clarion*, and beyond that he wanted *The Clarion* to help him advance in his chosen profession. He was a bullfighter.

Bill Whitcomb had taught me to beware of the adjectives "first," "only," and the like, but John Thompson claimed to be the only American Negro bullfighter. Certainly, I had never heard of another.

He said he had been discharged from the Navy and drifted to Mexico. There, he became fascinated by the bull ring, and soon took up the sport himself. There was no doubt he was genuine. He showed us posters and clippings with his picture, but even without them, Walt, with his hearty Negro skepticism, had not been inclined to doubt him. "Bullfighter" was written all over his death-enamored face.

Thompson told us he had fought for a couple of years and had become well-known in Mexico City, but that he couldn't break into the higher ranks without a stake. I gathered that he was in the position of a club boxer who wants to become a serious professional. He had come back to the United States in search of a financial backer, and got as far as Jose's when his funds ran out.

At first, we thought he wanted us to arrange a local fight for him. "Look," Walt laughed. "You know bullfighting ain't so big in this part of the country."

Thompson replied soberly that he was aware of that. "I want to fight in Mexico City," he explained. "I thought if I could meet Joe Louis, he might back me."

We, however, did not have access to the Brown Bomber, even if we had been sold on Thompson's plan. There must have been a lot of people trying to get to Joe back then, when what was needed at that point, as we understood it, was someone to back Joe.

But it was the only plan Thompson had—he was a bullfighter, not a businessman—and he stayed on at Jose's for six weeks, talking about bullfighting and about getting to see Joe Louis. *The Clarion* published his story and picture, and that was all we could do for him. He was an attraction and a conversation piece at Jose's bar but the patrons couldn't help him either.

Walt kept hinting to him that he should move on to some other area. It wasn't that we didn't want him in town, but it seemed such a hopeless place for his project.

Finally, I had an idea. Without much difficulty, I arranged for Thompson to appear on the television program *What's My Line?* It wasn't Joe Louis, but it would give him some publicity that might be helpful. And it would get him out of Jose Stanton's bar and to New York.

So the last time we saw him was on the television screen. The panel guessed his occupation rather quickly, which I feared was not a good omen.

30. Bad Changes, Good Changes, Sickness

The life into which my black friends and I kept trying to settle more or less comfortably—of getting out *The Clarion* with its exposure of injustices, of carrying on NAACP campaigns, even of sports-page crusades—was based on the idea of progress. We felt that through our small efforts and those of countless other people everywhere, things were getting better in small ways and would cumulatively get better. There were gains and victories, but the more our society was changing, the more it was remaining the same. We had to take another look at our activities and either give up in despair or cast about for stronger means of shaking the colossus.

One such recidivist event took place in Stilesburg. An aging black man went out of his mind and shot at his wife in their home. She escaped, ran to neighbors, and summoned the police. When they approached the house, he opened fire on them. The terrified woman said he had what the radio newscasters described as an "arsenal" of weapons and ammunition in the house. The police called in reinforcements, cleared occupants out of other homes in the area, and settled in for a siege.

As the day went on, the radio broadcast news bulletins on the battle as if it were a sporting event. More police and a sheriff's force came to assist. The chief of police was at the scene, and other notables made appearances at the firing line, taking the cover of trees and bushes. The house was now ringed solidly. What was worst for me was that *The Clarion* men followed the developments and laughed. Mr. Talbott, Pierce, and Brown actually seemed to be enjoying the fight the man was putting up. It struck me that for them he was acting out a dream I had often heard expressed by Negroes in one way or another.

After the incredible day came to its end, when the crazed man finally caught a bullet in his head, somebody reported that ten thousand shots had been fired into the house. The madman, in taking up violence, had released such violence in the city as I didn't know existed. I was sickened.

It was Bill Whitcomb who agreed with me. This wasn't his Kentucky vein of violence. "Things like this wouldn't happen in England," he observed with a frown. "Why they bound to shoot him like a turkey? Y'all station four or five bluecoats around that house, he'll come out sooner or later when he gets hungry. He ain't gonna starve to death in there."

George Talbott laughed. "Why they got to do that?" he said. "Shoot the bugger down. One bugger the less." And when Bill made a reply, George said angrily, "They got to enforce the law, don't they?"

The advent of George Talbott hadn't made life any easier for *The Clarion* staff. After his boyhood, he had been sent to live with relatives in Detroit to go to high school there. He must have run into trouble in our school system, or maybe Mr. Talbott wanted to get him away from segregated Dunbar. No matter how angry Mr. Talbott became with his sons, he never ceased to maintain that segregation had ruined them. Added to the street vices he had already acquired in our town were those of Detroit's. Underlying them all were the character flaws of the eldest son, knowing he was designed for the editorship of *The Clarion*. He was a self-indulgent and overbearing young man. To top it off, he had been drafted and had served in Korea. His father had pulled every wire he could find to get him out of it, and through our senator (the same man I had insulted in the Victory Edition), at last had succeeded in cutting his tour short.

In line with the Stilesburg shootout, George told a group of us, with his snickering laugh, that it had been a common practice to shoot prisoners of war in Korea. "I shot one myself," he said. "The sergeant told me to. Took the gook behind a tree and blew his brains out."

"Didn't it bother you?" asked Walt Evers.

"Man, are you crazy?" George retorted. "You want us to drag that gook all over Korea with us? That's war."

To me at least, the way George Talbott had turned out was a crushing blow. Was this the New Negro for whom all of us had been sacrificing ourselves? Of course, it was possible to look through his façade, that he saw himself as "a gook" and he was fat, so he was compensating for the murky lights that had been given him. But how far can you go in making excuses? We had a thug on our hands.

Then came a day when Hancock and George Brown got into a quarrel. Both were drunk: Hancock loquaciously and Brown pugnaciously. From my desk, I could hear them in the composing room; Hancock whining on; Brown muttering. Then there was the sharp sound of a fall. Several of us rushed to the scene.

Hancock was sitting on the floor, rubbing his jaw, looking up at Brown. With a drunken smile, he said, "Now look what y'all done did! Y'all done knocked me down. This is a pretty mess, Mr. Brown. People in *The Clarion* hitting each other—my, my!"

Brown, frowning with temper, growled at him, "I told y'all don't fuck with me, and I meant it."

This incident had no particular meaning for the two men, neither of whom bore a grudge the next day. But it seemed to me a kind of watershed for *The Clarion*. It was followed in a few weeks by another ugly scene. This took place on a Friday, Bill Whitcomb's "don't-disturb day." That week there had been a testimonial dinner for Senator Bancroft. We hadn't covered it, but a story had been sent in by the sponsors, and when the new paper was gone through, it mysteriously hadn't made it in. This brought to mind Bill's undying animosity for the senator. It was one thing in Bill's life he never talked about, and you were inclined to forget it was very much alive in his mind.

That morning, Mrs. Lewis had charged Bill with intentionally leaving out the story. She charged it with all her vigor, standing in the newsroom door and going on at length about "no-good, lazy niggers."

Bill had a great regard for Mrs. Lewis, and on most days he would have taken this with a smile and a murmuring of "Pshaw!" But this was one of his nervous days, and he replied angrily and hoarsely. He said that the Bancroft story had never reached him, and that in this gawddamned nigger place, run by her gawddamned shiftless relatives, that was the way everything happened. And he was tired of getting the gawddamned blame for it! "You Talbotts would make a preacher sass a grizzly bear. You would drive a man to drink!" he shouted, whereupon Mrs. Lewis, with redoubled spirit, started in on his drinking. "Bill Whitcomb, ain't nobody got to drive you to drink, you know it ain't, you sneakin' out an' nippin' that gin all day long, everyday. Everybody knows it. Drive you to drink! That's like drivin' a bee to honey! You just a ordinary, lowdown drunken nigger, an' that's common knowledge over seven states!"

Mrs. Lewis at last left, still calling revilements behind her. It wasn't two minutes until Smitty came in. He had no inkling of what had gone on before he arrived. And he, too, had the shaky nerves of sobriety. Smitty was pro-Senator Bancroft. I had the impression he might be in the senator's debt for drinking money now and then. He looked through the paper, and burst out, "Goddamn! Where's the Bancroft story?"

Nobody answered. "Lost!" exclaimed Smitty. "How could it get lost, tell me that! There's some hanky-panky here!"

He might have said more except that Bill, leaping up, yelled at the top of his voice, "Gawddamn it, I've heard enough!" He seized a folding chair and hurled it across the room at Smitty. It missed and crashed against the wall. Pulling his bullet from his pocket, Bill roared: "I'm goin' out to my car an' get what goes along with this, an' when I come back, there better not be any niggers askin' about the Bancroft story! Now gawddamn it, I've had all I intend to take. You niggers can push a man too gawddamned far!"

The shouting and the sound of the chair hitting the wall had drawn a silent crowd into the composing room, with the others looking through the newsroom door. All at once, I was half-blindly threading my way between them. I felt that I had to reach the air; I had to reach the sunlight.

I went to the parking lot and got into my car and drove away, at a rough, lurching speed. Up and down streets aimlessly. At last I took a highway going east from the city. It wasn't so much, as George Weyhouse told it later in jest, that I was afraid of Bill shooting up the place, although I did think he might finally have reached the point of using that gun. I had found myself, in the shouting and the crashing of the chair, driven beyond my endurance. The dirt, the poverty, the death hanging around. A picture flashed through my mind of the young stabbing victim we had seen on the sidewalk in front of *The Clarion*. His blood flowed out and made a pool. People were waiting for an ambulance. Then I remembered how Dunbar reverted to losing. James was denied the job. Willie Hempstead was unemployed. Nips of gin. Filth and gypsy turds. Black, still stay back. Shooting the old man. George Talbott. And through it all, except for the cards in Lehman's face, I had kept control. I had sat calm and polite. But it was too much.

I drove very fast, straight out east, ten miles, fifteen miles into the country. It was a pleasant, mild spring day. There was a married couple I knew in a town out here, old college friends, the woman an old love of mine, the man a onetime roommate. Should I go to their house, somehow take up again that old, other identity? What was I doing with my life? There was no revolution, no great progressive movement. Nothing but violence and dirt.

I wanted to drive on and on, a thousand miles to somewhere else. It would be easy for me to break away. Why shouldn't I? I had served my time.

But when I had gone a little farther, my panic and bad humor began to die down. No, it wouldn't be easy, I told myself. The ties that bound us together were not the trivial ones of skin color. And the only time was all time. What had I been thinking? I approached a crossroads, turned around, and headed back to town.

About that time, the NAACP also crossed a watershed.

The branch's labor and industry committee, working with *The Clarion*, had won small successes in opening jobs Negroes hitherto had been barred from. It was tedious work. The black population of the city was increasing by much larger numbers than the few jobs we could wrench loose from prejudice. The campaign seemed to be—to use the street phrase—scuffling backward.

One group of employers who appeared to be caving in at long last were the owners of supermarkets in black and "changing" neighborhoods. The A & P, Kroger, and other chains had been sensitized to the resentments and loyalties of their black customers and decided to get aboard the Freedom Train. None wanted to be caught lagging behind, and in the scurry, sometimes our problem was finding applicants for the jobs.

An exception to this welcome development—a stubborn, irritating exception—was the independent proprietor of Lauter's Supermarket, which had a 90 percent Negro clientele plus some white customers who passed by on 12th Street, the wide thoroughfare leading them to or from the suburbs. Gus Lauter was a self-made man, with the fierce individualism of the immigrant who has fought up the ladder. Like Papa Avakian, he was more American than the Americans. Not only wouldn't he hire a Negro, he wouldn't even see the delegation.

The NAACP executive committee sat around the table one Friday night. Spirits were at ebb tide. There was indignant talk of Lauter treating Negro women customers familiarly, even slapping them on the ass. Somebody suggested calling on the Mayor's Commission, but nobody thought it could handle such a tough bird as Lauter. And then somebody else said—who could it have been, that man or woman or youth deserves immortalizing—"Negroes ought to boycott Lauter's."

Whoever it was, everyone else looked startled. In those days, we were afraid of the word "boycott." People recalled that the NAACP National had said boycotts were illegal; or, at any rate, it was not considered "respectable." It might disgrace the organization.

Would it involve picketing? The NAACP in our town had never picketed. All those Negroes out there on the sidewalk, messing it up for business.

"Negroes won't do anything unless they have leadership," observed Ruth Reynolds.

There was a silence. Then Cinq drawled with a smile, "Well, maybe some folks would say we ought to give 'em leadership."

"No reason why we should call it a boycott," said Sanford Black. "Call it a Selective Buying Campaign. 'Don't buy where you can't work.' That's old stuff in Chicago and Detroit. Happens every day."

"Never happened here," said Dorothy Wendell.

"Baby, there's a first time for everything," replied Black, and two or three people murmured their agreement.

"Would we have to picket?" asked a woman.

"Just an informational picket," said Black with a sly smile, and moving into his preacher's tone, "not to physically prevent anyone from entering the store, but merely to inform them that the management refuses to comply with the request for an enlightened policy of fair employment. Nothing illegal about that, is there, Pat?"

"In my opinion, nothing whatever," said Pat, and he added with a nervous laugh: "Let's do it."

"Negroes won't come out for a thing like that, they'll be scared to," said Ruth. Her trait of compulsive pessimism was like Mr. Talbott betting against Dunbar. You realized she already had made up her mind it should be done.

After a half-hour of discussion, the vote was unanimous, or at least nobody voted no. There were several withholders.

So that was what launched the great boycott of Lauter's. Later, when the nation and even our town broke apart with fire and bombs, it was likely forgotten, but it shouldn't have been.

Contrary to Ruth's forebodings, the Negroes did turn out for the picket line. Without being asked, from nearby Stilesburg came Clarence Bailey and a half-dozen of the Co-op Community League. Attorney Peckham appeared with a sign proclaiming the support of the David vs. Goliath Society. Walt Rowland was there. Conservatives as well as progressives took their places on the line. And the masses—young, dark, anonymous men in brown or grey sweaters, black housewives, little girls. *The Clarion* photographers were there to spread pictures over two full pages. Sanford Black and Henry Watford stepped off in front, and when popular approval of the movement swept the ghettoes, appearances were made by many of the black preachers, and even a couple of white ones.

There was, as the daily newspapers put it, no violence. A good-humored, holiday spirit prevailed among the scores of people on the line. One heard some sharp remarks called in the direction of the office where old Lauter was presumed to be; now and then, a picket snapped at one of the few shoppers who crossed the line. But these outbursts too were more often than not couched in humor.

The city fathers apparently had decided that Lauter, who was a maverick anyway, must fend for himself. There might be a lot of Negro voters identified with this thing, just as there had turned out to be with the People's School Committee. And so, only a pair of black policemen were present, and they lolled at a corner of the building and talked with the picketers. The dailies, seemingly ill at ease with this unusual story, carried very brief but factual accounts, or none at all.

On 12th Street, the cars slowed as their suburban drivers looked out and wondered what all the niggers were up to. Then, true to the traditions of our state, they moved on.

There were two of us who didn't picket for a long time. I was in that awkward position of so many enthusiastic supporters who "were then or had ever been members of the Communist Party." I was apprehensive that my participation might not only get me into trouble but also somehow bring harm to the cause. The other was Ruth Reynolds. She sat for hours every day in her car, parked a little way from the store, where the picketers would come and confer with her. She was ready to run errands, to take people home, to go and get anything that was needed. I realized I had never fully understood her fiery militancy and the deep depressions that immobilized her. I remembered her with the housing chairperson, marching at the head of the group into discriminating restaurants, and telling off Steve Caron.

Now, in contrast to the picketers with their light-hearted camaraderie, Ruth was holding herself tense, waiting for something evil to happen. She was worrying with every pace taken by every man, woman, and child. She was watching for what would come around the corner. Not to run away, I knew she had no thought of that. But to throw herself against the catastrophe that only she foresaw, and hurl it back.

And indeed, Ruth, with her great, sad eyes, was seeing more than the rest of us. I stood at the car chatting with her one day. "The Negroes have their spirits up," she said proudly, and she added, "Preston, this is the way to do it. No more passing resolutions. Go into the streets."

She paused, looking at the people, and went on: "They don't know what's ahead of them, and that's just as well. I don't mean old Lauter. But y'all have built yourselves a country full of big white castles, and now us darkies got to shake 'em all down."

The line continued, shuffling and tramping. "Twenty million colored folks," said Ruth, "reached a place until they're more angry than scared. Come on, Preston, we're supposed to be Negro leaders, let's get in line."

So we picketed after all.

Lauter held out for eight days. Even then, he didn't want to see a delegation, but tried to have them meet with his son-in-law. Cinq, who was chairman, in his mild way put his foot down, and as it turned out, they got on rather well after the openings were over. The old man was allowed to make a speech about what a friend of the colored people he had actually been all along. He agreed to hire three Negroes at once and more as time went on.

Not long after that, one morning when I had hardly settled down to work in the newsroom, I felt a dull pain between my shoulder blades, a sudden sickness, and broke out in a cold sweat.

Smitty was the only other person there. After a time, he said, his voice coming as from a distance, "Pres, you look like you better go home. You want me to drive you?"

"No, I can make it," I answered. "Maybe I better go."

I drove home and tossed on the bed a while. I was good and sick. It happened that we had called Solomon Adams, the father of the Adams boys in the baseball league, to repair the television. While working, he looked at me once or twice and said: "Excuse me, Mr. Preston, but I think you'd better see a doctor."

I telephoned Susan and she came home and drove me to the doctor's. He told me to go to bed and stay there. That was a rough night, and in the morning, two nurses arrived from a laboratory with an electrocardiograph machine. Dr. Goldschmidt arrived in the afternoon, and he brought along a specialist. I had had a heart attack.

31. A Son's Confession— A Prodigal Comes Back Home

I was a long time getting well. Quitting smoking, watching cholesterol, taking steps one at a time and walking a little farther down the street each day until I finally circled the blocks, all that. In hindsight, with the attack on my life, I had got off on a different track.

For one thing, there were all kinds of solemn deference, by others and by myself. The NAACP workers made up a scrapbook entitled "This Is Your Life." Jim LeFever, who had broken the preachers' monopoly of the branch presidency, presented it to Susan at a social affair; a picture of the presentation was run on page one of *The Clarion*. The book was decorated with a black-ruled photograph of Walter White, who had recently died. The pages were autographed by my fellow activists of the branch. It was that winter, when I was able to get out to a basketball game, that Will Wilson awarded me the Capital City Officials' trophy.

Meanwhile, in the very depths of it, we had decided to move again. Our second neighborhood had become almost entirely Negro, and Michael was ready for junior high school. I seem to have dropped back in time a couple of years from the finish of the Meredith Mansions.

Eight blocks north of us, and a little to the west, lay the so-called Carlton-Meredith community, a pleasant neighborhood of tastefully designed homes on broad lawns under stately maples. It was, indeed, a showplace of the city, where the likes of us hardly had aspired to live. But now this community, too, despite its proximity to the university, with faculty members living in many of the homes, because of the relentless black tide moving northward, had come under the seller's gavel.

The school, No. 96, was rated one of the "best" in the city, attended by professors' children and other college-bound youngsters of the middle class. From that point of view, it seemed just the place to begin the sharpening of Michael's mind that might lead him to Harvard. The drawback, the really terrible thing, was that it was all-white. But the alternative if we did not move, School 34, had become practically all-black. It was a choice with no good outcome, the rotten fruit of segregation. Susan and I chose 96, consoling ourselves with the prospect that as the neighborhood changed, the school would soon be integrated.

The house we found—or rather which Susan found, since I was incapacitated—was a bungalow under two tremendous old trees. It was sold to us at a moderate price by a couple who were moving to California for their sunset years. They had put a lifetime of loving care into their home, which was attested to by such details as the brass door fixtures.

Meanwhile, we put the sale of our house at 4032 Stilwell into the hands of Walter Rowland, and he brought us Mrs. Worth and her husband as purchasers. And so everything went swimmingly.

But not for Michael. It was bad enough, I suppose, transferring from School 34 to 96 under any circumstances. The districts were adjacent and many of the boys of the two schools knew each other, but as, so to speak, enemies. Thirteen is the wrong age to change sides. And on top of simple gang and sports rivalries was the whole race issue. When a neighborhood is threatened with "change," as this one was, there is a downright war psychology from which no inhabitant can escape. I remember a few days after we moved in, a pretty blonde girl from down the block, the daughter of a YMCA executive, hung around our house after school to talk with Mike. Whatever happened, two months later, the girl gave a party and everybody in the class was invited but him.

What happened? Susan, who was often more perceptive than I where Michael was concerned, said she wasn't so sure he was all that discriminated against. She thought much of the difficulty was in his own head. As time went by, it became clear that this wasn't the temporary estrangement of a boy in a new school. When, two years later, he went on to high school, he became a part neither of the white group of students nor of the black. He wound up associating with a Jewish circle, but he wasn't one of them either and wasn't taken into their social fraternity. He often played cards with them, and one year placed a paid advertisement in the fraternity's yearbook—"Greetings from your Poker-Playing Friend, Mike Preston."

One afternoon when I was lying in the porch swing reading a magazine, I became aware that Michael had been sitting across from me for about ten minutes with some thought in his mind. Our eyes met, and he stammered:

"Dad—I want to tell you I did something wrong—I'm ashamed of it."

He dropped his eyes, scowling miserably. "I've got a new friend at school, Nick Cohen. We were talking, and—I told him you worked for *The Tribune.*"

Startled, I could only mumble something about it being all right. Michael's lower lip was trembling, and he said with vehemence: "I hate myself when I do something like that. Dad, I'm proud of where you work. I'm for the Negroes."

I told him that I understood it all. I didn't tell him that I was filled with self-loathing at having put him in a place where he had said such a thing.

That autumn, with this Michael problem and my enforced absence from work, my mind was weighed down by depression. Somehow, I had got to reading Trollope, the most cynical of the English novelists. Susan and I began attending the Unitarian church. I put my questions one day before the minister, an affable and knowledgeable man, younger than I. I asked him whether he had happened to read Trollope. Not lately.

I reminded him that Trollope wrote of people who gave their young lives to causes—in *Barchester Towers*, the cause of the High Church—and then, as middle age came, were overwhelmed by the rot of second thoughts.

The Reverend John Beatty made the sensible suggestion: "Why don't you see a psychiatrist?" I thought he would have done the same had I consulted him about working for *The Clarion*. And in my depression, I was disposed to add, "and rightly so."

And I did see one, a well-to-do man in his sixties who had been a hospital administrator. I saw him for about eight months. I don't know whether that happened which was supposed to. Probably not.

Meanwhile I did something else, which, in retrospect, suggests I should have been seeing two psychiatrists. I quit *The Clarion*.

It was Claudia Tubman who told me there was a job open at *The Bulletin*. The little paper had gone through one of its periodic financial crises. This time, it had got entirely out of Tansy's hands and into those of its printer, Paul Gibson, a man I didn't know. Claudio said he was a Democrat and a nice guy. The office and presses occupied a small clean building on a quiet side street not far from our new home. Altogether, I saw an attractive picture of light work in pleasant surroundings, free of *The Clarion*'s turmoil. And, of course, that was very much what I was looking for, in my post-coronary state of self-indulgence.

It even seemed to me it might be a fresh start. As for *The Clarion* and its people, in the cocoon of my illness, I felt no concern for them. Such was my eagerness to escape "that place" that I put off talking with Mr. Talbott and finally told him my decision by telephone.

Gibson was a tall, fleshy, brown-skinned man with a soft and gentle voice. He offered to pay me what I had been earning at *The Clarion*, which, as I recall, was then sixty-five dollars a week. I was styled the news editor and sat before a rickety typewriter making stories out of other people's notes. There was a dark and saturnine young man, Ronald Jones, a resourceful youth from a black college in St. Louis, who was the managing editor. At first, I supposed he was with *The Bulletin* because with the Talbott sons coming along, there was no room at *The Clarion*; but as I worked with him, I came to think it was simply that some chain of circumstances had led him there. It seemed to make no difference that *The Clarion* was the "real" Negro newspaper.

Jones held more sweeping views than the local black youths I had met. It was that autumn that Autherine Lucy, enrolling as the first Negro student at the University of Alabama, was threatened by rioters. President Eisenhower issued a statement "deploring" the riots, but he took no action to protect Miss Lucy. I remember Jones reading the headlines and saying bitterly: "God damn it! I'm going out and start me a country of my own!"

The Bulletin had Tansy's column; Kitty Curtis sent in society notes; Jones produced a few firsthand stories; and he and I rewrote freely from *The Clarion* and other newspapers. And that was all there was to it. The photoengraving was done in Chicago, at a cut-rate place Gibson knew about. We bundled the pictures and sent them off by air on Tuesdays at 4 p.m., and the engravings were picked up at the post office Thursday nights. There was one week they were not there by press time, and we faced the prospect of a paper with no illustrations. This was especially disastrous, because the front page always carried a large, and preferably sensational, photo.

Ronald Jones solved the problem with a daring, if somewhat crude, joke. He took a plain block of wood, almost page-size, inked it and thus printed an entirely black rectangle. Over it he put the headline "Washington Park at Midnight," and beneath another line: "Sex Perverts' Paradise." The presses rolled, and presumably some readers got at least a laugh for their money.

After one look around, I had concluded that *The Bulletin* couldn't go, but Gibson had to be convinced the hard way. He had a wife and four children to support, and it had to go; something had to go. He put a full eighty hours a week into it, operating the linotype from early morning until midnight, besides coping with the production and financial problems. We staff members thought that, with his excessive weight, he was literally working himself to death before our eyes.

If *The Clarion* owed Hoadley's, Gibson owed everybody he'd been able to get credit from, in town and outside of it. The time arrived when even his paychecks bounced and Ronald Jones drifted off somewhere. Six months had gone by. I felt able to be more active, and I went to Mr. Talbott and told him I was ready to return. In my self-absorption, it hadn't occurred to me there might be some difficulty about this. John Elliott had taken over the sports page, and was doing a first-rate job.

"Of course, but I'll need a little time to have a place for you," said Mr. Talbott. It was only by a fleeting look on his face that I at last sensed what I had put him through. But he held no grudge; by "a place" he meant simply the money to pay my wages (and the agreement of George Lewis).

I only had to wait two weeks. John Elliott had ability, but he had never become a member of *The Clarion* family and was having really thunderous scraps with the management. He was restless and ambitious, and it appeared he was "too big" for *The Clarion*. (He left the following year, taking a position as manager of a housing project.)

Elliott was moved to a reporter and I was given back the sports page.

PART THREE

It may even be that white involvement in civil rights began in response to some dim awareness of deficiencies in our culture—an awareness that whites needed to learn something from blacks about how to live. In other words, blacks, being imagined to have a more pure, less warped and contaminated libidinal existence, are seen—very ambivalently, to be sure—as a source of revitalization for the total society.

—PHILIP SALTER

32. School Integration

One night, I was coming away from a football game in which Northridge, which by then was heavily integrated—and its football team mostly Negro—had lost to Cold Stream, a white suburban school. Not fifty yards from the gate, and not five minutes after the end of the game, were two badly bruised white youths supporting each other on the busy sidewalk. I recognized one of them as Robert Trask, who lived in our old neighborhood and had once played in the baseball league. His friend's face was covered in blood.

"They jumped us," said Robert, whose face also bore the makings of a pair of black eyes. "I don't know who they were. They jumped us from behind."

I ran to get a policeman to summon an ambulance. When I returned, a crowd had gathered. The other youth was lying on the ground pressing a handkerchief to his cheek. Blood flowed copiously onto his sweater and shirt. Someone told me he was the son of Reverend Beatty.

Robert stood half-dazed, answering the policeman's questions. "There were about five of them," he said wearily. "Is an ambulance coming for Johnny? No, I didn't recognize them." And in reply to another question, he said matter-of-factly: "They were niggers."

At that, we heard the siren and saw the red light of the ambulance, and the crowd silently fell back.

The irony of the incident was that they were not only Northridge students but integrationists. I knew Robert to be one of the few white youths who had taken a stand against racism. It was for this reason that his family had continued to live in the neighborhood after it went black. In fact, if the two hadn't been pro-Negro, they probably wouldn't have been in a position to be jumped. Many of the white Northridge students had stopped attending the games after the team became predominantly black. Others, suspicious and fearful of Negroes, kept a sharp lookout around them as they went to their parked cars after the games. But Robert and John had set out blithely to walk home through a black neighborhood.

Another time, I had left Carlton field house after a Dunbar-Winette basketball game when I came across two Winette fans, a man and a boy, who had been similarly attacked while walking on a rather well-lit and well-traversed street. The man's face was bleeding, but he shook his head, saying: "No, I'll just drive home." He wasn't accustomed to this sort of thing in Winette. He was so surprised that he hardly seemed angry.

The town soon filled with these assaults, which had nothing personal about them; they were rarely preceded by provocations or name-calling. They seemed to be racial violence at its simplest level, black against white, in which—perhaps related to partisanship and perhaps not even that—the games were used as hunting grounds for victims.

There were various ways of reacting to the problem. The first, and most common, was to call for stronger policing and more severe treatment of the culprits by the courts. But as time went on, this proved to be ineffectual. Few of the assailants were apprehended, and their punishment (usually meted out behind the doors of juvenile court) didn't deter the others. This being the case, there followed a rather widespread attempt, in order to protect attendance at the games, to play the whole thing down. The assaults were called "post-game fights." In particular, frightened school officials and city officials felt it necessary to deny the racial angle. Statements were issued that the outbreaks were "not racially motivated" and that "whites as well as Negroes took part." And, of course, they did; at first, in the sense that they were being beaten on, and then some white youths ganged up to assault blacks in revenge.

The daily newspapers by this time had come round to the policy, which the NAACP and *The Clarion* had so long been urging on them, of dropping racial identification in stories. They also adhered to the practice of withholding the names of juveniles who were arrested. As a result, their columns were filled with stories of attacks by "youths" upon other "youths." This may have confused the upstate readers, but the people of the city knew by word-of-mouth that the niggers were assaulting the white kids, even when it happened to be the other way around. My own feeling was that, as always, it was dangerous to trifle with the truth; hysteria fed on the partially known. The hiding and glossing over the racial nature of the conflict, it seemed to me, was preventing the city from paying attention to it in order to learn what it represented. What was eating these youths that they were carrying on in this way? Was it a rudimentary, half-instinctive movement of inarticulate protest? If so, what were they trying to "say"? And who were "they" anyway? Students or dropouts, athletic fans or "delinquents," from one part of town or from all over town? The city seemed uninterested in asking these questions.

The Clarion's position was a complicated one. Actually, no one in town was more disturbed by these goings-on. The youths with their clubs and tire chains were making things difficult for everybody, and not least for the struggling Negro newspaper. Mr. Talbott, in particular, although I knew he was inclined to the theory that "it doesn't hurt for the niggers to raise a little hell," was utterly opposed to brutality, which he thought stupid and counterproductive. He always put down with contempt any suggestion that the Negroes, outnumbered as they were, could better their lot in America by attacks on the whites.

At the same time, his life experience in the ghetto and especially at *The Clarion* had made him so that he accepted every occurring act of violence as a reality about which it was pointless to become indignant. And at the same time, these were black youngsters, and their parents and friends were his people and his readers.

Mr. Talbott was always aware of the great, respectable, white violence waiting to come down at any pretext on the helpless black masses. Nothing could tempt him or fake him into lending support to white prejudice.

The resulting policy tried to take into account all the factors in a difficult situation. *The Clarion* published news stories of the incidents but without its usual gusto, making certain to include the cases where whites attacked blacks. I wrote editorials strongly criticizing the youths, leaving no doubt that we were opposed to their actions. Of course, it was doubtful that they read the editorials, but, at the least, it was important to put before the public where *The Clarion* stood on the issue. And in his column, St. John Ashley reproved the erring youths in down-home language that might get to them.

In my sports column, I had already advocated a change in respect to the football games that would have been an obvious remedy for the attacks. That was to shift the schoolboys' games from the night to the afternoon. My earlier grounds had been that playing under lights, in the cold autumn months, took all the color and fun out of football. Dunbar had moved its grid games to the afternoon. But for the rest of the city, and especially for basketball, this proposal was blocked by potent social and financial considerations. There was the massive objection that most adults could not attend the games during the day. Since schoolboy athletics had long ago been turned into spectator sports for adults, a virtual revolution in the adults' thinking would be required.

Not only that. The revenue from the games—including first of all the tickets of the adult spectators—financed the athletic programs of the schools. To replace this would have taken a big chunk of taxpayers' money. Therefore, the financial interests dominating the Public Schools Committee stood firmly against such a change and so did the School Board itself. The first and last law on the subject, regardless of the predictable bloody heads, was "Night sports must continue."

Meanwhile, I was intrigued by the question as to who the youths were. One saw groups of lower-class young fellows on the street corners with smirks on their faces that made one suspicious, but this wouldn't do. They were "thugs," as *The Clarion* men called them. From my acquaintance with some circles through sports, I knew it would be a mistake to lump them all together as head-whippers.

I did not think the violent ones, in general, were from Dunbar. This was in sharp contrast to the view of most white people of the town. The conservative white people, whom I sometimes estimated at about ninety-five percent of the local white community, supposed that all-Negro Dunbar, in the heart of the west side ghetto, was a hotbed of rebellion; the liberal white people thought the same thing, but considered it justifiable. It wasn't true. In my sports reporting, I was in and out of Dunbar almost daily, and I never saw a more amiable, well-behaved body of students.

I thought I sensed what we would now call a "brotherly" feeling among the Dunbar faculty and students. I noticed on so many occasions the quiet, deemphasized, and informal way that many of the teachers spoke to their students. Ephraim Carter was one I remember especially as having no "discipline" in his voice when addressing a student, and Paul James was the example par excellence. This was so different from what I had known at "white" schools that at first I thought it a delinquency, a failure to require the proper respect for authority. Frankly, I sometimes thought Carter was afraid of the students. But if this was to a certain extent true, it was based on the recognition that these were not middle-class youths, enjoying an extended period of sheltered childhood; rather, most of them already for years had been battling a hostile world, sometimes for daily bread itself.

This acceptance of the students perhaps was accompanied, as many parents charged, by a failure of the school to challenge the young people intellectually and to set before them high goals in life. It may be true that many bright minds perished there. I would not say, however, as some did, that the students were being "taught to be good niggers." Dunbar had its pride, and both faculty and students were well aware of discrimination. But they were not in constant contact with the open manifestation of racism; most of them spent the majority of their time, after all, in environments that were almost entirely black. Except as an oppressive foreign power, it was possible almost to forget that white people existed.

When Dunbar students got into fights and scrapes, they were likely to be all-Negro affairs, against black youths from the east side or other parts of town. Walt brought in one afternoon the shocking report of a gang rape by Dunbar students and ex-students, including a former basketball star. The victim was a Negro girl. Another example of Dunbar-style delinquency was the riot at the Debutantes Ball. This dance was an annual Dunbar event, held in a privately owned hall near the school. One year, hundreds of street youths, who resented being denied admission, formed a mob and laid siege to the hall. They shouted obscenities, threw rocks and bottles, and when the ball was over, assaulted the departing dancers, going so far as to tear off some of the girls' beautiful gowns and to beat up their escorts. It was all between Negroes and didn't even make news except in *The Clarion*.

If not Dunbar students or dropouts, who were the "bad Negroes" who were tearing up the white folks? I came to the conclusion that they were mostly from the districts of the recently integrated schools. Certainly, a good number were from the abysmally poor east side community, the Vo-Tech district. This observation was so embarrassing to the cause of integration that I kept it to myself. What had happened? It seemed to me that the mere physical integration of Vo-Tech and Northridge and other schools, without a program of human integration of the black and white students (and of integration and reeducation of the administrative staffs and faculties), had served to bring latent conflicts into the open. It had only brought the blacks and whites face-to-face. The white principals, teachers, and students (in the main) proposed to continue business as usual, with the addition of a certain number (a minority) of black youths to the scene. The exception was athletics, where they were welcomed, at least to a certain point. The blacks found themselves rigidly segregated in the cafeterias (by practice, of course, not by rule) and in the social affairs of the schools, in everything but sports. In the classrooms they were subjected to humiliation by white teachers, some of whom were bitterly racist; they did not understand the black poverty culture and had no curiosity about it. Instead, these administrators and teachers, except for a few who shone in the night like stars, in their insecurity and fear, fell back on procedures of order and discipline. They could have used a quiet word from Ephraim Carter on that.

The black youngsters, who had grown up in the black slums and hitherto had attended all-black schools, now found themselves in institutions where, for the first time in their lives, they were made to feel pariahs. It wasn't too surprising that some of them reacted with violence.

This theory, which put the blame on foot-dragging integration, was the best I could come up with, but I recognized it had its limitations. At the games, I used to watch the Negro students of the integrated schools to see whether their sympathies lay with "their own" teams or with Dunbar. I found their school loyalties surprisingly strong. The masses of black youths, especially the girls, cheered for Vo-Tech, for example, as if Dunbar were just another opponent. To paraphrase Joe Louis on Hitler, it was obvious that whatever was wrong with their schools, Dunbar couldn't cure it.

I then further observed, however, that at a game in which their school's team was not involved—let's say it had already been eliminated from the tournament—the Negro youths almost unanimously pulled for Dunbar. In this way, they held a kind of dual citizenship. And in this they were joined by a certain number of whites who had been fervent Dunbar partisans ever since the Big Team.

And, of course, all this did not apply to the street youths, who didn't cheer for anyone, but stood about looking cool.

The Negro athletes in the integrated schools sometimes felt that they had to stand up for their manhood. One who did so was Tom Maxwell, a clean-cut, dark-skinned star in several sports at Northridge. The basketball coach, Leon Basey, had an extremely vulgar way of speaking, including the use of racial epithets. He would cry to his players, "Hurry up, Jew-boy!" or "Get the lead out, Snowball!" Some said he had a theory of arousing their anger to make them play harder. At any rate, he called Maxwell "Lightning" just once. It was in the gymnasium, at a basketball practice. The youth straightened, walked to him and said, "Come on out and fight, Mr. Basey." The coach stammered and, regrettably, some of the onlookers thought, apologized.

At what might be called the other extreme was a story I heard about Steel High School's football team. This institution had recently been established on the near south side in a grimy old building vacated a few years earlier by Elliston High School, which had moved to the suburbs. Steel's constituency was surely unique: it served the children, white and black, of the surrounding slums and also "retarded" children from throughout the city. Steel had the best racial integration program in town. Jack Hudson was hired as the basketball coach, making him the first Negro to give instruction to white athletes in the state. Another "first" was Les Keltner, a man in his fifties, who was held by the black community in a respect almost amounting to awe. Bill Whitcomb had told me he was such a brilliant mathematician that he undoubtedly should have been teaching at a university. Instead, he had been teaching at Dunbar for as long as anyone could remember. In spite of this, or perhaps because of it, he had remained a free spirit so outspoken in his hatred of segregation that he often got into difficulties with the school authorities, both white and black. He wasn't active in any organization in my time, but the NAACP workers didn't hold it against him. They seemed to take it for granted that Les was "right," and, furthermore, that he had to keep out of the public eye or he would do something that would cost him his job. People were even a little afraid of associating with him, thinking of his great frustration and the troubles he had risked because of it.

When Steel High opened, Keltner was transferred there from Dunbar and thus became the first Negro in the city to teach mathematics to white students. It was a far cry from a university, but perhaps it was justified on the ground that unusually backward students needed an unusually good teacher. He was an inveterate football fan, and I used to talk with him when I covered the games. A large, heavy-set man who wore thick glasses over protruding eyes, he spoke rapidly and with a frequent boyish smile. His conversation, with me at least, was an unending sardonic rumination on The Question, as if it was on his mind constantly and he was only waiting for an audience. But that may have been because of my known position as a reporter for *The Clarion*.

In spite of this, I wasn't prepared for the story Keltner told me in the stands one night as we watched the game. I knew he served as mentor to the Negro boys on the Steel football team. At Steel, it was the football players who chose the Homecoming Queen to ride a convertible at the head of the procession and reign over the festivities. Throughout the school's brief history, this always had been a white girl.

"Pres, we're the majority on the team this year," Les began in his drawl. "It's the first time. I guess the way even the poor white folks are running, we will be from now on." His shoulders heaved in a sound-less chuckle.

"The boys came to me and said," he continued deliberately, "'Look, we can elect a Negro queen.'"

"Of course they can," I said.

"And I told them, yes, you can, but do you think you ought to? I mean, is it the right thing to do? Whites elect a white queen, Negroes elect a Negro queen?"

He shifted in his seat, and the lights from the field fell on his woolly white hair. His brown face wore a twisted smile. "They took my advice," he said, "They picked another white girl. I guess she deserved it."

Stupefied, I said without thinking, "Maybe next year."

"Maybe so, maybe not," he answered, taking his pipe from his mouth to laugh. I realized I had not understood him. "If she's the best girl, Pres," he gently reproved me.

My own ideas on these subjects were less philosophical. Not in a million years, I thought, would I have persuaded the youths to elect a white queen. And at the same time, I was in favor of a stern crackdown on the ruffians. Where *The Clarion* people tended to fall silent, I was rather shrill about it.

This was all the more true when, on the very first day that Michael attended Northridge High School, his expensive new bicycle, with gears and shift levers, was taken by a thief. This happened in broad daylight, and from the school's bicycle rack just outside the building. According to eyewitnesses whose testimony was reported by Michael, another boy's bicycle was taken at the same time. The other boy was a Negro. Two black boys had come, removed the locks from the bicycles, jumped on them, and ridden them away.

The next day, Michael said a story was going round that Coach Cochrane had seen the thieves in the act and had recognized one of them. Cochrane had then, it was reported, taken unknown and unofficial steps, with the end result that the Negro boy's bicycle was returned to him. But Michael's bad luck, or whatever it was, with Cochrane was still running; nothing had been done about his bike.

A few days later, Michael told me he had learned—on the good authority of schoolboy gossip—who had taken his bicycle and where it probably was. The thief was said to be Billy Hester, who lived in the 2900 block of Washington Place, not far from our original home. Billy, the boys said, was a member of a ring that stole bikes, exchanged the parts so as to camouflage them, and then sold them to fences. It was reported that there were "fifty bikes in Billy Hester's backyard."

I took up the matter with the principal. Still baffled by Michael's relationship with Cochrane, and still thinking that some evil spirit of coincidence must be at work, I left his name out of it. Whatever he was up to, I wasn't going to bring him into difficulty with his white superiors. The principal referred me to the vice principal, another white man. The vice principal kept telling me every day over the telephone that there was no progress in the case, and his tone of voice implied that none was to be expected.

The combination of official ignorance and boyish knowledge was maddening; and it spurred me to one of my "enterprising reporter" moods of direct action. I was determined to recover the bicycle myself.

I looked up the Hester residence in *The Clarion*'s city directory and proceeded in my car to the neighborhood. Before reaching Billy's house, I spied two Negro boys with bicycles walking into an alley that slanted up a little hill. On an impulse, I turned in behind them, and they jumped on the bikes and pumped hastily away. This confirmed my suspicions that I was on a hot scent.

Then, having located the Hester house, I drove through the alley behind it. There in the yard, I saw a number of bicycles, but too far from the alley for me to examine them without trespassing.

At this point, I thought it the better part of valor to call a cop. I went to a street telephone booth and put in a call to headquarters. After about ten minutes, two white policemen pulled up in a cruiser. One of them was young, husky, and hostile, while the other was an older and quieter man.

We went to the residence, a rotting frame house like the rest on the street. I guess I had expected Billy to answer the door. Instead, we were met by a tall, black, frowning man who must have been about thirty years old.

We went just inside the door, and the policemen turned to me to do the talking.

I asked whether this was Billy Hester's home, and the man said, "I'm his brother. What y'all want, anyhow?"

I explained about the bicycle and said, "I have reason to believe it's in your backyard." The brother, however, wasn't at all friendly and said, "Billy ain't here. What right y'all got coming into my house?"

I looked to the policemen, but the young one, to my surprise, said, "Mister, we can't search this man's yard just on your say-so. Now, have you seen your boy's bicycle here?"

I had to admit I had not; moreover, I was thrown on the defensive by the young policeman's unaccustomed attitude of respect for Negroes' civil rights. For a moment, I wondered whether an editorial I had written recently on the subject might not be getting results. At the same time, it flashed through my mind that a well-organized bicycle ring would have paid off the police.

In either case, I was the fool of the story, and there was nothing to do but back out, mumbling apologies. "Yeah, all right," the young cop said ungraciously.

Two or three days later, I went about retrieving the bicycle in the proper manner, by calling on Attorney Johnson Dennis, the Democratic precinct committeeman in our former neighborhood. Attorney Dennis, a fleshy brown-skinned man, was in the NAACP—

he was to be president one year—and also had a boy on our baseball team. "It's a God-damned shame," he agreed with me. "I can't give Johnny nothing but what disappears in a week. Ruins the neighborhood for decent people."

Huffing a bit and frowning angrily, the attorney escorted Michael and me to a police substation in the basement of City Hall, where there was a vast assortment of bicycles. We couldn't find Michael's among them, but we left a description of it and Attorney Dennis lodged our complaint in a voice of thunder.

Mike and I had some other downtown errands that took a couple of hours. When we got home, the bicycle was sitting in the yard. The gears had been removed from it, but Mike, possibly to avoid further trouble in his boys' world, said he didn't want them anyway.

I telephoned my thanks to Dennis and the police but made no inquiries about the particulars of the bike's return. It was the swiftest act of justice I have seen in my whole life. I certainly knew which party to vote for to facilitate the recovery of stolen goods.

It was the following spring that Billy and two of his ragged friends from that neighborhood showed up for the baseball team. Michael and I recognized him at once, and I judged from his look that he knew who we were, but nothing was said on the subject. I never liked him personally. He was a rogue, without discipline or respect for the team, but I had to admit he could hit, field, and throw better than Michael, and he went into the lineup.

As some came storming up in the bright, brief flash of their youth, to contend by strength or stealth for the places and possessions of our city, others, quietly or raising hell to the bitter end, made room for them.

Thus, one frosty morning Pierce met me at the time clock with the stammered news: "Eddie's dead."

After I expressed shock and dismay, he said, "They found him this morning. It was too cold out there where he slept. He died like an animal."

George Brown smiled. "Eddie lived and died like an animal," he said.

"Well, he didn't have much of a life, but he was free," Pierce replied. And using a nickname the men sometimes applied to Mr. Talbott, he added, "Cap saw to it he wasn't in no institution." I thought Pierce was remembering the orphans' home.

Little more was said about Eddie. I suppose he had a pauper's burial, without services.

Smitty, on the ether hand, was restless and troublesome. The time was long past when he had shown he could quit drinking. His swings became more violent. He disappeared for six weeks, then reappeared in the newsroom one Thursday night, gaunt, his eyes wilder than ever, his hands shaking. He was argumentative, apocalyptic. "Don't tell me what to do," he shouted, although no one was telling him. "I know what I'm doing! I am perfectly conscious of all that is happening. I'll call the President—do you doubt me? I am Smitty Smith!"

Pierce attempted to soothe him, and Mr. Talbott, appearing from the front office, complained, "Come on now, Smitty, these men are tryin' to work. This is press night, man! Come on out here and talk to me if you've got to."

Smitty wouldn't budge. "Work!" he yelled. "Mister, I've worked all my life, and where has it got me? All these men working for you—what are they doing?" His eyes fell on the papers on Bill's desk, and he leapt back in horror. "What is all this?" He raced his hand through the papers, mixing them together, making them fall to the floor. "Not by work shall ye be saved," he shouted. "Oh ye of little faith!"

It was half an hour before Mr. Talbott could get him out of the way, and then he refused to sit down and talk, but rolled off into the night. We didn't see him again. He had left the Talbotts, and no one knew for certain where he was living. Pierce once speculated he might be "shacking with that woman"—a person in Smitty's life whom I had never heard of.

A year went by. Even then, we weren't prepared for the news. For one thing, as Mr. Talbott reminded us, we hadn't known Smitty's age—I gathered he was in his sixties. And while we assumed his drinking had got the better of him, I think no one had imagined he was really ill. Somehow, it didn't seem right that Smitty had to be an old man or to suffer from a physically wasting disease like other people. As he said, he was Smitty Smith. But when I looked into his coffin, he had become so small that I would not have known him. Even his head seemed shrunken.

"Third man out of the poker game," was Pierce's lugubrious note. Besides Bill Baxter, there had been Mike Gale, who had passed away in the fullness of his years one night as he sat in a storefront to rest while taking a walk on the Avenue.

33. A Most Unusual Man

Although I had signed the membership book of Everyman Unitarian Church, some Sundays I wouldn't go there, but would slip off just a block east into the decaying residential district that surrounded it. There, some white Christians who relocated to the suburbs had sold their church to a most unusual poor people's congregation, the Brotherhood Believers Temple. I had become acquainted with the pastor, a twenty-five-year-old white man named Robert Robertson.

The Brotherhood Believers were an independent church, of the type called Pentecostal—that is, with shouting and speaking in tongues. The congregation had been composed originally of lower-class whites from Kentucky and Tennessee, or "hillbillies" as our city called them. But Reverend Robertson was one of those young white people who were just then rising to battle segregation. Under his leadership, the Believers had integrated until they were actually about fifty-fifty. In itself, this was amazing—to see Southern whites and blacks joining so intimately (at the end of the service you embraced your neighbor, and all the better if he or she was of the other color), but it was only the first amazement of the Brotherhood. The first miracle, a Believer might say.

The second miracle, as I had heard for myself, was that Bob Robertson was leading his fundamentalist flock in the most advanced campaign of social action and progressive politics I had ever witnessed in a religious body. More, he was preaching an extremely radical theology to them. He was breaking down their literal faith in the Bible, itself; he was actually exhorting them to "live as atheists," by which he meant to do good for its own sake and without expecting reward from a heavenly Father or in a future life. "Don't expect a man with a long gray beard to come out of the skies and solve your problems," he challenged them. "You must solve them yourselves, through brotherhood!"

And, at the same time, he was practicing faith healing.

I met Reverend Robertson when he came to *The Clarion* to place an ad for his church services. I was attracted to him at once. He and his wife Genevieve, though they had as little "social life" as Susan and I, found time to be dinner guests at our home. Bob was a handsome man, overflowing with a charisma that related to rural life; he reminded me strongly of my cousin Jackson, who had been a very popular young man among the country people. As he told me his story that evening and later when I interviewed him for *The Clarion*, I learned that my impression was correct.

He was a native of a tiny community in the eastern part of the state that was lily-white; that is, it was one of those towns where a Negro could not stay overnight. He told me that even when there was a black player who lived in the county on the high school basketball team, the boy could come into town only for the evening of a game.

I knew little about Bob's childhood except that he said his father was a harsh man who mistreated him, and who was a member of the Klan. He had died during Bob's adolescence. After high school, Bob went to the state university. It was there that he, who had seen hardly half-a-dozen Negroes in his life, saw the great light of integration. He said that a talk given by Eleanor Roosevelt, and the activities of the campus NAACP, were instrumental in preparing his mind for a new line of thinking. He was quite explicit about the event that changed his being as instantly as St. Paul's.

"I was sitting in a classroom when a dark-complexioned girl [this was his chosen term for Negro] took a chair alongside me. She was the most beautiful person I had ever seen, and I was overwhelmed by attraction to her."

That moment was Bob's vocation. He responded to it totally (although as far as I know, he never even spoke to the girl). With him, segregation took the place of sin and the cause of the black people that of virtue, to be espoused on every occasion, and when it was lying dormant, brought out with trumpets. He didn't tell me much more about his activities as a student, but one incident was typical of the Bob Robertson I came to know. He was getting a haircut in a barbershop operated by a Negro, when the proprietor mentioned that he served only white clientele.

"What!" said Bob. "Do you mean you wouldn't cut a Negro's hair?"

"That's right, suh—only white people's."

"Then you won't cut mine!" cried Bob, leaping out of the chair with half a haircut and the apron still around his neck. And he strode away.

This little story illustrated a difference between Bob's viewpoint and mine. He would give battle even to Negroes who were upholding the system of oppression, while I still considered such persons as coerced by my own group, the whites, and was hesitant to attack them.

The barbershop incident recurred in other forms during Bob Robertson's stormy career, perhaps most notably when he was being admitted as a patient to University Hospital. That was early in his tenure as executive secretary of the Mayor's Commission on Human Rights. Despite the title, he was countrified enough to be ignorant of many things in the city.

He was suffering from acute hepatitis and was nauseous with a high fever. The admitting clerk, as she went through the routine procedure, made the mistake of reading off the question "Race?"

Bristling, Bob said: "What do you want to know that for?"

Then the woman, who he noted was "a confused light-complexioned person from the South," made the greater mistake of answering: "Because I have to know what room to put you in."

"Is this hospital segregated?" Bob said ominously.

Thus began a full four hours of scenes, telephone calls, and conferences on ascending levels. Sick as he was, Bob refused to get into bed. The doctors could not prevail on him. Sitting in a wheelchair in the hallway, he demanded to see the director of the hospital. After some time, that man was summoned from his home, and when he arrived Bob told him: "I am a city official appointed by the mayor, and I will not go into a room until this hospital is integrated." And, he added: "I have a friend who's a reporter on *The Clarion*. I'll just call him and this will be all over *The Clarion* tomorrow. We'll just see what the Community Fund thinks of that." Then he did call me, but requested, apologizing—he knew I hated to "sit on" a story—that I hold off writing anything until it was over.

And that's how University Hospital, and soon the other hospitals in town, came to integrate their patient facilities. No doubt they had been considering the step, but they might have considered it till Doomsday if it hadn't been for Bobby's stand. He was as good as his word and didn't get into bed until they put him into a room with a black man. And he exacted a promise that no reprisal would be taken against the woman at the admitting desk.

Bob Robertson had first come to our city as a welfare worker after graduating from university. Soon thereafter, he met Genevieve. She was a woman of delicate beauty, an ash-blonde with a very sweet expression that bespoke her kind and gentle temperament. She was older than Bob. There was no exhausting the paradoxes of this couple—she was a registered nurse, and a most efficient one, capable of superintending a small hospital; and she was devoutly religious. After we got to know the Robertsons well, when my mother was in their nursing home, I was told that Genevieve had refused to marry Bob until he came to religion. She and her mother had "prayed over him" for six months, at the end of which time it was decided he had reached an acceptable state. I was tempted to ask how they could tell, since Bob must already have been many times more religious than the average clergyman, if they were measuring real morality; and if not, he never did become "religious," but rather "anti-religious." In fact, one of his strongest sermons was against literal belief in the Bible. "Paul said, justifying slavery, 'Servants, obey your masters,' and I say," he said, slamming the Bible on the pulpit with a gesture of disgust, "To hell with Paul!"

I think it was Genevieve's prayers, and her influence, that brought him to the ministry. He took some courses at Carlton Theological Seminary and obtained a charge in the Methodist Church, a small congregation in the white south side suburbs. He then proceeded to integrate it. And it wasn't as if he had put a few blacks in the back row; he brought them right down front and called attention to their being there. A furor ensued in the congregation. The district superintendent took a hand to squelch Bobby. He was a tall, spare man in his seventies. Bobby wouldn't give an inch, and in short order, he was turned out of the Methodists.

There went with him, however, not only his black recruits but a sizeable number—about a third, he said—of the whites. This was the nucleus of the Brotherhood.

He next took over the pastorate of an independent Pentecostal church, whose minister was retiring. Here the pattern was gone through again, except this time it was the church board instead of the municipal board who put him out. And yet he had picked up some more members.

It was at this point that the accumulated congregation decided to found its own church and bought the building near the Unitarian church. I have often been asked, usually by suspicious liberals, how the Brotherhood managed this operation, and later the acquisition of two nursing homes, then the massive brick and stone temple they bought from a Jewish congregation that was moving to the suburbs, as well as the establishment of a free restaurant and free clothing store. I must say that I never felt moved to pry into their financial arrangements, but I made a few rather general observations.

Their motto, Bob sometimes enunciated, was from the Acts of the Apostles: "They had all things in common." This Christian communism wasn't absolute, for most of them maintained their own homes and families, but they practiced it on a large scale, sharing articles of clothing, seeing that no member of the congregation (or outsider who came to them) went hungry or needy, maintaining a "church car" for anybody's use, paying up people's insurance premiums, and the like. This was their secret. By itself, I felt, it might well have been a secret for going broke together, not for amassing capital to launch more operations. The other part was that they were not dummies, as my middle-class friends supposed, but many of them were enterprising, active persons—electricians, carpenters, nurses—skilled at this and that. They held jobs, or operated small businesses, and I assumed they gave whopping tithes to the Brotherhood. Few of them were idle. If nothing else, they took foster children or aged people under the welfare grants program into their homes. Of their own labor, they gave to the Brotherhood projects without stint. Men and young people worked at construction, repairs or clean-up in their free time. The women contributed their services to the nursing homes, without pay or at subsistence wages. One whom I knew only as "Esther" seemed quite happy in that life; she reminded me of my grandmother. Others, especially black women with family responsibilities, were paid well. The Brotherhood women as a group acquired a reputation for catering such events as pancake breakfasts for civic groups; these brought in good-sized sums to the coffers of the church.

It seemed to me that the Brotherhood, rejecting the obscene reality of the present and reaching toward Bob's vision of the future, thereby had released the community vigor of pioneer times, which I had seen in the collective grain threshing of my boyhood. And that was the third miracle.

Also like the country people, they lived simply and economically, with the church providing all their status and recreation—and, although Bob and Genevieve weren't opposed to doctors, much of their medical care. I did not at that time witness any of the faith healings, though I am certain Bob was practicing it. He obviously was anxious to conceal this side of the Brotherhood from me. He was apologetic even about the speaking in tongues that I witnessed at the church. "Doggone them, they have to have that kind of stuff," he said. On one occasion, I arranged with Reverend Beatty for the Brotherhood to worship with the Unitarians, and for Bob to speak. Beatty was pleased with the idea, and assigned me to write the sermon title for the announcement board in front of the church, which I did as "New Wine in Old-Time Bottles." Some of the conservative

Unitarians were skittish at the prospect, but the congregation was soon won over by the service. They were reached by the forthright mixing of black and white. They were surprised and caught up by the joyousness of the singing and preaching. For another outstanding trait of Bob and the Brotherhood was that their religion was a happy one. There was just no solemnity about it. The music was played by a jazz combo, and the "psalms" were mostly popular tunes with new words written by Bob. To the strains of "The Beer-Barrel Polka" they sang: "There's a new world a-comin'..."

It was like a blast of fresh air to the Unitarians, who, for all their vaunted liberalism, had grown rather staid (and were halfway aware of it). They responded with enthusiasm to the soul-felt witnessing and the rest of it, and at the end, they applauded Bob's sermon. But there was no return visit. To my surprise, I seemed to be the only Unitarian who wanted to continue the relationship, and there was resistance from the other direction too. Bob had been pleased to accept the invitation, for one reason because he needed some support in recognized church circles, even from such an unorthodox group as the Unitarians. But he said he had had trouble with some of the more fundamentalist Believers. One of them, an elderly white woman, told him, "I won't stand for goin' unless you preach Jesus's blood!"

Later on, under different circumstances—we visited the Believers after they moved in a body to California—Susan and I witnessed an entire Sunday of Bobby's faith healing. We were disgusted, at first mentally, as Bobby went through all the tricks of the magician's repertoire. And then we were disgusted physically, when Genevieve paraded through the hall displaying on a gauze pad a bit of bloody issue that Bobby said was a "cancer" a black woman had just "passed." We were the Robertsons' house guests, and in a moment of intimacy, Susan asked Genevieve about it all. "The people demand it of him," she said. It seemed to us, though, that the Believers were promoting the demand. From this experience, however, I did not conclude that Bobby was a charlatan, nor was I in the least reconciled to the practice. It remained a door to which I found no key.

In the early years of our friendship, I had been able to help Bobby to a minimal recognition by the power structure. His draft number had come up, just a few months before he was to turn twenty-six, and Selective Service was refusing to exempt him as a minister. It fell to my lot, as an "objective" newspaper reporter and a member of another, recognized denomination, to write a letter to his draft board. I stated that I had attended services at the Temple and that the Brotherhood was a bonafide religious organization, as evidenced by preaching, praying, hymn singing, collection taking, and other activities of groups of this nature; and that Reverend Robertson was its principal and foremost founder, minister, and the regular leader of its services. In the nick of time before his scheduled reporting date, Bobby was granted his exemption.

From such beginnings, he and his Believers made their way in the course of a few years to a point where they were granted affiliation and partial funding by a large denomination that had its national headquarters in our city. At the same time, Bob was named to the Mayor's Commission post. Several powerful persons of the town had come to realize that the Believers, and only they, had what it took to cope with the problem of the "inner-city" slum dwellers, black and white, which was then mushrooming beyond the control of the traditional methods of management. To reach this place, as must anything new in the world, the Believers had suffered and stood firm, endured calumny, and let their good work speak for them. There was no compromise. Bob became even more forthright and radical in his preaching. "I stand for Jesus and for Vladimir Ilyitch Lenin," he cried out from the pulpit. "For Buddha, for Mohammed, for Karl Marx, and for Martin Lather King, Jr.!"

Bobby's reception in the black end of town was at first no more cordial than in the white one. He was seen as another white man with a gimmick. The good news that the Brotherhood Believers were truly a brotherhood was slow in spreading. Bob had three assistant pastors. One, Will Toms, was a fat white Kentuckian, a jolly deputy sheriff who had totally gone over to integration, although this was hard to believe until you knew him. Another was Reverend Joe Oliver, a tall black man whose entire family played an active and leading part in the

Brotherhood. But they had been Seventh-Day Adventists and weren't widely known by the Baptists and Methodists who made up most of the community. One of Oliver's daughters worked for *The Clarion*. The third pastor was a white fundamentalist, and he dropped away from the Brotherhood after a time.

In his drive to reach the black people, Bobby took the tactic of challenging the "do-nothing" Negro ministers, including the powerful Baptists, but, of course, not men like Sanford Black and Henry Watson. This brought the Ministerial Alliances down on him, giving him a certain bad reputation. However, it ultimately served his purpose, since a number of Negroes, already critical of these ministers, pricked up their ears. Several of his all-out statements on "hot" civil rights issues were printed in the newspapers and made good reading for people like Cinq who were fed up with pussyfooting. Meanwhile, individuals here and there learned that he was a man who did such things as perform interracial marriages, which were forbidden by an antiquated state law. Not everybody was in favor of interracial marriages—most Negro women opposed them, since they usually joined Negro men and white women. Regardless, I think everybody was impressed by the way Bobby contemptuously defied that law.

What clinched it though were the enemies he made among the Kluxers. The Robertsons lived in a decaying poor-white neighborhood between the black east side and west side. Negroes began moving in, and the whites battled them, but Bob and Genevieve put signs on their lawn reading: "We Welcome Our New Neighbors" and "We Like Living in an Integrated Neighborhood." After that, rocks sailed through their windows. Dynamite was at one point discovered in the Temple's coal bin. This was something the Negroes understood. People like Cinq decided the Believers were real.

For several years after their marriage, Bob and Genevieve had no children, although there was a teenaged girl who lived with them as their daughter. Then, they began adopting what they called their "Rainbow Family." First, they took in two Korean orphans of the war, a boy and a girl. The little girl was killed in a traffic crash, and they went through a miserable battle with the proprietors of three "white" cemeteries over her burial. Then, they adopted another Korean girl. All this didn't attract the attention of black people, but finally, they adopted a Negro baby whom they named Bob Robertson, Jr. And then, as seems to happen, Genevieve had a "home-made" child as they put it, and the house was full of infants. *The Clarion* published a picture of the family group—"The Human Family"—on the front page of its Christmas issue.

Genevieve, as she wheeled Bobby Jr. on the sidewalk, often was subjected to jibes from racists. One day, while she held him in her arms in a doctor's waiting room, a white woman spat in her face.

The incident was reported in *The Clarion* and was quickly the subject of conversation throughout our part of town. Had the woman known it, her spittle had sealed the compact between the Robertsons and all the Negroes of the city.

34. A Troubled Young Woman

I was never particularly conscious of an age difference with the Robertsons. If Bob sometimes deferred to me, it was because I had knowledge of the political field that he was only then acquiring. For example, I understood which legislation to support between the Right-to-Work Bill and the Civil Rights Bill. But with the coming of the early 1960s, it seemed to me that I looked around and suddenly saw much younger people everywhere. Many of these youths were doing things my friends and I had been advocating for twenty years, and thus were a great and surprising new source of energy. They were reinforcements we had long given up on expecting. Some of them, on the other hand, were doing things that were very wrong, and those that were doing things "right" occasionally were found to be doing other things that were infuriating.

And whatever they were doing, I thought further, they were sitting relaxed, laughing, "goofing off," and altogether behaving as if the world was being created anew and I was a kindly but rather irrelevant old gentleman.

One of these was John Barry, who came to work at *The Clarion*. John is now a columnist for one of the nation's leading newspapers. He was then a handsome, neat, well-mannered youth who hailed from Mississippi. (But he so entirely lacked a Deep South accent that I once jokingly accused him of being an FBI agent from somewhere else.)

I gathered that his parents were educated people, perhaps teachers. He was an excellent writer; his spelling and grammar were without blemish. He was a kind of bright young Negro I hadn't seen before, a saner Robert Morgan. Like the other youngsters (he was twenty-two), he seemed to be easy about everything. He was easy about his work and about Dunbar winning the tournament; he went with a white girl, and was easy about her.

John had been with us several months before he casually, as if he had just recalled it, told the story about his graduation from the Negro high school in Mississippi. "I was first in the class, and so they gave me a scholarship of what do you think? Of five dollars." He laughed, not bitterly but almost giggling. "Take this, my boy, and go off to college."

This sense of the ridiculousness of racism did not desert him in facing our city's powerful whites. On one occasion, at Mr. Talbott's angry insistence, a confrontation was arranged between a Negro who charged he had been beaten in the city lockup and several policemen, including the chief inspector. John Barry was assigned to the meeting at police headquarters.

The prisoner's face was "a mess," John later told us. The man declared that he had suffered, among other injuries, a black eye. Looking straight at it, Inspector Lisant dictated to the stenographer, "Let the record show I don't see a black eye."

And John, the cub reporter, interjected quietly and drily, "Let the record show I do see a black eye. Also a blind eye."

Another time, word came to the newsroom that there was a disturbance at Northridge High School, some kind of riot, with blacks and whites supposedly fighting in the cafeteria. John and I jumped into my car and drove there. We walked into the school, and John began interviewing some Negro students, taking notes on a pad. The youngsters told him excitedly that a "Negro strike" was being held to protest discrimination in a dramatic production. A large group of black students were sitting in the cafeteria and refusing to eat. There hadn't really been any fighting, but somebody had thrown a water glass and it had broken. They had spoken quickly, eager to get back to the cafeteria before they missed all the happenings.

At this point the principal came up, a very nervous man, and the youths skittered away. The principal recognized me, and one of his many concerns at the moment was that no reporters, especially from *The Clarion*, should come directly into the building and start talking with students. This was a rule that recently had been promulgated to help keep down "racial unrest" and thus prevent parking-lot thuggery. The daily newspapers had agreed to it, but as usual, the school officials had forgotten to ask *The Clarion*. Another rule forbade students of other schools from entering.

The principal talked with me without invoking the reporter ban; after all, I was one of his student's parents. Then he turned to John, whom he didn't know. "And what is your name?" he asked.

"John Barry."

"And where are you a student?" the principal went on.

"I am not a student."

John eyed him levelly and might have been still doing so if I hadn't introduced them. The principal decided to put a good face on it and invited us into his office, where we listened to his account of the situation. He was really quite cordial because he had fallen for the badger-game variant in insulting John, and never thereafter could do enough to put things right. From then on, the daily newspapermen asked permission when visiting the school, but John Barry just modestly walked on in.

Another young person whom I came to know well was John's white girlfriend, Karen Davenport. If John often was taken for a bit younger than his real age, Karen was one of those persons who seem tremendously older than they are. She was actually a student at Northridge— a classmate of Michael's—when she and I were going to civil rights meetings together and talking them over the next day at *The Clarion*, where she spent much of her free time.

Although she, too, now and then with a gesture or a laugh reminded me of her light-hearted, childish side, Karen was far from the
"cool" of John Barry. In fact, I once put the figure to myself that she
was a Joan of Arc, on fire in a world that turned colder to her the more
she burned. She was the daughter of peace-activist parents, or, rather,
a mother and a stepfather. Her own father had been killed in the
Korean War, and she had three—eventually four—younger half brothers and sisters.

I had become friends with the Davenports through the Fellowship
of Reconciliation, a pacifist organization that I had recently joined.
They were Unitarians. Catherine was a crusader, a conscientious and
brave woman who would speak out for peace, human brotherhood,
and her other moral passion, which was atheism. Richard was lacon-
ic, with a lurking sense of humor. It was quite a while before I learned
he had served in prison as a war resister during the Second World
War. Their children were lovely, and their family life was one of the
most beautiful I had ever seen. With one jarring note, which wasn't
apparent until you got to know them intimately, I finally realized in
amazement that it was one of those families in which mother and
daughter don't get along.

Karen came into several things—high school, civil rights, sex—
simultaneously and already troubled. I had first met her at the school's
Open House when she and Michael were sophomores. Our families
were talking together. She and I got into a conversation off to one side.
Even then she had a way, as children of civil rights parents often did,
of talking with adults as equals rather than with her peers. She was a
good-looking girl, peaches and cream, sexually developed beyond her
years, and one, in turn, was inclined to forget that she was a child. She
seemed distressed and lonely. She told me a story about her boyfriend
of the previous year, who had been drowned in a boating accident.
Her mother later advised me this was a fantasy, that she hadn't known
that boy. I accepted Catherine's statement, but looking back on it now,
I'm not sure whom to believe.

Karen and I, along with her parents, soon were actively engaged in
"The Humans'" anti-segregation wave in the city. It was one of those

movements that bring their participants together for a time like a band of lifelong friends. In our function as political workers, Karen and I almost lived together; the disparity between our ages disappeared (helped along by the powerful new idea that one shouldn't look down on young people). I found myself, of all things, powerfully attracted to her. I remember one summer night when I watched her speaking to a group and my penis came straight and quick to an erection, which was a nearly forgotten occurrence at my time of life. She wasn't aware of this aspect of our relationship. In fact, she once confided to me that another middle-aged man, a Negro, had made advances to her. "I was so surprised because, Pres, I wouldn't think of him in that way any more than I would you. It was awful." I could do nothing but ruefully swallow these words. I tried to put her sexiness out of my mind, but it continued to disturb me—especially when she seemed to be flaunting it (though she wasn't, quite the opposite). She had big legs, as the black people said, and in the summertime, she wore short shorts—it was before the time of miniskirts—that revealed them in all their length, shapeliness, and soft attractiveness. In her innocence, she was not conscious of the ribald comments she was occasioning when she walked along the Avenue and to *The Clarion* in this garb. I don't mean that Karen wasn't screwing John Barry, because I think she was. But she didn't appreciate the impact of her legs.

I certainly did, with that extreme and peculiar anguish—a compound of lust, fear, and who knows what else—that comes over a man in such a situation. Finally, one day in the office, after sitting and looking at her bare legs for half an hour, I suddenly shouted at her: "Will you go home and put some clothes on!"

Otherwise, our time together was spent in desegregation activity, and to a certain extent, when she was on the outs with Richard and Catherine, I suppose she used Susan and me as surrogate parents. For that matter, I was also using her as a surrogate daughter. Michael went into high school in such a frame of mind that he did not take part in organized activities, even around civil rights. And so, when I was struck by an inspiration to launch the Student Human Relations Council at Northridge, I imparted it to Karen. She immediately set to work and did it.

Like many of us who had the low boiling point requisite to start things, Karen wasn't suited to work in them after they were going. It was a couple of things. She tended to have all her associations with the Negroes, and nothing whatever to do with the whites. Even I had always kept up some white connections; I was a member of the Round Table and the Historical Association, and some other white groups. With Karen, it was the blacks against the whites. Needless to say, this wasn't the proper approach in building a Human Relations Council. For one thing, the Negro youth of our town hadn't yet awakened to the civil rights movement. The NAACP couldn't even keep a Youth Council in existence. The black youngsters of Northridge had more in common with the ordinary white youth in their interests, socializing, and the like. They looked on Karen as some kind of kook.

The poor child grimly persevered and made a few friendships among the Negro girls. From what I heard of these relationships, she was being tolerated. There was one girl and her family who seemed to like her, but over the years, Karen became too shrill and tiresome even for them. And there was an afternoon when I drove John Barry to a west side house where he had to see a teenager about something. An after-school gathering was going on. Karen's name was mentioned, and the black girls laughed. I looked at John and he was laughing too.

The Human Relations Council, composed of the Northridge line-up of blacks, whites, and Jews, grew into a constructive organization of its type, which passed resolutions against discrimination and tried to moderate the school's ethnic conflicts. But it had no place for Karen; she was considered a troublemaker. Despite being the founder, by the second year she was passed over in the election of officers. Her position had become so uncomfortable that she dropped out of the group. From then on, she associated almost entirely with adults. She spent even more time at *The Clarion*, where Mr. Talbott had quietly noted that whatever else "little Karen" might be, she was a wholehearted soldier against white racism. As always, that was enough for him.

Karen had shown an aptitude for drawing and painting, and after high school, she went to an art school in New York City. For a time, I heard of her activities through her parents. There was a story that she had been raped in a hallway by a Negro, but in the light of subsequent developments, I never knew how to evaluate it. For a little later, she was pregnant, and by a black man. With that bare and grudging news, her family turned terribly against her. To talk with Catherine, you would think the girl no longer existed. Karen twice called Susan and me from New York just to hear the sound of friendship. She was nineteen years old and, it seemed, utterly alone. We gathered that whatever had happened, there was no father for her child. I reflected sadly that she hadn't been any more successful in making friends in New York than in our town.

It wasn't, after all, as if the Davenports had conventional views on the subject. They continued to hold their places in the vanguard of those who militantly approved of interracial everything. They would have been the first ones, it seemed to me, to come to the defense of any other woman in such circumstances. To my surprise, because they came from religious backgrounds and had the manners of churchly people even though they were atheists, I had discovered while turning over books in their library that they held a Swedish-style reverence for sex, keeping a volume of photographs of nude lovers, which they handled as if it were the Bible. At first I was amused, but when we discussed it, their gentleness and clean-mindedness made me feel intolerably crude.

I had heard of integrationists who sang a different tune when The Question came home to them, but I couldn't believe this of the Davenports. It was a hard time for Karen; it was a hard time for Catherine; it must have been a hard time for Richard. And then, Susan and I were given the brief word that the child was born, and Karen was going to live with her aunt in Florida. We didn't think she would take a Negro infant to that Dixie state, and so surmised that there had been added to the population another brown orphan, whose hard times were only beginning.

Several years later, Karen returned to New York and, after a time, was married. Her mother attended the wedding, and stopped off afterwards to see us where we now live. She didn't tell us, and we didn't ask, but we learned later that Karen's husband was a black man. It was good to see that the mother and daughter were reconciled. There is only so much misery human beings can stand.

35. The "Humans"

The "Humans," to whom I have already referred, were, so to speak, the Human Relations Committee extended to the Everyman Unitarian Church. "Human" was the "in" word then, as people were getting away from "race." The members of the committee were mostly young—married, unmarried, and tentatively married—with a sprinkling of us oldsters. The group was interracial and crusaded against Jim Crow in a spirit of hilarity. One of its first actions was to integrate a beer joint.

The Humans didn't believe in segregating on religious lines either, and therefore the committee included quite a number of non-Unitarians. One of the most faithful attendants was Claudio Tubman. He was a member of the Second Christian Church, but his heart went to the Humans. He liked the drinking, the poetry readings the group sometimes engaged in, and above all the "humanity."

Richard and Catherine Davenport were also active on the committee. Nondrinkers, they brought quite a laugh when, on the capitulation of the beer joint's proprietor, they ordered ginger ale.

With their free and fancy behavior, the Humans outraged the bourgeoisie of Everyman Church. But they couldn't be stopped, because they attracted Negroes who were conspicuous by their absence from other functions of the church. It was a chronic sore point that only a precarious token number of blacks could be recruited into such a liberal congregation. The Negroes just wouldn't come, or wouldn't come back. There were liberal Negroes, of course, but they either went to black churches, with all the traditional trappings, or stayed home and slept off their hangovers. The situation wasn't helped when Everyman—over the protests of the Humans—built a new edifice seven miles out in the country. It was in an area where, according to a physician I knew, "even German Jews couldn't live." The planning committee delivered bracing reports on the new church once a month, but they were silent on this subject: it seemed a likely embarrassment that Negroes, who had never come to the inner-city church in any numbers, wouldn't come to the new one at all.

And so it was that Mrs. Morgan Delacroix, the most powerful pillar of the church board, was arrested in mid-sniff when she started to give her candid opinion of the Humans. For the Humans had not only established some credit in the black community, but their actual leader was a young black man who had recently come to town and was finding instant acceptance. His name was James Bridges Blake. He was an attorney. And, he was blind.

I have searched my memory in vain for my first meeting with James Blake, whom I was to know and marvel at, to follow and to love, to politic, and demonstrate, and drink with as I had Pat Johnson ten or fifteen years earlier. By now Pat, absorbed in his duties as manager of the Trotter Company, seldom appeared on the civil rights battlefronts. It seemed to me not so much providential as a matter of revolutionary fecundity that James Blake arrived at this juncture, when it seemed the black people were throwing up charismatic young leaders as rapidly as their cause demanded. James was twenty-seven, with a brilliant scholastic record. He had graduated from the state university with one of those superlative achievements that Bill Whitcomb had taught me to avoid citing and had then gone to Columbia University Law School on a fellowship. Like Pat, he was both a race man and an integrationist; his affliction brought him at once the devotion of the Negroes, who have a particular tenderness for the blind, and the compassionate white people of all sorts and manners. He had lost his vision at the age of three, when his mother accidentally poured scalding water over him. Although I never discussed it with him (except to rib him once, "You're no more blind than John Barry is from Mississippi"), I am quite certain his lack of sight was total, and that the amazing things he did were all spirit. He would have no truck with white canes or seeing-eye dogs. When you walked with him, the two of you kept your shoulders touching, and that was all. A good deal of the time, he made his way by himself around the town, like any other active young man.

Once, on the way home from a party, I saw him at three in the morning, alone, going into a public telephone booth. When I stopped, he explained he had been at another gathering, which he was the last to leave, and he was calling a cab.

One rarely saw on James Blake's face the signs of struggle, although in off moments I caught him looking pensive. Usually he wore a smile, although I sometimes thought it was a rather frozen one. I believe he had hit on this great challenge, to be black, blind, and filled with a zest for life—all of it—and to carry it off gallantly and even flippantly. The family was from M— (the site of the lynching). His brother Tom was an outstanding athlete, a collegiate champion quarter-miler. James, who was also tall and strongly built, told me that in younger days he used to play football, with the other fellows helping him into position between plays. Once, he said, on a country road, a friend let him move into the driver's seat and he drove a car for a moderate distance. He went often to the movies, and would remark, "Yes, I saw that picture."

Because he brought out the best in all factions, James was a popular choice as chairman. It may have been this was how I first encountered him: I have a vivid recollection of a gathering of about fifty people, at Everyman or some other church, with James Blake granting the floor to speakers by name, as he recognized them unhesitatingly from their voices.

I must finally note on this subject a small anecdote, but typical of his style, that sticks in my mind. I had once picked up James, along with several other people, to go to an NAACP meeting. While we were still not far from his lodgings, I asked, "I wonder why that driver is blinking his lights at me?"

"Pres, because you're going the wrong way on a one-way street," James replied mildly. And, of course, I was.

All these marvels in themselves tended to pull the liberals out of their lethargy and self-centeredness, to inspire them to a surge of energy and unity. But they were merely James Blake's entrée, because his brain was the sharpest thing in town. He had come from the universities and New York; he had a fresh approach to the civil rights struggle; and it was keener and more vigorous. Some of the big liberals were deceived by his cheerful personality; underneath it, as time went on, they found a foretaste of the strange new militancy of the Sixties. As they discovered him to be harder and more radical than they had bargained for, they became uneasy and began to drop him. But it was too late—James was already off and running. He had rented a law office across the street from City Hall. He practiced little law from it, but a good deal of civil rights politics. He had the Humans with him, and it proved surprising what this small, active group could do in a town where there was a vacuum in ways of dealing with The Question. We had then a Democratic mayor and majority of the City Council, all of whom wanted to keep Negro votes, but who were as "at home" with actual Negroes as they would have been with Martians. There were also by that time Reverend Carroll and Remus Hazelwood, who had finally gotten themselves nominated by their respective parties and elected to the council, and thus could push from the inside. The first action under James's leadership was the establishment of the Mayor's Commission on Human Rights. The Humans mounted a campaign, the mayor "bought" the plan, and the council enacted it. After the council meeting in City Hall that night, there was a boisterous victory celebration of the Humans in James's office. Not that a commission was all that great a thing, but more would follow. Pretty soon, James Blake seemed to be "running the town."

When the mayor got around to appointing the commission, it turned out that neither James nor any other Human was named. The members were big liberals and even conservatives. The Humans accepted this without resentment. They felt they were too radical, and perhaps too pure, to be in the city government. They remained an independent force, free to criticize, agitate, and make proposals. The next shove was to get a salaried director for the commission. Once again, the mayor appointed a right-wing liberal who tried to make everybody happy—discriminators as well as victims of discrimination. It was too late in the day for that. He resigned, and the post went to Bob Robertson. Things began to hum.

Through these and a dozen other campaigns, James Blake was taking care of everybody's interests but James Blake's. How he paid for
the office I couldn't imagine; I concluded he must have a benefactor.
It was my observation, and confirmed by one or two things I heard,
that he wasn't functioning too well as a private lawyer. He could make
light of his practical difficulties, but when I saw him at work, I realized
they were formidable. He had to rely on his secretary for the reading
of mail and documents, and even of the newspapers—of everything
that wasn't printed in Braille. Stemming from this, I suppose, and
from his entire situation, there was a certain development of character
in which it now and then appeared that he had let things go. His true
forte was speaking and working with people, and fortunately he
obtained a part-time position with a law school in a nearby state, to
which he commuted weekly by plane. As I understood it, he lectured
on constitutional law and civil rights. Here he was in his element.

And yet, despite the brilliance of his public leadership and university teaching, it was only after I observed James among his Negro
friends that I felt I really knew him. The big liberals might have understood him better if they also had been privileged to do so. There hung
out at his apartment a group of quiet young men who were listening to
records, drinking beer, thinking long thoughts, and talking the nights
away. Aside from one law student, most of them held humble jobs or
were simply unemployed, waiting for the world to turn. They were
intelligent, hip to every leaf that stirred in America, and also attuned
to those that were stirring in Africa.

They accepted James as their friend without feeling pity for him or
granting him immunity from criticism. They recognized and cher-
ished his talents, but he wasn't the only one of them who was "handicapped." And that was good for his soul.

He had defied so many barriers that he was tempted to defy all barriers. Some of these had to do with the diligent practice of law. Others
had to do with women.

After he had been in town a couple of years, James married Dorothy
Jackson, a bright and cheery activist who came from the Mercer region
and from the state university. She was a teacher in an elementary

school. I don't know what that marriage consisted of, but I would think it entirely possible that to James it inevitably presented another barrier: he was black, blind, and married. At any rate, after two or three years, Dorothy divorced him. Another year or two passed, and there was a surprising development. There was a young woman—I thought she was Negro, but because of her light complexion I was never certain— who was secretary of the Mayor's Commission on Human Rights. We Humans didn't know her very well and even thought she was rather backward. One would have never connected her with James. But it appeared, as the reports became too well-based to be doubted, that he had gotten her pregnant.

And suddenly, James and Dorothy were remarried. In the course of nature, the secretary bore her child and prepared to raise him as a single mother. Later, Dorothy moved out, although she and James continued to be friends, and legal spouses.

There are all kinds of ways for a man to fall. One afternoon, we at *The Clarion* received word of a spectacular and terrible event. It centered around a petite blonde girl who had come from a country town. She spent time in James's office, read to him, and helped him with the mimeographing and such work of the Humans. Her name was Kathy Hancock. There had been some talk about her when her parents, disapproving of her associations in the city, had her confined to the Seven Steeples mental hospital. James, as her attorney, had got her out, but the case was continuing.

On this summer afternoon they had walked from his office to Kathy's car, which was parked alongside the courthouse. There, in broad daylight, before the people on a busy sidewalk, a crazed white man ran across the street, pulled open the driver's side door, and began slashing Kathy with a knife. James, from the adjacent seat, reached over and was able to grapple with the assailant. He sustained one or two cuts himself and his coat sleeve was ripped. Then the man fled.

These were the facts as James came by to tell them to me about two hours later. He said he wanted *The Clarion*, of all the media, to get the true version of the occurrence. He seemed to be exercising great self-control, and my admiration for him had never been deeper: I couldn't keep my own mind from dwelling on the horror the attack must have been, as it came with the girl's screams out of the dark. We didn't speak of that, but I did of that other horror, the bestial race hatred that had seized the man when he saw Kathy and James walking together and, of course, touching shoulders.

"Drove him out of his mind, Pres," James said with a wry shrug. And, he added, "He'd been following us, across the street. Of course he had. You and I forget that we have these specimens among us."

James told me that as a matter of fact, Kathy and he had been conferring at his office on her legal case. It made a powerful headline: "MAN ASSAULTS WHITE WOMAN WITH BLIND ATTORNEY." But I found it did not bring the response I had expected; for some reason, the story was a dud. For a while, I speculated that people might be shying away from it because it was too god-awful. There are such cases. Then, it seemed to me that even James was content to let it die. A week passed and no suspect was apprehended. Were the police even trying? I put the question to James, who was the champion at prodding the police in such matters. For once, he sat silent. I expressed my indignation at the city's indifference to such a barbarous act. He agreed with me but went away and issued no statement. Nor did he bring it before any committee, not even the Humans. After Kathy got out of the hospital, I never again heard him refer to her. Her parents must have dropped her case, for in a short time she moved to Chicago, where I had the impression she went into an institution. Strangely, I have received a Christmas card from her every year since, which is appreciated but surprising, because we didn't know each other that well. Or maybe in the end we did.

The dailies gave the story the barest coverage and no follow-up. I rehashed it a time or two in *The Clarion* with nothing new to say. But in the quiet workings of the "Black Dispatch," some angles were making their way to light if not to print. For instance, there was the time element of the incident. Although Kathy was bleeding profusely, it appeared that James hadn't called a cop for an ambulance, but instead they had gone to the nearby office of Dr. Simpson, a Negro physician.

An hour and a half had passed before James telephoned the police, according to this account.

That, of course, could be understandable, if a little risky, given Negroes' suspicions of the police. Certainly, James had a complicated problem to protect his client, considering all her known troubles. He didn't want her back in Seven Steeples. I deduced that he must have at first hoped he could keep the event quiet, then realized or been persuaded by Dr. Simpson that he could not.

He had concealed this from me. But though it gave me an uncomfortable feeling to think that James was deceiving me, I had to concede that my capacity as newspaperman was something other than my capacity as friend. It couldn't be helped.

Nor did it make much difference to me when a more down-to-earth version was pieced together by Mr. Talbott in very close-lipped talks with Negro detectives and one or two street characters. It was that Kathy knew her attacker. He was her former boyfriend. She had put him down, a young black man or men had been subsequently seen calling at her apartment, and this was what had crazed him.

I reflected that it really didn't matter whether this man or one of these men was James Bridges Blake.

None of this was publishable, even had *The Clarion* been so inclined, but Mr. Talbott and Walt Evers accepted it at once as the true explanation and dismissed the whole affair from their minds. Not only did they have confidence in their informants but it squared with their conceptions of the nitty-gritty facts of life.

I don't know how far this story got around. The tide of public opinion already had been turning against James. What with this on top of that and the other, he found himself no longer running the town but just a citizen like the rest of us, with his strong points and weak ones. He had to give up his office; he now worked out of a dilapidated house he rented on Stilwell. Unfortunately, his teaching position also somehow came to an end at this time. He went back to M— for a while. He returned to town, and after some time he obtained a place as assistant in the legal services office of the War on Poverty.

As James ceased to blaze like a bright star, and the big liberals increasingly cold-shouldered him, he spent his time all the more in the brotherhood of young and dispossessed blacks. What if his career had been badly bent if not shattered? What if he had in some ways made this happen? Hadn't similar disasters, and the worse disaster of not starting at all, befallen them? It is in the society of the broken that one can develop perspectives of more thoroughgoing, more fundamental, solutions. James continued to show up at the meetings and functions of the NAACP, where he was his keen and cheerful self. He also turned out to be the coworker of Vincent Julian, a hitherto silent young man who launched a local chapter of the Congress of Racial Equality (CORE). No one knew just what CORE was, but it seemed to be more militant than the NAACP, more in tune with those black college students we read about who had a sit-in at a drugstore in South Carolina (although they were SNCC). Julian was not a fire breather. He spoke amiably enough, but he always gave an impression of having behind him—or being on the point of recruiting—a following of other young Negro men who, although it was hard to say what they would do, would be more implacable than the familiar old NAACP. The white folks were frightened and did not think it wise to encourage Julian; the colored folks wished him well but didn't intend to get too close to him. His organization lapsed after a couple of years, but not before it had brought this new kind of Negro to the scene. And there was James Blake right beside him, serving as his attorney when the peckerwoods pushed on him, helping write his press releases, and appearing with him on television programs.

The Humans at last came a cropper. The church board, which was controlled by the conservatives, one year made arrangements to hold the annual meeting at, of all places, the Town and Country Club. There was actually a stipulation that Negroes could enter the club that night to attend the meeting. The Humans came up fighting and started a petition to change the meeting place. We talked of picketing the meeting if this were not done.

An angry, cold confrontation was held between the board and the Humans. The board all along had watched the Humans' activities with displeasure, and now it, too, had reached its fighting point. There was a rumor that a prominent board member was tied in with the ownership of Town and Country, but that wasn't necessary. In the church's new location, the club was its neighbor and fellow suburbanite, with all that that carried with it. To begin the conference, Mrs. Delacroix snapped, "The first thing the Human Relations Committee needs to learn is human relations." From there, things ran downhill.

Telephones jangled; a call was made to Reverend Beatty, who just a month before had taken a position at a church in Chicago. At first, he said he agreed with the board, but the next day he called back and said he agreed with the Humans. His successor, an older man who had formerly been a socialist, kept hands off. Moderates advanced compromise proposals, which fell with thuds. It was a fight to the finish.

The board refused to reverse its decision and the Humans appealed, in a gesture of principle, to the congregation. A special meeting was held after services one Sunday. There were two speakers for each side. Catherine Davenport was one of ours and, fighting off tears, made a moving appeal although it was in vain. The congregation voted, by 297 to 142, for the board. The annual meeting was held at the Town and Country. The Humans didn't go, but we didn't picket either.

Catherine and some others resigned from the church. In a couple of months, the board abolished the Human Relations Committee, establishing in its stead a branch of the national Unitarian Fellowship for Social Justice, which elected a different set of officers. James Blake and I used to attend their meetings, because they weren't a bad group of people; only they were not Humans.

36. More Sports Stories and the Prodigal Son

In the world of sports, there were some novel developments. One day, there came into the office a youth who resembled a Greek god. He had a friend with him, and we soon learned why. When the handsome youth tried to talk, he stammered so badly he couldn't get a word out.

This was my first meeting with Loren Hary. He was an ordinary Negro youth from a poor family, and a junior at Northridge High School. He was a poor student, like Tony Madison and the others from the baseball team. But from the depth of his adversity, he had drawn an ambition. He was going to become Mr. America.

I knew little about this kind of human endeavor and did not have a high regard for it. But Loren told me, through his interpreter, that no Negro had ever been Mr. America. That was good enough for *The Clarion*. I wrote a feature story and Walt took his picture, and from then on we promoted his career to the best of our ability.

He had been encouraged by the Northridge track coach, Abe Royerson, one of the few white faculty members there who took an interest in the black students. Loren did most of his training at home, out of magazines and books he sent away for, and with equipment he rigged himself. For hours every day, for years on end, he worked to build those dazzling muscles. For the school, he competed in wrestling and weightlifting, but he explained that his specialty required a different discipline.

There isn't much more to tell. Loren was modest, unassuming, and necessarily somewhat quiet. There was only one thing he insisted on: that he would be the champion. We at *The Clarion*, though fond of him, were inured to people who thought this about themselves or could rationalize endlessly as to why it hadn't come true in their cases. The consensus, behind Loren's back, was that since his success depended on the decision of white judges, the nigger wouldn't make it.

But Loren kept placing higher and higher, first in the regional contests and then in the national, until one year, when he was nineteen, he was runner-up in the junior division. And the next year, he stood on the center platform, the first Negro to be named Mr. Jr. America.

I left *The Clarion* around that time and lost track of his progress. I don't know whether he went on to the very summit of the senior division. At any rate, he had made his point. And it seemed that as Loren rose to the top, his stutter died away.

Then, two colored boys shook the mighty High School Athletic Association to its foundations.

The Porter Brothers of Greeley, in the southern part of the state, were natives of Kentucky. They were sixteen and fifteen years old; their father was a janitor; and, as far as I know, they never said a word. What they were was tall. What they did was play basketball.

William was a sophomore at Greeley when the storm broke, and he was already six-foot-five. Joseph was on the freshman team, and he was six-foot-three.

With William scoring heavily, Greeley won a string of games that year, including the Sectional, in which it upset the favorite and its traditional rival, Mount Vernon.

Considering how many playing years the Porter boys had ahead of them, the prospects were bleak for Mount Vernon. It was a civic disaster. But after the tournament, when commerce was restored between Mount Vernon and Greeley, a certain rumor circulating in Greeley came to the ears of visitors from Mount Vernon. What they heard impelled a group of public-spirited people from Mount Vernon to make a trip to Kentucky in order to gather evidence.

In due course, the story broke on all the front pages in the state that Mount Vernon High School had filed a complaint with the HSAA, charging that Greeley High School had on its basketball team a player who should be declared ineligible for further competition in any and all interscholastic sports: William Porter. And that went for his brother too, one Joseph Porter, even though he was only a freshman and hadn't yet participated in varsity sports.

The allegation was that the entire Porter family, including the parents and several younger children, had been improperly induced to move from their old Kentucky home to Greeley so that William and Joseph might play on the basketball team. The inducement, said to have been proffered by a Greeley industrialist and sportsman, was alleged to have been a janitor job for the father in a Greeley factory, where he was indeed then employed.

Scandal! This was just the sort of thing the HSAA had been set up to prevent. The HSAA Board of Control scheduled a formal hearing. The principals, athletic directors, and coaches of Greeley and Mount Vernon high schools were summoned to it. But not the Porters—they

were not considered parties to the case, which was between the
schools. An HSAA investigator took the Porters' testimony and that of
other material witnesses. There were no lawyers.

Since the hearing was held behind closed doors, I can't report
what transpired. The ruling was as expected. Greeley High School
was suspended from the association for a year. The Porter boys were
barred from interscholastic sports for the rest of their high school
careers.

In all previous cases, that would have been the end of it. But times
were changing. The two colored boys from Kentucky went to court!
They got a lawyer. The NAACP, with Pat Johnson and James Blake as
counsel, entered the case as a friend of the court. Pat came by the office
one day and showed me the brief. It was a strong one, and I thought it
pretty well stripped the emperor of his imaginary clothes. But I couldn't
see it winning, not in our state.

For obvious reasons, the suit could not be heard in the counties of
Greeley or Mount Vernon. It was sent to the eastern part of the state,
and by sheer good fortune to a hill county where a rather poor brand
of ball was played and the residents weren't, so to speak, civilized. The
judge turned out to be a backwoods character—sort of an Abraham
Lincoln type—who took a long look at the arguments. He found that
the HSAA was a privately constituted organization having no legal
jurisdiction over who should or should not play basketball. Further,
he found that the Porter boys were residents of the state and of the
Greeley school district and that to deprive them of sports participation would be to curtail their education discriminatorily and to cause
them loss of possible future earning power. He ordered the HSAA ruling to be set aside.

The decision resulted in a statewide panic. The future of basketball as we had known it—even the tournament—had been thrown into
utter chaos. More than a few newspapers published indignant editorials. Black people and odd whites like me threw our hats in the air. It
seemed that at last life, the real life of poor brown-skinned and even
white-skinned youths, had come into its day of ascendancy over the
rigid dreams of senile men.

This only lasted for a short time. The verdict was appealed to the state supreme court, and that body of three politicians quickly overturned it. Pat told me it had been an unfortunate mistake that the suit had been brought in state rather than federal court, where the new wind of respect for civil rights might have been felt.

And so, the ball was taken out of the hands of the two colored boys, and they played no more in the high school gymnasiums of our state, but an honest and an upright judge had spoken. The HSAA was no longer divinely ordained, only upheld by a higher court. We were in a time in which even when the old order won, it lost something in the process.

The Clarion's newsroom was acquiring the atmosphere of a youth hangout. Bill and I huddled behind our typewriters, hemmed in by what he grumpily called "chillun." Besides Barry and, much of the time, Karen, there were George and Cashy Talbott, now grown into young men and entering, more or less, into their prescribed slots in their father's business. Cashy, like Mr. Talbott before him, had fizzled out in his year at the state university. He was mild and pleasant, like his mother. He liked to stand around and make small talk with Marguerite Woodson, a bright and sweet-tempered girl who had came to us after her graduation from Dunbar. And from Lord knows where, there appeared one day Don Hill.

Don, at twenty-three or -four, seemed to be already what Bill Whitcomb called a "lost ball in high weeds." He had buckteeth, somewhat slanting eyes, and he was light-brown, about the color of Smitty Smith. He was always not only broke but deep in debt, a predicament that *The Clarion* did nothing to relieve. I believe Mr. Talbott thought Don was so poor already that he must know how to live on next to nothing. Don once unwittingly confirmed this, when he was planning to go to a dance, by taking one white shirt to the laundry.

Another reason for not paying Don was that he was so irrepressibly happy learning the newspaper profession. He was perpetually breaking into laughter over nothing, starting arguments on the most absurd grounds, and inquisitive about things other people took for granted. Even during a deadline. "Now, Mr. Preston, excuse me—I

know you're busy, but this just occurred to me—assuming there is a
God, do you think He is a white man or a colored man?"

"Shit!" interjected George. "Pres is a Unitarian, and he don't
believe in no God at all. That's why the niggers shy away from him
when there's a thunderstorm."

"Not young Negroes," said Marguerite crisply. "We don't believe in
all that old crap. We have a cool, modern God, who knows where it's at."

"Shit!" said George again. "Girl, many's the time I've seen you
when Pres is in here, and one of those old lightning bolts comes
crackin' down, and you scoot on out to that front office quicker'n a cat."

"What I think is this," said Don, who had asked the question really
in order to give his opinion. He enjoyed holding the floor, and for that
reason had an irritating habit of slowing down when he was about to
make a point. "What I think . . ."

"Say what you goddamn think, you damned fool!" George would
shout in rage.

"Well, there you are—you got to call me out of my name," Don
protested. "But what I think is . . ." and he broke into a smile, as if it
were all ludicrous, "that God, assuming He exists, isn't white, like Mr.
Preston—begging your pardon, Mr. Preston—and He isn't black like
the Muslims say, but He's, well, sort of my color." And he added hastily,
"Because if you average out all the people in the world, that's the color
you'd get. What do you think, Mr. Preston?"

But at that point, Bill would jump up. "Damn, boy, you talk like a
fellow that plays with himself. Call this a newspaper! I can't work in
this madhouse!" And he would stalk out.

With a shrug, Don would say, "I'm just trying to learn. Now listen. . . ."

"Damned fool" was the role Don was cast in. You could see before
he told you that he had been a child of a broken family. If he had been
white, you might have called him neurotic, but he was just a poor,
brown boy, and so everyone—Mrs. Weyhouse was about the champion
at it—gave him a tongue-lashing. Although I didn't approve of this, at
times exasperation got the better of me, and I, too, joined in. He waited, smiling as if he enjoyed the attention, until you finished, and then

said something artless that turned the tables on you. "Can't tell him anything," said Lehman, "knows everything already." But then, he began to laugh in spite of himself, thinking about Don.

After he had been there three or four months, he told us one day that he had a "bad" case of gonorrhea. No, he hadn't been to a doctor—even if he had money to pay one, he didn't know of any doctor.

"Then you stay out of the goddamn can," shouted George. "On second thought, I'll stay out of it myself."

Mr. Talbott arranged for him to see Dr. Sherman and gave him a lecture. "You've got to take care of yourself, Donnie. You're twenty-four years old, and been in the Army—you know better than that. You can't just let things like this go. It don't make sense, man!"

"Well, Mr. Talbott, maybe if you would pay me a little more I could take care of myself," said Don, but with his Chinese smile that took the bite out of it. And as Mr. Talbott left the room, with the stock answer of "Shit," Don added, "Besides, I was in the Air Force. And I was only in four months."

He had been discharged, he told us, because of his "nervousness."

But when you looked behind the shaggy-tailed puppy dog, there was a sensitive human being, famished for life and creating it out of such scraps as he could find. Like the rest of us, he had a "desk," which was a place at one of the sawhorse tables. Soon he had covered the wall next to it with a collection of photographs—women, musicians, sports figures. It was the first time anyone had done that in *The Clarion* newsroom. He was universally criticized for "cluttering up the place like a teenage girl," but soon it was tacitly realized that Don had made a bright and attractive corner.

Don always treated me with respect—he was interested in my views even if he didn't accept them; he was interested in everything. We had many long talks. He had been a football player at North City Central High School, and among his other duties as *Clarion* jack-of-all-trades, I gave him some sports assignments. His stories were very lively and exciting, if factually erratic. What he dreamed of was a column of his own, filled with names, hot tips, and wild rumors. I didn't know then, of course, that I was training my successor.

What we oldsters went through with Don was mere comedy compared with Mr. Talbott's travails with his sons. I think I have never witnessed another such gargantuan struggle on this earth as he had with George.

Cashy, although the younger, was the first disappointment. He enjoyed looking on at *The Clarion* scene, but had no stomach for it as a way of life. After a couple of years, he and Marguerite were married, and then Cashy went out and got an ordinary assembly-line job at General Motors. He earned twice the pay he would have made at *The Clarion*. I thought it was more that he was able to live quietly and steadily, without harsh battles.

Cashy's defection wasn't fatal, but it left the whole Talbott saga depending on George. If for some reason he didn't eventually take over as editor, the control of the paper would go out of the family. Or, what was the same thing in Mr. Talbott's eyes, it would go to George Lewis, who was not a patrilineal Talbott. This would mean not only Mr. Talbott's final defeat in his long warfare with his sister, but, as he saw it, betrayal of the sacred trust he had received from his father.

And George was impossible; he was a holy terror. He was the first person on *The Clarion* staff who lived as a "thug," which not even Smitty Smith had done. By this time, he had a ménage somewhere with a street woman who had several children, we understood, without the benefit of matrimony. Mr. Talbott blamed it on segregation, the school system, and the Army; the staff blamed it in part on Mr. Talbott, reviving the stories of his youthful wildness and pointing at his current untidiness. Whoever was to blame, never did Cassius M. Talbott have such a time forcing a crooked peg into a round hole as he did with his son George.

He was at first assigned as the crime reporter, this being a field in which he was felt to be certainly knowledgeable. Week after week, he would come strolling in on deadline day at eleven-thirty or at noon, with a smirk on his face, and when his father remonstrated with him, he would retort hotly: "I'm here, goddamn it! We'll get it out! Lay off a me!"

Then, he would sit down, laugh, read the papers, and, as often as not, disappear. He had gone out for a drink. Later, unhurriedly, he would begin making his telephone calls and finally, write his stories. The linotype machines sat idle waiting for him, and Hancock and Pierce exchanged vigorous shakes of the head. "We won't make it, Pres, we'll never make it through George Talbott," Pierce said gloomily. "We got through everything else, but he'll be the end of us."

"You better believe it," echoed Hancock, again shaking his head.

When George's story did at last appear, it was like one by Tansy or Smitty—hopelessly mistyped, with letters transposed, words and whole phrases left out. Hancock, leaning forward and frowning at the illegible copy, would mutter as he set it. Once he threw an entire story on the floor. "Retype this!" he demanded. "I can't set this copy!"

But George was gone for the day. It was up to Bill or me to retype the story. If you had to consult him on some question of fact, you knew where to look for him: in the bars.

Through all this, Mr. Talbott was hovering in the background like a mother hen, afraid of the workers, now and then shouting at George, but afraid most of all that he would walk off the job, so that the shouts lacked edge.

I came to understand that George fully appreciated the situation and knew his father was afraid of him. Whatever he might choose to do or not do, he would someday, if he wished, be editor of *The Clarion*, which for all practical purposes meant that he was head of it already. I thought it was his recalcitrance, his stubborn egotism that was the essence of the power to command and thus might become his chief qualification for the post. You couldn't imagine Cashy doing it. That was just the point.

He gave orders like Louis XIV. "Don, run over to the Milk Maid and get me a chocolate malt, heavy on the malt."

"Why should I get you a malt, get your own motherfucking malt," Don would object, but George would cut him off: "I'm busy. Go on now!"

If we were witnessing the blooming of executive ability, it was long coming to fruition. One day, George didn't show up. A check of his haunts gave no results. After three days, Walt Evers quipped, "Drag the canal." Mr. Talbott was very nervous. "Goddamn, I don't know," he said, and with bitter anger, "I don't give a fuck, either."

George was gone a week, and it turned out he had been in Detroit with some of his drinking friends. "Another Smitty," said Pierce. George came into the newsroom with for once a rather subdued expression, but in two minutes he was his old self, giving orders.

He repeated this episode, taking off for New York, Kansas City, even once, they said, Mexico City. Where did he get the money? Was he actually connected with a burglary ring? But the men said he was writing bad checks and his father was making them good. And in a quarrel with Mr. Talbott one night, Mrs. Lewis shouted that George was helping himself from the cash register, and she added, "I'm going to put a stop to it. You'll see what I do, you and that no-good bum of yours. I'll tear down his playhouse! That fat shit-ass won't be let to ruin this paper that my daddy built, you heed what I'm telling you!"

"That's a goddamned lie, and you ain't going to do shit!" Mr. Talbott said, by way of calming her. And she didn't. But I imagined the family conferences at that time must have been worth hearing.

It was sometime toward the following Christmas, as we were in the newsroom, only Mr. Talbott and I, that for once in our association I saw him weep.

"Pres, he's beyond all control," he said, tears streaming down his rugged face. "He's cost me twelve thousand dollars in the last year, not only here but other places where I have to go behind him and bail him out. The boy is sick! What in the name of God will I do!"

It unnerved me to see Mr. Talbott like this. I muttered something about many people having trouble with their children. I knew it was entirely inadequate. This was the crisis of his life, of his unremitting effort to pry up the huge white stone that blocked the entrance of light and air into the ghetto, so that pestilence thrived there and his people sickened and died. And while he pushed at the stone, the pestilence had engulfed his first-born. It had been all for nothing! And he was helplessly watching it.

Then, Mr. Talbott raised his right hand, and, his face contorting terribly, he said, "I swear to Almighty God that if he does it one more time, I will let him go to prison. And that will be the end of it! May God strike me dead!"

It was a measure of his agony, which something in the universe had to answer. George did it again, not once but several times. Mr. Talbott hadn't the heart to carry out his threat; but he repeated it. The conflict raged on for two more years. Everyone but Mr. Talbott had long ago given up hope. Then, at last, there began to appear a change in George. He wasn't whipped, he couldn't be whipped, but the out-of-town jaunts became fewer and he gradually took on a more responsible attitude toward *The Clarion*. He even at times had a way of talking things over decently with the employees. There was nothing dramatic about it, and you couldn't say when it had happened, but there he was running the newsroom, as a sort of coequal boss with his father and George Lewis. "I want you to call the prosecutor at Mercer and find out about this nigger that shot his wife," he would say crisply to Don, or Barry, or even to Bill or me. "I'm goin' out for a little while, but I'll be back." And after a short time, lo and behold, he would come back. He carried still, and would probably carry forever, the marks of a "thug," but basically, Mr. Talbott's ordeal had ended.

37. A War on Black Children

Did the real estate people actually have a secret master plan to control the expansion of the horde of black locusts that kept pouring up from the Southland? If so, at some point a decision was made that ravaged logic, on the face of it, although it may have been quite reasonable from the standpoint of who owned what real estate. On the near east side, in the neighborhood of Mr. and Mrs. Avakian, there stood on the bank of a meandering creek the resplendent new headquarters of a life insurance company, presided over by a man who was very rich and also very active in running the town. It was nothing one could prove, but some of us thought that the building towered like a castle by a moat, guarding the fading middle-class homes north of it from Negro irruption. At any rate, on the east side, the blacks stopped at the creek. This meant, of course, that somewhere else their remorseless steam pressure had to be allowed to break through. Under all the circum-

stances, the only place left was our west side community of homes surrounding Carlton University. This was a showplace neighborhood of
the city, near our own modest bungalow. Most of the dwellings were
far finer, on much larger lots, than those of the east side. One might
have thought the university would have been their protector; but
Carlton was a backward, business-dominated institution, which exercised no civic clout.

"Well, Pres didn't run far enough," Walt Evers announced with a
laugh in the newsroom one morning. "Nigger done bought in his
block."

One was followed by several. Next door to us lived a man who had
had a coronary about the same time as I. We had become friends as we
fearfully walked the block together and compared symptoms. Now he
told me with profuse apologies that he had sold out to a colored
preacher and was moving to the suburbs. From there, he again moved
shortly to the next world, hopefully for him, to a white part of it.

The first newsworthy reaction to this arrival of our black fellow
citizens was the bombing of a neat and well-painted house the day
after a family, who happened to be cousins of the Talbotts, had
moved there. Walt and I dashed out to survey the scene and take pictures. No one had been hurt, and not a great deal of damage was
done. The people were nervous but inclined to laugh with us about
it: the event confirmed their view of race relations. They had no
thought of backing out.

The woman of the family said they had reason to suspect some
white youths who lived across the street. And indeed, although no one
was arrested, there was no more violence. It was not a neighborhood
to plant bombs, when all was said and done. Quite the contrary, the
Carlton-Meredith Neighborhood Association (CNMA) was soon
formed, which was among the first of its kind in the United States. I
don't remember just how the constitution put it, but its general purpose
was to enable the whites and Negroes to live together in harmony. Susan
and I became active in it. There were all kinds of subcommittees
engaged in "working together for a better community," drawing up
plans, sponsoring projects, and going in deputations to City Hall for

the erection of traffic signals or a more frequent trash collection. What one recalls most clearly, however, were the public meetings, overflowing with polite smiles and good will.

Undergirding the CMNA's expressions of idealism—so that the organization, if not exactly helped by the power structure, at least wasn't hindered from proceeding—were some solid motivations. There was the physical beauty of the neighborhood, as well as the cultural advantages of its proximity to Carlton. The university refused to lift an official finger for the cause, but some of its faculty members took part. And a number of the other householders were retired or soon-to-retire business or professional people, who owned fine, in some cases almost palatial, residences upon which they had lavished care for decades. Their grounds were immaculately tended and adorned with shrubs and flowers in which they took an absorbing and loving interest.

In these people, whiteness had finally reached a stopping point: they were damned if they were going to run because a few colored families had moved in. It was too bad, but in a world changing out of all recognition, you sometimes had to take the bitter with the better. They were determined to keep their homes.

Most of these conservative people remained aloof from CMNA. Occasionally, the organization got roundabout word that one of them had spoken favorably of our doings, because if the Negroes were going to be there, the scene might as well be kept peaceable. Meanwhile, several liberal white families, young people, deliberately moved into the neighborhood out of enthusiasm for integration. It didn't hurt that they often got a house at a bargain, as we had.

The CMNA was such an oasis of fellowship in the desert of hatred that only rarely did one reflect on the logical conclusion of its program. And then, one tended to turn his thoughts away, for this conclusion raised troublesome questions. Keeping the neighborhood integrated in these circumstances soon would mean halting the influx of Negroes, or at least greatly reducing its rate. Whether they realized it or not, the white members were, in effect, saying: "We will live peacefully with you as long as you unite with us to keep any more of you from coming in; the neighborhood must not go black." There wasn't any likelihood of its going white. Nor was the cry for integration being raised in other parts of the city where blacks had not yet shown up.

And it wasn't only the white people. The Negroes in CMNA, by virtue of some nest egg or unusual earning power, had made their perilous way to our neighborhood from more or less slummy ghettoes on which they looked back with horror. Now they saw these ghettoes, with their overcrowding and their unkempt houses and yards, their filth and their noise, approaching to overtake them. However they might feel about The Question, this filled them with fear. I remember a querulous talk made by Jim LeFever, who as an NAACP activist could hardly be called a Tom. He said, "I moved into my house two years ago [it was in the neighborhood of our former home at 4032] and already when you go out in the evening, the trucks are parked bumper to bumper. Now, they all have garages, but they won't use them. I'm ready to call the police. But if I do, the cops won't do anything about it, and the only result will be I'll get a bad name."

One of the things the CMNA people fulminated against was "blockbusting." This was a practice in which "unscrupulous" real estate men, usually blacks, would negotiate the sale of one house in an all-white block to a Negro, and then would "spread panic" among the other white householders so that they too would put their homes up for sale. Maybe it was because I had a good friend who was a hungry Negro real estate man, but I never could see what was so "unscrupulous" about these operations. A black salesman came to my door once and gave me an advertising leaflet; the only way he "spread panic" was by the color of his skin. I guess that was supposed to be enough. It seemed to me the CMNA hadn't thoroughly examined the scruples of the white "realtors," who wouldn't sell the house of a Negro until another house in that block already had been sold to one.

I met one such Negro woman who had access to money, which she used as a revolving fund in the purchase of "first" homes. She would buy a house in her own name and then resell it to another Negro. I wasn't told where the money came from. I thought of some secret benefactor, or perhaps a legacy. I now realize that I was romanticizing her out of my own revolutionary imagination. She undoubtedly was working as a blockbuster for some Negro "realist," maybe my old friend Hatteras Thompson. Come to think of it, she might have even been white. At any rate, she was further underground than any Communist. Most of the civil rights activists did not know of her existence, and the few who did spoke her name in whispers. It was Ruth Reynolds who put her in touch with me. This was before any houses on our block had been sold, and she had an eye on the home of my friend next door. She and I had to meet clandestinely, in a restaurant in a white area, and guard our conversation as if we were plotting a murder. I described the layout of the house to her as well as I knew it, and I also told her something about my neighbor's state of mind. Ruth told me later that the woman had two or three meetings with him, but that he appeared suspicious of her purpose.

A bit of a hassle developed in the association over a project that represented, or purported to represent, Negro advancement.

On a large lot in the south part of CMNA's "territory," there was a moldering old mansion, the remnant of a millionaire's estate, which had descended to the status of a cheap rooming-house. It formed a notorious eyesore in the otherwise lovely community. It had been for sale from time immemorial, but since it was adjacent to the historic Negro district west of Washington Place, who (that was white enough to afford it) would want to buy it?

But, as the black people of the city began to feel their oats, it developed that the Gamma fraternity wanted to buy it, for the purpose of erecting an apartment building. This, however, would require a zoning variance, since apartments were not allowed in our neighborhood of one-family homes. There was also a question of the proposed building being too tall for the available parking and recreational space. The Gammas insisted that this had to be, in order that it might contain enough apartments to be economically feasible since moderate rents were to be charged.

In such a matter as this, the view of a community organization, especially an integrated one like CMNA, was bound to have considerable weight with the municipal zoning board. And CMNA's view of the project tended to be quite dim. Several members, Negro as well as white, said they didn't want an apartment building, least of all an overcrowded one. They didn't want larger throngs of inhabitants and more cars parked in the streets. They preferred to let the old mansion sit there until someone came along and tore it down to build houses.

At first, I was inclined to agree, on practical and aesthetic grounds. At the same time, I was strongly drawn to listen to the Gammas because they were Negroes. We held a meeting in our home of a CMNA subcommittee with the fraternity brothers and the architect, a young Negro who was the son-in-law of Phoebus Greenlea. As they talked about the plan awkwardly and defensively, with great enthusiasm but no expertise, it seemed to me they might be about to erect a shoddy structure that would disfigure the neighborhood. I was overcome by suspicion, wondering whether the Gammas had that much money, or were fronting for some white operators who wanted to get around the zoning regulations. And then I thought some more. Damn it, these were black people, and they were trying to do something. How would they ever vault into the stream of accomplishment if they had to conform to the rules applying to rich white capitalists? Where would that architect find another such commission?

And so I flipped over to their side, but it did them no good. The association took a vote and as a result it was denied and the project was abandoned. At this distance in time and space, I have to admit that I suppose the neighborhood is the better for it. I'm not too sure about the nation.

The truth is, there was no "right" solution to the problem presented by the Gammas' ambition. Nor to anything else the black people wanted to do, unless it was starting a basketball team. It was in the nature of things in our society. Americans wanted to travel first-class, but the Negroes could only come up, in Mr. Talbott's expression, "with a boot and a shoe." I will defend our association's members as the brightest and most generous people in town, but they couldn't solve the Gammas' problem. And in default of solving it, they—the white ones and most of the black ones—settled for the status quo. In rejecting imperfect, halfway measures, they left a hole in the sky that would be there until something came along to fill it, something that would be necessarily quite different from our beloved integration.

Speaking of new neighbors, we acquired one at the next corner west. Soon the Skipper was holding forth at association meetings, speaking out of turn and bullying the chairman. He knew more of the CMNA members than I, it seemed; those he didn't know, he asked me about. Shortly after he moved, he was forced to retire from the YMCA because of age. His reaction to this was terrible to behold. He carried on an unconscionable campaign against his successor, Howard Hurst, a mild man in his thirties who had come from another city to take the post. Leadership of the Congress Avenue Y—or Cataract Creek Y, as it now was called, having been relocated in a splendid new building at another site—was a difficult job at best, demanding the talents of a United Nations diplomat. As a new man, Hurst made mistakes. The Skipper pounced on them, dwelt on them in conversations and telephone calls, and exaggerated them. He could not forgive life for driving him out of his seat of power; in blind revenge he was determined to drive Hurst out of it. Hurst was humble and deferential toward the Skipper, but it availed him nothing. His crime was being in the position.

Susan and I paid a courtesy call on the Skipper and Mrs. LeFever, although Susan could not abide him. He treated her, too, as a "dear comrade" and tried to pump information from her. And he began to take an interest in Michael. One summer Michael was looking for a job, and the Skipper offered to intercede on his behalf with the manager of a supermarket. "I know him well, he's an old friend of mine, I'll just have a word with him," the Skipper said. The manager was a white man, but, of course, to hear the Skipper tell it, his "old friends" in the town, white as well as black, were legion. However, nothing came of this project.

It was only natural for the Skipper to concern himself with youths and their development; but the thought of him questioning Michael, about our affairs and even more Michael's, nearly drove us wild. Under the circumstances, there was nothing we could do, beyond giving Michael an explicit warning against him. And still, after all those years, I couldn't get out of my mind the feeling that he might just be a gossipy old man and I was being paranoid, perhaps with an underlying race prejudice. One afternoon, amid the falling leaves of October, we had a long talk about ordinary matters on the sidewalk between our two homes. Afterwards, I had no sooner got into the house than the telephone rang.

It was the Skipper, and he said breathlessly, without so much as a hello, "Pres, where did you say your brother is working?"

This was not one of the things we had been discussing. The shock of it this time didn't catch me mumbling but nailed down my intention to give him deliberate, fantastically wrong answers. Taking the first city that came into my head, I said firmly, "Boston."

"When did he go to Boston?" he asked. "I thought you said he was in Pittsburgh."

I replied that no, he had been in Boston all the time. I judged that was an outrageous enough lie to let the Skipper know there was nothing further to be got out of me.

But to the end of his days, which was only three or four years in coming, he never stopped asking me questions, and I never stopped giving him false answers. This was somewhat more difficult now that we were near neighbors. When Mike went to college, the Skipper got wind that he was at the state university, where the Skipper had many interests and connections. I invented an entirely different situation that had him at Asbury and a member of dear old DKE.

Standing at the Skipper's grave after his funeral, I felt again the strength of his personality and had the thought that suppose I was wrong about him after all?

Besides the residential problem, the northward swarming of blacks brought about a racial crisis at Northridge High School, through which Michael was then making his way. And to deal with this from a liberal adult point of view, another organization was formed. It was called the Northridge Parents Human Relations Council.

This group had a considerable amount of overlapping membership with the Carlton-Meredith Association and also with the

Unitarians, so that some of us were seeing almost more of each other at meetings than we were of our own families. Since it embraced the entire high school district, the council was a larger organization than the CMNA. It also had more of what I called "big liberals," and even a vociferous conservative woman, a doctor's wife, whom some of us suspected of being a member of the John Birch Society. Her opinions, expressed in a rasping voice, were infuriating to several of us, but we had to admit that she showed a sincere concern for the Negro students according to her lights. She was a backer of the wrestling team, and when I heard her talking of her activities one night, I was obliged to swallow the bitter pill that she spent more time actually aiding the students than I did.

The promotion of "human relations" at Northridge was even more complicated than in the neighborhood. Northridge historically had been the city's foremost "academic" school, sending its graduates overwhelmingly to college, even to the Ivy League schools and to Europe. Nationally prominent historians, writers, and scientists were alumni of Northridge, as well as droves of lawyers, other professionals, and businessmen. In short, everybody who was anybody, including, not the least, Susan.

Moreover, Northridge still served, besides the region the Negroes were inundating, areas farther north and northeast in which really wealthy white people held solid. The governor's mansion was in that district. There was a large community of prosperous Jews. All these people, unless they sent their children to private prep schools, of which the city had only one, were obliged to send them to Northridge. They wanted to send them to Northridge, but they wanted to be damned well sure it was to a Northridge whose "academic standards" had not been "lowered." I place these words in quotation marks, not because they didn't have a real meaning, but because one heard them so often that they became shibboleths.

How were Northridge's standards to remain high, and how was Northridge to continue to be a pre-Ivy League school, when its student population was coming to be thirty or forty percent Negroes, whose minds had been irremediably ruined before they got there?

How were you going to conduct a "public prep school" with a student body half consisting of Tony Madisons (and also white Tony Madisons, since a lower class of white people was moving in on the fringes of the black advance)? A very live nerve is touched when you tinker with people's dreams for their children, and although it might stamp me as a Charlie, I knew that I wanted for Michael the "high standard" of education for which Northridge was renowned. I still had visions of sending him to Harvard.

Without getting into the inferno of controversy that soon was raging around this question of "standards," it seemed there was little that could be done. This was a direction in which the Human Relations Council plunged with all its energy. But it didn't seem this would be enough; and it was hard to get it going. The faculty members of the school, especially the older ones, were up in arms against the Negroes and what they "were doing to Northridge" even more than the white parents. Many of these teachers, who had spent years or decades in the aura of a superior school, took the coming of the Negroes as a personal affront. They were utterly bewildered and their life plans shattered. Yet they had tenure: you couldn't get rid of them if you wanted to (I thought it better to attempt to convert them). If you transferred them to other schools and brought in more open-minded beginners, you would thereby lose the patina of scholarship that distinguished Northridge, which resided or was thought to reside in their persons.

Teachers in such a state of mind weren't likely to do anything to help black boys and girls enter the world of higher knowledge. Included in their number, incidentally, was the principal, a longtime teacher of Latin, who was flabbergasted at the turn of affairs. While the council members and black parents were more or less aware of this hostility shown to the Negro students, none of us had any idea of its virulence until John Barry and I made *The Clarion*'s yearbook survey. Mr. Talbott instructed John to buy the yearbooks of the integrated high schools in order that he might identify from their pictures the Negroes who were about to graduate. Then, I conceived the project of surveying "school-life integration" by going through each book and counting all the white and black photos, first with respect to the sheer numbers and then with regard to class officers, club members, and participants in social affairs.

Northridge was the school we were most interested in. What we discovered was shocking, even to us. "A war on children!" John muttered.

I still have the faded sheets of copy paper bearing our tabulations. In a student body of 2,148, there were 623 Negroes, or 29 percent. But of all the boys and girls pictured in extracurricular activities, only 12 percent were black. And this included the athletic teams, which were predominantly Negro.

The Student Council consisted of 112 white youngsters and one Negro girl.

The following organizations were totally white: the Junior Counselors; the True Blue Club; the Key Club, which was the top boys' organization; the History Club, the Junior Policy committee and Senior Council; the Drum Majorettes; Marching Northridgettes; Cheerleaders; Reserve Cheerleaders; and Frosh Cheerleaders.

On the other hand, we found that in two organizations, the Red Cross and Y-Teens, Negroes made up heavy majorities. A black girl at Northridge explained this to Barry: "Those are clubs that Negroes can't be kept out of because of their policy. But when us kids join them, the whites mostly quit."

John and I agreed, however, that the most damning discrepancy in the yearbook was in spot photographs showing informal and incidental scenes at the school. The editors and photographers of the book were white students, and the advisor was a white teacher. For these pictures, they were not limited as to subject matter: they chose the scenes that to them best illustrated the school's life and spirit. And in this category we counted the pictures of 261 whites and only 11 Negroes, including several in crowd shots.

There were a great many more figures, all pointing to the same conclusion. The black minority was being permitted to attend the school, to play on the athletic teams, and drill with the Reserve Officers Training Corps. Beyond that, the black youth were invisible; they were not "there." Worse, they were there and being daily and hourly rejected and denied.

It was this exclusion from school activities that had led to the "cafeteria strike" John and I had walked in on. For example, the Junior Vaudeville was an annual entertainment made up of singing and dancing skits prepared by groups of students. Yet, for three years in a row, black students had entered skits in the competition, and each year they had been rejected by the teacher-student committee of judges. This was, in part, the working out of "high standards," that is to say, a cultural verdict. Some committee members were heard to remark that the black skits were "vulgar" and "too explicitly sexy." However true that might have been, they were, naturally, influenced by the Negro idiom.

Meanwhile, as our statistics showed, not a single black girl had been selected as a cheerleader. There came a night when the Junior Vaudeville was being staged, and at the same time the Northridge basketball team was playing Elliston. The team consisted of four Negroes and, as the saying went, a token white boy to count the baskets. The cheerleaders absented themselves from the game because they all were taking part in the Junior Vaudeville. They were the kind of popular white girls who were in everything. The team was left without a cheering section. Some black girls who were not involved in any organized squad moved from their seats in the stands to perform a few impromptu, ragged cheers.

This was on a Friday night. The following Monday, nearly all the Negro students in the school (with the exception of the athletes, who were forbidden by the coaches to take part) went into the cafeteria at lunch period, but either refused to eat or ate lunches they had brought from home. Some displayed signs asking, "Is This Little Rock?"

In response to this action and protests by a large group of black parents, as well as the Parents Human Relations Council, a black skit was accepted into the Junior Vaudeville the following year and one Negro cheerleader was appointed.

Then, the whole issue came to a head again and set the school boiling, in regard to the Senior Prom.

Each year, there reigned at this dance, which was Northridge's leading social event, a couple designated as Marigold and Bluebeard.

After the candidates had been nominated by the prom committee, which had a faculty advisor, they were elected by a vote of the senior class. It usually came out that Marigold was a popular girl from a good family and Bluebeard was a prominent athlete. The year that Tom Maxwell was a senior, he was Mr. Everything in sports: basketball, football, and track. He was also considered to be of exemplary personality, and we at *The Clarion* certainly thought he would be elected. But he wasn't even nominated.

The Negro students seethed with indignation, and somebody got word to *The Clarion*. A rumor was going around that there had been some jive with the committee. John Barry and I made another trip to Mr. Harlan's office. He appreciated the seriousness of the charge and summoned the prom committee advisor before us. This wretched woman admitted having "suggested" to the committee that a Negro boy should not be nominated, "since they didn't have in mind any Negro girl." To her, it was unthinkable that Tom should lead the promenade with a blonde young thing on his arm.

I don't recall that any redress was made in this case. Perhaps the woman was removed from her post for future dances.

With such teachers setting the tone, it seemed to me little wonder that the Northridge students didn't integrate themselves. Michael reported that the seating in the cafeteria, for instance, was strictly segregated, not by rule but by voluntary action of the students: white tables, black tables, and a Jewish table (where he found refuge).

From all this, it will be seen that the Parents Human Relations Council, as well as the Student Human Relations Council, had their work cut out for them. However, in the parents' organizations there appeared at once a distinct split. Some of us had in mind what we thought was a straightforward goal: integration of the Negro and white youths that lived in the district in all activities of the school. It didn't occur to us that there could be any other way of looking at it.

It was with something like astonishment that we learned that there was another group, and, indeed, perhaps the predominant one, because it was made up of big liberals and civic leaders. These luminaries had another goal, namely, the maintenance of "high standards." It would be evil of me to say that this group was not for integration, because it was. Mrs. Lloyd and Mrs. Fielding spent more time promoting interracial student activities than I did. But, they were for integration in the current proportions and looked with alarm on any additional influx of Negroes. Their reasoning was as follows: We have now a school that, if truly integrated, offers cultural advantages to those Negro children who can avail themselves of them. But, if more Negroes come in, the white people will move out and we shall have another ghetto school, and the Negro children will once again be stripped of their chance for quality education. They assumed it as a first law of nature that Northridge would no longer maintain its reputation as a "high standard" school if it were to become all or largely Negro.

Our side realized that they probably were right about this. Still, the Negroes were coming, and the white folks were fleeing. It seemed to us that the others were striving for a fantasy, and this could be dangerous. We tried to persuade them to come to terms with the reality of the changes that were occurring, and to defend their "standards" some other way. Sadly, we argued in vain.

I differed also with the other group on their stand of "reducing tensions" within the school. My position wasn't popular; everyone's first impulse in the presence of tension is to want to reduce it. But, as an old revolutionary and a *Clarion* man, I knew that the proper course was usually to increase tensions, as a motivating force to solve the problems that caused them. If it worked out, you got rid of the tensions once and for all, instead of burying them where they would continue to operate. That was, I believed, the only chance for an underdog.

Such a doctrine was anathema to the right-wing members, if I may call them that. That was why they didn't like *The Clarion* in the first place; and they thought I was an especially venomous representative of it. It was just too bad I was a parent and couldn't be kept out of the meetings.

I remember giving a short answer after Mrs. Fielding expressed her view that the Student Human Relations Council should be established "not now—there should be a thorough study and preparation first—but next year." I had only to support something for her to oppose it, and I'm afraid it was mutual. There were three women, all big liberals, who were thorns in my side. Besides Mrs. Fielding, the other two were white—a Unitarian who had sided with the board and a long-winded member of the Mayor's Human Rights Commission. One night as I drove home from a meeting, there sprang irresistibly into my mind a limerick:

> Fielding, Ralston and Brooke
> Are three reasons why all up I'm shook.
> Now Rosemary counsels avoidance of haste,
> And Helen observes it's a question of taste,
> And Nellie—oh, Nellie —what words you do waste!
> Which is why I'm not high in the book
> Of Fielding, Ralston,
> Of Fielding, Ralston,
> Of Fielding, Ralston and Brooke.

Despite these Queen Canutes of the civil rights movement, as I considered them, the black children continued to be born, and the black families continued to come up from Alabama. They continued to move into the Northridge district and to show up the day after Labor Day for enrollment in high school. The white folks continued to move away. Michael went, not to Harvard, but to the state university; and Tony went into the Army. I heard he was sent to Vietnam, where neither the loss of his fast-ball nor his inattention in class greatly mattered. A few years later, after we left town, a project that had been moving along underground among the conservatives was realized when Northridge's neighborhood lines were wiped out and it was designated an "academic" school for the entire city. However, in a couple of years more, a federal court overruled that. The next and weirdest proposal, as it appeared to me, was made when the School Board voted to eliminate both Dunbar and Northridge as high schools, turning them into junior highs. This was in an effort to meet federal desegregation standards for the city. There were two Negro members of the board, and they both voted for the measure. One of them was The Skipper.

Everybody in town went to court to stop that, including a white organization on one side and the NAACP on the other.

When I visited *The Clarion* not long ago, Mr. Talbott said the plan still envisaged the building of a new Dunbar in a different location, where it would be integrated, but the proposed change for Northridge had been abandoned. He said the school had become more than eighty percent black.

38. Romances in Black and White

I did at one time find myself fancying a young white woman or two. In the interracial movement, few young black women showed up, and those who did were inclined to be rather conventional. Either they were looking for social life with their peers, or they were tremendously idealistic in a way that their parents might approve.

Young white women, however, were overturning the world, as their prototypes had been ever since Penny and the John Reed Club, and if they could find anything of which their parents disapproved, they did it. They were conflictual and dramatic, and like anyone who is living this way, they were interesting. We men leaped to the conclusion that in their unconventionality, they were accessible. At any kind of gathering, they drew men like flies.

One of these women whose path and mine crossed briefly was Trudy Boche, who lived on the campus of the state college at Harlington. I met her at a conference of some kind at the Lucy Terry YMCA, and we continued our conversation at the after-party in a private home. She was twenty-five, a tall lanky girl, not unusually pretty but pert and lively. And there was something else about her, a quality one sometimes finds in effective organizers: she seemed to show a genuine affection toward every person, Negro or white—this emotion of hers was an almost tangible thing.

I remember at one point a young Negro, sitting on the floor beside her, accidentally brushed her knee with his cigarette. "Hey," she said, "that's my knee."

I looked at her, thinking she meant his hand was on her knee and he should remove it, but she caught my look and added, "Nothing special about a knee, but I don't happen to want mine burned."

As the evening wore on, Trudy and I had a great long talk, finding ourselves more and more to be "soul mates." Such things will happen, even between girls in their twenties and men approaching fifty. She told me that she was working for the Wesley Foundation on the Harlington campus, a sort of missionary to the youth and especially the black youth. I was surprised to find her religious, but then she explained that her father was a college professor and her mother a psychiatrist, and she had rebelled into Methodism and integration.

As eleven o'clock drew near, Trudy said she had to leave to catch the bus for Harlington. I couldn't abide that. "Oh, stick around," I said. "I'll take you home."

"But it's seventy miles!"

And so it happened, sometime after midnight, that the two of us rode through the moonlight all the way to Harlington, chatting away about the NAACP, the Freedom Riders, and our experiences with black people. At one lonely place, I stopped the car and tried to kiss her, but Trudy politely declined and we went on. I left her at her rooming house and headed back for home, which was now seventy miles away.

Trudy was pure at heart, but I don't want to leave the impression that all "integrated" white women were like that. I don't think those words would spring to your mind, for example, in describing Margie Allison.

Not that Margie was sexually promiscuous, but she was an entirely different sort of woman from Trudy, or from Penny or Winifred, for instance. It was my observation that, with respect to people crossing the color line, many roads led to Rome. There were people who acted out of the most highly elaborated religious or political principles. And there were others who, you might say, didn't know any better. I thought that Mr. and Mrs. Duke of the state NAACP, and Clarence and Margie Allison, were examples of this.

I had known Clarence as a Dunbar basketball player a couple of years before the Big Team, and all I knew about him was just that he was tall, dark-skinned, a good player, and rather quiet. Margie came from one of those rural counties in which Negroes were rare. I think her father was a banker, or he might have been a well-to-do farmer. They were of German descent.

Margie was not political, not religious, and not an intellectual. She was a fox: tall, pretty with her black hair and blue eyes, and above all, smartly dressed. Her passions were jazz, buying things, and Earl, who was her baby boy. I supposed that when she attended the state university she was the kind who went to all the dances and never cracked a book. In our city, she may still have frequented dances, or jazz concerts, and I guessed that's where she picked up with Clarence.

She was a merry woman. She had a way of talking frivolously about her own affairs, no matter how bad they got, and they got pretty bad. When I met her, she and Clarence were already divorced, and she was living with Earl in a new little one-bedroom house not far from our home. She was teaching in an elementary school, taking Earl each day to a babysitter. I gathered that Clarence had been unable to find a job and had gone to seed, drinking and carousing. He sometimes came to her house at night, drunk and argumentative, she said. I was alarmed on her behalf, and she made it clear that she was frightened too. But then she laughed, "I can handle Clarence. I can handle everybody but myself, ain't that the truth?"

She could handle me with her little finger. She knew that I didn't stop by her house so often just out of pity for her situation, and there were times when our eyes talked, but she would say, "Well, run along, Pres. Been nice seeing you." And after I introduced her to Susan, they were friendly in what I thought was a demonstrative manner, putting me in my place without a word.

Margie was one of those people with whom America had been filling since the war, people who lived ahead of their incomes. One day when Susan and I were calling on her, she showed us a vacuum cleaner she had bought. "I don't really need it for this little house," she giggled, "but just yesterday I finished the payments on the washing machine. I don't feel right if I'm not making payments on something." The thing that really got her into financial hot water was the car, a big and sporty one. Although it was in her name, she foolishly let Clarence use it, and he demolished it. It was about half paid for, and Margie had to continue making the payments, although the car was useless junk. But with her cheerful devotion to style, she soon bought another one, brand-new and even bigger. "Afford it? Well, I can afford the payments," she said.

But there was one thing she couldn't buy, either for credit or cash. Margie never mentioned it, but from something she said about the neighborhood and the school Earl got into in a few years, I realized she was constantly thinking of the problems he would face because of his color. And from the way she looked at him now and then, you could see she hoped he would grow up white, or so light as not to be noticed. It was pitiful, because it seemed to me there wasn't a chance. Earl was a jolly four-year-old boy, in color he was somewhere between yellow and light brown, with nappy hair. Such children, I had been told at *The Clarion*, tended to become darker as they grew older.

Not that Margie would have cared if he had been green. Margie Allison didn't give a damn about race; she wasn't either for or against integration. I could get her to only one or two meetings, and she didn't even keep up with the news on the subject. She wasn't interested. On the other hand, she never displayed the slightest regret that she had married a Negro, and she continued to take her friends, black or white, as they came. Her family, at first, had excommunicated her and refused even to let her bring Earl for a visit. In time they relented, and she told me they had become very fond of him. One summer, she moved down there, and then got a teaching job in a large city nearby.

We haven't heard from her since. On a recent visit back to the old town, as I was coming out of *The Clarion* office, I met Clarence. He looked to me as he always had. We smiled and exchanged a handshake. I couldn't tell from his expression whether it was from the basketball days, or whether he was aware of the extent of my association with Margie, and that I knew he was a man who had lost a wife and a son.

But, as I have said, interracial marriages by no means always ended tragically. It was my observation that they were like other marriages, except that they were under a spotlight; I once joked that the trouble was not that they were interracial, but intersexual. Black women almost universally disapproved of them, because they were generally contracted between Negro men and white women. There was at least one in our city that was the other way around. A young white man of our neighborhood, who was a public relations promoter, shed his white spouse and married a black social worker. This alliance seemed to be eminently successful. He crossed over in lifestyle, and most of his promotions from then on were in the Negro community.

Another attempt at mixed marriage turned out to be a tragicomedy, or at least it was so regarded. This also involved a promoter, but a black one, named Colorado Thompson. I never got it straight what relation he was to Hatteras, if any, but he was in the same line of business, only lower down. Among other enterprises, he owned a small print shop, which made him a competitor of *The Clarion*, and for that reason he stayed away from our office and I never had the pleasure of meeting him. He promoted various entertainments, and I heard also that it was he who printed the numbers tickets.

The story about Colorado, as told by St. John Ashley and others, had to do with his mail-order German bride. In a magazine, he saw a photograph of a svelte blonde fräulein who was advertising for a husband to bring her to the land of the free. He entered into correspondence with her, confirmed that she had no color prejudice, and soon all was arranged.

Colorado drove to New York accompanied by his lawyer, and met the boat. Then, he saw coming down the gangplank a woman whose features were vaguely recognizable—but who weighed, he quickly estimated, three hundred pounds!

He turned to flee, but the lawyer wouldn't let him.

They were married by a magistrate, and Colorado drove home with his new wife. I don't know the circumstances of their living together, but it wasn't long until she divorced him, getting a handsome chunk of his property. Mrs. Frieda Thompson was in the real estate business for years, being another of those white persons who were identified with the Negro community. As for Colorado, I guess every black woman in town thought he got what he deserved.

39. Odds and Ends

When my mother's teaching days were over, she lived for five years in a small apartment in Winette, going each winter to a retirement resort in Florida that was maintained by her college sorority. She missed the students who had filled her life after Harry and I grew up and left home.

As a teacher, Mother had always been unusually friendly toward the Negroes in her classes. She told us how she had once changed a boy's grade from F to D so he would be eligible for the track team. "He couldn't tell parts of speech," she said, "but I couldn't run the hundred-yard dash."

Mother also told us that she had once been at her desk after school, alone in the room except for a black student who had been summoned to make up some work, but instead was pacing the floor behind her. Suddenly he said, "Mrs. Preston, I'm going to kill you."

"Oh, I don't think you are," Mother replied.

"Yes I am," said the disturbed youth, "with this knife."

Mother said she didn't look up from the papers she was marking, but merely replied, "I don't think you are, William, because there wouldn't be any sense in it."

The boy quietly put the knife away and departed. And my mother didn't report the incident to the principal. She had a keen sense of personal relationships, which I thought had been sharpened by her childhood readings of Dickens and Thackeray.

After retirement, she found a way to continue this identification by sending a small sum each month to a very poor black girl whom she somehow met in Florida and who was struggling through college. Mother, who had been short of funds all her life, looked on this not only as a benefaction but as a bond of fellowship. It must have been she who had taught me noblesse oblige, but her own variety had a great deal of humanity in it.

The time came—she was seventy-seven—when she could no longer manage for herself. She lived with us for six months, but she was subject to falling (I told her what she needed was a football uniform). She would have to enter a nursing home. First, Susan and I arranged that she went into one a cut above the average, with hardwood floors and Japanese screens. She was able to do so because of her teacher's pension and a matching check each month from her sister Iva. But she was treated coldly there, and we moved her to the Brotherhood Believers home, where, if there were not glistening floors, there was human love. During her first years at the home, Mother used to go around and help care for the bedridden patients. Then, she too was bedridden. She objected only to the choir that came and sang hymns at her on Sunday afternoons. When I reported this to Pastor Robertson, he said with a frown, "My goodness yes—those people!" But under the circumstances, he told her he could only sympathize.

With Mother living at the home, I came into closer association with Bobby and Genevieve. Although I didn't know it, they were already thinking of their exodus in search of a haven from racism that was to take them to Hawaii, Brazil, and finally the new stronghold of the Brotherhood Believers in northern California. One day, Bobby came to *The Clarion* and disclosed to me that they were planning a visit to Cuba. He said he hoped to have an interview with Fidel Castro and asked whether I might be of assistance toward that end. It wasn't quite so outlandish as it sounded, because Cuba was then represented in the United States by a black public relations firm—Joe Louis Associates—headquartered in Harlem. I wrote them a letter on *Clarion* stationery, in which I tried to make clear what manner of man Bobby Robertson was. However, nothing came of it.

The Robertsons went anyway, and after their return, I was able to provide Bobby a forum of sorts for his report (which may or may not have been a favor, in those hectic days, from a practical point of view). I then was a member of a luncheon group called the Labor and Religion Circle. It was about as small and ineffectual an organization as ever I took part in. Some of our city's labor leaders had started it with the idea of corralling a few ministers to make pro-union statements during strikes. Meanwhile, they had to talk about other things, and organized labor had become so conservative, since my days at the General Motors sit-in, that the labor men were continually being put off their ease by the radical language of the few idealistic preachers who attended. There was one exception, a onetime Communist who I thought had working-class instincts, but then he went off on the Krebiozen cancer-cure crusade before my very eyes.

I don't know what I was doing there but going to meetings—I used to say I was a member because I was neither a laborer nor religious. I had gotten into it originally when the organizers invited Mr. Talbott, no doubt because it would be a good idea to have the black newspaper on your side during strikes, and for the price of a cheap lunch at that. Of course, he had sent me in his stead. Usually, I sat near the foot of the table, and kept my mouth shut except to eat. But before one meeting, I received a postcard informing me that the Reverend Carroll Tyding, a black minister who had just returned from a visit to Cuba, was scheduled to speak. I don't know how this had been arranged. The subject was the last one in the world the labor leaders wanted to hear about, unless the talk turned out to be a denunciation, which seemed doubtful, as Castro was reported to have abolished the color line.

It was true that Reverend Tyding often appeared at predominantly white gatherings because he was one of a handful of blacks who had been designated by the power structure as "Negro spokesmen." It was a peculiar case; his middle-class manner allowed him to be seen as a white liberal wearing greasepaint. However, the sentiments he expressed weren't Tommish. He did speak in a soft voice, and perhaps this was soothing to white nerves regardless of what he was saying. In the present instance, it was also reassuring that he had gone to Cuba with an official group of Presbyterians.

I took Bobby along to the luncheon and pointed out to the chairman that he, too, was a minister who had visited Cuba. Thus trapped, the chairman made way for him and the talk became a symposium. To the consternation of the labor leaders, both of the speakers gave glowing accounts of Castroism. I remember that Reverend Tyding said he had found one Cuban clergyman who was living in fear. "He wouldn't talk until he had taken me into the middle of a field where we couldn't possibly be overheard. There he told me that since the coming to power of Castro, he had lived in a state of mortal terror. But not of the government, he said—the government protected him. Because he had always stood for the old regime of landlords and exploitation, he was afraid of the people."

Bobby and Genevieve had taken a particular interest in the social services established by Castro, the childcare centers, schools, and hospitals. Bobby also remarked on the closing of the once notorious brothels of Havana and the program to rehabilitate the prostitutes. He and Genevieve had "adopted" a former prostitute and sent her money so she could return to her native village and establish herself in another way of earning her livelihood.

I couldn't say then, but I think I can now, what it was I disliked about the Freedom Rider. He came into the newsroom, a white, plain-dirt farm boy, and told his story. He didn't know about John Brown; he didn't know about the self-determination of the black belt; I doubt that he even knew about Dr. DuBois or Paul Robeson.

He was just a dried-up little kid from thirty miles west. That was solid Klan country, and how he came out of there to go on a Freedom Ride—and his wife too—was a mystery. He wasn't articulate about it. I had a feeling he was religiously motivated through some kind of sect.

"Well, you know how the mob stopped us and turned over the buses and burned them," he said. "The papers called it a mob, but there was state troopers right in it, watchin' and even helpin' 'em out. They loaded us all up and took us to Jackson and had what they said was a hearing. I haven't seen Myra since then, but they let her write a letter to me once a month, an' I can write to her. I know how she's getting' along."

"They took me to Parchman (State Penitentiary). I was in Parchman eighty-three days. I lost thirty-seven pounds, from a hundred and sixty to how you see me now. Parchman is hell on earth. It's awful hot there, and there ain't no shade. The food wasn't nothing. A couple of weeks I was on hard labor, breakin' rocks and things like that, but most of the time there just wasn't nothin' to do. I got to know some Negro fellows, though."

Then he told me about the three black men who had described their experiences with white women. It didn't seem to occur to him that most integrationists discounted such stories and assigned the cases as frame-ups.

His penitentiary stay had been ended through legal action to force the acceptance of bail. His trial was still to come, and after a long delay the date had been set.

"Yes, I think I got to go back for it. I might not, even though it's the right thing to do." He flicked me an unsmiling look and continued, "but there's the chance they would take it out on Myra. She doesn't say so in her letters, but I can tell she's gettin' sick. They've had her in there a hundred an' seventeen days."

There was more along the same lines. I wrote the Freedom Rider's story, and George gave it a page one display. He never came back, and I was unable to learn how his case and his wife's turned out. The other *Clarion* people didn't have much to say about him, as if he made them uncomfortable too.

The NAACP by this time had gone blah. Faithful, but blah. First, a young man active in the lodges was president, and then Mrs. Worth, and then Mrs. Victoria Cox, a loyal, hardworking woman who was afraid to sneeze without authorization from the national office. The organization no longer packed a punch. James Blake was on his uppers, and his CORE friend had left town. The Humans were wandering around like lost souls. Dunbar was losing the opening game in the Sectional. A Negro attorney, Mrs. Coretta Langley, and her two teenage sons were denied membership in the First Friends Church after having been members in Birmingham, Alabama. It seemed that in our local meeting, unanimity could not be reached. Bobby Robertson was under fire in the Mayor's Commission for being too radical, and the mayor wasn't defending him.

Into all this, as I look back, the Freedom Rider had injected a crude note, as if sounding the end of a played-out game and the advent of one with different rules.

And yet, the old game continued alongside the new one. A certain number of the players couldn't stop until they died, and even then they might get involved in a segregated cemetery fight. I was one of these, as Ruth Reynolds had long ago observed. In my youth I had been a participant in an organized Communist movement, then had gone through a stage of political guerrilla warfare that had finally become an individual's second nature. It was for this reason that, short of abolishing racism or Negroes, there was no way to prevent people like James Blake and me from "agitating." We would start out the morning innocent as babes and before noon, life would present us with some situation, perhaps commonplace or trivial to others, in which we would at once see a handle to The Question. And we would reach for it without thinking.

Some of these incidents, I suppose, contained an element of the ludicrous, but that didn't matter. There was, for example, a day when I had come home to lunch. Michael, who was beginning to drive, had borrowed the car. He was gone about half an hour when he telephoned. He had been in a collision.

He said no one was injured, but the other car was badly damaged. By the time I called a taxi and got to the scene, the car had been towed away. The windshield of our Studebaker (a successor to the first one), which fortunately was of shatterproof glass, was smashed out in such a way that Mike must have hit it with his head, although he didn't remember doing so.

He said the other car was driven by a woman, with her teenage son as a passenger. Mike had plowed into it from behind. The way it had happened was that he was crossing a bridge that was so humpbacked he couldn't see what was on the other side of it. And what was there was the woman's car, stopped on the highway as she waited to turn left into—the Town and Country Club!

Michael should have taken precautions crossing the bridge blind, and he had admitted at the scene that he was to blame. But the circumstance that the woman was intending to patronize the citadel of racism caused a light bulb to flash in my mind. In preparing a news story, I had recently learned that it was illegal in our town to turn left in the middle of a block. If the woman was, herself, thus breaking the law, it was she rather than Michael who was at fault. Mike said it was common practice for drivers to turn there as she had been preparing to do, but I replied so much the worse for them. Maybe we could get a court ruling that would inconvenience everyone going to the club from that direction, by obliging them all to take a longer route in order to approach the club from the right-hand side of the road.

I put in a call to James Blake but he didn't answer. I anticipated he would be gleeful at getting a stick with which to beat the Town and Country. Meanwhile, the woman telephoned me, and there began a comedy—not so comic to her—that continued for several days.

"Mr. Preston, I want to see about getting my car repaired," she said.

"Yes, I know," I answered. "I am so sorry. But I have to talk to my lawyer."

"But your son admitted it was his fault. He smashed right into us while we were standing still. He said so at the time."

"Yes, he told me he did, and I'll take action just as fast as I can. But there's something about it you aren't aware of."

The next evening, after I had talked with James and he was checking it out, she called again. She was frantic. "Mr. Preston, I don't know what you're doing, but I wish you could see my car. It's just a pile of junk, sitting out here in the garage. My husband is a traveling salesman, and he's out of town, and I can't do a thing. I can't do my marketing. I can't take the children to school."

Thinking "and you can't go to the Town and Country Club," I answered, "I'm really very sorry about it, but there's nothing I can say at the moment. My lawyer is working on it."

Then, she said something I hadn't expected. "Mr. Preston, I wonder if you could come out here and look at my car. Then you would know what I am going through."

I declined her invitation.

The next day, James called and said the statute banning left-hand turns had an exception by which it did not apply to that area, which was considered to be rural. We commiserated with each other on the collapse of our case. I telephoned the woman and at last was free to tell her what had been on my mind. And while I was at it, I told her why she ought to be ashamed of herself for belonging to that club.

It was about this time that Lucille Fields left us. That, of course, is a white folks' way of putting it. She had come when Michael was little more than an infant, had served as his part-time mother until he was almost a man, had kept our house, cleaned it and washed the dishes and scrubbed the floors (Susan had always prepared the breakfasts and dinners), and now she departed for a life of her own. She had several years earlier moved out of her squalid slum into the neighborhood of Cinq's home, where if her house was rotting at the edges, it was at least doing so on a large lawn shaded by trees. She was able to do this because her younger daughter Patricia had grown into a well-trained social worker and had landed a good job in Washington. Patricia was the one who was devoutly Catholic, almost like a nun, and who scrimped and saved to get her degree. I wish I could say that we had something to do with it, but I'm afraid we didn't, except maybe in the negative sense of giving her something to get away from.

Through that long period when Lucille was a surrogate mother to Michael, she had four children of her own: two daughters and two sons. For them, the surrogate was Lucille's mother-in-law, who lived with them. They turned out well, on the whole. The sons, Harold and Bruce, held jobs and headed families. I remember Lucille telling me they wouldn't let her iron their shirts, because, they said, she didn't do it properly. They did it themselves. In short, they were cheerful and self-asserting men. The other daughter, Emily, was a bit on the wild side. She married a postal worker and moved to Detroit, where her husband eventually was convicted of theft and sent to prison. They had a couple of small children, and Emily then went through a troubled time—and so did Lucille.

"Lucille is the slave of a slave of a slave," Susan once said to me in an angry moment.

When Lucille set off to begin her new life with Patricia, we gave her in parting our only heirloom, a mahogany sofa that had belonged to my grandfather and had been stored in our attic. It didn't go with our furniture, which was modern. Years later, I visited Lucille in Washington; she was living in a housing development apartment and she sat on that sofa and asked about Michael. To tell the truth, I had for the moment forgotten that she was his "other mother." On his part, I think he has kept a fond memory of her.

Lucille's place in our home couldn't be filled, but her domestic duties were taken over, in a manner of speaking, by a most unusual woman. Mrs. Molly Smith, who was sent to us by the Muffin House, was a slender, demure, thirty-seven-year-old black woman from Georgia. Despite having two children and four grandchildren, she never had learned to cook! She was also entirely unfamiliar with the operation of a vacuum cleaner. Or so she said, and while I was aware that domestics sometimes professed ignorance in order to prevent too much work being piled on them, there was about her a naïve sincerity that convinced me she was telling the truth.

One day, Mrs. Smith told Susan that she had enrolled in night school at Dunbar. What courses was she taking? English and algebra. There, it seemed to me, everything was said about the future of domestic service.

My mother died in the Brotherhood nursing home on her eighty-second birthday; it was a bright September day. Her funeral was held two days later in Winette. We were touched that the Robertsons and some of the workers from the home drove there for the service, while *The Clarion* staff sent a display of roses.

When it was over, I had her little estate to administer. It was the first time I had ever personally been in need of a lawyer, and I called on Attorney Peckham. He assured me it was only a matter of waiting out the statutory time.

But, as it turned out, the six months were only the beginning of the waiting. As always, Dave Peckham was active on many fronts, challenging the gas company, challenging the President, even challenging the NAACP, but he was not active in administrating my mother's estate. He even got married, for the fourth time, but he didn't get around to filing that piece of paper in Superior Court.

It wasn't as if there was anything to it. After her long retirement and medical expenses, my mother had left thirty-four hundred dollars in a mutual fund, and this was to be divided evenly between my brother and me.

Peckham had recently moved his office to an unsightly building on the Avenue. After I found that telephoning brought no results, I used to drop in on him. His secretary was a middle-aged woman with a sad face and a manner that indicated she knew what it was to deal with him and could hold out no hope.

Peckham sat at a very large desk that was more cluttered than Mr. Talbott's. When reference was made to our business, he would start searching through the pile of papers, pick up two or three of them in turn and then say, "It's in the files." Sometimes he would call to the secretary, "Get out Mr. Preston's papers tomorrow morning. I want to take care of that while I'm at the courthouse." It occurred to me that he had lost the documents, but one day he triumphantly produced them.

With my admiration for him as a gifted personality, when I went to see him I didn't like to come straight to the point of the petty matter at hand. And, of course, it wasn't necessary; my presence was reminder enough. I sat down and we talked of other things. Mostly he reminisced about political events and characters—he had known them all—and told anecdotes of the civil rights struggle before I had arrived in it. "Did you ever hear about the time the Kluxers were going to parade up Illinois Avenue? Yes, this was in the Twenties. But the Negroes were ready for 'em, waiting in the second-story windows with rifles and shotguns and nuts and bolts, and when they found out about that they called it off. Went on the other side of town," he chuckled.

After half an hour of this, he would say offhandedly, as I was preparing to leave, "Oh, by the way, that business of yours, it's just about ready."

Nine, ten months went by, a year, fourteen months. Although I couldn't really be angry with him, I was so exasperated by the situation that I wrote him a letter. "Dear Dave, I simply have to get my mother's estate cleared up. This is to notify you that if you don't take action on it immediately, I will be obliged to put it into the hands of another attorney."

He called me the next day. Without mentioning my letter, he said, in a businesslike manner, "Pres, I just wanted to let you know that I filed the papers on your mother's probate today. I had a word with the judge, and it will be disposed of shortly."

It was impressive, though I came to doubt that he had done so. I told myself I could not blame all the law's delays on him. Two or three more months passed, and the day at last arrived when Attorney Peckham and I consummated our professional relation and reverted to private status. We had gotten through it successfully, and remained friends.

At a Mammoth Meeting not long afterward, I heard Peckham use the expression "good white friends," and after the program I drew him aside. "Dave," I rebuked him, "you know there are no good white people and damned few good Negroes." His laugh was uproarious.

40. The Muslims

The coming of the Muslims was the first phenomenon that drove an absolute wedge between me and my *Clarion* friends.

The Muslims polarized us into two camps. As I read about the doings of Elijah Muhammad, Malcolm (until his last year), and their followers, I was horrified. This was, to me, the Negroes accepting segregation, glorying in it, and institutionalizing it. It was, I believed, a march straight to the rear disguised as an advance. To the extent that it succeeded in gripping the imagination of the masses, I thought it would nullify all that the NAACP and other integration movements had won at such a cost in a painful struggle.

All this was in such contrast to the NAACP, with its democratic forums, its parliamentary procedure, its acceptance of all comers regardless of color. I was even inclined to honor Marcus Garvey's nationalist movement, the Universal Negro Improvement Association. Its great days had passed before my time, but it was still represented in the community by Reverend Pote—a Jamaican and a self-styled preacher who wrote long letters to *The Clarion*. I could see at a glance that he hated me. I thought he would have loved to kill me, but we were active together in the NAACP and other organizations, and besides, he had to come by me to get his effusions into *The Clarion*. So, he had put on a forced smile and we had found a *modus vivendi*.

The Muslims shut the door in my face. They were the first black organization to do so, and I was deeply upset. And as time went on, I realized to my dismay that my Negro friends had an entirely different reaction toward them. Hancock, Pierce, George Talbott, Archie Cinq, even such a professed integrationist as Mr. Talbott, when they read about the Muslims, or learned that the Muslims had opened a store-front headquarters (across the street from *The Clarion* parking lot, incidentally), broke out in smiles. These smiles contained a certain amount of derision. "Oh, pshaw," said Bill Whitcomb. But all the same, they were genuine smiles of happiness.

The most telling thing, it seemed to me, was that while the men did not avowedly identify themselves with the Muslims—nobody whom I knew joined—they never tired of talking about them. I would go into the composing room and find Pierce standing at a counter, absorbedly bent over a copy of *Elijah Speaks*. This was even truer of the people on the streets. They found their spirits awakened by the antics of the Muslims as they never had been by all the pronounce-ments of the NAACP.

"Us colored folks never did think integration was goin' nowhere," Hancock explained to me. "We knew y'all didn't want no niggers around, not in a million years. But we thought the NAACP was right, like a preacher, an' we was sinners. A sinner don't have to do like the preacher says, but he's bound to admit the preacher's right an' that hurts his conscience."

"Then along comes the Muslims an' says integration ain't nothin' but a game. That means we right all along, Mr. Preston." He poked his forefinger at me and said, "It don't matter whether it's the Lord or the Devil, it makes you feel good just for somebody to say you right." "But it's scuffling backward," I objected. He turned away and sat down at his machine. "Humph!" he said. "What else we doin' nohow!"

The Muslims were at first written of in the daily newspapers as if they were subversives. An effort was made to equate them with the Klan, by speaking of white and black hate groups. Some Negroes joined in this campaign. When the city denied the Muslims a permit for a meeting, Attorney Fielding made public a statement applauding the action. "Forward-looking Negro Americans," he said, "who have fought, bled, and died in all this country's wars, have no more use for black racism than they do for white racism. Any and all organizations based on skin color have placed themselves outside democracy."

The NAACP, while also opposing the Muslims' philosophy, took a stand along with the American Civil Liberties Union that they should be given a permit. When the meeting was finally held, there was an uproar because the Muslims would allow only black policemen and newspapermen to enter the hall. The daily newspapers had no Negro reporters. Rather than hire any, they took up a concerted policy of ignoring the Muslims' subsequent meetings. The police department yielded and sent black cops. Beyond this, it was found that despite the Muslims' flamboyant rhetoric, they were well-behaved citizens. The white folks got over their scare and decided it was one more "harmless colored thing."

The Muslims continued to get under my skin though. I remember one summer night when Susan and I were attending an outdoor concert in the Carlton Bowl. I saw Leslie Kaltenborn talking with a thin, modest-looking Negro whom I didn't know, and I went over to chat with them. Kaltenborn introduced us, and I thrust out my hand. But the black man, his face screwed up with a look of extreme distaste, kept both his hands behind his back.

One afternoon at *The Clarion*, shouts came from the composing room. I rushed in there along with everyone else. Pierce, almost incoherent, was standing over Hancock, who sat at his machine. "You wh-wh-what?" Pierce was saying.

Hancock, drunk to the nines, was smiling. "Now I've done it, I've gone and done it."

Pierce explained excitedly that Hancock, in reaching for his whiskey bottle, had got hold instead of the bottle of carbon tetrachloride he kept at his other hand for cleaning the machine and had taken a swig from it.

We stood around him expressing our concern and dismay, and asking him questions he was unable to answer. He was too drunk. It was our belief that the chemical would burn a man's insides.

Everyone was waiting for Mr. Talbott to do something, but he took one look, turned, and went back to his desk. Pierce and I exchanged glances, and Pierce shook his head in criticism of Mr. Talbott. Still, we stood there.

At last, a young man who had come to *The Clarion* only a few weeks before, and wasn't used to our way of "waiting for Cap," said, "Well, for God's sake, ain't somebody going to take him to the hospital?"

After this man had put Hancock into his car and driven off, I wandered into the front office. Mr. Talbott was sitting staring out the window. "Goddamned drunks," he muttered to no one in particular.

I went out and drove up the Avenue to Hancock's home and broke the news to his wife. We got into the car, and I drove toward the hospital. But we were no more than halfway when we saw a sight we could hardly believe. There, on the sidewalk across the street, was Hancock walking erratically toward home.

He was all smiles and apologies, in the way a man can be at a certain stage of drunkenness if he is fundamentally good-natured. We had a hard time getting out of him that he had been examined and apparently was none the worse for the experience.

He couldn't get through having his laugh at himself and apologizing to his wife, not in the car and not at home. He kept shaking his head and saying, "Well, honey, y'all win. Y'all said the nigger'd go to the well once too often. Look at what Hancock has gone and done. Hancock's a big God-damned fool. But y'all done told me. Y'all done warned me many a time, but I wouldn't listen—I was too God-damned stubborn. Just a stubborn nigger—begging your pardon, Mr, Preston—begging y'all white folks' pardon, but I'm nothin' but a no-count, stubborn nigger. Can't tell me nothin'. But I done got my comeuppance, yessirree bub."

He was still going on when I left. When I arrived at work the next morning, he was sitting at his machine, sober, pecking away at the linotype. He didn't have a word to say. Pierce told me he had suffered no ill effects. "That stuff ought to have burned his mouth and throat to hell," Pierce said. "I reckon he had too much whiskey in him."

That was the consensus: "You can't hurt a drunk."

Another observation was, "What's eatin' Cap? That ain't like him. The man might a' died. He's hot at Hancock about somethin'."

Despite his self-abasement, Hancock made little change in his habits. Perhaps after it was all over, he was fortified by the realization that he had survived the worst. He moved the cleaner to a shelf where he couldn't reach it without getting up. He observed a sort of Lenten day or two of sobriety and then returned to his nipping.

Mr. Talbott was, indeed, hot at Hancock. After twenty-five years of it, he was fed up with Hancock's drinking on the job. But what shook me to my bones was what he said to me one day about Pierce.

How we got on the subject I don't recall. We were alone in the newsroom, and suddenly Mr. Talbott was whispering hoarsely: "He's against me, he's always been against me. You think he's a hard worker, but what you don't know is that he's a thief. My God, Pres, I've watched him doin' it for years. One of these days I'll have it out with him! Thousands on thousands of dollars."

Flabbergasted, I must have moved away from him. He pursued me, his gray eyes blazing with frenzy, spittle standing at the corner of his mouth. He nodded rhythmically for emphasis. "Man, what he does is slip my type-metal out and sell it. He's sold it to Tansy, he's sold it to Colorado, Paul Gibson, he's sold it to every printer in the business. Do you think I don't know what happens to the metal? Good God, man, Pierce sells the metal. He's been selling it from the minute he walked in that door."

I made some protest, though I could hardly speak. I had so often found him right when I believed him wrong, that for an instant I thought it was happening again. But it couldn't be. If there was an honest man in the world, a painfully honest man, it was Harold Pierce. And he lived *The Clarion*, worked it, played it, slept it, and dreamed of it in his sleep. "It's not so," I said.

"It's true," he answered, and left the room. No, for once he was dead wrong. Then, what was it all about? Why had he gone mad on the subject of Pierce? Not George Brown, not Bill Whitcomb, not his son George, not even Hancock, but why precisely Pierce, on whom the entire *Clarion* depended, who made it go from day to day and week to week?

I was upset, more than I had been for a long time. I thought for a moment of following him to the office, to have it out with him. Instead, I took my hat and coat and went out the back door, through the parking lot. I began walking north, toward the Trotter Building. It was an Indian summer afternoon at the end of November. When I passed the corner, I saw that off to the right a crowd of street people had gathered, enjoying themselves in the mild sunlight.

I believe I had had some notion of taking my problem to Pat Johnson, but instead I strolled up the Avenue. I was thinking of Mr. Talbott as he grudgingly handed out the paychecks. It once had flashed into my mind, watching him, that, at that hour of the week, he hated the employees. He seemed to regard them as so many infiltrators who had taken over his shop and were compelling him to support them. It struck me now that they had done so by making themselves as indispensable as the machines. Because they produced *The Clarion*, in a sense, they controlled it. Pierce above all.

During all the years I had heard *The Clarion* men grumble, there had never been the first whisper of a strike. But suppose circumstances had arisen in which they took other jobs? That would have put Mr. Talbott out of business, as it had Charley Howard. *The Clarion* would have gone under. I began to see another reason, besides black humanity, for his toleration of their irregularities, his never firing anyone. He had recognized, if they hadn't, that he was at their mercy, that his only chance lay in their brotherhood.

I reached the Johnson housing development and took a seat on a bench that had been fixed in the sidewalk for bus passengers. In fading stenciled letters, its back proclaimed: "Reynolds Brothers Funeral Home." Across the street in a small plot worn clear of grass, half-a-dozen youths were playing basketball at a netless rim nailed to a vacant house. Papers and dust swirled in the street. There was just one key to the personality of Cassius Talbott, I realized at last, and that was his fanatical devotion to *The Clarion*. He was a monomaniac. And that was what it took—a crazy man to walk a crazy mile. He had upheld his impossible venture against the weight of the great white world, and against the clawing efforts of fellow blacks to pull him down. He had fought to a standstill the drive of his sister to install George Lewis, because he saw that the young man wasn't insane enough; and he had fought to bridle the insanity of his son George, and turn it in *The Clarion*'s direction. Humbling himself before white power-wielders and lowly street Negroes, he had also humbled himself before the workers, whom he feared and hated because he saw them as a threat to *The Clarion*. Now his true feelings twice had broken loose momentarily, when he turned his back on Hancock and when he slandered Pierce to me. But he would get those feelings in hand—he wouldn't say to Pierce what he had said to me, and he wouldn't fire Hancock until the day came when he could do so without hurting *The Clarion*. He was cunning and harmless.

The basketball was passed too high and came bounding to my feet; I arose and tossed it to a jet-skinned youth. And suddenly I thought I understood Mr. Talbott's motives in employing me. In the first place, he had seized the opportunity to acquire for *The Clarion* the benefits of my WASP habits of work. And he'd hoped, vainly, that through me he could somehow get a foothold in the all-powerful white world.

This was the basis, on his part, of our famous friendship. For a moment, I felt a comedown from the fantasy of two men surmounting the color line. But then, I realized that the line was there and couldn't be surmounted; it could only be destroyed, and we hadn't arrived at that point. Meanwhile, I was useful to him, in his simple and straightforward need.

I was already starting to walk back when another conclusion struck me as if the basketball had bounced off my head. Wasn't he useful to me? Wasn't it time to put down all the high-sounding phrases and face the fact that *The Clarion* had given me a job and a life?

For a number of people who have figured in this account, it had come to an end. The generation of our parents was gone. Aunt Lottie McPherson had quietly died of cancer. The terrible cough of Mrs. Lewis became worse and worse, resounding through the building as if she were trying to give birth from her lungs. Then she no longer came to the office, and in a few months she died. These women had been leading personalities of *The Clarion*, and yet it seemed to me that their deaths were accepted quickly, almost complacently. The chief concern was they should have "nice funerals."

At Mrs. Lewis's service, her son George and his little son and daughter were broken up by grief, but the rest of the people acted almost as if she were still alive. Bill Whitcomb, called on to speak on behalf of the staff, delivered the most unusual address I ever heard at a funeral. It was one of his stern Christmas talks. "This woman was very hard to get along with," he recalled. "She caused a lot of trouble for everybody in the office. There was no escaping her sharp tongue. She was a willful and obstinate woman." He went on enumerating her faults until one feared he would have nothing good to say of her. I couldn't decide whether he was demonstrating his oft-expressed passion for the sincere portrayal of the dead or was carried away by his role and didn't realize what he was saying. Many times, he had declared to me his admiration for Mrs. Lewis as the most able of the Talbotts. I looked at the family pew and at Pierce and the other workers to see how they were taking it. They were hanging thoughtfully on every word.

Finally, Bill said, easing his gruff tone only the slightest, "She was a strong person, and held to her course no matter what came in her way. She had a vision of *The Clarion*, inspired by her distinguished and beloved father. To that vision she remained faithful unto death, and she passed it on to her son." (There was just a flick of sadness in his eyes; I thought that even here he was thinking of himself, as he was compelled to do so often, and remembering that he had no son.) "And now, it's all over," said Bill. "Let bygones be bygones. Her life was harsh, but whatever you believe, she's found the valley of peace."

The people sighed and looked pleased at his conclusion. Bill was no Baptist preacher, but in his way he had made an eloquent speech, and they were satisfied.

And then one snowbound Friday morning, Mr. Talbott told us Lehman had died while delivering papers to the stations. He had been wrestling with the cursed *Clarion* truck in the icy streets and the snowdrifts when he complained of a terrific headache. He was taken to the hospital, where he went into a coma and didn't last out the day.

His funeral was held at St. John's Episcopal. The coffin was closed. The minister said, "I'm not going to preach a sermon. There's the sermon!" George Brown and Pierce and I, sitting together, with our eyes followed his index finger until we came to the grayish-brown box that presumably contained Lehman. It was enough of a sermon for us, but the minister went on to string scripture together until he might as well have preached one. The three of us were pallbearers, along with Mr. Talbott, the Saint, George Weyhouse, Walt Evers, and Hancock. Before turning for the cemetery, the cortege proceeded south in order to pass *The Clarion* office, which sat in its faded green paint unblinking like a toad. Looking out the front window as we passed were Miss List and the young people, who had been left to mind the office. I was told *The Clarion* had closed only once, on the death of its founder, George M. Talbott I.

41. The End of My Saga

I always had the intention of someday leaving *The Clarion*. I had pictured this event as taking place in something of the following way: the integration movement would get larger and more prosperous, and publishers or organizations somewhere would found integrationist or otherwise "progressive" magazines or newspapers, with higher salary scales than *The Clarion* and situated in New York or other big, interesting places. One of these publications would come to my attention— or better yet, one of these publishers would learn of my career and my work—and negotiations for a job would ensue. And thus, I would move on and take Susan and Michael into a more "normal" life, not only with a greater income but with acceptance into broader circles, that is to say, integrated society with a larger proportion of white people. Then, Susan could stop winning the bread and devote herself to the artistic photography in which she had aborted a promising career because of the necessity to help support me. Michael, no longer tempted to lie about his father's occupation, could find a liberal but remunerative spoke in the great American wheel of commerce, and I, myself, would be recognized as a white man who gallantly had served for a time, at considerable sacrifice, with the forces of the Negroes—had "paid his dues"—and then had returned to the company of his peers. Look at this interesting chap who worked for a black newspaper; he is a model of noblesse oblige.

I recognized that this fantasy contained the secret betrayal that the Negro held against his white comrade-in-arms: "Y'all can flee the battlefield, and are studying it right now, but there's no way in the world I can get this black off me."

On the other hand, in self-defense, my dream solution never for a moment contemplated the possibility of actually turning on the race question. Indeed, far from being ashamed of my connection with *The Clarion*, I looked on it as the ace with which I would take bigger pots, so to speak. And while I may have been too enthusiastic in this notion, I think my experience has shown it wasn't altogether a delusion. Men and women here and there, most of whom could do nothing about it, were quietly thinking in the same direction, and I was destined to meet some of them.

The other thing about my escape hatch was that it was stuck off in a corner of my mind and forgotten, for years at a stretch. It was as if it had to exist but not to be acted on, in the contentment of my middle-aged life at *The Clarion*, from day to week to month, from sports season to sports season. For, of course, no knight came riding in for me, white, black or indigo; nobody reached down and plucked me up. Virtue was its own reward. People in our town had gotten used to me being where I was, and people in cities who started "progressive" magazines didn't know of my existence. Now and then, I had a brainstorm and sent off a letter of inquiry. One year in the McCarthy period, Susan and I grew alarmed at the specter of American fascism and proposed to move to Canada, and went job hunting in Toronto for a week. I also used to "write," but only when the spirit moved me. After my heart attack, I dusted off a few short stories and wrote two or three new ones to add to my lifelong collection of rejection slips. I stopped this as soon as I got back to work. The truth was that my occupation suited me fine, as long as I had this exception tucked away somewhere.

And then, suddenly, it all changed. I would like to explain it clearly, but I simply can't; perhaps the explanation has already been given in these pages. There was no dramatic incident, the nearest thing being, fittingly enough, an experience with the Dunbar basketball team. The coach was young Bill Winslow. I had known Bill for years, had gone to Mosbyville to interview him when he was still in high school, had met his mother, had written extravagant praise of him as a player. Now he was stumbling along in Paul James' shoes, and under the stress of being unable to fill them, his bad temper was showing. He was becoming the sort of Negro who took out his frustrations on *The Clarion* because it was Negro, and on me because I was *Clarion* and "a white fool" in the bargain. He chewed me out for points in my stories that were mistaken in a minor way— not to mention criticisms of his team—as James had seldom done and then very politely. At the same time, judging from the evidence of stories published in the dailies, he was becoming buddy-buddy with the daily newspapermen and giving them scoops over *The Clarion*. The vendetta came to a head one day when he refused to let Walt Evers take photographs of his players at practice. He said we hadn't made arrangements in advance, and they were too busy. Walt wasn't used to such treatment at Dunbar and shot back in a loud voice, "We got to take 'em quick before y'all motherfuckers get beat in the first game!"

I found myself not so much angered as disillusioned. Where had it all gone? Besides, Bill Winslow was in his twenties, and I was crowding fifty. What was I doing anyway, planning to report on a squad of schoolboy athletes who weren't even going to make a basketball revolution? It was dreary, it was boring, to hell with it. With the fans' fever mounting and the tournament only two weeks away, I stopped writing about Dunbar, and Walt never went back for the pictures. A reader from Winette sent an alarmed letter, asking what was wrong. I printed it, but I didn't answer it.

I realized that I had lost interest. And not only in Dunbar. For the first time since coming through the Special Edition door eighteen years before, I had lost interest in Negroes.

This should have been an astounding discovery, except that losing interest isn't astounding. The young people with their chatter in the newsroom, the Muslims burrowing into self-segregation, the petty quarrel with Winslow—it all seemed to me trivial. I looked at the blacks, and they were only people. The gnarled old *Clarion* was no longer where it was at.

And at the same time, like Rip Van Winkle awakening, I found myself looking on the white world with new eyes. The glacial Eisenhower years were over, and the Kennedys were in the White House. The ice was breaking up not only in politics but in other areas of life. The daily *Herald* had at last abandoned its tiresome policy of me-tooing the conservative press and at least was printing both sides of questions. A young publisher was reportedly hoping to launch a liberal newspaper in the city, and I planned to go to see him. Susan and I were increasingly drawn to the theater, especially the local Theater of the Absurd—a shoestring dramatic group on the south side that was challenging the moribund Civic Playhouse, which for decades had been devoted to worn Broadway hits. And to everyone's surprise, from the state university where Michael was now a junior—from that hitherto parochial institution attended by the sons and daughters of Middle America—were being heard the first rumblings of a great student revolt.

The white people were coming out of their holes. As they did so, I became aware that they, too, were hurting and that a good many of them were struggling, according to their lights, against the same enormous enemies the blacks and I had been wrestling with. With this realization, the rage at them, which had sustained me for so long, began to lift. If, after all this time, they were going into a new edition of the 1930s, I wanted to be a part of it.

As for helping the black people, I thought that I could now do this better among the white people. That was what the collective conscience—the Marxists and the black leaders—had been saying for a long, long time. Finally, it appeared to me, things were shaping up so that it just might be possible.

If it had been impractical for me to go to work for *The Clarion*, it was, of course, ten times as impractical to leave. My pay had crept up over the years, until I was earning about eighty-five dollars a week. With Susan's considerably higher office-worker salary, the rent from 3006, and some income her parents had left us (and my mother's small contribution), we were living comfortably on a modest scale, vacationing in Canada, and putting Michael through college. And then looking fifty in the face, I was, or should have been, fearful about getting another job, especially if my *Clarion* years should turn out not to be an asset on my resumé after all. It was a long time since I had been unemployed, however, and I couldn't really anticipate such difficulties.

At any rate, like Robert Morgan, I had to go, and just then appeared a knight of sorts. In *The Herald*, I read of a new magazine venture that was being organized in our city. It already had a name: *Sienna Squire*. It was to be a magazine of the *Playboy* type but "strongly interracial." That is, it would publish "quality fiction and articles," interspersed with cheesecake photographs of black and white young women.

The formula put the magazine within my field of consideration, and I was attracted by the prospect of fiction in addition to articles. Among the feelings assailing me in a rush was one that I had been in newspaper work too long. I didn't believe the publication would succeed, but I had an idea it might last a few months, by which time I could have something else lined up. (I wasn't yet familiar with the "*Playboy* syndrome." It was later explained to me by a man who came into the magazine's headquarters and introduced himself as a professional hack writer. He said the example of Hugh Hefner in founding his famous magazine with only enough capital for the first issue, and immediately getting such a response that he was able to make it to the big time, had inspired literally hundreds of Americans to go and do likewise. They had all, of course, lost their shirts. By the time he told me, it was too late.

I was deliberately overlooking the poor prospects of the magazine; I didn't want to think about what a risky venture it was. If I could just take it at face value I would be able to wrench free from *The Clarion*, a thing I never could do otherwise. So, I must have appeared a naïve mouse in the trap when interviewed by the publishers, an adventurous-looking couple in their thirties, and an impressive beatnik-type who had come from Chicago to be the editor. It was obvious there was little money, although the name was dropped of a well-to-do sportsman who was said to be putting up twenty-five thousand dollars, which was due any day. In a corridor, I met Dick Rudy, and he told me he had come aboard the enterprise (while holding on to his regular radio job). And I saw girls, black and white, being ushered in to be photographed in the nude. These things satisfied me that the project was at least straight on integration.

I was offered the post of fiction editor, and I bargained with the beatnik over the salary, which we set at $125 a week "to start with." For the present, however, I would receive $62.50, with the balance to be made up as soon as the twenty-five thousand came in. (I understood the *Playboy* syndrome even better when the $62.50 check bounced, and then bounced again.) The irritable young man pressured me to leave *The Clarion* to work full-time at once. He didn't know what he was asking; I insisted on giving Mr. Talbott two weeks' notice. I said that, in the meanwhile, I would work for the magazine in the evenings.

Then it was time for me to inform Mr. Talbott. Although those hectic weeks of the changeover have always been a blur, I remember clearly one scene where he is sitting at his desk and I alongside it, just as when I had been hired. And around us the familiar darkness of *The Clarion* office, the familiar soot on the walls, the humility—what I remember as home.

I don't know what he expected, maybe a request for a raise, but when I told him, a look of shock came on his face.

"You're what!" he said in hardly more than a whisper. "You're leaving!"

I was disturbed by that look of Mr. Talbott's, though I guiltily knew I had it coming. In line with the conclusion I had reached about his motives, I thought he was shaken for *The Clarion*. I knew I wasn't irreplaceable as a sports editor or in my other capacities; I had found that out. But it was our "partnership" and its special meaning. It was that link between the black man and the white man, through all the years and struggles, through life and death. It was where *The Clarion* stood on white people. It was where white people stood on *The*

Clarion. It was what we had striven for. It was the future. Negroes could come and go at *The Clarion*, but this would change something. It would break something. It was the end of something.

But, of course, it was just one person trying to find a way in all the tangled circumstances and practicalities. Heroics and betrayals were not for the likes of us. When Mr. Talbott spoke again, he said quietly that he understood.

And yet, that first look of his had burnt itself into my mind, as they say an atomic fireball will do on the naked eyes. I have seen it again and again in the years that followed. Only gradually have I come to realize that there was something else in it: that he was, indeed, struck with terror, but not only or chiefly for *The Clarion*, not only for integration, for his people—that when he said, "You're what!" he was concerned for me.

The world of the adventurous white people shortly proved itself to be quite unstable. They didn't have the capacity of *The Clarion* in making bricks without straw. The magazine, after I arrived for full-time duty, lasted exactly three days. The twenty-five thousand had not come through, nor apparently had twenty-five hundred. For a time, I was unemployed. Mr. Talbott helped me by lying to the authorities about the manner of my leaving—he told them I had been laid off and thus was eligible for benefits. Then, I got on with the new liberal newspaper, whose lifespan was four months. By the end of the year, Susan and I had decided definitely to chuck it all and move to a civilized country: Canada.

That we didn't move after all is irrelevant. With these plans, it seemed to us that for once we might throw a big party, on New Year's Eve. We invited about fifty people—our black friends and our white friends, NAACP coworkers, Carlton-Meredith coworkers, erstwhile Humans, old radicals, and some of the new theater buffs with whom we were getting friendly. We laid out a stock of all the kinds of liquor we could think of.

It was a grand success. The lights blazed, and the din was boisterous. Ruth Reynolds and James Blake and Margie Allison and the Davenports, who took only fruit juice, were all there. I, on the contrary, had resolved as an experiment to have one of every sort of drink I dispensed in my capacity as bartender. Soon, I was looking at a rapid succession of brilliant faces. The weather was unusually mild, and strolling neighbors began dropping in; at one point there appeared, of all persons, a visiting South Korean army officer, in uniform. Politics was forgotten, and he too was made welcome.

Among the guests was Winston Waverly, a handsome brown-skinned man with a neat mustache and tortoise shell-rimmed glasses. Winston was a young teacher and an NAACP activist. He was always impeccably dressed and groomed. He lived in the Carlton-Meredith and had—but was in the process of losing—a wife and a couple of kids. I had not so long before made a terrible gaffe at *The Clarion* in connection with this. Winston, who was chairman of the NAACP labor and industry committee, had told me he was unable to attend a meeting because he was "having trouble at home." I didn't know this euphemism for marital difficulty and took it to mean illness in the family. In reporting the meeting and explaining his absence, I had quoted his words in the paper.

As the hour of midnight neared at the party, I went to the kitchen to get the champagne. There was Winston, falling-down drunk. I hadn't seen him in that condition before. I happen to be one of those people who become affable when drunk or, as Susan says, fit to live with, but with Winston it was the opposite. All his bitter troubles with his wife were boiling out, and in addition, other, more profound troubles: deep, black troubles that one had never known possessed this neat young man. As he went on, he seemed demented and at the same time filled with strength and power.

While I was putting the champagne bottles on a tray he disappeared, and when he returned, he was carrying a shotgun.

"Hey, Winston!" I said. "What's that for?"

"Shoot out the back door," he replied.

"No, now wait a minute," I said; "Let's not do that."

"For the New Year," Winston said with a surly grin. "At midnight, everybody shoot out the back door. Tomorrow, cabbage and hog maw. Old Southern custom. Shit, man, get out of my way."

I kept trying to dissuade him, but he was growing angry. "Fuck the motherfuckin' neighborhood," he shouted. "Fuck the white folks and fuck the niggers. It's New Year's, man, time to shoot your gun."

Suddenly, he whirled and half-pointed the gun at me. I wouldn't have thought he recognized me, so dead-drunk he was, but he said, "Yes, I'm gonna blow your fuckin' brains out! You put it in *The Clarion* about Edna and me. And I'm tired of your shit anyway. I'm tired of everybody's shit. You don't want me to shoot out the back door, okay, I'll shoot your fuckin' head off."

I was looking at the muzzle of the gun, which was wavering between my chest and the floor, and just then I noticed something. "Now, wait a minute, Winston," I said, "just take it easy, old buddy." Of course, I was drunk too, although by now frightened almost into sobriety. I continued: "Everything's gonna be all right, and you can shoot out the door if you want to, but right now your shoelace is untied." He looked down at it too.

"I'll tie it for you, Winston, good friend," I said.

I knelt down and tied the lace of Winston's right shoe. His mood passed, and he took the gun back to his car.

I put the bottles on the tray and went into the living room, which might be as good a place as any to close this story.

—York, Pennsylvania, 1974